THE

Memoir Club

ALSO BY
Laura Kalpakian

NOVELS
Educating Waverley
Steps and Exes
Caveat
Cosette: A Sequel to Les Misérables
Graced Land
Crescendo
These Latter Days
Beggars and Choosers

SHORT STORIES
The Delinquent Virgin
Dark Continent and Other Stories
Fair Augusto and Other Stories

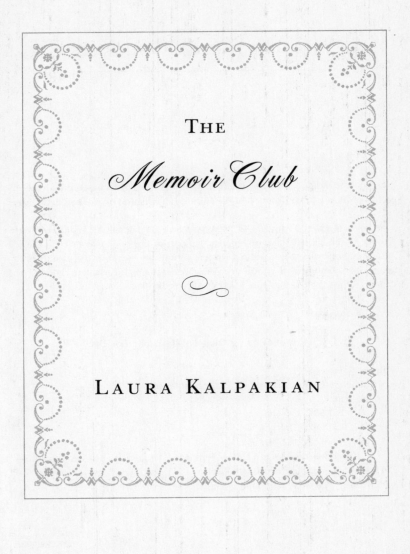

THE

Memoir Club

∽

LAURA KALPAKIAN

St. Martin's Griffin 🙰 New York

THIS BOOK IS FOR MURIEL DANCE

Note to Readers: This is a work of fiction. All of the characters and events portrayed in this novel are either products of the author's imagination or are used fictitiously.

www.stmartins.com

Library of Congress Cataloging-in-Publication Data

Kalpakian, Laura.
    The memoir club : a novel / by Laura Kalpakian.
      p.   cm.
    ISBN 0-312-32275-5 (hc)
    ISBN 0-312-32277-1 (pbk)
    EAN 978-0-312-32277-9
    1. Women—Societies and clubs—Fiction.   2. Autobiography—Authorship—Fiction.   3. Female friendship—Fiction.   4. Loss (Psychology)—Fiction.
    5. Women teachers—Fiction.   I. Title.

PS3561.A4168M46   2004
813'.54—dc22

                                                        2003022725

First St. Martin's Griffin Edition: February 2005

10 9 8 7 6 5 4 3 2 1

Contents

PART IV
An Uneasy Relationship

Writing Your Memoir

PENNY TAYLOR, INSTRUCTOR

Things to Remember

A memoir is an act not just of preservation
but of invention. The memoir is a narrative construct:
literary shape that you give to the past.
Much is left out, much is subsumed,
much is demanded.

PART I
Preservation and Invention

1

The St. Bernard

Our annual picnics look like any other. A little early in the season, perhaps. The ground is often spongy and the trees reluctantly budding, but if the weather's at all decent, we gather in the park, the picnic tables down by the lake. We have the red-checked tablecloths, the plastic coolers, the potluck tubs of coleslaw and potato salad, the little grill for hot dogs. The kids bring dogs and Frisbees. Maybe even a ball, a football often, though it's April and most people haven't yet unpacked their picnic baskets after Portland's long, wet winter. The park is pretty empty, and down at the lake, the ducks are not yet overfed and a filthy menace. (That's the nurse in me talking; can't be helped, hygiene, hand-washing fanatic, that's me.) But really, you would not have guessed that we all convene to commemorate a tragedy. We started out that brutal day five years ago, staring at one another, strangers newly endowed with our collective, our terrible title, the Families of the Victims. Slowly, we have become survivors. Most. Not all. Some have died. Some by their own hand. Some cannot bear the sight of the rest of us. But for those of us who live here in Portland, we find a bit of strength in numbers.

We keep it low-key. No grandstanding speeches. From the beginning, the first anniversary, everyone had enough sense to stay clear of that. Words would not bring back the dead. Often there's a priest and rabbi, prayers before we part. But you probably couldn't tell that this was a gathering of people who five years before had

no connection whatever. Then, suddenly, we faced one another in
an airport lounge that cordoned us off from people who had not suffered what we had suffered. All our lives were suddenly thrust into
one another, rammed into each other as the plane had slammed
into the sea.

From a distance people wave to Caryn and me as we get out of
the car. We are a sort of duet. We have the same short hair, light
brown, nondescript, no-fuss haircuts, and we have the athlete's
springy walk. Instinct and training combined, I guess. Except that
Caryn is blue eyed, broad shouldered, and long legged, and I still
have a goalie's body. Big Nell they used to call me in college. Respectfully. Women's soccer MVP. Women's soccer was my ticket, all
right. How else does a Polish-Irish girl from Gary, Indiana, get into
Notre Dame where she meets the likes of Caryn Henley from
Grosse Pointe? I put our macaroni salad on the picnic table and
the beers and bottled water in the cooler while Caryn embraces
everyone. We all hold each other just a little longer than necessary.
We bite our lips. We smile. We tell everyone how great they look
and they say the same to us. And in the midst of all this we peer
into one another's eyes and ask the unasked and unanswerable:
How are you living with this? Are you doing better than I am? Are
you living past, living through, living beyond the crash?

And of course we notice the changes. Five years have passed.
Fatherless kids have grown up. Sometimes these kids have new fathers, the widow remarries or shyly stands beside a boyfriend she
didn't have last year. There's nothing ever said, but all of us, the
Families of the Victims, we want the others to like the new people
who have come into our lives. Once that's accomplished, then often they don't return. I've noticed that. And this year, I thought
our numbers had seriously diminished. One hundred and twenty-
two victims can have a lot of friends and family, though not everyone was from Portland, of course. That was the destination. I look
around today's picnic and I start counting. Not just numbers, but
faces.

The family that always brings the rabbi brought a different rabbi,
and I wonder if the original rabbi got tired of these old prayers.
The family that always brought the priest wasn't even here. Some
people had new babies or toddlers, and I always hoped to see

Caryn pick up one of these babies and hold it. But she didn't. She held back.

For me, this reunion picnic is a seminar. Really, like those update-your-triage-technique seminars that hospitals are always giving for nurses. I want to know what's worked for others, their survival strategies. I tuck them away to use for or with Caryn. She isn't my sister or my wife or my partner or any of that, but I see her as my responsibility. I'm the one still here. Five years later.

Caryn goes off to talk to another doctor. I wander among small groups, inquiring in a general fashion, asking in essence, who has found the Wonder Weapon to Slay Grief? Well, this year yoga is very big, but we've tried that, and the outcome was that Caryn could stand on her head. That was nice. Was it the Wonder Weapon to Slay Grief? No. Therapy is always a big topic. Someone has always found the most wonderful therapist or counselor. I hear the name of Kim Ogilvie with an all but audible round of applause. Caryn has done Kim Ogilvie. A couple of years' worth. In my opinion, Kim is an okay counselor, but really she's just as limited a human being as any of us. Kim talked a lot about grief abatement. Time does that. She was supposed to do more. When Caryn quit seeing Kim, she wasn't back to square one, no, but she was still treading water there in the sea of grief, and she still had not had the energy or wish to swim to shore.

So beer in hand, I move to another group. I overhear discussion of a book one guy endorses, called, oddly, *The Laughing Cat*. He's rattling on about the laughing reflex and the author who maintains that humans are porous creatures, that experience and emotion come from both inside and outside the individual, and you needn't confine yourself to one or the other but approach the more accessible. "You have to think about the ordinary in an extraordinary way. You have to become not just conscious, but cognizant."

"What's that got to do with the cat?" I ask.

"Have you ever seen a cat laugh?"

"I don't think so," I replied, "but I've never tickled one, either."

I moved along to another group, hoping I'd find something better than guru rehash. Holding my beer, I join some remodelers, people who are really get-down engaged with the kitchen, the bath-room, the contractor. These people are really animated and into it and stepping out of grief, but we've done that too, Caryn and me. Years ago. Tore off the wallpaper, tore out the fixtures, redid her bedroom and her bathroom after Steve moved out. It was fine and cathartic, and expelled Steve (worth doing), but did it lift her from the sea of grief? No.

I find a pretty large gathering of people, maybe fifteen or so, who are concentrating on the lawsuit. Oh, yes, the Families of the Victims Lawsuit, which has been dragging on for years, dragging all through the courts and boardrooms like Marley's ghost drag-ging his chains. Class action. Or inaction. They're discussing the proposed settlement. Some people who had retained their own attorneys are doing better than those of us who went with the class action. These people are all pissed off. Their strategy for grief is to channel it into the courts and indignation and float it on a sea of briefs. It seems to help them. It's not Caryn's style, or mine.

I'm on my second beer when I start to understand that the peo-ple who really are doing fine are not here. They're doing so fine they don't need to come commemorate their losses with the other survivors. Those people will not be back.

I find a group who have been traveling this past year. That sounded promising. I can't remember the last time Caryn went anywhere except home to Grosse Pointe for the holidays. I haven't been to Europe in fifteen years. But best of all, said these survivors, it wasn't just Greece or Fiji, but that they could leave their sorrow at home. "We were on a cruise," said one woman whose fiancé had died, "my sister and I, and she said to me, no one knows. Isn't that wonderful? No one knows about the plane crash unless we tell them."

"Did you?" I asked.

"No. I can't bear the obligatory condolences. When people find out what happened to you, they're shocked and they all say how sorry they are, and I can't bear it." She gave a rueful glance to the new bride of a man whose first wife had perished.

I looked at the bride and her husband; they would not be back next year.

Just then, I get accosted by Sam Fredericks, the Dirty Old Man of the survivors. I can write Sam's dialogue by now.

"If it isn't Nurse Nelly!" Sam pats me on the back. He's about eighty. He lost a middle-aged son in the crash. The son's widow remarried three years ago and moved to Texas. She is not here. Nor are his grandchildren. "Well, I guess I can have my heart attack now." Sam turns to the others and confides, "I always want to have a heart attack so Nell Faraday will give me mouth-to-mouth. If that's the only way I can get Nell to take me in her arms, well, that's fine." And he clasped his hands over his heart and put on a stricken look.

"Well, Sam," I reply, "unless you were going to be on top, I don't think you'd survive." Sam weighs about ninety pounds. I tip the scales at one hundred ninety.

They call me the St. Bernard. The big furry one with the droopy eyelids and the fleshy lips and committed to rescue. My ex-boyfriend Mike gave me the name. We were at the Women's Uptown Christmas party a couple of years ago, and he had too much to drink and he thought it was all very funny. So did everyone else. Put the brandy flask around the St. Bernard's neck. The nurse rescues the doctor. The name stuck. Oh, not to my face, of course, but I know that's what they call me, Caryn's friends and everyone who works at Women's Uptown. It was the only thing Mike gave me that lasted. I still sometimes see him. Sometimes I even sleep with him. Sometimes I still love him, but he wanted me to let Caryn go, let Caryn find her own way through her grief, and I could not do that. I said she was my friend for twenty years and I wasn't letting go and I wasn't giving up. He said that for me Caryn came first. And I thought about it, and said yes. He said he didn't want to be second in any woman's life.

My attention strays toward some nearby picnic tables where some mothers are setting up balloons and banners for a children's birthday party. I wish they'd move. I'm tempted to ask them to move, but what can I say? Please don't set up here near us, a children's birthday party is too cruel so nearby.

Then I spot Caryn. She's sitting on the bench with the new girlfriend of a man whose wife had died with the other one hundred and twenty-one. Caryn is listening, but her eyes are downcast. She's playing with a bottle cap. Caryn uses up every bit of her energy at Women's Uptown. It's how she can live. I'm fairly certain that she's more or less pinned here by this woman who is maybe thirty, pale with anxious blue eyes and a knotted brow, and she doesn't have the energy to extricate herself. Big Nell can do this.

Caryn introduces me to Angie or Audrey or something like that who is in the middle of a fascinating description of her pancreas, certain that Dr. Henley is spellbound as she recounts her naturo-path's suggestions. I butt in. "Caryn doesn't know you well enough to hear about your pancreas."

"I was just saying that my polyps—"

"If you want to see the doctor, make an appointment. At Women's Uptown we don't require insurance." The woman leaves, and Caryn and I amble back to the picnic table.

"You were pretty rough with her." Caryn manages a wan smile.

"So what? I'd rather be a pushy bitch than a thoughtless bore."

"Oh, Nell." Caryn smiled. "You always have things nailed down, don't you?" We each got a beer and a handful of potato chips. She turned and watched the nearby women setting up for the birthday party. Bunches of kids tumbled out of minivans and ran toward the tables. Their voices filled the air, carried over water. "How old do you think they are, Nell?"

"I don't know."

"Maybe Elise's age."

"Maybe."

"Maybe Scott's."

What can I say: Do you mean Scott's age when he died, Caryn, or Scott's age had he lived? We wander down to the lake. Caryn flings potato chips into the water, though most dribble to the mud at our feet. The noisy ducks squabble over the chips. The swans sail away, across the glassy lake, their faces to another shore.

So that was how we happened to be in Bologna some four months later and met Fabrizio. He was not on my itinerary. He was spontaneous. He was good for Caryn. Never mind she had not wanted to go to Europe in the first place. I insisted. The women at the picnic, who said that Greece or Fiji freed them, had convinced me that travel was not the Wonder Weapon to Slay Grief, but still worth a try. Besides, we both had tons of vacation accumulated from Women's Uptown. Money was not a problem. I did all the exas-perating work, booking the tickets and the hotels, and since I was the one making the plans, I slipped in Eastern Europe too, Prague, Budapest, places that conventional travelers didn't go. And since we were at it, and having paid some small homage to my East European forbears, I slipped in a last stop in Dublin before we returned to Portland. The trip was a success. You couldn't leave your grief at home, but you did not need to confront it every day. You had to think about other things: schedules, maps, ordering in a foreign language. And Fabrizio didn't hurt either, did he?

However, my sense of well-planned strategy crashed that fall. I'm a nurse. I keep charts. And somehow, the success of the trip seemed to trigger an equally steep downward curve for Caryn in the fall. I don't mean she couldn't work. She could always go to Women's Uptown and hold the place and herself together, and in that there was a kind of dignity to her suffering. You could see the suffering, but none of our staff could allude to it, any more than you could look at a woman in a wheelchair and ask, how does it feel to be a cripple? These cycles of crashing depression came and went. This was the worst in years. We were in for a bad time. The St. Bernard does not take no for an answer, but rescuing Caryn when she didn't want to be rescued?

I'd done it before. I outlasted everyone. Her friends, our co-workers, finally, exhausted, gave up on her. Her family—well, the Henleys just couldn't comprehend a set of troubles that wouldn't respond to money. I outlasted her lover Steve. He couldn't understand why fabulous and ecstatic sex with him wouldn't end her grief. But he left over the swing set. He was standing there at the kitchen window one Saturday morning, she told me, drinking a cup of coffee. He said to her, you need to take down the swing set. Those kids are not coming back. Give it to someone who can use it. And then he said, either the swing set goes or I do. He said that sleeping with Caryn was like fucking a dummy.

I wasn't sorry to see his muscled butt out the door. I could not help thinking—even Caryn cannot help thinking—if she had not had an affair with Steve in the first place, her marriage would have remained intact, difficult, yes, but intact for the sake of Scott and Elise. Caryn and Andrew were both good parents, and they both adored their kids. And then Andrew and the kids might not have been on that plane . . .

But that way lies madness. Caryn might go there, but I can't.

No, I'm the action half of this duo. I am more physical. I like to clean. I opened her freezer a year after the catastrophe and threw out all the awful hamburger casseroles well-meaning people had left. Caryn is a vegetarian. The lids bulged, the contents thick with hoarfrost and freezer burn after a year. They landed in the trash with a thud. That was satisfying. I'm the one who threw out all the prescriptions in names that weren't Caryn's. I dealt with Andrew's family when necessary. I did this adequately. Not great. But better than Caryn could have, since they certainly blamed Caryn for breaking up the marriage to sleep with Steve, and thus their son's death. If that way lies madness, they went frequently. Thank God they lived in Michigan and not in Portland.

And was Caryn eternally in my debt and grateful for all this effort? No. She resented it. She was pissed off. She wanted the grief to kill her, and I was determined it would not. I am the St. Bernard. At Women's Uptown they say of my loyalty that I am like an old dog who would rather be beaten with a well-known slipper than petted by an unfamiliar hand. Loyal Nell. Admirable and annoying. Among Caryn's friends, all of whom leaped into the fray at the time of the tragedy but who were not equal to the strength of Caryn's grief, I'm equal to it. Big Nell. They don't call me that for nothing. There were all the whispered lesbo rumors. I was in love with Caryn. I wanted to move in with Caryn. I had no life of my own. Especially after Mike left me, all this circulated. I don't care what they think. I outlasted them all. The grief and the gossip.

In the annals of depression, Caryn's crash and burn that autumn after the European trip was a new experience. Worse, she went home to Grosse Pointe for the holidays. Her parents always had a bad effect on her. She came back to Portland querulous and prickly and easy to offend, and she had designer labels on everything. So unlike her. I once found a whole cupboard full of designer soap under the sink in the bathroom and asked her what in hell they were for. She laughed. It did me good to hear her laugh. Finally we took them all to Women's Uptown. When we have a patient who is a little less than up-to-date on her hygiene (many of them, I'm afraid; most everyone who comes to Women's Uptown is really pretty down-market), we give her a bar of designer soap. A gift.

While Caryn was still in Grosse Pointe for the holidays, I was sitting in the Women's Uptown lunchroom reading the arts section of the paper, and I saw this notice about a class in writing the memoir taught by a famous New York author who was moving to Portland. He was published and reviewed everywhere, and his memoirs had been made into a movie. They had a picture of him too. He was handsome in a pale, intellectual way. University Extension was offering his class in winter quarter. Memoir, I thought, as I savored my nutritious Gummi Squiggles. Hmmm. This might be a new avenue. Caryn would never have gone near anything so frou-frou as poetry. And neither would I. I mean, we're athletes and medical women, not kids seeking life lessons in espresso cups. But *memoir*. I liked the antique, Frenchified whiff to the word. I said it so often that afternoon that a couple of my patients asked me who I was talking to.

I signed us up.

"You're wasting your money," said Caryn when she got back just before the class was to start. "There's nothing I want to remember."

"You can write My Summer Vacation, about our trip. Write about Fabrizio if you want."

She gave me one of her looks. After twenty years, I know this look, and all the others. Caryn can speak volumes and not open her mouth. She would not be writing about Fabrizio. Count on it.

"It'll be good for you," I went on, undaunted. "There'll be good reading, and other people we don't know to talk to, and you can express yourself."

"I don't want to read. I don't want to write. I don't want to talk. I can express myself at the Women's Uptown."

"It will be an exercise in articulation. Like yoga with pronouns."

I didn't tell her the class capped at fifteen, and such was the luster of the teacher's New York name, it had filled up fast. Five other people besides us were wait-listed. Extension had told me to go the first night, that people might drop.

So Wednesday night after work, I brought Chinese takeout, which we microwaved in the lunchroom of the Women's Uptown. Flushed with MSG, we went to the memoir class, Caryn telling me more than once she didn't want to do this. Give it a try, I insisted. Just give it a try. I had high hopes.

I drove, paid the parking, and found the classroom in one of those great old buildings that had been renovated by soulless bureaucrats who had carved up all the proud proportionate rooms and put in fluorescent lighting. This room was high ceilinged; all the heat rose. Though we were at least twenty people, it was still cold. The desk chairs were proportioned for nymphs and uncomfortable for someone of my bulk.

That first night there was an interesting array of people, mostly professional, I suppose, people who, like us, had come from work. Having changed out of our scrubs at Women's Uptown, we didn't look professional, but comfortable. There was a woman in a sari and an old woman with great blue veins standing out on the backs of her pale hands and streaks of pink and purple and chartreuse in her white hair. A man and a well-dressed woman walked in at the same time, laughing, talking; clearly they knew each other. He was a lawyer and she had been his longtime client and they were surprised to see each other here. She also knew another woman here, an undistinguished matronly sort, and their connection was the Portland Symphony. Neither of them looked like a musician. The well-dressed woman went into instant hostess mode and introduced these two people she knew and her attorney recognized two other people and they all shook hands and exchanged names and firms. Lawyers.

Caryn loathes lawyers. Who can blame her after all that divorce mess? She gave me one of her looks encoded by twenty years of friendship: You must be kidding. Are we really going to do this?

Maybe not, I thought, but I didn't say anything, because I hadn't told her we were only wait-listed, or she never would have come. I didn't think we'd get in, anyway. Look at all these people.

Then there came in a middle-aged woman, unremarkable in every way. Portly. Gray hair. Doughy complexion, dark eyes, and a beaky nose. She did not take one of the little chairs but went instead to the front and placed her battered briefcase on the table in front of her. "I am Penny Taylor, the teacher. I have saved Extension's bacon," she announced, "by filling in at the last minute to teach this class for He Who Shall Be Nameless. This gentlemen is not teaching the class, because he did not move to Portland after all. He decided to stay in New York and get married."

I might have been mistaken, but I thought I detected a little sigh rippling through the crowded classroom; many of the women seemed audibly disappointed.

"Anyone wishing to leave the class may do so now and get a full refund. If you stay after this, you may still leave, of course, but there will be no refunds." Penny Taylor busied herself after this, pulling from the bowels of her briefcase wads of papers and books while the room emptied out. She did not look up until the door had closed on the last student. I looked around; there were so few students now, we were definitely in the class. Couldn't get out of it.

Penny gave something between a self-satisfied snort and a derisive grunt. We never did learn to read her moods or anticipate them. At least I never did. That first night and ever after she wore black wool slacks and a fine-weave sweater, nice clothes that contrasted oddly with filthy athletic shoes, all caked with ingrained dirt. She bounced slightly on these when she walked, and she exuded the confidence of a young aerobics instructor facing a room full of middle-aged flabbos. This was misleading, really, because she could be acerbic and insightful in the same moment. She took little care to soften her observations or flatter the student. She spoke too with an odd, old-fashioned formality, phrases and expressions you might read, but don't expect to hear.

Once the class cleared out, Penny began in a declarative fashion. "Since this is a memoir class and self-revelation cannot be avoided and so must be embraced, let me say briefly that I am long divorced, an episode to which I will never again allude, I have raised three children, and I am a grandmother. I have earned my gray hair. I have earned my wrinkles." There was a titter of uncertain laughter for that. She went on at length to liken writing to gardening, all things coming to beautiful fruition in the spring etc., etc., while she directed our attention to a variety of handouts. Penny's favorite metaphors were always taken from the garden: experience being the compost of your life, how to tell the weeds from the wildflowers, keeping your borders trimmed, and the like. She must have spent hours in the garden. She said she had long thought about the memoir, about the rendering of the past, of trying to live as though the present was the past and you could see it all clearly, with all the weeds pulled. She rattled on compulsively about narrative voice, which apparently was different from narrative and different from, though allied to, the narrator. I didn't understand a bit of it.

I hadn't counted on this. I mean, I really did expect yoga with pronouns. Penny clearly expected, well, work. Everyone would turn in a paper on a schedule; the class would read, critique, and comment. This isn't the kind of reading Caryn and I do. For what we read, you need your material to follow logically and in a concise fashion. You need your paragraphs numbered, your sources correctly cited. Cause, effect, conclusions sequentially presented. Science demands that you purge the inessential.

"The memoir presupposes a first-person narrator," Penny went on, her light tread belying her bulk, "and a structure. It cannot be formless or amorphous. Only you can put the structure on your experience. Your experience becomes your material. Your narrative voice must be compatible with your structure. We will be doing a lot of writing in this class, and I'd like to know what each of you is working on. You wouldn't be here if you weren't working on something." She began with the back of the class. Caryn and me.

Caryn shot me a defiant look and said, "I'm not working on anything. I'm not writing. I'm not a writer."

"Ah, you're beginning, then?"

"I am past beginning. I don't even want to be here."

Penny gave a grave, noncommittal nod and remarked, "Ah, but you lived to tell the tale. Otherwise, you wouldn't be here, would you?"

I knew right then we should have left with the others. But when she moved along to me, I offered up cheerfully, "I'm writing about our trip, that is, we, Caryn and I, went on a long European jaunt together."

"Recently?" asked Penny.

"Last September."

"Travel writing, good travel writing, is a form of memoir. Were you looking for something particular on your journey?"

Release? Respite? An alternative to grief? Travel as an antidote to suicide? I couldn't say any of that, so I maundered on, yes, I'd been looking for roots. The old family ties. Whatever I said, it was enough to set Penny off pontificating about the pleasures and difficulties of a family memoir, offering many suggestions for further reading in this genre and asking if anyone else in the class was writing such a memoir.

The balding, blue-eyed lawyer, Ted, said he had taken the class to write a memoir of his late father, a judge well-known in Portland.

The woman sitting beside him who was his client said she too was writing a memoir about her late husband, Marcus Hellman. She was Francine Hellman. Marcus was a great scientist who had never got the credit he deserved. She was perhaps sixty-something, well preserved, with cool green eyes, manicured fingernails, a strong jaw, and a mouth set with both conviction and suspicion.

To all this Penny nodded soberly. Really, her demeanor reminded me of Caryn when we're seeing a patient for the first time and nothing's been established except that this woman is sick.

Another middle-aged man, also an attorney and who spoke in a rich baritone, wanted to write about his grandparents' escape from the Nazis. A woman lawyer wanted to write the life of a brother who had committed suicide. The woman in a sari, with thick gray hair wound in a bun and a lilting accent, was writing about the partition of India and the death of her parents. Jill McDougall, a tiny young woman with spiky black hair cut short and alive with static electricity, said she was an orphan. Not born an orphan. "No one is born an orphan," she said in her quiet voice. "To be born at all you must have parents, but I was in a Korean orphanage and then adopted by Americans, John and Mary McDougall. I guess I want to find something of my roots too." She glanced at me quickly, then looked away.

I wanted to say ha ha, I was only kidding, and there is no family— unless you count the Polish Micks in Gary, Indiana—but Jill's voice was so fragile, and she hugged her own thin arms, that I didn't dare. Jill looked like a small sunflower with her black hair with blue tips radiating out.

Next to her was the matron from the symphony. Her name, Rusty, seemed to fit her. Her clothes had all the style and color of tofu. Rusty seemed not just physically compact and solid but also compressed. She said plainly she wanted to write something about herself to send to her estranged daughter, Melissa. "One day maybe Melissa will be interested in who I am."

"Well, you'll find out, even if she isn't interested," declared Penny. "Once you start digging about with your narrative spade in the past, you'll find things you never imagined."

Worms? Stones? Bones? Things best buried? All this talk of loss, people dead, departed, estranged made me sweat with misgiving. I had hoped the memoir class would serve as a life jacket to keep

Caryn afloat, to help her paddle her way out of the sea of grief. But this high-ceilinged classroom was full of angst and unhappiness. Caryn's had enough disaster. I listened to all of them, one by one, describe what they wanted to write about: death, divorce, defeat, abandonment, the suicides, illegitimacy, insanity, religion, marred childhoods, and blighted youths, all of them grim or sad. Beside me, Caryn slumped in her chair, no pen in hand. In the old codes of twenty years, I could all but hear her say to me, I know why you brought me here. I can guess what you thought this class might do, but look at them, these people will never help me. They cannot help themselves. They are a bunch of losers looking for cheap therapy and someone to blame for their own inadequacies.

And I have to say, I thought she was right. The last student Penny called on was the old woman with the chartreuse streaks in her wispy white hair, Sarah Jane Perkins, and to hear her talk, I thought there might be hope yet.

"I had a very unusual childhood. I started teaching when I was ten years old, and I've never really stopped. I thought I'd write about my work and about the Laughing Cat that chased the mice out of my schoolroom."

One of the women, the lawyer whose brother had committed suicide, tentatively raised her hand, and Penny acknowledged her, but her question was for Sarah Jane. "Are you Sarah Jane Perkins, the therapist who wrote *The Laughing Cat*?"

"I'm only an informal therapist, my Ph.D. is an honorary degree, not earned. But yes, I wrote *The Laughing Cat*."

I remembered someone at the picnic talking about that book. I looked at the old girl with more interest.

"Oh, if you wrote that book, you earned the Ph.D. I have to thank Dr. Perkins," the woman attorney explained to Penny Taylor and the rest of us. "*The Laughing Cat* didn't save my brother's life, but it saved my sanity after he died. My mother's too."

Penny Taylor too seemed to regard Dr. Perkins with a more lively interest. She pondered for a bit, as if zapping through a mental Rolodex. "If you've already written about your career in *The Laughing Cat*, then you'll have to write about something else, won't you?"

"Will I?"

"The central difference between fiction and the memoir is that in fiction, you can take the same events or concerns and truss them up time after time," she went on, though the connection escaped me. "You can keep writing the same book over and over if you've a mind to." She sniffed at this; clearly she thought these authors tedious and unimaginative. Then she went on, glowing a bit, if that's not too strong a term for Penny Taylor. "The memoir isn't like that. You get one chance to write your memoir. You can't go back and redo the memoir any more than you can undo the past. It stands in for the truth."

Everyone, even the lawyers, looked puzzled, and then Rusty Meadows, the dun-colored matron, asked timidly, "What does that mean, exactly?"

Penny gave Ms. Meadows a cryptic smile and an even more cryptic reply and then she returned to Dr. Perkins and asked after her childhood.

"My father was a bootlegger." Sarah Jane Perkins laughed. She had bad teeth. "And I lived for about ten years in a honky-tonk hotel on the Skagit River, a speakeasy, really."

Now this was more what I had in mind for memoirs. It would be nice to read something idyllic, remote, and humorous.

"Then there was a flood and we lost everything," Sarah Jane went on. "My mother had started out as a schoolteacher and she went back to being a schoolteacher."

"And what about your father?" asked Penny Taylor. "Did he die in the flood?"

I thought this was a pretty brutal inquiry for the first night of class, and I was dismayed to watch what I'd thought would be a charming story get submerged in yet another family catastrophe.

Dr. Perkins took a bit before replying, though she kept her tone light. "No, he didn't die then. My father was a cripple. Lost a leg in a logging accident, and there's no such thing as a one-legged logger. That's how we happened to move to the honky-tonk hotel. My dad made bootleg hooch. Perkins Finest, it was called. He painted the labels for the bottles too. But after the flood, well, Prohibition ended; there was no call for Perkins Finest. It was the Depression. It was all a long time ago."

"That's the point of the memoir," Penny said.

Her oblique meaning, if she had one, was lost on me. I eyed the door. Depression, floods, crippling, suicide, orphans, and the horrors of history? Calamity all around.

Caryn looked at me and shook her head, as much to say, are we really going to spend our Wednesday nights for the next ten weeks here?

Well, yes, we did. And it wasn't as bad as I'd thought.

Caryn and I were the worst writers in the bunch. Since neither of us was going to go near the events that had brought us here in the first place, Caryn took up something along the lines of My Summer Vacation about our European trip. Fabrizio was not mentioned. I wrote some anecdotal slop about the Micks and the Polacks in Gary, Indiana, which everyone seemed to think was a great story. I must say I couldn't understand their enthusiasm, and it made me wonder if I had underestimated the comic possibilities of my decidedly unfunny family. Since people were kind enough to take our writing seriously, we took theirs seriously. Caryn was an especially good reader; she had a doctor's sense of logic, a doctor's belief in causality and linked sequences, and I was a little in awe of gifts I didn't know she possessed.

Throughout that winter, we looked forward to Wednesday nights. We became comrades with some of the other students. Not friends, perhaps, but comrades like soldiers are comrades, or people working a dangerous job or a difficult shift become comrades. We built up an affection for people I couldn't have imagined meeting in our everyday lives. We were made privy to their pasts, and there was an enforced intimacy in that. When the ten weeks of the memoir class were over, a lot of us were really sorry to see it end. And Sarah Jane Perkins said, well why should it? We won't have the classroom, but we could meet elsewhere. And then Francine Hellman asked Penny if she was free in the spring, and Penny said yes, she could continue to teach Wednesday nights in the spring. Francine said, well, we could all chip in for Penny's fee, and Francine volunteered her house for us to meet.

I said yes we'd go on meeting with them, and Caryn said no.

We quarreled on our way home that night. I always drove Caryn to her house and picked her up on Thursday mornings so we didn't have to go back to Women's Uptown at night to pick up her car. Not a good neighborhood, Women's Uptown, day or night, for that matter. We always quarreled in an old-fashioned connubial way, like spouses who know their union is so durable it can withstand oath or snotty jab, but tonight was different somehow.

At first I thought she was just tired. She had come out of the autumn's terrible despondency, but now, March, I feared that as the anniversary of the crash approached, she might go under again. So I throttled along with all the reasons she should continue with the class, ending up quoting Penny Taylor. "You have to bring some order to your life. Penny's right. In writing a memoir, you automatically put a kind of order, a structure over your life and you understand it better."

"Penny is full of bullshit. She can't be telling me what I need, and neither can you."

"You need to do something useful with your life."

"Most people think being a doctor is doing something useful. Most people think—"

"Yes, yes, you're wonderfully noble, Caryn. Working twelve and fourteen hours a day on behalf of the Women's Uptown Clinic makes you a saint. What about yourself? What about Caryn?"

There was a brief bitter silence. "You ask too much."

"Maybe."

"I don't want to write anything more," Caryn insisted. "I just want to live. Isn't that enough? Isn't it enough that I don't commit suicide?"

I drove along in silence for a while. When the plane first crashed, Caryn's friends kept a twenty-four-hour suicide watch on her. Not just me, lots of her friends, even the faithless Steve. Then, as time passed, people understandably feared less for her. I feared more. I feared more ever since last year's picnic when I could see that everyone except Sam and Caryn was getting better, and that slowly the number of people who came together to commemorate would diminish. One day it would be me and Caryn and Sam Fredericks. Then old Sam would die, and it would be me and Caryn. For all of the Families of the Victims, some fundamental part of their lives could never be reconstructed. But some people, most maybe, constructed a fitting memorial around that place and waded out of the sea of grief. They were, of course, forever altered, but they pulled up, somehow, on that other shore. After six years, I could see this as a process. But Sam and Caryn were not doing this. Sam and Caryn continued to confront the devastation: the loss of their children, and for Caryn the loss of Andrew with whom she had much unfinished business. Still—now always—unfinished. The devastation was always fresh.

She reached over and put her hand on my arm. "Don't worry."

"I do worry."

"Don't. I'll go to the stupid class. I'll write some other tripe. If it will make you happy, I'll do it."

Ordinarily, here I'd say some hogwash like, oh, don't do it to make me happy, but I'm beyond all that self-serving autonomy stuff. I'm the St. Bernard. I know my job.

"I won't commit suicide," she said. We drove a bit in silence. "I'd be afraid to. Not afraid to die. Afraid of losing heaven. What if it's true, Nell? I don't have much religion, but if it's true and killing yourself is a sin, then I wouldn't ever get to be with Scott and Elise and Andrew. I couldn't bear that. I can bear this world only because I feel certain that somewhere I'll be with them again."

"You will."

"I don't want to be unworthy of heaven."

From Dr. Caryn Henley, the consummate medical functionary, this was such a strange phrase, I had no answer for it.

"Besides," she added, "the class is a little like a Wednesday night vacation, isn't it? Not Europe exactly. No Fabrizio." She sighed. "But it's like going to a little island, that class. An island in time. No one there knows anything about me, except that you and I have known each other forever. We went to Europe, and we work together at Women's Uptown. They know nothing of my losses. The only other place I can go where that's true is working with my patients. They know nothing of me, and they don't need to. All my other friends, even just acquaintances"—she drew a deep breath—"I always feel like, when they look at me, they think, that's the woman who lost her children in the crash."

"I don't think that's true," I lied.

"Of course you do. Liar." She got out her keys as I pulled up in front of her house. "See you in the A.M."

"Six-fifteen."

As I drove away, I tried to think back. What had I wanted for Caryn from this memoir class? Whatever it was, it didn't happen. But there had been another strange and unexpected gift, and I was surprised that Caryn could first articulate it. The simple gift of these Wednesday nights was the chance to share something of yourself, yes, but to choose what that something was, though you couldn't always know how the class would respond to it, that's for sure. If you wanted to tell how your mother abandoned you at birth, or your brother was a drug addict, then fine, you could write about it in this neutral place where we were supposed to be thinking not what a bastard wastrel your brother was but about the narrative voice you used to portray him.

And so, on Wednesday nights, since Caryn and I did not choose to discuss the tragedy, we were, in a way, free of it. Wednesday nights were a small island in the old sea of grief. No one in the class knew that Caryn Henley's dead family had no tombs. That Caryn's only son, her only daughter, her only husband shared their graves with the millions the sea had already claimed, certainly with the one hundred and twenty-two other people who had been on that flight, returning to Portland from Orange County, California, the one that plunged into the sea. Why? How? Who was responsible? Our tragedy was so far in the past, that back then the first fear was not terrorists. Mechanical failure? Human error? Fatal safety flaws? At first everyone, the FAA, the media, the Families of the Victims, airline officials, all felt a pressing need to know. The airline, while professing every sadness and cooperation, did not want to admit culpability in what finally seemed to have been a case of overconfident pilots and underinspected aircraft. In time, the catastrophe, the unthinkable losses all went into the hands of lawyers who wanted to assign blame and monetary value to that blame. The families of these one hundred and twenty-two dead, the Families of the Victims, became our partners in pain. And the people in the Memoir Club became our partners in eluding that pain.

2

Heartburn at the Greasy Spoon

My husband was a great man and a brilliant scientist.

They all hated that for an opener. They said it gently, of course, everyone except for Penny Taylor who had the most annoying habit of pouncing—literally, athletic shoes and all, pouncing—on one's work and declaring it inept. Penny's praise was perfunctory and stilted, while her suggestions for improvement were verbose. She could zap immediately on the weakest part of anything you wrote, and she was always right.

Damn it.

Even Francine's compatriots in the class—who were careful always to mummify any negative observation in wads of praise—assured her that they did not doubt that her late husband was a great man and a brilliant scientist. They were certain of it. But wouldn't it be better to draw a portrait of him? To show him in action, they suggested. To put forth a picture of him so that readers could be convinced by their own judgments that the late Dr. Marcus Hellman, chair of the Department of Astrophysics, was a great man and a brilliant scientist.

"What's wrong with Francine's beginning?" Penny inquired of the class. When an answer was not immediately forthcoming, she went on, "Instead of backflashing, telling us he was this or that—"

A great man. A brilliant scientist, thought Francine, her teeth grinding while she smiled.

"—she should show us how he came to be. How does a man get interested in astrophysics? I mean, it's not like being a fireman, is it? No one knows at age five, oh, I think I'll be an astrophysicist. How did he discover this as a boy?"

I didn't know him as a boy, Francine inwardly protested.

"Maybe Francine didn't know him as a boy," offered Sarah Jane, giving her toothy smile. "She can only write about what she knows."

"Nonsense. No one is asking her to footnote," Penny snapped. "The memoir is the art of using detail to evoke."

So for her next submission to the class, Francine began at the beginning, what she knew of Marc's childhood and youth. She began with the irony of a great ocean scientist being born in Idaho to a haberdasher and his wife, dreadful people who smelled somehow always of mothballs. Francine could not abide them. She did not say this. She did not even allude to mothballs or his mother's nasty inflection on the word *goy*.

Still, the class hated that opener too. Francine had written enough to be interesting, they judged, but not enough to be satisfying. Jill McDougall gently asked, "What were they like, Marc's parents?"

He had become Marc to Jill, to Sarah Jane, to Caryn, Nell, Rusty, everyone. This was an odd and gratifying aspect to the memoir class. They spoke of Marc as if they had known him. They asked questions about him. He became familiar, like a friend not present. Even if they criticized Francine's presentation of his life, they gave her the opportunity to talk about him afresh. He had been dead for three years.

"Why don't you start with when you two met?" That was Caryn's suggestion. "It's your memoir."

Stung slightly that anyone would think she wanted to write about herself, Francine's thin lips pursed in a smile and she denied this. "I want to write about my husband. It's Marc's memoir."

"It's Marc's story," Penny butted in, "but it's Francine's memoir. The author's need to write the memoir is implied in the form itself."

Francine found this irritating but instructive. For her last submission to the class, she began with Gonzaga, a Catholic university in Spokane, Washington, where they had met as undergraduates. Mary Francine Sullivan was part of the majority, as she had been all her life: a Catholic girl who had gone to Catholic school among a homogenous white population of Northwesterners. Then, naturally, she went on to Catholic university. Marc Hellman was Jewish. He had the resilience and the secretive instincts of a man who had grown up Jewish in Idaho. A real minority. Marc Hellman was also the most interesting person Francine Sullivan had ever laid eyes on. And the most beautiful. She had seen him first at the university pool. He was a lifeguard. Mary Francine decided she needed rescuing.

Her children thought this story tedious beyond belief, but the class loved it. Beginning Marc's memoir with herself, with how she had first met him was a great hit. Even Penny Taylor loved it. Francine basked in their praise, which bolstered her confidence considerably. Taking strength from the applause, she felt such a wave of pleasure and connectedness that she offered her home for a meeting place so the six of them and Penny could have class in the spring. "If you can stand the mess," she added, knowing full well there was no mess and never had been. It was a beautiful two-story Edwardian home, high on one of the city's hills, near the rose garden and with a fine view. "I'm getting the house ready to sell."

"Where are you moving?" asked Nell.

"I'm going back east. Without Marc, I have no one here. So I'm going east to live near my sons. One son is a scientist like his father, a researcher at MIT." Francine waited for the import and significance of this son's achievement to have its effect and then added, "My youngest son is a stock broker in Manhattan. Upper West Side. That's where he lives."

"You'll miss Portland."

Francine toyed with her pearl drop pendant. "I should be with my sons. They're all I have now."

Nell, in her throaty way, laughed. "You have us! For the next ten weeks. Wednesday nights."

In fact, so confident was Francine that she volunteered to have some pages for discussion that very first night. She expanded her opening chapter to tell the story of having dropped out of college in her senior year to type her husband's senior thesis. She did not add that they had gotten married in August before their senior year against the wishes of both sets of parents, the Jews arguing for time, the Catholics flatly objecting such a union. But they were both of age by then, at least in Idaho, and a Post Falls judge performed the ceremony. Afterward, Francine's parents withdrew all support; the haberdasher and his wife paid the young couple's rent.

Marc's thesis was a hundred pages long, the longest thesis any student had ever written at Gonzaga. Of course, it was full of all sorts of equations, all of which had to be done by hand or on a special typewriter that was only in the Physics Department. One little error and the whole page had to be retyped. This was daunting in itself, but worse, I didn't know how to type! So I went from being a student at Gonzaga University to night school at Spokane High to learn to type. I always intended to go back to college, but Marc went to Berkeley for his graduate work and the out-of-state tuition in California was very high. At Berkeley, we lived in the married student housing projects. I got a job in the university cashier's office. Every morning before we left our apartment, I made sandwiches for us, and we ate lunch together every day. We rode the bus home together unless Marc was working late. On those nights we got a quick bite at the Greasy Spoon, and I went back to the lab with him. We were inseparable.

That first Wednesday night the students convened in Francine's picture-perfect living room. Francine had tea and madeleines, also the picture of perfection. The other women were dazzled by what she had created. Sarah Jane actually called her house a masterpiece. They all praised her hospitality. More important, they praised what she had written. Francine flushed with happiness, confidence she had not felt in a very long time.

However, when Penny Taylor returned Francine's manuscript to her, she had circled the name of the restaurant. Francine informed her that the Greasy Spoon really was the name of the place. Penny didn't care what they called it. "More, Francine. Heartburn." Penny insisted on a paragraph of heartburn. What did the Greasy Spoon look like? What did it smell like? "Be candid, Francine. Be specific. Why would you remember such a place?"

There were about eight booths lining the walls and a long counter with ashtrays for every two seats. Everyone smoked in those days, but

Mabel, the waitress, couldn't abide dirty ashtrays and emptied them continually. Marc and I would wait for a booth when we could. We would
stand by the coatrack, not side by side, but Marc behind me, his arms
around me, and I would lean gently into him and feel him there, bracing
me, bracing my whole life, protected in his casual embrace. I didn't care
if we waited. I liked to wait for the booth. To have him behind me,
holding me. Sometimes Marc would whisper to me, look over there, that's
Professor so and so, the Nobel Prize winner. That's Professor whoever,
who did this or that. Ignited the atom, for all I knew. I nodded and I
listened. I was interested. Not in which genius was grabbing a hamburger
at the Greasy Spoon, but in the sound of Marc's voice. The low purr of
his voice in my ear. Now, when I look back at it, there was probably
more brilliance collected in the Berkeley Greasy Spoon at that time than
anywhere on earth. Not just with the professors, but the men who were
students, who would sit at the counter and jab the air with cigarettes
and talk about philosophy and science and language, about linguistics
and semantics and astrophysics.

Marc and I would always get a booth because Mabel liked us. We
would order. Hamburgers and french fries and Thousand Island dressing
on wilted lettuce, hard scrambled eggs and runny cherry pie. We'd be
eating and Marc's friends would come in—he was always wonderfully
charming and popular—and he'd say to his friends, come on, squeeze in
here. There's room. Six of us, seven sometimes squeezed in there, all of
them talking science, like its own thrilling language, and just because
you can't understand it doesn't mean you can't be thrilled. I was thrilled.
For me it was the coming together of head and heart.

Head and heart and lower than that. Thigh. Haunch. Groin.
Could she write that? Francine asked herself this. Not could she
write it for a bunch of women she scarcely knew, but could she
write it at all?

Marc would ask me for a match, put the cigarette in his mouth, light
the match with one hand, and with his other hand he would stroke my
thigh. He talked with the other students, maybe eight of us packed tight
in the booth, me against the wall, while his hand went up and down my
thigh, longish strokes at first and then shorter and shorter, moving in
short caresses down between my thighs till I thought I would melt into
a puddle under the table, until I could hardly control my own breathing

and my every pubic hair was electrified and my skin burned and I was gushing. I wanted to close my eyes, though I knew if I did I would swoon and everyone would know what he was doing to me. I should tell him to stop. It was a public place. But I couldn't make him stop and I didn't want him to stop. He kept talking while he was stroking me, but when I reached over to him under the table, when I felt for his hardness inside his pants, he withdrew his hand from me. Just like that. He brought his hand up on the table and lit another cigarette. It took my breath away. The stroking and caressing and his fingers had taken my breath away, but now I had to go the rest of the evening—the rest of the night if he had to go back to the lab—just so hungry and wet and needing him so bad that I sometimes got him to do it standing up in the closet at the lab. And then again, of course, when we got home.

She could write it. She could not, of course, turn it in for Penny Taylor and the Memoir Club. Her revised paragraph about the Greasy Spoon ended with the intelligent conversation all around her:

I sat there in the booth at the Greasy Spoon in Berkeley and smiled, while all around me the great minds of that generation smoked cigarettes and put forth theories that would change science forever.

This revised paragraph collected for Francine an all but standing ovation from the other students. They said it had everything: great description, great emotion, lots of energy and detail. Jill said it made her want to cry.

"Why?" asked Francine, who could see nothing sad in her account.

"You were just a handmaiden, a nonentity to these men, and you didn't even know it."

Francine paused, feared for just a moment that she had turned in the long description of the hands under the table. She laughed with some difficulty through her nose. "I was not a nonentity."

"It sort of sounds like it," Jill replied, her thin, low voice losing conviction. "I mean from what you've written, Francine."

Francine reread her paragraph quickly, and her lips pressed together in a seam. When she remembered what the others had not read, her heart crawled up into her throat and stayed there. She had been the maid to his hand, all right. She knew suddenly that all his cronies and associates, those great minds, they had all known what Marc was doing under the table. For all the talk of science, they doubtlessly knew that Marc was foraging about between his wife's legs. Francine colored and fought the shame of it. Thirty-odd years too late.

"It's like you were just content to sit there and take it all in and ask nothing for yourself."

"Take what in?" Francine's body flooded with a sticky chagrin.

"Well, all those 'great men.' " Jill shrugged in her self-effacing way. "Why did the men all have to be great? And the women . . . Well, what were the women?"

The fine old grandfather clock in the front hall sounded a disapproving hour. It was suddenly all too clear to Francine what the women had been. Certainly what she had been. A typist, a breadwinner, and a hand-job maiden.

"It was a different time," Sarah Jane declared. Sarah Jane changed the streaks of color in her hair according to her mood. Now they were a goldenrod yellow and blossom pink. "You're too young to remember that time, Jill, but women thought of themselves as handmaidens to greatness. It was enough. That counted as ambition for a woman. No one asked if she had potential. Back then, when Francine was a young wife, you were someone's wife and that could be your life. You weren't obliged to make a lot of choices and balancing acts. You didn't have to choose between being a wife and mother and a doctor." Sarah Jane smiled over to Caryn. "You couldn't have it all in those days. You got married. You chose the man and the life that went with him."

"Marc's career was my career," said Francine.

"That's what I mean," said Sarah Jane.

"Did you see yourself as a sort of Dr. and Mrs. Corporation?" asked Nell.

"Yes."

Caryn laughed, a genuine, easy laugh, "When I got married, my mother was beside herself with joy. She thought no one would ever marry me, that I was too brainy and picky and I was better at sports than most men. But she loved saying Dr. and Mr. My husband wasn't a doctor."

All the women in the class smiled, even Penny. No one observed that this was the first mention ever of a husband in Caryn's life. Or at least in her past.

"I chose to be Mrs. Marc Hellman." Francine said this with some aplomb. She did not add that she adored him, that she would do anything he asked. He didn't have to ask. Before she had exhumed the under-the-table activities in the Greasy Spoon, Francine had forgotten how lustrous and lusty those early days of her marriage had been. Perhaps the first five years while they struggled, Marc as a grad student, Francine in the university cashier's office, and then when baby Eric came along, they had only Marc's research assistant salary. And yet, those days—before everything they had achieved together, before this Edwardian home, before his university position, before his reputation in the scientific community was established, if not secure—those were the happiest days she could remember. Francine looked around her perfect living room, fresh flowers every week, soft carpets, gleaming granite framing the fireplace. Ready for the pages of a magazine. Her whole house was like that. Her whole life, for that matter.

"Well," said Rusty, reaching for a pale, scalloped madeleine, "you know what they say. Behind every great man is a woman and a lie."

"I was Marc's CEO," said Francine. "Socially speaking."

But with the great man gone, what was the woman to do? Francine's life, since Marc's death, had increasingly narrowed. When Marc died, she lost her husband, yes, but she also lost, in a manner of speaking, her job. She was no longer the CEO of anything. She had also lost her standing in the community, at least such community as she cared about. She began to wish she had been kinder in the past to other women whose husbands had died, or who had been divorced. She began to wish she had not cooperated in making them invisible, and she could see now that's what it was. After the big bouts of sympathy end, you find yourself stranded. A little invisible. An embarrassment to your friends. Even to yourself. Francine had taken the memoir class to recoup the pride and pleasure she had known in Marc's shadow. But she had found something else. She found she was not invisible after all. At least not to her class compatriots. They liked her. They liked her for herself and not because she was Marc Hellman's wife. Imagine that.

In offering her house for the Memoir Club to meet, Francine Hellman had acted impetuously. How long had it been since she had done anything impetuous? She couldn't remember. But the thought of having the Memoir Club on Wednesday nights gave her a certain amount of happiness, anticipation. She knew how to create a charming atmosphere where people could feel at ease and welcome. She could do that for company. She was indeed a social CEO. Francine was a fine hostess. Everyone said so. At least people to whom she was not related said so.

The people to whom she was related—her sons and her husband—never suggested anything to the contrary. At least they never did to Francine. To their therapists and their girlfriends and their feng shui specialists, counselors, masseuses, personal trainers, office assistants, research fellows, racquetball partners, hairdressers and bartenders, colleagues and graduate students, they told a different story, the story of a woman who created for her family a tense, uneasy atmosphere. Her sons' memoirs—had they chosen to write them—would have provided a very different narrative perspective for Penny Taylor and the Memoir Club.

But the sons lived far away. On the East Coast. They had impressive careers. They were grown men. Francine still called them her boys. Her boys adored her. In the Hellman family, there was only one girl and she was it.

Dear boys,

I think I told you I took a memoir class in Extension this winter to work on a memoir of your dad. In fact, we're meeting now at my house, still a class, but it feels more like a club. I haven't had company really since your father died, and everything looks very good right now, manicured and immaculate, the way I like it. The realtor has great hopes for our beautiful four-bedroom house, and he's certain, especially in springtime with the spectacular gardens, it will sell right away. When he told me that, I said, hike the price up another ten thousand! I don't want it to sell before the class ends. I wanted to tell you I won't be coming to Cambridge or New York to look for an apartment until then, when the class is over in June. You probably think I am making a great fuss over nothing, but the memoir of your father is important to me, and it's something I would like to finish before I leave Portland and come east to live. I am giving up thirty-five years in this house, but first I will preserve your dad's life and work.

My fellow writers think that more of *us* is needed in the story of *him*. I've broadened the concept of my book about Marc. It's going to be a memoir of our family's life, keeping my focus of course on your father's work and research, the great discoveries he made, and for which he never got proper credit. In fact, I'm writing now especially because I need your help. The teacher, Penny Taylor, can be a little rough around the edges, but the way she talks about the memoir has made me rethink the past.

It's not what you think, the past. Penny says, it's like a swamp, and you have to have a sturdy little boat, an oar, and courage to navigate all the shoals and rapids. And, she says, even the shoals and rapids are constantly changing. Anyway, it made me wonder if there are shoals and rapids that you two remember differently, or even better than I do.

I'm writing to ask you if you can think of particular instances, memories of your father, of our family, and send them to me. They don't need to be beautifully written. I will attend to that.

> Love,
> Mother

P.S. To help me with my work—there, doesn't that have a nice sound, boys? My work—I've written to many of Marc's friends and colleagues from all over the world, asking for their recollections of him too. The list is attached to this note. Can you think of anyone I've missed? I'm really looking forward to this project. It's going to be a wonderful tribute to Marc.

When Francine's sons read this e-mail, they were on the phone to one another within minutes. Their concerns were not for their mother, for her selling the house before coming east to live near them. After all, Francine insisted on her independence. She wouldn't dream of being a burden to them. She sometimes jested that she wanted to be near her grandchildren. Except that she had no grandchildren. Her sons had never married, either one of them, and she sometimes voiced her thoughts—not complaints, of course, just her thoughts—that it would be nice if they got married. Certainly they were of an age to be married. They ought to be married.

The youngest son, the stockbroker, had a string of women, each beautiful, glamorous, and fugitive. He treated each girlfriend with respect and courtesy, and then in a few months, there was someone else. No hard feelings. At least not for him. The eldest son did virile and athletic things like sculling on the Charles River, and his women came and went with the sports and the seasons.

Each son dreaded Francine's moving east. They had put three thousand miles between themselves and their parents in the first place. Neither wanted her nearby. They could not say these things, not even to each other. They could not say they loved her. They didn't. Or if they did, it was a love so complex, so riddled with unspoken resentment, that it was easier to call it something else. They could not say they hated her. They didn't. They dreaded her, and they could not say this either. They could not say that she had—and always had had—a way of withholding her approval, her lips pressed together so the strong jaw became forbidding, the green eyes darting, looking around, seeing everything you had done wrong or left undone, seeing all the ways you were wanting and inadequate, and so making her approval, the gift of her approval, all the more valuable, making you slaver and struggle and sweat. She could make you compete and perform, endure any obstacle to gain that approval, even if, in fact, you really didn't give a shit.

"That's what I say. I don't give a shit. Let her find out."

"You can't mean that. It would kill her. Dad was her whole reason for living. He was her whole life."

"She certainly didn't have any time for me. But maybe you're different. You're the eldest. You're the fucking scientist, just like Dad and so—"

"Oh, shut up. You're so tedious when you whine about no one ever loved you."

"No one ever did," said the younger brother, Jesse.

There was a brief silence. And into this well there fell, echoing, the unspoken *Yu-Chun,* the name elegant, enigmatic as the woman herself.

Jesse spoke. "Mom has included Yu-Chun on this list. Mom has written to her asking about Dad. I think we should call Yu-Chun. Or write. Or something. Warn her what Mom's up to. Do you have an address for her?"

"How the hell should I know where she is?"

"You're the fucking scientist," Jesse repeated. "Did she go back to Taiwan?"

"I don't remember. The question is, how does Mom know where she lives?"

"The last time I was home for Christmas, right after Dad died, I think I remember seeing a Christmas card from Yu-Chun. You know how Mom always arranges them on the mantel? I saw one from her."

"She sends Mom Christmas cards? She sleeps with Dad for fifteen years and then sends Mom a Christmas card? What a hypocrite!" The elder son, Eric, came down on each word with bicuspid finality. "Did Yu-Chun send Christmas cards when Dad was alive?"

"I don't know. Why are you asking me?"

"I'm asking you, Mr. Stocks and Bonds, because maybe you don't remember our last conversation with Dad. You remember that conversation? Well, do you?"

Jesse resented being pushed into the child's corner. "Of course I remember it. It's just—"

But Eric cut him off. Eric was on a roll, heaping abuse on Yu-Chun's hypocrisy and her general loathsomeness, her having started out as their father's grad student and climbing into his bed. Staying there for fifteen years unbeknownst to their mother.

"I don't know," said Jesse. "I don't think she's that bad. I liked her."

"Oh, that'll be a great help to Mom. You liked her."

"Shut up."

"Anyway, what is Yu-Chun going to say?" Eric continued, inflecting his words with an Asian lilt, " 'Ah, Yes, Missy Hellman, I remember some things about Dr. Hellman you don't remember. Let's see, I remember a lovely day in Honolulu. Yes, my daughter was born there. Do you remember that, Missy Hellman? No? Dr. Hellman remembered. He never forgot.' "

"She'll never say anything like that. She was scared shitless of Mom."

They talked for an hour, the conversation creaking, straining under all the old freight of long-standing, stagnant bitterness. In the end, though, they managed to reassure one another that even if Yu-Chun bothered to reply to Francine's inquiry, she would never allude to the daughter she had borne. She would not disgrace Marc Hellman's sons by saying that their father had asked them to take half from their generous portion of Dr. Hellman's estate and give to his daughter, Marcella. When they had protested, *half???*, their father pointed out the rest would all eventually come to them. When Francine died, Jesse and Eric would get everything. Their father said that this way he would not hurt Francine. He could take care of his daughter without hurting Francine, and he could help Yu-Chun who, Jesse and Eric later decided, would never risk Francine's rage. Yu-Chun would never say or write anything to demean the memory of their father who was a great man and a brilliant scientist. Everyone agreed on that.

3

A Memoir for Melissa

All the girls got married. Usually you married your high school boyfriend because it was all right to go all the way if you were going to marry the boy. My older sisters, Faith, Mercy, and Patience, went all the way and married the boys. Married young. Even as a kid, I could look at their lives and know I didn't want to live like that. I could not say as much, of course. Not that I wanted a career. Even the boys I grew up with didn't say career. They said jobs. For a girl, you took typing and shorthand and maybe bookkeeping, skills that would get you a job if you needed it one day. If your husband died young, or some other catastrophe. When I went to high school, I didn't think about my husband dying young. I didn't think about a husband. I wanted to take the college prep courses, but my father said girls didn't go to college. Girls got married. I did not know until I was twenty that my mother had been to college. She was a graduate of Coldwell Christian Teachers' College. She mentioned this one day. I have forgotten how it came up, but I remember exactly what we were doing. Hanging sheets in the backyard.

Penny Taylor got hung up on the sheets. In her embrace of scenic detail and narrative voice, Penny seized on these sheets and wanted to know all about them, just as she had wanted to know about Francine's heartburn at the Greasy Spoon.

To please Penny, Rusty Meadows tried her best to do something lovely and metaphoric with the sheets. She was surprised at how much she valued Penny's good opinion. Her efforts came to little more than sheets blowing in a stiff wind. A dusty wind, the only kind there was in California's central valley. It was a farming town, but the family farms were long gone, and most everyone there, Mexican, white, black, Chinese, Japanese, worked in the fields, their backs bent, hoisting loads, running tractors and combines for agribusiness conglomerates with offices in San Francisco and Sacramento. Her father was an irrigation mechanic, but the endless curtains of water that fell over the crops still couldn't moisten the dry, dusty wind. As soon as you hung laundry up, it would be thinly coated with fine blond grit. These sheets, the ones Rusty and her mother were hanging, were just out of the wringer. Still damp and still white. Like sails, Rusty thought, like the sails that would unfurl, catch the wind, and take her far away, *The sheets like galleon sails . . .*

She put that last line in her memoir, pausing, pen to her lips. Smiling. Penny Taylor would like that. The other students would applaud.

Rusty still used a pen to write her first few drafts. She liked the feel of the pen. Made it seem less like work. The computer was work. She was an organized, efficient woman, assistant to the administrative director of the symphony, Ronald Oliver, and protective of her boss. When Rusty began working for him three years before, she knew nothing of music beyond the hymns of her youth. She had started as a temp and moved into the permanent job. Ronald, young enough to be her son, valued her skills, her discretion, and he was dazzled that she could actually take shorthand. He appreciated, too, the fact that she made the Symphony League matrons, women like Francine Hellman, feel at ease. Dealing with the league matrons was a big part of Ronald's job. A woman younger than Rusty—a woman in high heels, short skirts, sassy clothes, cute butt, pert breasts—would not have suited the Symphony League matrons at all.

Classical music, the symphony, the splash and color of it, the excitement, were all wonderful to Rusty. She went alone to the concerts. When she first heard the symphony perform Ravel's *La Valse,* she thought she was having a heart attack. She thought she was dying, and the music was both killing her and saving her life. For Rusty, the symphony was not a social occasion, to go with someone, murmur between pieces, take a stroll at the intermission, a drink beforehand, a bite to eat afterward. None of that. The symphony served for her what church had done for her parents: a place to release your own private emotions into a vast pool of others' emotions, experience, response, reaction. In short, a great private bath you took publicly.

The memoir class offered her something of the same sort: the once-weekly pleasures of camaraderie, a sort of intimate anonymity, or anonymous intimacy. The class was a form of discipline too. Without it, Rusty would not write the story of her life, so important for her daughter, Melissa. Even if Melissa did not know this.

By the end of ten weeks, the other students were not anonymous. They were her compatriots, and their stories stayed with her. Their responses to her own story either rankled with her for days, or made her think, or both: stabs of insight, some of which delighted her, most of which were painful. Insights she would not otherwise have endured. Indeed, that she might have shunned. At Penny's insistence, Rusty wrote:

The sheets like galleon sails billowed. My mother was very particular about the wash. Whites with whites. Coloreds with coloreds. All the whites were washed with bleach and so I could smell too the scent of bleach, harsh, chemical, bright. My mother pinned one end of the sheet to the line and I pinned the other and we moved along to the next and the next and we talked a bit about a boy from church who was going to Coldwell Christian College. My mother said, "Well, of course, it's not like it was when I went there. It was harder to get into Coldwell Christian when I went there."

I nearly dropped my side of the sheet. *I* was stunned. I said, "What do you mean? You went to college? You have a college education?" She put a clothespin in her mouth so she wouldn't have to talk anymore. She knew she'd said too much.

By the end of the day, before my father came home, I got it out of her. She spoke without any particular feeling. She just said she had never mentioned going to Coldwell Christian College, because it wouldn't do for a woman to be above her husband. I asked her if my father knew she was a college graduate. And she said yes, of course he did, but it wouldn't do to make an issue of it. If you were married, then it wasn't right to have something of her own that your husband didn't have.

And I said, "Even an education, Ma?"

And she said, "Especially an education."

> She had a degree from a teachers college, but she never taught any-
> thing except Sunday school. She raised six children to adulthood, four
> girls and two boys. Of these, I am the black sheep.

Rusty crossed that out. Penny Taylor always said the narrator is
not the author.

Rusty put down her pencil. As the author, she knew that what
her mother had really said: *It's not like it was when I went there, Charity.*

That was her real name. Her older sisters were Faith and Mercy
and Patience. As a girl she had always secretly loved the line in the
Bible, *the greatest of these is charity,* secretly took pride in being the
greatest. Charity. Though in truth she knew she should have been
named Headstrong Pride, because she went before her own destruction and her haughty spirit was never quite the same after her
fall.

She had named herself Rusty on arriving in Portland years before. She wanted out of California, but not someplace cold. She
had not reckoned on the rain. With two suitcases, one in each
hand, she walked to the front door of the Portland bus station,
dismayed to see the rain coming down in sheets. A genial guy,
actually a bum, a beggar, but genial just the same, shared his umbrella with her. He held it over her head as she walked to the taxi
stand. She ought to have tipped him, but she didn't. He didn't
seem to mind. He remarked she would rust up here if she wasn't
careful. She would grow rusty.

A pretty dumb way of naming yourself, her husband always said.
Letting a bum give you a name.

"He wasn't a bum. He shared his umbrella. A bum wouldn't do
that."

Her husband, Tom Meadows, had lain back against the pillows,
his cigarette caught in the grin, the curl of his lips. He was shirt-
less, shoeless. He'd worked the late shift and he was still feeling
frisky. Those were good days. Tom grinned. "He was charitable to
Charity."

Later, when their marriage dissolved in divorce, Tom himself was
not so charitable to Charity, who by then had been Rusty Meadows
for so long she'd all but forgotten Charity Manning. Their marriage did not so much end as tatter, fray, fall apart, grow soggy,

mildewed, and yes, rusty. For Tom and Rusty Meadows, there was
no country-western song heartbreak, no drunken nights or smoky
bars or pickup trucks parked in front of motels. Just an endless
round of peeled paint and broken plumbing, busted appliances,
balogna, white bread, Hamburger Helper, Tuna Helper, macaroni
and cheese from a box. Too little money, too many medical bills
to pay for their youngest daughter, Diane, who suffered from rheu-
matic fever and weak lungs, recurrent pneumonia, asthma, and
persistent ill health. Tom had health insurance, but there were big
deductibles, co-pay prescriptions, limits on the amounts the insurance company would pay for any one family member. They mortgaged the house for Diane's pacemaker at age seventeen. Getting
Diane well, keeping her well, was an expensive proposition, and as
with most crises, not until it was past did Tom and Rusty see the
wreckage.

Their other children, Kevin and Amy, resented the time, affection, attention they had been denied. They couldn't go to the
prom or the class graduation party or the band trip to Disneyland
because there wasn't any money. Financially, the family was drained
by Diane's medical bills. The family's time and attention were con-
sumed by Diane's illness. No one came to Amy's choral concerts
or Kevin's track meets because their parents were at the hospital
with Diane. There was no Little League for Kevin and no Brownies
for Amy, because there was no money, and certainly no time, for
these extravagances. No friends could come over, because Diane
was sick. And then, after the pacemaker, Diane miraculously got
better. She stayed better.

But Kevin and Amy moved out as soon as they could. They got
jobs and apartments they shared with friends. Tom and Rusty, the
house, the family, and the marriage were all shipwrecked, as if the
sheets like galleon sails had blown Rusty only to destruction.

It was then, in the midst of the shipwreck, that she told Tom
about the daughter. The other daughter. Melissa, the lost daughter.
The one taken from her. She told him the truth of it: how she had
almost died of the pain and the shame of giving Melissa up. She
told him of the hole in her life that nothing could fill. Not him.
Not Kevin or Amy, or even Diane. She told her husband she always
believed God would not take Diane from them because He had
already taken Melissa from her. That couldn't happen twice.

Tom Meadows was not a bad man, not cruel, only limited, as the Bible says, weighed in the balance, and in this instance found wanting. But this long-buried secret? This he could not bear, not endure, not accept. Tom and Rusty parted, divorced. The house was sold. They divided the money, such as it was, after paying off two mortgages.

Rusty rented a three-bedroom first-floor apartment in a rundown complex. Diane, healthy but not altogether strong, moved in with her. Rusty got a job in an insurance company. She lied about her computer skills. By the time the insurance company moved its offices to Wichita, her computer skills were competent. She scanned the want ads for another job, but they all looked boring, dead end. So she went to the temp agency. Even if the jobs were boring, they would be finite. Then she got the symphony job. Ronald Oliver was jaw-drop astonished that as he talked, Rusty's pencil squiggled down the page, and then she read it back to him. He didn't know anyone could still do that.

Tucking away a portion of her salary each month in a special account, adding it to the divorce settlement, Rusty saved enough to pay a private firm that specialized in locating adoptees. It was expensive. It took ten months, but they found Melissa. Melissa was unmarried, divorced, actually, a librarian in an elementary school in a town called Aptos, California. Rusty got out the map. Aptos was on the beach. This pleased her. She liked to picture Melissa walking on the beach. She imagined a little dog by her side. It was troubling though that her name was not Melissa. Her name was Suzanne Carol Post.

The letter Rusty set out to write to Suzanne Carol Post, who was really Melissa, was very difficult. *One page, keep it short, keep it even, don't frighten her, don't leap, just cautiously approach. Think of those spacey, orange-robed, shave-headed Zen guys who used to panhandle in the parking lots with a smile, a little prayer attached to a wilted carnation, a gift to you, even if you did not donate. Aspire to that, Rusty. You offer a little prayer and a carnation and you are not at all threatening, not pushy, beatific as a Buddhist.* Took a month to write. After six months and no reply, Rusty had sent another copy with return receipt requested. S. C. Post signed the green card, but Melissa did not reply. Ever.

This was when Rusty began to think she'd done the letter wrong.

Melissa didn't understand what Rusty wanted. No interfering. Not at all! No clinging, no tears, no begging to be part of her adult life. Absolutely not! Never. But she wanted Melissa to know something about how she came to be given up. That abandoning her wasn't Rusty's wish or choice or because Rusty didn't love her. Rusty wanted to write the story of her life as it related to Melissa. A memoir for Melissa.

In the memoir class, as the story of Melissa unfolded—her accidental begetting, the shame and uproar of the pregnancy, the heartache and mental illness occasioned by her loss—the students were respectful, sympathetic, and they judged Rusty's parents far more harshly than she had ever dared to judge them.

"It's appalling the way they treated you," said Sarah Jane, after they had read Rusty's first draft.

"It's not as if you killed someone," Caryn offered.

"It was a mortal sin," said Rusty. "God would never forgive me. I could never forgive myself and still be part of my church. My parents prayed the baby would be stillborn. I was sent to my father's sisters' house in Elko, Nevada. My aunts met me at the bus station. They stuck a wedding ring on my finger and told me to shut up. They told people in Elko my husband was in Vietnam, and I was too broken up to talk about it."

"A memoir is an act not just of preservation, but of invention," said Penny Taylor, ignoring the emotions Rusty had roused among the others. Penny returned always to questions of craft. "Of course it aspires to be the truth. It claims to be the truth. But it's the truth seen through a particular prism. Time is the prism that all things must pass through. And in doing so, they change. The past is never the same. It always changes according to the present."

Rusty took these words down in shorthand, underscoring them, grateful for them, still thinking about them as she returned to her apartment after class that Wednesday night.

She put her key in the lock and opened the door. She could hear voices in the living room. Laughter. Someone had burned popcorn in the kitchen, and the little blackened kernels lay all over the counter. There were the remains of a bakery cake with the words WELCOME BABY in both pink and blue frosting. All the sugar rosettes were gone. There were beer cans, a few pop bottles, and a wine of uncertain vintage on the kitchen table. As were the plates.

A bouquet of balloons announced there had been a surprise baby shower. The balloons had already sunk midway down from the ceiling. They beamed and bounced and danced with the drafts Rusty brought in with her.

Rusty put her coat over the back of a kitchen chair and wandered into the living room where all sorts of tissue and paper and cute little baby things lay on the floor. "I'm home."

The party was over, but the girls were all still there, girls watching TV. Not girls, Rusty told herself. Women. Young women. They wanted to be called women, but they wanted to act like girls. Amy and Diane and their friends. They were sprawled on the couch and the floor watching MTV. They were going to community college, or they had jobs, or both. Even Amy. At six months pregnant, Amy was going to community college. She'd been a barista, but then the doctor told Amy she should not be on her feet. Without a job, Amy had no money for rent. Rusty said of course, come live with me. Tom had remarried. His new wife's two kids lived with them and there wasn't any room for Amy, and his new wife didn't get along with her in any event.

Amy wanted to show Rusty all the adorable presents her friends had given her for the baby, but Rusty said tomorrow would do. She had to get some sleep. She had to work tomorrow morning. Amy said okay, kissed her cheek, and went back to her friends, exactly as if this were a middle school sleepover. On MTV they were watching tattooed boys with chains, lip-synching to angry lyrics, jumping up and down and pointing with stiff fingers to their crotches.

Rusty left Amy and Diane and their friends in the living room and went to her bedroom, closing the door against their levity, their ignorance of the pain the world could inflict. What was it Caryn said in class, when Rusty had referred to herself as a pregnant girl? There are no pregnant girls. Once a girl is pregnant, said Dr. Caryn Henley, she's a woman. She faces a woman's choices and a woman's needs, a woman's pleasures and a woman's anguish. So why, wondered Rusty, was there so little anguish for Amy? Rusty did not wish woe for her daughter. She would never wish on another human being what she had endured. But it still seemed a question she should ask. Not out loud, maybe. But to herself.

She could ask why Amy's girlfriends could give her a surprise shower, just as if this pregnancy were a planned, happy event for a married couple. She marveled that Amy described herself cheerfully as preggers. Oh, there'd been bouts of weeping in the beginning, but Amy decided she loved Chuck, though she didn't want to marry him right now. She still slept with him, though. She said they didn't need marriage to know they loved each other. They were too young to marry.

But they were not too young to bring another life into the world, were they, thought Rusty. To be responsible for a helpless infant who would look to them for everything. No one said this. Certainly not social services that provided Amy with free prenatal care. Not so much as a thought, a glance, a moment's wasted rebuke that Amy was pregnant, unmarried, and should consider the serious social implications of this new life and its effect on Amy's own life. There weren't any effects or implications. Or there didn't seem to be. There was talk of Amy's social security number. Not her soul. Preggers was not only not a sin, it was scarcely a stigma. Preggers Amy came to live with Mom and Diane. Chuck had an apartment with his cousins, and sometimes he came to see Amy. They went on dates. Sometimes Amy spent the night at Chuck's apartment. Chuck was thinking of joining the navy. Amy was thinking of being a dental hygienist. No one was thinking of the baby.

Except maybe Rusty. Rusty thought about the baby all the time. The prospect of this baby made her think of Melissa. Constantly. In the beginning, Rusty had advised Amy to have a nice legal abortion; whatever the pain and mental anguish, it would not be lifelong. A child was for life, she added. Amy didn't think she wanted an abortion. She wanted to go ahead and have the baby. When that was decided, or at least when the time for legal abortion had passed, Rusty said that Amy must not, under any circumstances, give the child up. She did not tell Amy about Melissa, but she was thinking of Melissa all the time. Always.

Amy's nonchalant pregnancy brought back to Rusty all that heartbreaking pain. The loss. Not just of Melissa. Since Rusty ran away from home, she had not seen any of her family. One sister sent a yearly Christmas card. That was all. And the card, with its cherubic Christ kicking up his little fat heels in the manger while everyone adored him, even that seemed to Rusty a sort of implicit rebuke.

Two years ago when she wrote her short letter to Melissa, Rusty had vowed if there was no reply, well, fine. She would accept that. It would be God's will. Rusty still thought like that. She tried not to, but she did. Clearly, God had not forgiven her. Why should He? She had not forgiven herself. Her punishment was not to know the child she had abandoned. Punishment for the abandonment. That was the sin. When Amy got pregnant, all Rusty's vows crumbled, and she signed up for the memoir class through Extension. And when Penny Taylor gave her little speech tonight in class, time being a prism through which all things passed, and in passing, all things changed, Rusty had feared she might cry.

She put on her nightgown. She went into her bathroom to wash her face. Pulling her dripping hands away, she looked up into familiar reflection. The bathroom was kindly lit, so the light was warm and flattering. Her face was still her own. Oh, there were creases and bags, sags and pouches, and her hair was a lusterless salt-and-pepper gray, but her blue eyes were still bright and intelligent. "I can't accept this punishment," Rusty said to herself or God. "I'll endure more punishment if I have to, and even if I have to inflict pain on Melissa, I'll do it. I'm sorry, Melissa, but I have to do this."

She would send the memoir to Melissa. As soon as it was finished. She would not wait for Melissa to respond to her two-year-old letter.

Like looking through a new prism. Time's prism.

Rusty went to the desk in her room where the computer sat. She picked up a pen and a legal pad. She began to write her next offering for the Memoir Club. Not a revision of what she had already written, but a revision of her very life. She began in a simple and direct fashion.

My real name is Charity Ann Manning, and once, a long time ago, I fell in love with a boy. I was not allowed to love this boy. He was not allowed to love me. But we did what was forbidden, and from this love, I, Charity, bore an illegitimate child, a daughter I thought of always as Melissa.

I had to give her away when she was only a few days old. Maybe less. I lost time. They put me under with some kind of drug, and when I woke they had taken Melissa away. No one would tell me anything. I nearly died of grief and guilt and missing Melissa. I so regretted losing Melissa I hardly ever thought about the boy I had loved. He was gone, anyway.

He never knew about Melissa. I never told him. I never told anyone outside the family. I never had a close girlfriend I could share secrets with. In our family, you shared your secrets with God or you kept your mouth shut. I kept my mouth shut. God was not interested.

I remember very little after Melissa was born and taken from me. I kept no journals or records. Sometimes, though, to this day, if I have the radio on, the oldies-but-goodies station, there will come on a song, a stupid doo-wop or let's-go-surfing song, that reaches up and squeezes my heart in a fist so that I think it will burst. I cannot breathe and I hear her crying. Melissa's crying comes back to me. Not for long. I always know it will fade when the clenching at my heart eases and I can breathe again.

For three years or so after Melissa was born, I heard the baby crying. Day and night. I could not find the baby to pick her up. She just kept crying. Her crying never left me. Day or night. I cried too. All the time. I cried out for Melissa. I called her name. I called out, I'm coming, Melissa, but I could not find her or comfort her, and her wailing drove me to beat my head against the garage wall. They stitched me up. I still have the scars from the stitches. They sent me to the state hospital for the insane. As for the scars from the state hospital for the insane, I have those too. Somewhere. The drugs they gave me must have worked. The baby quit crying.

When I was finally released and returned home, I wanted to go back to high school, but my parents said no. I was too old. Besides, they said, the story would get around, and my brothers Luke and John would be shamed. They were already shamed. And Faith and Mercy and Patience? My sisters were all married. When their babies cried, they got to pick them up. I hated them. My mother said I should pray, and I'd find out what God wanted me to do. Besides housework.

Hanging wet white sheets on the long clotheslines. The sheets like galleon sails billowed.

Rusty was too tired to continue now. She put the paper in a drawer and set the alarm, turned out the light, got into bed. In the dark she thought it remarkable that Penny Taylor and her fascination with sheets on the line should have turned out to be metaphorically correct.

After that day, discovering that her mother too had abandoned something important, not her child but her education, Charity

Manning had started to think again. Slowly. Not always clearly. But the conviction grew within her that surely God must have wanted something from her besides housework. Certainly Charity Manning wanted more than that. Eventually, she packed two suitcases and put them under the bed. One Sunday when the family went to church, Charity feigned illness. Then she called a cab. A bus ride to Portland. A bum who held the umbrella for her and said she would get rusty. Charity became Rusty. Rusty became Mrs. Tom Meadows, mother of Diane and Kevin and Amy, now pregnant, unwed, and happy as a clam.

Everyone was happy. Tom told Amy he was delighted to be a grandfather. Tom wanted her to marry Chuck. Kevin Meadows told Amy and Chuck, way to go! Diane was happy. Diane, now in good health with a good bookkeeper's job, was going to Lamaze classes as Amy's coach. Amy was happy. Social services was happy because Amy was taking good prenatal care. Amy's girlfriends were so happy they gave a shower with balloons and a cake and presents. Chuck was either happy or he was too immature to realize that to be a father was more than just a fun time in the backseat of the Camaro. Everyone was happy.

Rusty did not wish suffering on Amy. She was not a vindictive woman. But now through time's changed prism, she thought it utterly and completely unfair that the world could be so changed that boys on TV could stiffen up their index fingers and point to their crotches, that girls could be knocked up and everyone think it was all fine and dandy, and it didn't matter if you were married or not. It was utterly and completely unfair that being pregnant some thirty years ago had cost a girl her sanity, her soul, her parents' love, her sisters' affection, her brothers' goodwill, and finally her marriage. It was utterly unfair that unwed motherhood had wreaked and wrecked and changed her entire life. Had left her with a great shattered hole in her life, anguish that left her panting always after the one person she could never have. *Melissa.* Now to be an unwed mother was just another life choice. All Rusty's long-ago sacrifices were ridiculous. She should just let go of them. But she couldn't. They were hers. They were hers and Melissa was hers in a way that nothing else could ever be.

Rusty knew she ought to be ashamed of caring so much about her suffering. But didn't everyone who was taking this memoir class care about their suffering? You had to, or you wouldn't be here. Rusty cared. She cared that the suffering seemed so quaint now. Comic. Silly as the heroine tied to the railroad tracks while the mustachioed villain cried a husky *aha!* over her squealing. The villain chortled and the silly girl kept looking down the tracks for the hero. Instead she saw the train. She struggled, her little feet kicking in protest, her little fists clenching. Everyone in the audience laughed at her little efforts to save herself. She was helpless. They believed that the hero would come and save her. But the girl knew the train would come, and the hero would not, that her life would be torn apart, that she was as powerless as she was pathetic.

4

The Talking Kimono

CHALLENGING. FOR PENNY TAYLOR WRITING WAS AL-
ways challenging. If you didn't succeed in achieving what you set
out to do, she would say you were ambitious. Penny applauded
ambition as she embraced challenge. Sometimes Jill got exhausted
just listening to Penny.

"You always have to recognize the difference between challenge
and bravado, between severe assessment and incipient despair,"
Penny said the night they were discussing Jill's memoir. Penny always talked like that; she could never be casual, or crack a joke.
She spoke formally, as though giving a commencement address.
"You have to give yourself enough confidence to write, to order
and structure your experience, to begin to see your life, your own
past as material, and still keep enough judgment so you don't get
too complacent. In gardening, it's the same thing."

Jill wondered how gardening had any bearing here, but she said
nothing.

"Jill has taken on a very ambitious project," Penny went on.

This means I've failed to meet the challenge, thought Jill.

"Jill is trying to describe what she does not have. A void."

Oh, don't say that, Jill thought, knowing, with a sickening intes-
tinal thud it was true.

"She has in these pages described a gap that memory cannot
bridge, and her imagination is not quite up to the challenge. How
can you write a memoir if you have no memory?"

I don't know. What am I doing here? I'm stupid, kimchi. Katherine wouldn't do this would she? *Not on your life,* Jill heard her sister's mocking voice, and wished she had Katherine's flip, irreverent manner. Lisa wouldn't do it. She wished she had the solid, lawyerly knowingness of her sister Lisa.

"How can you write a narrative," Penny all but demanded, "that will absorb what did not happen into what did?" To this perplexing question, there was silence. Frowns all around.

"Surely it's been done," said Sarah Jane at last. "Everything's been done once. Hasn't it?"

Penny declined to reply to this cheerful rhetorical inquiry and the gas fire hissed and the rain outside Francine's French doors pounded on the terrace. Jill took furious notes, eyes on the paper, looking at no one, wishing she had not tried to describe a past that in some ways did not ever exist.

Nell jumped in. "I thought Jill did a very good job, excellent really, describing the little kimono that her mother had found her in and the little toggle fasteners, and loops made of cloth and how tiny it was and embroidered."

"She made excellent use of an object," Penny concurred, indicating with her peremptory tone that Nell's comment was obvious.

Penny was going somewhere else with this, and to Jill McDougall, it seemed the destination was the abyss, because for her the little kimono was not an object at all. It was a being. Herself. All she had, all she ever would have of who she might have been. It lay there at the center of her life, tiny, pressed, neat. Penny's right, she thought, my life is a void and my memoir stinks. Jill wanted to ask to be temporarily excused to go to the bathroom. To throw up.

In the winter quarter class at the university, maybe she would have. But you couldn't throw up in Francine Hellman's bathroom. It was too beautiful. Too clean. Too pristine and color coordinated to fling up the toilet seat, fall to your knees, and barf. No one would. Probably no one ever had.

The Memoir Club was different from the class. It was March and the short, dark afternoons of the Northwest winter waned, as though the light nibbled away at dusk. The days grew longer and the spring grew tender all around them. They could see the spring budding through the French doors in Francine's living room. Meeting at Francine's made the class seem more like a social occasion. A sort of party. After all, they gathered here weekly, women who liked each other's company, though no one, except for Caryn and Nell, had any dealings outside of class. Francine treated them with a hostessy deference. She laid out cups (and saucers) on the table and she always had several teapots kept hot so you could have any kind of tea you liked, English breakfast, Earl Grey, green tea and floral teas and peach and orange teas. They each had their favorites and stuck to them, except for the adventurous Sarah Jane who chose a new one each time.

That first evening of the Memoir Club Francine provided madeleines from Portland's premier bakery. Penny had to explain the literary significance of the madeleine to the medical professionals, Nell and Caryn. Still, after that, by common consent, each week one person contributed something, cookies or chocolates, fine cheeses and crackers, for the whole group, the Memoir Club, as they had come to describe themselves. You wouldn't dream of bringing Doritos to Francine's house. Jill one night brought some of Colin's Empress Ice Cream. Caffè Amaretto. Everyone declared it was ambrosia, magical. Jill went home and told Colin, pleasing him. The Caffè Amaretto was still in development, so the endorsement was helpful.

Once the women arrived at Francine's and had a cup of tea, they began as friends might begin an evening. They chatted offhandedly about their various men, if they had them, children if they had them. They talked about their jobs. All except Penny Taylor. True to her declaration that very first night, she never again mentioned a husband or children or grandchildren; she never talked about anything, even the weather, alluding only occasionally to her garden. Standing around Francine's tea table, cheered by the soft clink of cups and saucers, a gentle, unique sound none of them heard during their working days, they drifted into class mode only after Penny took her place. Each had an accustomed, though certainly not an assigned place, Jill and Caryn on one sofa, Nell and Sarah Jane on another, Rusty in the chair closest to the fireplace, and Francine, in what was clearly Her Chair, on the other, and Penny in the great wing chair. Penny's papers and books and satchels lay on the floor beside her in an untidy heap that annoyed Francine, though she was too well-bred to say so. You could tell from the way she held her lips, in a prim, thin line.

Tonight the work at hand was Jill's. Tonight, despite Penny's exhortation to challenge, Jill knew she ought never to have tried to describe what she did not know. How could you write about a Korean family? How could you describe them in English? Jill had neither the language nor the culture. Jill was American. If her Korean birth parents leaped up in Francine's garden right now, burst through the French doors and embraced her, explained everything, what would Jill make of it? Nothing. She made ice cream for a living. How American could you get?

We were all three Korean orphans. For each of us, my mother saved the little garment we wore when she first held us in her arms. She made three separate trips to Korea to collect each of us. I am the middle daughter. My garment is a blue kimono. Not silk. Cotton, faded blue cotton, a thick fabric, quilted to keep me warm in the Korean winter. My birthday is in January. It would have been snowy and very cold. Mary McDougall did not collect me at the orphanage until July. Where was I for those six months? My kimono does not say. My kimono is stained down the front, probably from baby spit-up. There are four ties across the chest, and on either side of these four ties, there are little white flowers with green leaves, embroidered by hand. By my mother's hands. My Korean mother.

But Mary McDougall is my mother, isn't she? I have never called anyone else mother. Is she my real mother? Or is my real mother a woman far away and unknown to me. Does she look like me? Does she have a picture of me in my little blue kimono? Mary doesn't. There are no pictures of me from Korea. There are no pictures of any of us in Korea. Mary tells my sisters and me there are no Korea pictures of us because she was too busy with her beloved babies and the blasted bureaucracies to take pictures in Korea. Who am I?

In all my pictures, I am an American baby. An American child. An American girl. I am wearing Lisa's hand-me-downs. Very cute, but not mine. At least not originally. Sometimes I think I will never have anything originally mine. My mother says I am an original, and she is mine and I am hers. She says those journeys to Korea to take her daughters in her arms, to bring them home to America, these were the happiest days of her life, just exactly as if she had given birth. But she hadn't given birth even though she wanted desperately to be a mother. John McDougall could give her many things, a big house, a new car every other year, but he could not make her a mother. She always says she wanted to be, especially and particularly, our Mother: Lisa, Jill, and Katherine, the daughters of John and Mary. How American can you be?

Grammy Edna would make jokes about the Asian Invasion whenever she took us to the park or the movies or miniature golfing. Watch out, she'd say, to the ticket taker or the popcorn people, I'm bringing the Asian Invasion! Grampy Joe always sang the same song when we came to visit. It was clever and catchy and funny, and Grampy Joe taught me the words and he would laugh and laugh and applaud when I sang it. He said I sang it like a little trooper. When I was in high school and the Girls' Choir went to see *The Mikado.* I vomited all the way home on the bus. "Three Little Maids from School." Grampy Joe didn't even have the wit to get it right. We weren't Japanese at all.

But my mother always said, Jill has my eyes, Lisa has my nose, Katherine has hair just like mine. And of course we look nothing like Mary McDougall at all. Mary McDougall has light brown hair, graying now, and blue eyes. She is fair and fragile and irresolute, slightly stooped, as though her shoulders must round over to protect her heart. But we are hers and she is ours. We are so hers she didn't like to talk about our being anyone else's. When we would ask how she found us, or where we were living in Korea when she came to claim us, or anything about the orphanages, she said she couldn't remember. She couldn't even remember where the orphanages were. Korea. Who ran them? Missionaries. What kind? Missionaries were all the same. Christians. She said all she remembered of any of her trips to Korea was a bureaucratic nightmare. International red tape. Documents in Korean. How could Mary possibly read or understand them? The translator was drunk and dirty. Things were dirty and the water was bad, and all Mary cared about was holding her baby girl and returning to America with a daughter. Mary made herself sound very brave to go to Korea all alone. John did not go with her.

Last year Lisa and Katherine came to Portland to celebrate Mom's sixtieth birthday. After our little family party, Mom went to bed and the three of us cleaned up and sat in the tiny breakfast nook, drinking beer. Lisa declared she had decided that Mom and Dad weren't our real parents, and we should call them John and Mary. Lisa is a by-the-book type. By the book we don't know who our parents are, and of course we won't ever know. Lisa says we're not really sisters and we should give up the pretense.

Katherine said, oh yeah, and what do we call each other? Kimchi? Katherine is always very flip and witty. Very American. Very Honolulu and confident with a glamorous job. Katherine says either we're sisters or we're not. She wants to be sisters, so Lisa can just shut up. I had never thought of it as a choice. But it made me happy to decide to be sisters. Lisa's still not sure.

But Mom is still Mom, and not Mary, though it's easier to think of Dad as John. Our parents' marriage died in front of our eyes, slowly, painfully. Then one day Dad told us he was moving. He was going to live with Sybil. We had a big house in those days, and he told us in the living room, sitting us all three down in front of the big TV while he sat on the couch. Katherine and I waited for Lisa to ask: Who is Sybil? And when she did, Dad said Sybil was at the center of his life. So then we knew we weren't.

We blamed ourselves, we three little maids from Korea. Face it, we told ourselves, the divorce was our fault. Dad—blue-eyed, strong-jawed, stocky, athletic Dad—didn't want a bunch of slope-eyed, sallow-skinned, black-haired, skinny girl children. Dad didn't want us in the first place. Dad said that was nonsense. He said he loved us. He loved Sybil too. He said Sybil would love us like a mother, because he loved us. He'd still be our dad. But we wondered by then if he ever had been our dad. We took it hard.

Four women weren't enough for John McDougall. He had to have another. Sybil. One Sybil was worth four of us. Even if you didn't count Mom, one Sybil was worth three of us. Do the math.

After the divorce, Mom set about getting us another father just like she had set about getting daughters. Adopt-a-Dad. These adopted fathers did not come in little blue kimonos, but they did involve endless red tape, a sort of bureaucracy. Meals, dates, bring them home to meet the three little maids, "family" outings. Some of these men were better than others. None were satisfactory. Mom adopted them too. Mom adopted three kittens from a kid who was giving them away by the freeway off-ramp. She adopted an Australian sheepdog named Amigo when the neighbors were moving to Colorado. She adopted a yappy dachshund named Mona that she found in the park alone and friendless. She adopted an iguana named Fritz that some college students were going to "liberate into the wild." Mom is very good at adopting. The Adopt-a-Dad program was not a success, but everyone loves the dogs and the cats and the iguana. Finally she adopted Paul the Greek. She's still with him. He says his real name is Apollo, but everyone calls him Paul. Mom wanted us to call him Dad, but no one does.

Dad said that since Mom was our adopted Mom, we could adopt Sybil, too. We three said nothing. We didn't have to. We each knew what the others were thinking and it wasn't pretty. He said Sybil loved us. In time we would love Sybil. But Sybil could be a rock star, an angel, Santa Claus, and the Tooth Fairy all rolled into one, and we wouldn't love her. Ever.

Once a month, visitation weekend, we went to John and Sybil's house. After dinner Sybil would lead us into the family room, that's what she called it. She said we had to stay here and watch TV and be quiet till they came for us. These two hours after dinner were her time with John, and we weren't to interfere. That was theirs. So we sat and watched TV till Katherine, who was only eight, said Sybil was a bitch, and Lisa told her shut up. Lisa told us if Mom knew what we had to go through every visitation weekend with Sybil, it would make her sad. Sadder. Lisa was thirteen and understood these things. She said it was bad enough for Mom to let us go to John and Sybil's for the weekend, but if she thought for one minute we were treated like the Asian Invasion, she'd cry her eyes out and it would be too cruel. Lisa said if we so much as breathed a word to Mom, Lisa knew of a Japanese torture and she'd torture us till our Korean ancestors cried out for mercy.

I tried to picture my Korean ancestors crying out for mercy, all of them with round faces and black hair and narrow eyes, all wearing blue kimonos and black pants, but all I could come up with was Grampy Joe and Grammy Edna singing "Three Little Maids."

So we all came home after visitation weekends at Dad's, and we said to Mom, we had an okay time at John and Sybil's. Then, later, here and there, we'd let it drop that Sybil had bad breath, or Sybil's clothes were too tight across the butt, and she always had wedgies. That she didn't know how to set a table and she couldn't use chopsticks and she couldn't cook rice or anything else. Mom prided herself on her rice. We said the toilets were dirty at Sybil and John's. The cat box stank. The beds were lumpy. These things pleased Mom. So we kept at it. But we never said Sybil was a bitch and that every night that we were there, from seven to nine was her special time with John and we weren't to interfere.

We always wondered what Sybil and John did in this time, sacred from children even if we were there only once a month. Finally, Lisa said she'd had enough TV. She left the family room and wandered around the house just daring Sybil to catch her. Katherine and I stayed put. Lisa came back and said TV was better. What was so sacred? They were sitting around doing nothing at all. After that, Katherine and I joined her and tiptoed all over the house. It was a big house and we pretended to be spies and pirates, army commandos with two-way radios and the enemy was everywhere.

Fist over your mouth: Phhthh. Charlie company. Phhthh. Do you read me, Charlie?

Phht. We read you. Enemy in sight.

Phhhthh. Give me your location, Charlie. And keep clear of danger.

Phhthh. Enemy sighted in the bedroom. Door open. Do not, repeat, do not attempt landing.

What are they doing in the bedroom? (This, forgetting to be commandos.)

Nothing. Talking on the bed. Cannot hear them. The door open, just lying there talking.

Sometimes we'd creep outside and smash the flowerbeds peering in the kitchen windows where John was reading the paper while Sybil did the dishes.

Sometimes they were in John's study, or the living room, Sybil's bare feet propped on his knees while they talked and John rubbed her feet.

It didn't seem so very special to us. But still, one of Sybil was worth three of us. Do the math.

About this time, I was maybe eleven, I started to put my little blue kimono, my Korean baby kimono, under my pillow at night. I kept it in tissue paper and laid it out carefully, imagining that it had been hand-stitched and embroidered with these little white flowers by my own mother's soft hands while she waited for me to be born. She would have been happy waiting for me to be born. I thought if I put it under my pillow she would come to me in the night. In dreams. She would smile. She would tell me who I am. Speak to me even if it wasn't in English. I said, Good night, little baby kimono. I kissed the toggles. I told the kimono I would always be close by if it needed me in the night. I asked it to talk to me. To tell me who I am.

My mother found my kimono under my pillow one morning and she took me in her arms. She didn't say anything for a long time. She was crying against my hair. Then she said no one could love me like she did. I said no one could love her like I did. I told her the kimono had talked to me in the night. I had asked it some questions and it talked. Mom quit crying. She asked me what had I asked? I told Mom I couldn't remember. Just like she couldn't remember anything about Korea. My mother finally said, Jill, when you are married and happy and have your own home, you won't need this kimono anymore.

When Lisa turned seventeen she refused to go on visitation weekends. By now John and Sybil had their own child, a nasty, blue-eyed, freckled boy, Travis, who looks just like John, and acts just like Sybil. We had to babysit this brat when we were there. Lisa finally asked Sybil if she let Travis scream his rotten little guts out for two hours every night when she didn't have three live-in babysitters?

Sybil went to Dad like the tattletale that she is, and Lisa and Dad had a big fight. Lisa said she was never coming back. Lisa said to Dad: If you don't like it, take me to court. Maybe that's where she got the idea of law school.

Katherine and I could not do the same thing. And anyway, after that, John told Sybil they couldn't have any more sacred time on visitation weekend. He had to be a father. Only now that he had to be a father, we had to share him with nasty Travis. Then, somehow, slowly, like two small boats silently loosed from our moorings and floating into a wider lake, Katherine and I eased our way out of visitation weekends. We were in high school. We were too busy. We had summer jobs. We were too busy. We had tennis practice and tests to study for. We went away to college.

Lisa became a lawyer and married a rich lawyer in Chicago. Katherine moved to Honolulu and is always having affairs with married men and telling us about them so we'll be shocked. We don't care. We're not their wives. I've been with Colin for years now, and I suppose we could or should get married, but we don't. Colin makes me happy.

Colin and I live together and work together. We make premium ice cream, artisan ice cream, Empress Ice Cream. Ours is a high-quality, handmade boutique product. We have accounts as far away as Eugene and Corvallis but not beyond. We are local and proud of it. We work out of a small warehouse in Rose City Light Industrial Park, acres of windowless warehouses. We have a couple of employees to oversee the manufacturing, but the actual creation of each flavor goes on in our apartment. We have a long counter, about twenty domestic ice cream makers for experiments, and the sound of their whirring is a hum underneath my life. Colin is a creative genius in the kitchen, but he doesn't stop to think that time is money, that cream and sugar and vanilla and fresh peaches and lychee nuts are all money too. He knows this is true, though it doesn't seem to matter to him. He has a degree in business administration, Oregon State. So do I.

I went into business administration because I wanted to make money. I'm not ashamed of it. Why should I be? I like nice things and new cars, and it was nice to have them while John lived with us. When John moved in with Sybil, she had the nice house and the new cars. Mom had a crummy tract house, and our cars choked and smoked and dropped their mufflers on the freeway. It did not surprise me and Lisa and Katherine that one of the adopt-a-dads was a mechanic. By the time Lisa was fifteen, she vowed she was marrying a rich man, and she did. Katherine said she was going into a job that was rich and glamorous, and she directs executive bookings for a famous Honolulu hotel. All I said is I wanted to be rich. I failed.

Colin had no such wish or desire to make money. He changed his major, but he didn't really change. Colin started in chemistry at Oregon State, but the chemistry he was really crazy about was the chemistry of the kitchen. Cooking. Colin's great dream is to own a restaurant, a really fine place, small, nothing snooty, just excellent. He is an artist.

I fell in love with Colin at a picnic of bus ad students in the beginning of my senior year. My boyfriend and I were standing around talking, and Colin joined us, just sort of fearlessly. He didn't care about all that toe treading and fitting in and all the things other people lose sleep over. He was fair, freckled, blue-eyed. He came up and stood beside me and smiled. I didn't know him. No one did. Everyone looked at him weird, but he just smiled, held his plastic cup in hand, and listened as if he were interested in money and stocks and points and the dot-com revolution. At this picnic, I somehow got marooned with Colin. He was telling me about his passion for cooking and his father, who would go around whis-tling the tune from the ice cream truck, "Mary Had a Little Lamb." Colin whistled it for me right there at the picnic. I was embarrassed for myself and for him. But Colin didn't seem to notice that people were snickering. Finally, I laid my hand on his arm and said yes, it was a terrible song. It was the first time I touched him. I sympathized with him having a crass father. I had a few crass father stories myself, after all.

Oh, no, Colin said, it wasn't that his father was crass. His father just wanted him to find work that would make him happy, and if he wanted to be in the kitchen, then he should have a restaurant. He should know about business.

Colin never did know about business, never mind his degree from

Oregon State. His father was all wrong. From the time I first met them, I was prepared to despise Colin's family. But I couldn't. They are bois- terous and noisy. His parents call each other Tooter and Twinkie. I do not want to know why. His sisters are tomboys. They are all like a foreign country to me. Like Korea.

Even now, after nine years together, when Colin and I go to their house in the summer and the ice cream truck goes by playing "Mary Had a Little Lamb," everyone picks up the tune of "Mary Had a Little Lamb" and sings or whistles. They laugh and laugh. The whole family thinks this is the funniest joke ever. Tooter calls out, "Run on out there, Colin! Stop that truck! Ask the driver for a few professional pointers on your future career!" They make jokes about men in the kitchen. After his graduation from Oregon State, Colin went to culinary school and graduated with top honors and his family gave him an apron they had specially decked out with MAGNA CUM GRAVY. And when he didn't want to go to work for someone else, to cook to someone else's standard, they laughed and bought him a toy ice cream truck and told him to get to work. That was probably the idea for Empress Ice Cream. They tease me. They say Colin will make a good wife and say how lucky I am I never have to cook. They laugh and say they counted on me to reform him and I've failed.

I have failed, but not in the way they think. When I lost my dot-com job, Colin and I lost our apartment. Not as in we misplaced it. We could not pay the rent. Empress Ice Cream could not pay the rent. Colin said he didn't care about the dot-com job and all the money I made. He said we should be together. Work together. So now I do the books and man- age all the business for Empress Ice Cream and Colin does the creating. Every day after work, when our two employees leave, we get in our Empress minivan and drive away as if we still live somewhere else. We go have a cup of coffee and read the papers we can't afford to subscribe to and then we go back to the warehouse.

I had said I wanted to be rich. Now all I want is not to live in the windowless room at the back of the Empress Ice Cream warehouse premises.

It's illegal to live on the warehouse premises. Our apartment is fitted up nicely, cozy in the winter, stifling in the summer. There are Monet posters of gardens on the concrete walls. Colin has promised me windows and a garden. Soon. At least we have our own home, he says. I do not count the warehouse apartment as home, but I can't say so to Colin. He is happy. I am happy with him, but it's not like my mother said, that when I was a grown woman I would not need my blue kimono. I still need it.

Keeping it in its tissue paper, because it's old now, old as I am, thirty-three, I lay out my little blue kimono under my pillow, carefully. I hope it will speak to me in dreams. Colin teases me about this. He asks if he puts his sweaty old running shirt under his pillow, will it speak to him in the night. After we turn out the light, he makes growly noises at me. He pretends to be the voice of his sweaty shirt. But he is a good man and he never pretends to be the voice of my kimono.

Last Christmas Lisa and her husband came from Chicago, Katherine came from Honolulu, and we all had Christmas at Mom's apartment with Paul the Greek. Colin did the cooking. Christmas Eve, he made us turn out the light, close our eyes, and then he brought the plum pudding to the table with blue flames burning in a halo. Breathtaking. When the flames went out, we all applauded and Colin pulled out the sprig of holly and says, Why, look! There's a note attached to it!

There was no note. I am used to this.

He reads the imaginary note from the holly. It says there is another note under the plate. He looks very carefully and brings out an envelope from under the serving dish. What is this? Why, it's an envelope! It's addressed to Jill and it's from Santa! What can it be? When did Santa leave it? Colin carried on and on, asking these silly questions while I opened the envelope that said on it "To Jill, from Santa, love, Colin."

Inside were two round-trip tickets to Korea. First class. The most expensive kind of redeemable, refundable-whenever ticket you can buy. I asked: How did you ever get the money for this? He shrugged. He had planned it for a very long time. He had saved, squirreled away money for this ticket. I said it was too much. I could not go. Colin said I must go, and with the second ticket I could take anyone I wanted, Mom or Katherine or Lisa, or him, for that matter. He laughed. He said I could bring John or Sybil or Travis if I wanted. This did not get a laugh from my family.

Ever since Christmas Eve, I have put the talking kimono under my pillow, and I ask it the same question. Whom in my family should I take with me to Korea? The choice will be crucial. Each person will be a different journey. Each person will mean something else about who I am. Should I take Lisa, because she doesn't believe Mom is really her mother, and we could go there and be Korean together even though we are not really sisters? Should it be Katherine so we could go there and be American together because we are really sisters? Should it be Mom so we can find the place where she first held me in her arms? Should it be Colin because he is mine and I am his? If I go with Colin or Mom, think how weird it will be. Everyone in Korea will look like me. Mom or Colin will look out of place. Foreign and not like they belong to me. Just like every time I went somewhere with Mom, even if she held me in her arms, or held my hand, everyone knew I was foreign and out of place and I did not really belong to her. And what would I do with the talking kimono? Take it to every orphanage in Korea, unwrap it from its tissue paper and ask: Do you remember the child who wore this thirty-some years ago? Look at this, please, and tell me if you remember the embroidered flowers, the four toggle fasteners, the baby spit-up. A woman named Mary Mc-Dougall came for this child. Who is she?

"Your memoir ends inconclusively," remarked Penny Taylor. She had a sort of gimlet eye, a squint almost that made her seem to be always winking, completely at odds with her lack of humor. Everyone else in the Memoir Club agreed that Jill had done a superlative job of describing and invoking the blue baby kimono. Once the applause for Jill had run its course, Penny leapt back into the breach. "There's no shape to it, no implied understanding."

"Does there have to be?" asked Jill.

"Of course. That you would write a memoir at all suggests some sort of understanding, some sort of truce with the past. There's none here. The ending doesn't satisfy what you so carefully set up."

"What was that?" replied Jill.

"Surely you know."

Jill was embarrassed to say that she didn't.

Penny busied herself stuffing her papers back into her battered satchel. She had an infallible internal clock that told her when the three hours were over. She did not wear a watch. "An answer to the question you asked the talking kimono."

"I asked who to take to Korea, but it didn't answer me."

"Ah," said Penny without further comment.

"Do you mean I don't yet know who I am?"

"There's a central thematic quandary inherent in your work. That's why, when you quit writing—note I do not say you came to the end, there's still the void—you've only just asked the question. You have no answer." Penny always spoke in this antique, oblique fashion, and often Jill didn't understand. Penny snapped her brief-case shut. "Maybe you aren't getting answers because you're asking the wrong questions."

"How long have you been living in the warehouse?" asked Francine.

"I don't know. A few years."

"A few years! That's terrible."

Jill shrugged. "You get used to it. There aren't any windows to wash. The floors are cement and there's a drain so we just hose down. The bathroom's so small it's easy to clean. It's not bad in the winter. It's terrible in the spring and the summer."

"Colin bought these tickets instead of paying rent?" Francine's voice curled slightly upward like a plume of smoke seeking resolution and finding only ether.

"Yes."

"That's well, that's odd, isn't it?"

"He's an odd man. What can I say? How many men do you know who are passionate about ice cream?"

"He's passionate about you," said Caryn. "Whatever else you can say about him, you can say that."

"He said he thought this was a journey I had to make. Korea." Jill glanced at Penny. "To try to fill in the void."

Penny slid her reading glasses down her beaky nose, peered intently over them.

"And I thought if I took the memoir class and wrote about it, I'd know more what I was looking for. But that didn't really happen. I mean, in winter term I just floundered around writing about John and Sybil and their bratty kid, Travis, and how pissed off we get when John calls him our brother. Travis is nothing to me. To me or Lisa or Katherine, for that matter. We look at him with his round eyes and red hair and we think, who is this kid, and why does John think we're related to him? We're not. So after I wrote all that in the winter quarter, I knew who I wasn't. In ten weeks, that's all I'd accomplished."

Nell gave a short laugh. "That's a lot!"

"The author's need to write the memoir is implicit in the form itself," said Penny, quoting her own holy writ.

"Not knowing whom to take to Korea means I still don't know who I am."

"You're being too hard on your mother. And on yourself," said Rusty. "You were loved. You and your sisters. Isn't that enough?"

"It ought to be, I guess," said Jill, "but it feels like a void," she added, wishing again that she hadn't embarked on this enterprise.

"At its best," Penny addressed Jill's unspoken thought, "your memoir should reveal to you questions you have not heretofore been able to articulate. That's one of its functions."

"And answers?" insisted Jill. "At its best, shouldn't the memoir answer your questions?"

"Perhaps your mother's right and you are an original. Perhaps you are the Empress of Ice Cream." Penny smiled. She stood, bouncing lightly on her dirty athletic shoes. Said good night. And left.

"The Empress of Ice Cream," said Francine, a fugitive smile lighting her face, altering all her classical features into something less lovely but more pleasing. "That's a nice thought." Francine started picking up the cups and saucers, their jingling clatter amiable and intimate, as the notebooks closed and the pens were dropped in bags and people picked up the manuscripts for next week's class and said they hoped the rain had stopped.

Jill thanked everyone as she collected her compatriots' comments on her memoir, but she felt unsatisfied. They had given her no answers and hardly any direction at all. Who of her family should she take first class to Korea? What would she find? What would it mean to her? Who was she and how would she know until she went to Korea? How could she not have answers to these questions? She was over thirty, after all. You're supposed to have your life together, aren't you? You're not supposed to be living in a warehouse. You're not supposed to be living with a man who squirrels away thousands of dollars and doesn't tell you. You're supposed to have a career with benefits and retirement and colleagues. A home. A husband. Mortgage payments, and a car that doesn't say Empress Ice Cream on the side.

Jill looked around her at the other members of the class, and she felt suddenly foreign here, the only Asian in sight. She braced for the old remembered pang, the loneliness that could be assuaged only by the whispering of the talking kimono, even if she could not understand what it said.

5

Uptown Women

Caryn's first effort for the Memoir Club—that is, after the actual class ended and everyone had read as much of My Summer Vacation as would ever be written—ended up ashes in the kitchen sink. She rinsed the sink and fanned the smoke. This was not the kind of writing she did well. Oh, notes on a patient's chart, fine. Prescriptions, fine. But every time Caryn tried to write something more mature and responsible than My Summer Vacation, she came back to Scott and Elise and Andrew. She could not evade them, but they eluded language. She opened the kitchen window and fanned the smoke outside. From here she could see the backyard swing set still there, unused, summer and winter, the tire swing hanging from the copper beech, awaiting voices that would not return.

After the disaster her parents had insisted Caryn leave this house, move, they would buy the new house. She refused. They urged her to leave Portland altogether. She refused. They wanted her to take a year's vacation, they would absorb her financial losses. Caryn refused. She must stay here, right here, nearby in case Scott and Elise and Andrew wanted to find her. She waited for ghosts to seek her out, to assure her, in some wordless and as yet unknown way, that they were all right and waiting for her. Nell understood this. Nell believed Caryn when she said she'd felt or sensed or seen or somehow heard Something. Some breeze that lingered too long on her cheek, a shadow that moved without an object to cast that shadow, a scent, a voice—sound, anyway—rustling in the branches of the copper beech.

The phone rang, and to her surprise, it was Ted Swanson, the lawyer from the winter Extension class, the one who was writing the memoir of his august father, the judge. They chatted on inconsequentially and then Caryn laughed and asked if he were calling because he wanted to join the Memoir Club, meeting still on Wednesday evening at Francine's.

Ted declined. "No, I got what I wanted out of the class, some way to put my recollections of my father on paper in a coherent fashion that was neither eulogy nor obituary."

Caryn remembered the piece. The man who emerged from Ted's piece was, well, a judge: just, kind, grave, as if chiseled in marble and sitting on the courthouse steps with a pigeon on his head. She didn't say this. She said, "Penny wanted you to supply more context and texture."

"Partners in old Portland law firms don't believe in texture, only in precedent. I'd like to set a precedent and ask if you'd go out to dinner with me tonight."

Taken aback, Caryn fumbled through her mental Rolodex of excuses, and if he had asked a week in advance, she would have consulted the calender and come up with something. But she agreed, finally, to have dinner with him, though she said she would meet him at the restaurant, the posh downtown, La Gondola, at eight.

She almost called Nell to tell her but decided against it. Too adolescent. Still, having an attractive man ask you out to dinner improves the spirits. Caryn returned to the computer and the alleged memoir with a bit more vivacity and decided that since the personal was too painful, she would write a memoir about the professional. There she was on assured ground.

The Women's Uptown Clinic was founded in 1965 by a group of visionary medical professionals and social workers who believed in that era's concept of the Great Society, that good medical care should be available to all. When all that idealism dried up, the clinic struggled continually for funding, and in the mad money rush of the late 80s and early 90s it almost went under completely. But it was saved by the combined efforts of shrewd lobbyists and a few powerful benefactors and politicians. However, as director of Women's Uptown I spent far too much time writing grants, courting city, state, and federal agencies, and worrying about funding. I gave up that aspect of the job five, now almost six, years ago. The clinic has a Board of Trustees, wealthy volunteers, mainly, and their director of development does most of that work. I am able to return to my medical duties, though I still oversee the day-to-day running of the clinic and make policy decisions.

We are women's health exclusively, and largely reproductive health and crisis work. I've seen it all, the best and the worst that men and women can do to each other. All men. All women. Race, culture, creed, it makes no difference. Red, yellow, black, white, brown, men and women are all the same, tissue, blood, bile, corpuscles, tendons, ganglia, nerves, everything wet and electrical, zaps and gurgles, ten thousand things that can all go wrong. Women especially can go wrong. Our bodies drip and exude, droop, slough off, harbor. We take men into our bodies and expel children. I've seen it all: great swollen labia in the last months of pregnancy, the body readying itself for a new life. I've seen ulcerated cervixes and vaginal warts the size of quarters, herpes, chancroid, syphilis, AIDS, all the diseases and indignities men and women inflict on one another's bodies. I've seen tumors that are certain death, though the patient looks at me trustingly.

I keep a great box of tissues on the small table between the two comfortable chairs in my office where I interview patients. When a patient first comes to us at Women's Uptown, we interview first in the doctor's office. We take the family history, discuss her needs and circumstances. It's not an efficient use of our time, but we pride ourselves on it. Patients need to be people before they are asked to disrobe and get up on the table, legs spread, the rays of incandescent light warming up their pubic places. The staff here at Women's Uptown, we call ourselves the Uptown Women. Classy women. Our patients get treated like uptown women in the big expensive practices because the staff, we ourselves, are women of substance, style, and pride.

In my office beside the table with the tissues, I have the two chairs, several houseplants, all green and fresh looking. If they ever start to wilt or die, I get rid of them. The place has to exude health. I sit at a small desk with a computer off to one side, so the big computer screen does not come between me and the people I am talking to. I try not to use the computer when they are there. I use a pen on their charts. I have Monet posters on the walls. I prefer these museum reproductions to the pictures favored by office decorators who insist that the most soothing colors are peach and pink, cream and blue motifs, representations of dolphins and daisies, or high and distant mountains. Not in my office. I have Monet's haystacks and the Japanese footbridge. I have a big Monet print of a woman with a parasol shading her face standing in a field where the wheat and wind blow together. She seems fearless. She's looking into the future. My patients all want to be that woman. Hell, I want to be that woman.

In terms of procedures, we deal with simple office stuff. A minor mole, a bunch of warts, most gynecological procedures, pregnancy testing, prenatal care and termination, OB (saving for the birth itself), Lamaze classes, all that. Everything else is referred out. We are a neighborhood resource and not a gleaming medical facility. The neighborhood itself is the proverbial bad neighborhood, not a good place to be after dark. Women's Uptown Clinic is situated at the convergence of many bus routes, a low one-story building on a corner, our signs in English and Spanish.

I began working here about nine years ago. I am one of two MDs. We have three nurse-practitioners. I have been there longer than any of the medical staff. Nell, the next longest. Esther the office manager, she's the only one who's been there longer than I have. Our professional staff unfortunately has a high turnover. The pay is not great, and especially as the antiabortion forces have gathered momentum, Women's Uptown is an easy target for their venom. These ostensibly profamily groups can, more or less with impunity, rain abuse on our clinic. Our patients themselves are not always respectful or respectable and they are sometimes abusive of the staff, medical and clerical. Our patients' needs can be numbing. Even their crises can become routine. Crisis pregnancies, crisis VD, crisis OD, crisis lumps and bumps and broken bones and black eyes. Women's Uptown encourages their patients to get annual checkups by issuing birth control prescriptions for a year at a time. And we give away condoms by the truckload. For all of that, when their prescriptions run out (and yes, when the extensions run out), we at the clinic can all but predict who will come in pregnant and with another crisis.

At the Women's Uptown I have terminated pregnancies on girls as young as thirteen who come in with their mothers. The mothers bray and blather about a boy who got the girl into trouble, but when the girl is silent, everyone knows who did this. Oh, not the name. I do not ask the name. He's one of the mother's men, her boyfriend, her husband, her brother, some son of a bitch or another who ought to be arrested and jailed, the bastard, but who remains nameless. I do not threaten the mother with exposure. If I do, she will not bring the girl back to the clinic. The girl will suffer. The girl will suffer anyway. That bastard with his irresponsible prick will not be punished, while a fourteen-year-old girl, in one bright stab of pain, is drained of an embryonic life. The girl is drained as well of something for which there is no scientific name. Sometimes I see the same girls over and over. After they've left home and they're out on their own.

I have also terminated pregnancies on women of forty-five, forty-eight, religious wives of religious men, women carrying a sixth or seventh or eighth child. These men do not know their wives have come to Women's Uptown. Some of these women say they're not married. They laugh irritably and pretend to have had one-night stands with men they don't know. They lay their right hand over their left hand so I will not see the white band where their wedding rings have been. They suffer for the lies they have told, the lies they will tell, for the guilt that is preferable to yet another child.

Usually our patients know what they want. If they want birth control, so much the better. We hand out condoms in boxes. Our receptionist, Chantal, gives them out at the reception desk. No questions asked. Sometimes men come into the Women's Uptown asking for condoms, and that's fine. Some of these men strut in, thinking that the women in the clinic will be looking them up and down. Sometimes they ask Chantal, hey, baby, don't you got any French ticklers? And Chantal always says, that's your department, buster, not ours. The men leave laughing.

It was an odd sensation, a date. Entering La Gondola with its recessed lighting creating little lagoons of warmth in what was otherwise a room of silvery black-and-white motifs relieved only by colorful orchids on each table, Caryn felt like an ostrich climbing into a boat. Mercifully, Ted was already there. The maître d' led her back. Ted rose when she approached; he took her hand and told her she looked lovely, and Caryn thought to herself, what a civilized man.

Ted was nursing a martini. Caryn ordered a Campari and soda, and thought La Gondola suited him: a little austere but very much aware of everything, forms, manners. Ted took care that Caryn felt looked after and that the waiter felt respected. He managed this without being chummy. That was something, Caryn thought. Ted asked if she had acquired a taste for Campari and soda on her

Italian travels with Nell. There came to Caryn's mind a picture of Fabrizio and she smiled and said, well, yes, that was where she had first had Campari and soda.

Over dinner and an excellent wine, their talk ranged in a desultory fashion, beginning of course with what they knew of each other from Penny's memoir class and easing gently out into what they did not know.

"I took the class only because Nell insisted," Caryn volunteered. "I didn't want to, but I ended up enjoying it in a way."

"You continued with the meetings on Wednesday night."

"I look forward to Wednesday night," she said, though she did not say why.

Ted had a receding hairline that somehow accentuated his bright blue eyes and the smooth skin on his close-shaven face. He said he had been long divorced. Two children, now grown. Neither living in Portland. "I'm the first to admit my shortcomings as a husband and a father. I tried, but I found it difficult, even impossible, to put aside my working life. In that, I'm sorry to say, I'm very like my father, the judge."

"But you loved him."

"I respected him," Ted replied rather too quickly. He considered for a moment. "I loved him enough to want to grow up to be like him. And I did. Makes me glad neither of my kids wanted to grow up to be like me. I'm a little dismayed now, at fifty, to only just realize how much I really am like him. I'm trying to break the old habits. Taking the memoir class was a step for me to try and put my father's life in perspective, to understand the past. Now I'm concentrating on the future. I'm making myself do things I've never done." He smiled. "I'm going river-rafting later this spring."

"That sounds very adventurous."

"Well, I'm not an adventurous sort of man, so that's why I'm going. I have a lot of time to make up for. Are you married? In class, you never said."

"I was."

"Kids?"

"No."

"Hard to be a good doctor and keep a marriage together, I suppose. The same kind of occupational hazards as being a lawyer except you confront life and death and we don't."

Caryn told him a little of what she had written out that very morning, about Women's Uptown and the kind of place it was, and what the work meant to her. "It's an endurance test, really. Almost every day. That's why I like it. It's sort like an athletic contest, when I've long since passed the point in my life where I can be really athletic."

"You look to be in good shape to me."

"I'm not anymore. But I used to be. Nell and I both were fine athletes once. We were on the women's soccer team at Notre Dame."

"How did you end up at Notre Dame? Are you Catholic?"

"Catholic? The religion of immigrants? Never. My parents were strictly white bread Episcopalian when they went at all. No, I applied to Notre Dame because someone told me it was the hardest place to get into, especially premed, and especially for a woman."

"So you had to prove you could it."

"Yes. And my parents could afford Notre Dame. They can afford anything. We grew up in Grosse Pointe, and even there, the public high school wasn't good enough for my parents, so we all went to private high school. I hated it. I couldn't wait to get out."

"The snobbery?" Ted asked. "I don't mean to be asking leading questions. It's a lawyerly instinct."

Caryn savored the pasta primavera, sipped her wine. She considered sleeping with Ted. She felt certain, in fact, that she would sleep with Ted Swanson. Not tonight. But sometime. She would not take him home where there were pictures of Scott and Elise and Andrew everywhere, but his place. Yes. His place. She would have to get used to having a date before she could get used to having a lover. Before she could do that, she would have to take these first difficult steps, to tread into wholly new territory: to tell the truth—though not the whole truth, not the Scott and Elise and Andrew truth—to a man.

"At my high school," she began, "the girls were always in the bathroom, not smoking as any self-respecting high school student would have done in those days, anyone in a public school, no, at my school they were vomiting. Finger down the throat. My older sister was anorexic. My older sister loved her bones to show. She would look in the mirror"—Caryn reached up and touched her own collarbone—"and smile when she could see her bones sticking out. Her arms were like matchsticks. She thought it was beautiful.

I wasn't like that. I wasn't like any of them. I liked to see muscle on my body. I was an endurance athlete. Tennis. Track. Soccer."

"Stamina," said Ted. "You valued stamina."

"Yes, and competition. And when I got my MD, my mother wanted me to get a job in some posh clinic or another working with anorexic girls so I could help girls like my sister. But that's not what I wanted at all. I wanted to offer medical help to people whose lives I could barely imagine. I'd rather deal with people who are actually hungry, with women who struggle to survive, instead of struggling to efface themselves off the planet."

"Dessert?" he asked. "You have to have dessert."

And of course she did.

Nell approved of Ted. She encouraged the love affair. She said, after all, they knew something about him. They knew about his family from the memoir class. They knew, or could at least guess at, the kind of man he was. They had a kind of context for him.

"You sound like Penny," Caryn chided her.

"I suppose I do. But it's better than meeting someone at say . . ." Nell groped beyond the obvious.

"The tennis club?"

"Well, yes. Now that you mention it." The tennis club was where Caryn had met Steve all those years ago.

"Ted wants to take tennis lessons so he can play with me. He asked if I knew who was a good tennis coach, a good teacher."

Nell's brows shot up. "And you said?"

Caryn said she didn't know anyone. This was a lie. Steve Benson was the best tennis teacher in Portland. He had taught Dr. Henley a good deal more than tennis. She had had an affair with him that she excused by telling herself it was just an affair. Nothing more. She'd feel guilty of course, then it would be over and the guilt itself would heal. She told herself she was experiencing as a woman what she ought to have done as a kid, when, instead of sleeping around, she'd been so intent on grades and getting into medical school. She told herself many things to excuse her own egregious conduct, but the truth of it was, once she had gone to bed with Steve Benson, there was no turning back. Caryn had always been matter-of-fact about sex; she was a doctor, after all. She had borne two children. But on those stolen afternoons Steve brought her to sexual life. He was fearless. He used his hands like no man she had ever been with. He used more than that. Toys. Weird unguents, Kinky objects. Steve wakened in Caryn a sexual being, a ravenous voluptuary. *Physician feel thyself:* She was a doctor who only just discovered the pleasures that the body could render, how often and in which new and forbidden ways. She neglected her work and felt guilty. She neglected her husband and felt guilty. She neglected her children and felt guilty. And yet the overwhelming physical passion she felt for Steve drowned out everything else in her life, including Nell Faraday's repeated admonitions that he was bad for her, in every way. Caryn told Nell to butt out of her private life.

Andrew found out, of course. After a few months of scenes, Andrew moved out. He filed for divorce. He asked for custody of his children. Caryn's divorce was long and messy and actually went to trial where, in the custody hearing, Andrew's attorney brought up not only the affair and the fact that Steve was by now living in the same home with Caryn and Scott and Elise, but also various unsavory episodes from Steve's life that he had never disclosed to Caryn. Caryn's lawyer, admitting that Mr. Benson's character wasn't perhaps sterling, nonetheless convinced the judge that he posed no danger whatever to the two minor children, Scott and Elise.

The judge found for joint custody. Scott and Elise had two homes. Their parents worked on an elaborate plan of three nights one week and four nights the next at each parent's house, alternate weekends. And then Andrew got them for spring break. Disneyland. And then the plane plunged into the sea. Andrew and Scott and Elise were at the bottom of the ocean. Together. Caryn had lost her custody battle to God or Fate or Heaven itself. Caryn Henley was alone with her grief and her boyfriend. And then she was just alone.

Except for Nell.

After Steve left, Nell prescribed a ritual burning of all the sheets Steve had slept on. And they did. Then Nell prescribed the rituals of home improvement, and over the course of several months, she and Caryn redid Caryn's bedroom and bathroom so that no trace of her old life remained: from the fixtures to the curtains to the lighting and the wallpaper and carpet, the rooms looked entirely new, Steve vanquished. Andrew too, for that matter. The children's rooms, of course, remained untouched. Just as they were, those sheets unchanged. Sometimes Caryn slept in their beds.

Though Caryn could function as a doctor at work, she could not quite function as a human being. That's when Nell urged therapy. Dr. Kim Ogilvie. Give it six months. Let her help you. Caryn declined. She said she'd been once to Dr. Ogilvie, and her waiting room was done up in the profession's preferred peach and cream and blue framed pictures of dolphins. Tacky. But Nell would not be deterred. She was the St. Bernard. So Caryn went.

Dr. Oglivie insisted on being called Kim. She talked a lot about grief abatement. After a few visits, Caryn took a bit of backhanded pleasure in recounting to Nell some of Kim's suggestions. They were the very suggestions Nell would not like to hear: that Caryn should quit Women's Uptown, find new and more challenging work than these old routines. Move to a different city where the stimulus would be all new and exhilarating. Nell only growled or grumped or said pass the salt. Caryn did not add that she declined Kim's suggestions because she would not leave Nell.

To this Kim said, "Nonsense. You don't owe Nell that kind of loyalty." Kim believed Caryn should move from the house where she had lived with her children, seek and endorse a new life, be always occupied and not dwell on her losses.

Caryn said, "I like to dwell with my losses. It's the only place I can bear to dwell. Every day that I do not shoot myself I have endorsed life."

Oddly, Kim's notions of grief abatement returned to Caryn as she sat in Penny Taylor's class. Not that Penny ever used such a phase. But Penny used so many garden metaphors in talking about the memoir that Caryn began to think of her grief, of her whole life, as an unsightly weed-strewn lot: a bramble of bracken and thorny blackberries with thick, twisting sinews, nettles, belladonna, resistant even to the backhoe and the chain saw. The thought amused her. Surely the city would come in and demand that something be done. Put up a sign. Spray. Mow. Charge the property owner if she could be found. But Caryn's grief did not abate. Its roots were deep and reached down down to the core of her life, the choices she had made. If she had not been unfaithful, if she had stayed married to Andrew, then he would not have taken the children to Disneyland by himself. They all four might have gone. Or wouldn't have gone. Dead or alive, they would all be together. Caryn wanted them all to be together.

But she went forward, addicted to the numbing routines of the Women's Uptown and the more pleasurable routines of Saturday night with Ted Swanson. The whole of Saturday night at Ted's apartment. In Ted's bed.

Ted was a new experience for her, lover, companion, friend. The sex was satisfying but not consuming. She thought this must be what people meant when they talked about mature love. She wasn't sure.

After they had established a regular, satisfying Saturday night ritual, he asked if there were someone else in her life.

"What makes you think so?"

"I don't think so. I think you're too honest a person to be cheating. But I've never seen your house. We always come to my apartment. I thought maybe you lived with someone. Maybe not a lover, maybe a rottweiler, a horrible old crone of an aunty."

"No. There's no old crone aunty. No vicious dog. No crazy-jealous lover," she added, thinking of Steve who had been crazy-jealous of everything: her kids, her career, her patients, her education, her friends, who had needed to make himself always paramount. The one on top in every way. "I live alone. I was married once. I told you that. I'm divorced now. A long time ago."

"Where does your ex-husband live?"

She lay her head in the comfortable niche of his shoulder. She feared telling him. Feared losing what she had with him, that he would see her as she sometimes saw herself, a woman made a pariah, a woman whose guilty affair had cost her finally her marriage, her children, their lives, any hope of redemption or restitution, an individual somehow stained and set apart. He was a lawyer, after all, he would see that she was guilty. And then she decided that while all that was true, she had to tell him the truth, not the prim, tweezed truth one puts in a memoir, but the whole of it, and if she lost him, she would be no more alone than she'd been before they met.

Ted Swanson was not a spontaneous sort of man, so it was something of a surprise to Caryn when on a Wednesday afternoon, late, he called her at the Women's Uptown Clinic and asked her to meet him for a drink right after work. He had something important to discuss. Not over the phone. "Call me when you're going to leave work and I'll meet you at La Gondola."

He was there, his customary martini before him when she arrived. He always had one. Never more than that. He had taken a table way in the back near the white marble fountain where the walls were papered with life-sized gondolas covered in snow. He waited till she had ordered and the waiter had left them, and then he said he heard something very troubling on the radio: a local antiabortion group had recently started a new system of harassment of any clinic that performed abortions. Keeping their required legal distance from the clinics, they stationed true believers across the street and gave them video cameras and published the pictures constantly on the Internet. Anyone entering or leaving the clinic—staff, patients, the mailman, the pizza delivery kid—could be seen, day or night, around the world. Ted had gone to this site, and there was the Women's Uptown Clinic, Portland, Oregon. He wanted Caryn's permission to seek an injunction against the group and their video camera. He said it was a violation of privacy and possibly dangerous. He was concerned for her.

She was touched, but she did not think the cameras were dangerous.

"It's a legal issue too," he protested. "I can stop this."

"But I don't want you to pursue it."

"I'll work pro bono."

"It's not that, though it's generous of you, but really, I don't want to give in to these people. It's what they want. These groups, whatever they're calling themselves this time, Fetus Protectors or Freedom for Embryos, Family Champions, they want us to go to court to stop them. They want the media and the legal profession to make a stink over their tactics and call attention to their cause. Believe me, when you've been at this as long as I have, you see that they work in cycles, you might say. They flare up, they die down. But they're like their own disease. Sometimes they're more virulent than others."

"But they never go away."

"No. They never go away. But truly, they go in cycles."

"It could be dangerous for your staff too."

"It could. It probably is, but we can't be fearful. It's what they want. The worst of it is that one of our young receptionists thinks it's funny. Chantal calls out 'yo' mama' jokes across the street. I've told her, and everyone in the office, they absolutely can't do this. Esther, our office manager, made it very clear that anyone who engages in name-calling will find her job in jeopardy."

"Maybe some of the women who come to you would prefer that the whole world didn't know they were walking into the clinic."

Caryn gave a rueful laugh. "We're not exactly the Cedars of Sinai Hospital, Ted. No one wants be seen coming into our clinic. The women who come to us have no health insurance, no money. They are girls in trouble and old women who didn't think that lump was anything at all. They're women who never take care of their own health because they've got so much else to worry about. Their men are gone or just unreliable, and show up when they're broke and horny. Our patients have lost jobs, or never had them. They're bag ladies and drunks and drug addicts. If they have young kids, their kids worry them sick. If their kids are grown, they've probably abandoned Mom. Our patients are living on Social Security or disability, or under tarps beneath the freeways. They're women the world has forgotten, many of them, not all. Most. Would they be at the Women's Uptown if they had their own doctors? No. No one wants to be seen coming in or out."

"Except you and Nell."

"And our staff. We are Uptown Women. Besides, we've thought of a way to protect our patients. Nell and I came up with this." She smiled conspiratorially. "We've opened the back door for patients. Esther calls all the patients with appointments and tells them to park in the back, where it says Staff Only, and come through the back door, which also says Staff Only. We're leaving it open. That way they don't need to fear the cameraman. They're protected by the building. It's private property and the protesters can't trespass. If our patients take the bus, at least they're warned, and they can come in the back too."

"Where does the staff park?" He asked, ever the precise lawyer.

"Down at the Safeway. We walk to the clinic, so the patients can have the whole staff parking lot and come in the back."

"Very clever."

"We thought so."

"I could do it swiftly, Caryn. A talk with the judge—"

"They'll give up after a while. If we cower in front of these fanatics, they'll just take strength from it." She finished her Campari and soda. "Now, I have to go. It's Wednesday, and tonight the Memoir Club is doing my piece."

"So you finally found a way to write it."

"No. Not that. I didn't find a way to write that." She flushed slightly. "I'll never be able to write about my kids. I wrote about the clinic, about Women's Uptown."

"I'd like to read it."

"You would? I don't write very well."

"I'd like to read it."

She kissed him on the cheek before she left.

At the Memoir Club that night, Caryn's piece about the Uptown Women's Clinic collected applause. Even Penny said she had excellent narrative voice. Caryn wasn't certain what this was, but she was glad it was excellent. When Penny proceeded, critiquing her way from the piece's strengths to its weaknesses, she said only that Caryn had offered up the general; she should now move to the specific. "Detail," Penny emphasized.

"Like the Greasy Spoon?" asked Caryn, trying very hard to fathom what Penny wanted from her. "Like the sheets Rusty was hanging out?"

Penny pondered for a while. The silence hung among them like a slowly deflating balloon. At last she asked, "What are you especially good at in this work?"

This was not what Caryn expected, and she couldn't imagine why it would matter, although she certainly knew the answer to the question. "I'm careful with my patients. I treat them like people, not just bodies, not just a chart full of afflictions."

"You counsel them? Console them?"

"When necessary, yes. I let them know their options. But you have to tread a line with some patients. You have to be careful. Especially with those who don't know what they want."

"Then write about one of those cases. You'll figure it out."

"Figure what out?"

"What you need to know."

"Don't you have a garden metaphor for Caryn?" asked Sarah Jane with arch simplicity.

"Not for Caryn," replied Penny, ignoring the irony. "At least not for now."

Other than our regulars—the bag ladies who need to dry out, the homeless OD whose friends always bring her in because we're nearby, the woman who wants us to examine her doll—most of the patients I see are not memorable. Like the actor who remembers only his bad reviews, I remember the patients I can't help. The ones who come to me and then refuse any medical alternative, these are perplexing patients. I don't know what they want of me.

Take someone like Darcy Reeves. Darcy is about nineteen, I would guess, tall, stunningly attractive with dark curly hair, fair skin, and clear eyes. She carries herself with a self-possession that would make you swear she was thirty. At least she did when she first came in. She was with her husband, Daniel. He really was thirty. Maybe pushing forty. He was a solid, thickly bearded man, his hair once red now a dull sandy color, and angry skin beneath the beard. His eyebrows met at top of his nose. All in all, he gave the impression of a man in hairy camouflage. He was a terrible contrast to the beautiful Darcy. He skulked there beneath his wild hair while she looked at everything with a direct and unflinching vision. She was poised, and there was nothing goofy or ingratiating about her. Lots of eighteen-year-olds feel obliged to make jokes and you have to respond in kind, at least at first. Then at some point, you have to say, really, it's not funny. What we're about here, it is not funny.

But Darcy had none of that. She was newly pregnant, perhaps four weeks, her first child, and first pregnancy. She said she wasn't sure what to do. Terminate or continue. It was an unplanned pregnancy, and she just wasn't sure. I remember Darcy because her words, her stated dilemma, the dithering it implied were so completely at odds with everything else about her. The flat, clear gaze. The soft voice. The lift of her chin. I suspected that Daniel was the one who dithered, and that she had brought him along so he couldn't later complain he'd been left out. They were an odd couple. He struck me as a whiner. He grunted rather than made audible assent. He pressed his fingertips together till the nails went white under the pressure. He kept his blue eyes on the floor, nodding now and then, twitching to register some negative reaction. He said very little. Sometimes he would look up to the woman in the Monet print, and the eyebrows over his nose knotted.

I asked the usual questions. Leading questions in the sense that if the patient wants counseling, even consoling, that's an option I can offer. I do not leap over the desk and pat anyone's shoulder. But I tell the patient what procedures are medically possible within the law.

After I examined Darcy she kept her same composure. Most women told yes, they're pregnant, whatever their feelings about the pregnancy, they evince some emotion. Happiness. Chagrin. Wretchedness. Whatever. But Darcy thanked me without ever changing her expression. I told her we had a lot of literature to give her and to make an appointment for next month. Then, without emotion, not so much as a quaver in the voice, she said again she might terminate. She wasn't sure. I told her to come back in when she was sure. I told her she had twelve weeks to choose. I consulted the calendar and gave her a date. I told her to think it through, that an appointment to terminate couldn't always be had for the asking and advised her not let it go too late.

The next time she came in, I asked if she wanted Daniel in the examining room with her. She said no. She had come alone anyway, and he was not her husband, though she did live with him and he was the father of her child. Physically she was fine, a young woman perfectly poised to carry her child to term. I told her this. I said everything was fine and right on schedule. She should take her vitamins.

"I may have an abortion. I'm not sure."

"Take your vitamins anyway."

"Why should I, if I'm going to have an abortion?"

"Vitamins are good for you. Listen, Darcy, termination is an option, of course," I said, "but usually it's an emotional decision for women and you don't seem particularly vested in it, on either side."

She considered this with a studious sort of air. Like a high school student. Finally she said, "It's not like I don't have feelings in this."

"I didn't say that."

"I have feelings."

I waited for her to say what they were, but not much else was forthcoming, so I gave her the speech on prenatal care. I asked if she worked. "Some kinds of work you have to be extra careful when you're pregnant."

"My job is having this baby."

"That's fine. That's great."

"Except I might not have it."

"Yes, of course."

"What do you advise, Dr. Henley?"

"About?"

"Having the baby."

"Darcy, that kind of advice you have to ask someone else. I have told you the medical options within the law, but the choices are yours. You have to follow your own conscience and assess your own needs. I can't do it. If you want to talk to a counselor, I can refer you. If you want—"

"It sounds like you're reading my rights. The right to remain silent, all that."

Her equanimity was beginning to get on my nerves. "This isn't a television show, Darcy. This is your life. Do you have anyone you can confide in, besides Daniel, I mean? Where are your parents?"

"Daniel and I live with my parents. We all live together."

"How do your parents feel about your pregnancy?"

"My job is having this baby," she repeated. "Everyone has some kind of work assigned to them and that's mine."

"Assigned by who?"

She blinked. Was that the first time she'd blinked? I couldn't recall. I suddenly realized how beautiful she was. Not a sculpted fake face like a movie star, but the fresh and extravagant beauty like that of a poem or a painting that made you happy just to be nearby, to breathe nearby her. And yet, for all that dazzle, her smile was mirthless and not at all young.

"Everyone has something to do, Dr. Henley. Something assigned. You're a doctor."

"Yes, that's my job, but I wasn't assigned to it."

"You chose it."

"Yes."

She pressed her full lips tightly. I thought she might be going to cry, or at least that her unflappable poise might be deserting her. She was a kid, after all. I told her, "Having a baby is a huge life choice and your life and your body will never be the same." Then, trying not to sound didactic, as if I were attempting to say her decision, I added, "That's just a fact of life."

"I might have an abortion."

I closed up her chart. I asked her if she had any further questions. She paused, again sort of thinking it over. I got antsy, annoyed, and I said if she did, she could always call Women's Uptown Clinic, and we would answer her questions, assist her in any way we could.

I left the examining room. I handed the chart to Nell, but before I gave it to her, I took my green ink pen and made a check in the upper right-hand corner of the first page. This is what we use to indicate that the patient may be under some kind of unstated psychological stress. These patients always have to be seen by the doctor, not the nurse-practitioner. Sometimes the green check just stays there for years. People stay depressed or anxious or strung out or hungover for years. Sometimes they get better. Sometimes we just never see them again.

A week later, I saw Darcy Reeves's name on my colleague's appointments. For a termination. So she had made up her mind. Later I found out she was a no-show. I asked Chantal to call the home and just inquire in a general fashion if Darcy was all right. Chantal told me she got a message box, a computer voice with no names. Chantal asked if she should leave a message. Sure, I said, leave a message, but I also asked Chantal to flag this patient. Everything should be referred through me. I told Esther, next time Darcy Reeves came in, check her driver's license. She might look thirty, but we want to be certain that she's not a minor.

A week, ten days later, when Esther handed me her chart, she said Darcy Reeves was actually twenty years old. Darcy was in the waiting room. I told Esther I'd see her in the office, not the examining room.

This time Darcy Reeves was not composed or poised. Neither was she blubbering, but her face was all puffy from crying and her eyes were red. She was pale and her voice was shaky and she said she'd only come in to make an appointment for the termination.

"You've done that," I said. "You were a no-show."

"I changed my mind."

"You've changed your mind again?"

"Yes."

"Darcy, I feel like someone, I don't know who it is, Daniel or your parents or someone, is putting undue pressure on you."

"Are you an abortion counselor? Is that what you're doing?"

"No, I am not. I think you should see a counselor, though. I think you should talk to someone before you take this step. I don't think you want to terminate this pregnancy."

"I tell you I don't want the baby. I want an abortion. You have to give me an abortion."

"I thought it was your job, having the baby. Are you giving up your job?"

She laughed, only it wasn't a laugh, it reminded me of a rusty razor on tender skin.

I glanced at her chart. "Darcy, you have about ten days left to make this decision. Let me give you a referral to a counselor and then you come back here. Whatever you decide is fine, but it has to be your own choice." I wrote out the referral and handed it to her. I started to say something else, but she got up and left, her tall body swaying gracefully. She did not close the door.

"She won't be back." That's what Nell said before they went to the Memoir Club the night that Caryn's memoir would be discussed. They were in the clinic lunchroom, eating microwaved Chinese takeout, heavy on the cornstarch. Nell sucked thoughtfully on the end of her chopsticks. "Somebody is telling Darcy it's bad and wicked to be pregnant and unmarried, and she's all torn up because her mind and her body and her heart are telling her to keep the kid. Somebody at home, probably. Or maybe it's the opposite. They're telling her this is her job and she's only twenty and she doesn't want any part of it. Somebody is pulling her strings."

"It's not as if she's Rusty Meadows thirty-five years ago, knocked up and no help in sight. Darcy lives with the father. And her own parents. When she first came in with Daniel, she filled out the forms as Mrs. Daniel Phillips."

"A lie."

"Yes, but of the two of them, she was the more collected."

"That was weeks ago, Caryn. She has ten days to make up her mind. If she has the abortion, she'll be so guilty, she'll fall apart, and if she doesn't, she'll piss them off, Daniel or the parents or whoever, and they'll make her life a hell. She loses either way. We've seen it all before."

"I know, but she just seemed so, well, so . . ."

"Self-possessed."

"Yes. How did you know?"

Nell laughed. "It's in your memoir. You said it! Your writing is much better. You get to pass go and collect one hundred dollars! What did Ted say when he read it?"

Caryn looked pleased. "He liked it. He said it was very well written."

"An astute man. I thought they'd given up making that model. Seriously," she added more tentatively, "maybe he should go with you this year. You know. To the picnic."

Caryn rinsed off their chopsticks and carefully closed up the cartons before tossing them in the trash. "The anniversary this year is on a Tuesday, but the picnic won't be the weekend before like it always is. It has to be after. People are busy. Isn't that amazing, Nell? People are too busy? How can that be?"

"Things change. People's lives go on."

"But that day is sacred."

"Yes, but time doesn't matter to the dead. It only matters to the living. There will be fewer people there this year than there were last year. And fewer the year after that, and one day there won't be a picnic at all."

"Don't say that."

"It's true."

Caryn leaned against the sink, breaking into an MSG sweat.

"You should go with someone new. Not me. Maybe Kim Ogilvie was right about opening your life to someone new, Caryn. Ted is a good man. I felt that even last winter when we'd just met him. There's something first-rate about him, and he cares about you. That's a gift. He cares enough to want to go to court to fight those fucking morons with the video cameras. When did you last meet a man who wanted to protect you?"

"I don't need a man to protect me."

"Everyone needs someone, Caryn."

"I have you."

"Yes. You have me, the St. Bernard."

"I never called you that. I was the guy in the snow."

"But snow is melting. Slowly. Just like in the old Beatles song. You know?" Nell sang the first few bars of "Here Comes the Sun" as she washed her hands and mopped them dry with a coarse paper towel. "Come on, let's lock up. We don't want to be late, and we have to walk to the Safeway to get the car."

"Why can't I die of a broken heart, Nell? They say people can. Why not me? Why couldn't I just die of a broken heart? It would be so much easier than living with it."

"Because you are a doctor. You are a model of competence. You are a healer. Because you are an athlete and a woman of stamina. Because we are Uptown Women and we have each other and as long as we have that, we'll always have Scott and Elise and Andrew. But that doesn't mean you can't have Ted too."

6

Tiger in the Tree

I began my teaching career at the age of ten in a one-room schoolhouse in rural Washington State, a town now known as Thornton Euclid, though back then, in the Depression, they were two towns close by one another. I shared that first classroom with my mother. Not by choice. Pa built a low partition down the middle of the room, and eventually he painted my side. He was mad with paint, my pa. He said I could choose what I wanted and he would paint it for me. All right, I said. I'd like a jungle with animals. He limped away laughing, saying, I count on you, Sarah Jane, to stump me every time. What he painted on the partition wasn't the sort of jungle you would ever actually see, more of a Garden of Eden jungle with buffalos and cheetah-looking creatures, tigers and possums and a couple of fat bears who looked to be dancing with the monkeys. He put the tiger in the pine tree with the possums.

"Is that how you came by the name *The Laughing Cat?*" asked Rusty when we were all gathered at Francine's to discuss my memoir.

I said no, but then I reconsidered. "Well, when I think back on that tiger, I think he did have a smile on his face."

"Probably because he was about to eat the possum," offered Nell.

"The possum was not smiling. That I remember."

"What was on your mother's side of the partition?" asked Penny, coming down hard with her dirty athletic shoe on the untidy papers at her feet. It was a fine spring evening, so warm that Francine had opened the French doors and a little breeze had wafted in and rustled Penny's papers.

"The stove," I said and laughed. "I had the babies, kids who were between, say, five and eight. We called them the babies, anyone who couldn't yet read. Ma taught the older children. They might be as old as fourteen. Most children didn't go to school past that. Anyone in Euclid who wanted to go to high school had to go all the way to Mount Vernon, and you had to board there besides, at least during the week. In the Depression people just didn't do that. If you could read, and do your sums, enough math to get you through the world, if you knew the dates of the Civil War and the first sentence of the Declaration of Independence, that was enough for most people."

"What did kids do when they left school?" asked Jill. "I mean, fourteen is awfully young to be . . . well, cast out into the world."

"Not then. You'd be surprised what a fourteen-year-old can do. Most of the boys went to the logging camps, or they might sign on fishing boats, or work as day laborers in all the road construction in the Northwest. My brother Virgil drove a truck when he was twelve. The girls went to work in the canneries, or became shop-girls, or stayed home for a year or two and then got married. Narrow horizons," I added. "Most people never thought much beyond that. Never dreamed."

"But you did," said Rusty. "You clearly dreamed beyond that."

"Oh, yes," I said. "I went to the University of Washington, graduated summa cum laude in biology. Not too many girls could say that in those days."

"Well, your mother must have been very proud of you." Francine smiled. "When my sons graduated from college, I was so proud of them, even if their grades weren't very good. Jesse's were really pathetic, if you want to know the truth, but I guess the firm that hired him didn't look too closely. Eric got into grad school only with Marc's considerable help."

"Well, it wasn't really like that for me," I said after a time. I know how to wallpaper the truth with a few well-pasted falsehoods. Everyone does. But I object to it on principle. "Ma didn't want me even to go to Mt. Vernon to high school, much less to UW. Pa insisted. My father, who had no real education to speak of, fought my mother, the teacher, on this score. Finally, she agreed I could go to high school in Mt. Vernon if I got a job there and could pay my own room and board. Pa even talked her out of that. He talked her down to one or the other, room or board. He made her choose right there in front of me. But she had the last word on the subject. She always did."

"What was the last word?" asked Penny.

"Mushrooms," I said, biting down on the fragrant lavender cookies Francine had made for the Memoir Club. I chewed reflectively. "She said at least if I went to high school, I could probably learn to tell one mushroom from another. My father's whole family was wiped out by mushrooms. Everyone but him."

There was a sort of stunned silence then. I've had sixty-some years to get used to this idea. Pa's family graves are in the Thornton Euclid cemetery, and they all have the same date, so you know it was some kind of calamity or another. They're buried nearby my parents. My father always said it was a sorry way to go, killed off by something no bigger than your toe and just as ugly.

"That's terrible," said Caryn.

"I guess it really was," I admitted.

"What about your mother's side?" asked Nell.

"Ma was from Canada. That's all she'd ever tell us of her family. As a young woman she'd come from Canada to teach at that same schoolhouse in Euclid. That's where she met Pa. She married him and followed him off to the logging camps, and the river, but then, after the flood, we came back and she taught school again. I taught too."

"How could you be a teacher if you were only ten?" asked Jill.

"We're missing the point," said Penny, meaning that *we* were missing the point. She wasn't about to miss the point, or let us for very long. She pushed her glasses down over her nose, and eye-balling me in that piercing way, said, "I asked what was on your mother's side of the partition."

I laughed again. "I told you, the stove. And didn't we know it! All winter long."

"I meant the picture," said Penny, smiling in a peculiar, almost conspiratorial way. "What did your father paint on her side of the partition?"

"I can't remember."

"Remember."

Pa never would have discovered paint, never would have picked up a brush if he hadn't lost his leg in a logging accident. He even painted his wooden leg. Just a beautiful design of brilliant colors.

Pa also painted the cedar shake cabin that we lived in. It came with the teaching job. Then he built a nice big shed out back, behind the cabin and the school. He painted that too. He put up a sign: PERKINS FINEST PAINTING, a dazzler in red and blue and gold. When he wasn't painting signs for businesses, new and old, he painted great big ads on the sides of barns, a seascape for a man whose bride had been born on Lopez Island, a mural over the whole bar at the Euclid Hotel. This was his most ambitious picture, and it was a real picture, supposed to show pioneer days when these towns were scarcely more than a rail stop. The engine just gleamed in this mural, and the mules were all detailed right down to the flies on their butts. You could see it from the lobby. It was that big.

What Pa loved was color. He'd scarcely ever left the mountains or the river, but he drew that Lopez Island bride the finest seascape you can imagine. My jungle, that was an eyeful of jungle, all right. I asked him to do the other wall on my side of the classroom. Underwater, I said. I'd like the jungle on one wall and underwater on the other, and a lot of fish. I'd like a river, like the Skagit River where you and I used to go fishing, Pa, when we lived at Watson's Landing.

He drew it so the level of the river was just about as high as an eight-year-old is tall. Above the river there were blue skies and poplars. Just like Watson's Landing. A child, standing by that wall, could hold her nose and pretend to plunge under and swim with the fishes. And what fishes! Hundreds of them, some in great brooding schools, some alone, some peeking out from plant life and from under things the river had swallowed. Rowboats, old troughs and bins, some books and a doll, and the chassis of an 1917 truck. No bodies, of course. The river might have taken lives too, but Pa didn't paint that. This river was full of life. When I came into my classroom and saw what he had done, I said, Pa you are one fine painter. You do everything well, Pa. You made fine Perkins Finest hooch and you paint fine Perkins Finest paintings.

Pa said, thank you, Sarah Jane, but the true Perkins Finest thing I know of is you. You are my Finest, and don't you forget it. Then he stumped out.

So now I had a jungle and a river, but no stove in winter. One December, I asked if he could do me a desert on one wall and the floor. Pa had never seen a desert, had no idea what one might look like, but he said he figured he could do the colors and a couple of cacti and some coyotes. And since I'm at it, Sarah Jane, he said, you got one last wall there. What would you like there?

Whatever you want, Pa. Just paint me whatever you want. Surprise me.

And he did. It was not a picture of anything in particular, but the color just about leaped off the walls and danced with you. You could imagine it to be whatever you wanted. You had to imagine, and in order to do that, you had to bring something to the experience. And that's when I first started to think about how we're porous, humankind. I would never have said it like that, of course, not that young, but something of the sort came to me. You not only take things in, but you give things out. You gave to experience and you took from it. The flow can go either way. Both ways. That's what I posited in my undergraduate work for Professor Plunkett at the University of Washington: we are like membranes. But I was only ten when I found my way toward the practices that have guided my life working with the deaf, the autistic, with people suffering neural impairment from strokes or accidents, with those mentally captive in their own terrible worlds. I have found ways to use the body to free the mind. They say I am a great pioneer in the field. Well, I started young and unwillingly. I told my mother, I'm only ten years old, how can I be a teacher?

Ma said, Sarah Jane, you can read, can't you? You have read lots of books, haven't you?

The answer was yes.

So you can teach the babies to read.

But Ma! I'm not much older than they are.

But you can read, and they can't. It's easy.

But Ma! I don't want to read baby books. I want to read—and here I cast about, biting my lip and fighting my tears, because all those years we lived on the river, I could hardly ever get to the Euclid library. Now I lived here. I could walk to the library and read whatever I wanted.

Read those books later, Sarah Jane. Now I need you to teach the babies.

I knew I had lost. I knew any more fighting was futile and would get me smacked. I said, all right, how do you do it?

Just keep at them. Keep repeating what you want them to learn. By the time they move up to my class, Ma said, they had better be able to read. You see to that, Sarah Jane, I will take care of everything else.

And she did. On her side, the side with the stove, Ma's students sat at long tables facing the front where she stood. Ma kept a long leather switch on the end of a pole with a little possum tail tied to it. Expert fly fisherman could have taken lessons from Ma: how exactly to cast that pole and smack that offender. If a student just nodded off to sleep, he got the possum tail. If he were being in any way disrespectful, which covered just about everything else, he got the leather switch.

I had no such tool to keep the little ones in line. When my students mouthed off or nodded off or whimpered or whatever, which was often, I had no way to punish them except with threats. The babies knew though that if they made too much noise, Ma would come over to our side, switch in hand. Most of the time she didn't have to use it. Her look, and a few harsh words, sufficed. But she would use it if pressed. There was none of this tenderness, the nurturing you find in schools now. No one cared if you had low self-esteem. You had to know how to read if you were going to move up to Ma's class and be near the stove. This was no small consideration.

So to teach these babies to read and to keep them quiet, I started telling stories. Mostly about animals. One for each letter of the alphabet. I'd use the animals that Pa had painted on three of the four walls, the animals in the jungle, the fish in the river, the coyote howling at the sun. It was a brilliant burning red sun in Pa's desert and the coyote howled away. I made up others, nonsense stories mostly, like the tiger in the tree, stories where most of the words started with that one letter. I'd act these stories out, making faces, and walking or dancing or moving in a particular way, mostly to keep warm. But after a time, the babies could recognize the letter just by the way I'd use my body.

My brother Virgil had helped me stack up the benches and tables on my side of the partition in winter, so there was enough room for everyone, me included, to snuggle close together, in a circle on the floor. We pretended we were Indians sometimes on the desert floor, sharing our human warmth. Gave me new respect for the phrase "huddled masses." This was a good way to stay warm, all right, but for me, there remained a problem.

The school, and the cedar shake cabin behind, were crawling with rodents when we moved in. They were everywhere. I cannot bear mice and rats. I have a terrible aversion to them that amounts to phobia. When Virgil wanted to tease me, that's what he'd use. He'd put a dead mouse or a dead rat somewhere close by me. I told him it was not funny, but he didn't heed me. Finally I told Virgil that if he did it again, I'd take that dead mouse and I'd put it in the gas tank of that Dodge truck he was so proud of. He said I wouldn't dare, but he knew I would.

After the Laughing Cat came to live with us, the rodent hordes moved on, or elsewhere. She terrorized those mice and even the great big rats, she would just jump on them, and presto, her work was finished. She'd lick her paws clean. She sent shivers up my spine, though I was grateful to her. Every school morning after breakfast, I'd pick up the Laughing Cat—she never did have a name, just a title—and carry her over to the schoolhouse and let her loose on my side of the partition. By the time the bell rang, I could bear to sit on the desert floor without fear. When it came time for me to read to the babies, I'd join them on the desert floor, open a book, and point to each word as I read. Sometimes I'd ask one of the babies to act out the letters, using my animals stories. And they did learn to read. Even Ma said to me, Sarah Jane, you are just like me. You are a born teacher.

I did not want to hear this. I did not want to be like Ma. I have spent my adult life trying to prove her wrong. But I am a born teacher, though it was not what I set out to do in life. I wanted to be a great biologist, a scientist like Professor Plunkett. That was the glowing vision I had when I graduated from the University of Washington, the only summa cum laude grad among the biology students, and Professor Plunkett's prize pupil. I applied to grad school there. And they turned me down.

Professor Plunkett said to me, Sarah Jane, it's because you are female. That's their rationale for not admitting you. It is wholly wrong, Sarah Jane, biologically wrong, morally wrong, and certainly socially wrong. Should we squander female brains? Should we leave females to the mercy of their hormones? We don't leave males to theirs, do we?

I was so broken in spirit, I could not speak, much less say something smart that would prove I ought to have been admitted to the graduate school.

There may be more to it than that, Sarah Jane. I fear they are punishing you because you are my student. I wrote you a glowing letter.

I read it. I thought that with a letter like that, and everything else, I would be admitted for sure.

There's a political undercurrent here. I have made enemies over the years. My ideas have rankled with many. I've been here a long time. They can't get rid of me, but they don't have to endorse me. In refusing you, they're telling me that my recommendation is insufficient, no longer valid. That I'm finished and a has-been. It is as much a slap against me as it is to you.

Except, I said, I am the one not admitted to graduate school.

What will you do now?

I saw myself teaching the babies to read for the rest of my life. I said I had no plans, but I had no hopes either.

I can offer you work, Sarah Jane. I need an assistant. It won't be graduate school in the formal sense. A sort of private graduate school, you might say. I'm not as strong as I used to be, and I would be very grateful for your assistance. We can do much together.

We did. I stayed with Horace Plunkett, sharing his work, his writings, his ideas, though not his bed. He never asked that of me, and I never offered. For eight years, till Horace died—fell over one day, just attacked by his own heart—I worked with him, wrote with him, published with him, studied with him, becoming his colleague rather than assistant. And after he died, I knew I was finished at the University of Washington. But Reed College hired me to carry on his work. I have lived in the same house in Portland ever since.

I loved Horace Plunkett, thirty years my senior, bald, corpulent, with merry eyes and the most astonishing imagination ever. I loved him, though naturally, in those years, I fell in love with other men. I made all the usual mistakes and wrongheaded alliances, the errors of judgment and passion that people make, each of us believing our experience to be unique in the annals of humanity. I never got married, though. I never made that mistake.

And if I could, I would say to Ma, maybe I am a born teacher, but I am not like you. I have never used a leather switch with a possum tail on anyone. And except for my sister, I have never slapped anyone. I have never denied the ordinary old human warmth to anyone who asked it of me. In that school where I worked with you, Ma, warmth and color were kept apart, on either side of a partition. So all my life I have tried to keep them together. I paint my hair, so that even if I'm old and gray, I will never be drained of color. I never want to outgrow surprise and delight. I want to be able to see the tiger in the tree when he appears, unlooked for, surprising and delightful.

Penny Taylor pondered over my offering. She frowned. And though all my compatriots in the Memoir Club loved it—and said so—I could tell that Penny did not love it.

"Adequate, but still wanting," she announced in her odd, formal way.

"Wanting what?" I asked.

"Everything you've left out." Penny set the teacup down without looking, and you could tell Francine was about to pounce on her if she missed the saucer and put the cup on the inlaid side table. "You didn't even answer the initial question."

"I didn't?" I rifled through my own pages. "What more is there to say? On her side of the partition, Ma had the stove. She had the warmth. I had the color."

"So her side was utterly bare?"

"Well, no, of course not. It was your usual utilitarian schoolroom. There was a portrait of Abraham Lincoln and one of George Washington and one of FDR. There was a map of the world that pre-dated the Great War, and a guide to the parts of speech, and a copy of the Pledge of Allegiance just in case you didn't know it by heart."

"But nothing painted."

I got a little prickly at this, though it was a straightforward question. "Well, no. My father never painted anything on her side of the partition."

"Why not?" asked Penny.

I have been using the reflex of laughter in my work for nearly forty years, but there are some things inherently grave, resistant to laughter. But I laughed just the same, to deflect her attention.

Penny was having none of it. "It's not a death and destruction question, Sarah Jane. Is it?" She looked around, as if we were taking a vote. "It's a simple recognition, the sort of thing that lies," she pondered, searching for a garden metaphor, "not at the root of who you are, nothing like that. Maybe a weed you never bothered to pull. If you once do pull it, try to pull it, you're not sure how deep the roots are. Are you?"

I replied reluctantly, distilling a complex answer down to its simplest form. I am not a weeper. My voice was steady. "Pa was waiting for Ma to ask. He would have painted her anything if she'd asked.

She never did ask. If she'd asked, she would have had to say thank you, and it wasn't in her." I felt as though I had spit out some hard smooth stone I had carried under my tongue for years, maybe all my life.

Penny gave a little inward grunt and made some notes. "You remember that first handout I gave you? A memoir is an act not just of preservation but of invention. The memoir is a narrative construct: literary shape that you give to the past. You need to go back to the river, Sarah Jane."

"The Skagit River? Watson's Landing?"

Penny packed up her papers. "You should begin at the beginning."

"That wasn't the beginning. I wasn't born there. I was born up in the mountains."

"That isn't the beginning I'm talking about," she said almost merrily. "What does it matter where you're born, or where you die? Much is left out. Much is subsumed. Much is demanded," she went on, quoting her own handout. "That's what you want to remember. Especially the subsumed and demanded."

She asked after the time then. She said the time had got away from her. She always said this, though she never wore a watch. These Wednesday night class meetings went three hours exactly. No more. No less. Then Penny was done, and she left right on time. The rest of us never do. We always linger a bit. Helping Francine clean up, we slowly collect our things, make small talk. Everyone said to me they thought Penny was wrong, that my memoir was far better than adequate and not wanting at all. But I knew what she meant. And I knew that if I were to live up to what Pa thought of me, if truly I were to be Perkins Finest, I would have to follow Penny's suggestion, to find what the river had subsumed and demanded of us.

Writing Your Memoir

PENNY TAYLOR, INSTRUCTOR

Things to remember

The experience described in the memoir is not fresh.
Not raw.
The grit of daily life has been expunged,
polished, washed away.
The memoir has always the advantage of hindsight.
It recognizes the significance of people and events.
It pulls the past into a pattern.
It gives the past shape and meaning that it did not
have when it was the present.

PART II
Past and Pattern

7

Thankless Hordes

THE LETTER THAT FRANCINE HELLMAN HAD SENT TO Marc's old friends, former colleagues, associates and assistants, had not had the desired effect.

> Dear [fill in the name],
>
> I'm writing to you now especially because I need your help in broadening and better documenting Marc's life in my memoir. I want to expand on his work, his research, to detail the great discoveries for which he never received proper credit. I want this memoir to reflect not only the legacy he left to Eric and Jesse and me, his family, but what he left to each of you, to the world for that matter. I will welcome your personal insights and contributions, details, as my writing teacher is always saying.

In response to this carefully phrased, gracious (Francine was sure it was gracious) inquiry, what did she get? Brief, dashed-off, uninspired replies, notes accompanying reprints of scientific papers these individuals had written with Marc, who was nearly always first author. Sometimes there were no notes. Just the reprints. Sometimes the individual might scribble across the top, *For Fran, All best.* Especially galling, as she detested "Fran." Some sent the reprint with only their own signature scrawled across the top, as if it were some valuable first edition. Francine bristled to open the mail, and daily, her heart sank. On her desk she had a tray labeled THANKLESS HORDES. The letters overflowed.

Even those individuals who actually wrote back offered her nothing but dashed-off phrases. *The best of men . . . The finest of scientists . . . A brilliant mind . . . Best of his generation . . . A fond mentor . . . An exacting teacher . . .* These scribbled eulogies suggested, in truth, that in the three years since his death, Marc Hellman—the real, the vital, the incomparable Marc Hellman—had been all but forgotten, that he would, already had, diminish to a footnote. What remained of the man and the scientist was a collection of stale praise cast in conventional phrases. As these materials collected, Fran felt her dismay, her pique cinder down to sadness. Those few friends she still saw from her old Dr. and Mrs. Marcus Hellman life were not interested in the responses she'd received; they were not interested in her memoir, for that matter. But the members of the Memoir Club—that's how they thought of themselves now—were more than interested, they were indignant on her behalf. These women, who had never known Marc, shared her frustration at the paltry responses. They even shared her sadness. And this was a new sensation for Francine. Joy, irritation, dismay, all these emotions one could offer about with impunity, but sadness was an emotion Francine had never shared with anyone but Marc.

None of the Memoir Club could understand how Marc's former colleagues could be so thoughtless, heartless, and uncaring. Penny Taylor, adopting one of her favorite phrases, asked Francine if her note was, well, wanting. Penny Taylor said, "If you've had such a resounding failure, perhaps there was something wrong with the note you originally wrote, your original inquiry."

"No. It was simple and direct. It was gracious."

"Maybe it was too gracious."

Was it possible to be too gracious? "Would you like to read it, Penny? I have copy on my desk."

"No, thank you. But you want to remember, all of you." She nodded, and in her prim, steadfast way, regarded her students one by one. Very disconcerting when she did this. "Clarity is the responsibility of the writer. Not the reader. Maybe you need to try again."

So Francine sent out a second round of notes. In these, she thanked everyone who had taken the time to write in the first

place, even those who had merely autographed their stinking reprints, of which Francine already had copies in the files in Marc's
study. Since Marc was first author, of course she had copies. In her
second note, and in true Francine fashion, she indicated exactly
what she wanted done without ever quite offering instructions. Suggestions, yes. She stated her aims for the memoir and requested a
few moments of their valuable time to help her to coordinate the
various aspects of Marc's career and contribute to a memoir worthy
of him. As she filled in each name after *Dear,* she sometimes found
herself muttering. "If Marc hadn't given up his valuable time for
you, where would you be? Where would any of you be, but for him?
Without Marc there would be no prestigious research institutes at
Johns Hopkins and MIT and the University of Chicago and UCLA.
You needed my husband, you thankless wretch."

To this second note Francine received a brief flurry of short,
uninformative replies and a few desultory e-mails. Really, did no
one take the time to write anymore? Much less to write well. She
found herself going over these letters, marking them up, cryptically
correcting, as Penny Taylor might have, punctuation, grammar,
spelling.

Jesse and Eric knew, or knew of, most of the people to whom
she'd written. Francine often dashed off hurried e-mails to her
sons, naming names and casting aspersions: That ungrateful
Sharon Fadiman. And Curtis Field! Can you imagine? They owe
him their careers. As the second round of replies dribbled in, or
failed to dribble in, she excoriated Marc's former friends and colleagues, people whom she had endlessly entertained for years.
Where would these people be without Marc? And do you know
what they write to me? Things like he was a fine scientist. That's
all. Bye-bye. Of course he was a fine scientist! Don't they think I
know that? Why else would I be writing a book about his life? Are
they dense as well as rude, thoughtless, and thankless?

She wrote to Jesse and Eric when her indignation was fresh,
when it had not yet distilled to the sad realization that Marc was
not only dead, he had diminished. The sense of his presence in
the house dissipated. Even in his study. Francine spent hours in his
study, only to understand how alone she was, how alone she had
been for three years. She told the realtor to drop the price on the
house. She wanted it sold. She wanted to leave. To be near some-

one she loved and who loved her. Marc was dead, but Jesse and Eric were only far away.

Jesse and Eric did not know their mother was suffering anything more than pique on behalf of their father. Every time she wrote to them, for all her ire directed at others, they read, implicit in her words, what you two write about your father had better by hell be more detailed and more useful than these. And so Jesse and Eric wrote back that they were hard at work complying with her request. They asked after specific people on Fran's list, including Yu-Chun. "And after everything Marc lavished on her," Francine declared, "she can't even write back to me." Jesse and Eric breathed a sigh of mutual relief.

Realizing that her stack of Thankless Hordes was of no use to her whatever, Fran threw these disheartening replies in the recycle. Then she remembered Caryn Henley saying how there was a pleasant finality in burning one's old unsatisfactory drafts in the sink or over the toilet. Francine took the Thankless Hordes' letters into the kitchen, and one by one, lit the corners. Then she went and found the scientific reprints they had sent her, especially those autographed ones, and these she burned in the sink too. She left the kitchen window open and the smoke wafted out into the garden. She stood there for quite a long time, seeing them into ash. There. She had destroyed the evidence that Marc no longer mattered. She really must remember to thank Caryn for the tip.

After some weeks, she got a letter from Yu-Chun Liu in Taiwan. She burned that too. Not right away, but she burned that too.

8

Auburn #7

"Mom! Get the phone, will you? Diane and I are doing my breathing."

The least Amy could do was answer the phone, Rusty thought, fanning away the fumes. "You get it, Amy. Answering the phone isn't exactly heavy lifting." She set the timer and sat on the closed toilet. She was altering her life, one small step at a time. This step was Auburn #7. As a girl, Charity Manning had lustrous auburn hair. If time had dulled and grayed her hair, well, that was easily changed, wasn't it? Rusty felt the need for change. All this wading into the past, writing the memoir for Melissa, was difficult; she had not even thought of Charity Manning for years and years. Now, spending months writing about Charity, she remembered what lovely hair Charity once had. That was when she looked in the mirror at her own undistinguished locks. That was when she bought Auburn #7 and waited till Sunday morning to apply.

"It's for you." Amy brought the portable phone into the bathroom and returned to her breathing and MTV.

Rusty took the phone. A woman's voice inquired after Rusty Meadows. "Yes."

"This is Suzanne Post calling. I'm here in Portland."

Rusty closed the bathroom door and opened the window to let out the hair color fumes that might otherwise overwhelm her. *Melissa.* Certainly, she felt overwhelmed. *Melissa.* This was not how it was supposed to happen. She was not supposed to be standing here in an old T-shirt, a frumpy, overweight, a middle-aged broad with one hand on the timer and a head full of hair color. The whole carousel of what she had imagined played up and down before her, and she seemed to suffer from motion sickness, woozy, so much so that she had to sit back down on the toilet.

"Are you there? Rusty?"

"Yes." Are you there, Melissa? Are you really there? Melissa. O my beloved. Melissa. "Where are you calling from?" Rusty managed to eke out.

"I'm in Portland for a conference of media specialists."

"I thought you were a librarian. I mean, I'd heard—"

"Yes, well, whoever you paid to find me must be hopelessly behind the times. We're not school librarians anymore. We're information specialists, media specialists. I prefer that. At least an information specialist wouldn't automatically have dandruff and wear her hair in a bun."

Rusty laughed too long at Suzanne's wit. "I'm very happy to hear from you. Very." *Melissa. Melissa.* "I'm surprised, that's all. You've taken me by surprise."

"I know. It's been a long time since I got your letter."

"Two years." I must be harmless and cheerful, Rusty reminded herself. "But that's fine. I didn't really expect to hear from you at all. So I'm, well, I'm just delighted." There, that was fine. Convincing but not desperate. No pouncing or weeping.

"I came to this Portland conference not knowing if I would call you or not. I have hesitated and struggled with it, really." This tiny confession made her voice relax, just a bit. "I have struggled with the idea of making this phone call at all. I knew if I called, I couldn't go back."

Rusty smiled; tears lit her eyes. "Yes. There's no going back." *Melissa.* "I can't tell you how happy I am you called. Just to hear your voice." *Melissa.* "Are you alone? I mean, are you traveling alone? Are you married, or . . . ?"

"Divorced. And you?"

"Divorced."

"Was that your daughter who answered the phone?"

"That was my daughter Amy." And you are my daughter Melissa.

"So you have children."

"Three. All grown. Amy and Diane live with me. And you?"

"I suspect you know the answer to that." Suzanne paused. "You went to the trouble to find me. They must have told you all about me. Whoever it was you put on my trail."

"Yes. I'm sorry. I hope it wasn't intrusive, it probably was, it wasn't meant to be, I just needed to . . . all those years, I was . . . I was eager to find you." Melissa. Melissa: Suzanne Carol Post. Graduated Petaluma High, Petaluma, California. BA in English, California State University at Hayward. MA, library science, UCLA. Librarian, now known as media specialist, information specialist, at Aptos Beach Elementary, Aptos, California. Recently bought a small home, heavily mortgaged. Lives alone. Unmarried. No children. Drives a 2000 VW. Good credit. Clean driving record. No outstanding warrants. No court records saving for an uncontested divorce in 1999, irreconcilable differences; the couple owned no property to speak of and both waived spousal support or any future claims against either's estate. Public record.

The lump in Rusty's throat swelled, but she managed finally to push the words up to her tongue and past her lips. "I have missed you. I would like to meet you. Please." Melissa.

"I would like to meet you too. I guess I'm ready. As ready as I will ever be."

Rusty said she would make a reservation at La Gondola. One o'clock? Under the name of Meadows. Melissa agreed. La Gondola was convenient to her hotel. Then she said good-bye and Rusty held the phone until the tinny voice came on scolding her. She put it down. The timer for Auburn #7 had gone off, and she had not even heard it.

Rusty Meadows entered La Gondola as if it were a theater in which she would perform the most important role of her entire life, the production to decide her future. She had never eaten here. Far too expensive for any of the Meadows family, but she had heard Francine Hellman mention it. And Ronald Oliver. And Jill, too, since La Gondola featured Empress Ice Cream. She regretted the choice. La Gondola was more Frank Lloyd Wright than rustic Italian. It had a cool masculine atmosphere, lots of black and white, the walls papered with life-sized black gondolas covered in snow, the water gray. The tables were lit warmly and decorated with baskets of exotic orchids. From a fountain at the back came the sound of falling water. La Gondola might do very well for the Symphony League to discuss fund-raising, but for the kind of messy, weepy, fall-into-each-other's arms family reunion Rusty pictured? No. So maybe this wasn't a performance. Maybe it was just an audition: *Look at me, Melissa. I am your mother!* Fanfare! Drumroll! *See how good I would have been to and for you, Melissa! See how much I love you! For thirty-five years you are, you have been* . . . What? A loss. A void, as Penny Taylor would say. Yes, thought Rusty, sipping the herbal tea she ordered to steady her nerves. Melissa was the void in Rusty's life, and she had written the *Memoir for Melissa* to fill that void. In doing so, she reflected, Melissa had felt her mother calling out to her. The power of the pen. Melissa had to come to Portland and to answer Rusty's call. At last. That's how it had happened. Rusty finished a whole pot of camomile. She was half an hour early. She waited, a smile on her lips.

But who was this woman following the young waiter? Were they coming to this table? There were few other people in the restaurant. Could that be Melissa? She didn't look like Melissa. Did she? She was dark, short, a solid body. A firm step. Strong features. Tailored, casual clothes. Not especially chic but well made. Comfortable shoes. Rusty took this all in, her eyes sweeping up and down as the two came closer to her table. Melissa doesn't look anything like I did at sixteen. And how could she? Rusty's inner nag gave her a kick in the metaphorical rear. She's not sixteen. And Rusty realized then that though she'd known Melissa was in her midthirties, she had always pictured her the image of Charity Manning. Melissa and Charity had got, had become, forever entangled in her imagination, even in her memory, and she had expected somehow to meet them both.

"Melissa?" said Rusty when the waiter led the woman to her table.

"I'm meeting someone named Meadows."

"Meadows, yes?" The waiter inquired of Rusty, his manicured brows arching over the question. "That is my understanding. Has there been some error?"

"Oh, Suzanne!" Rusty burst out, "Yes. It's Suzanne. Forgive me! I had you confused with someone else."

The waiter pulled the chair for Suzanne and took her order for a mineral water. Nothing more at the moment. The two women stared at each other.

"I don't look like you," said Suzanne, frowning.

Rusty, undone, her shock shattering such little composure as she had collected, laughed. Stupidly. "The shape of your face? The mouth, maybe?" Suzanne vaguely resembled Rusty's own awful father. The thought was too terrible

The waiter, despairing already of a tip from these ladies, brought the mineral water and resolved to leave them alone. The younger one was not at all gracious and the older one was mushy and on the edge of tears. La Gondola did not encourage tears, except perhaps on behalf of the artichoke frittata, which he recommended for a first course. He waited pen poised for their order. Rusty said she'd have whatever Suzanne was having.

"I haven't read the menu."

"I'll be back," said the waiter, leaving them.

"Were they good to you?" asked Rusty. "Did you love them?"

"Who?" Suzanne looked up, puzzled, from the menu.

"The Posts. That's your name, Suzanne Post, isn't it? Suzanne Carol Post. Those people who brought you up?"

"Those people," she lingered tartly on the word, "are my parents. Carol and Stan Post. My mother and father were very good to me. Always."

"Thank God." Rusty actually sank back in her chair and used her napkin to wipe her brow and her eyes. "Good. I'm so glad to hear it. I'm grateful to them. I worried, you see. You can't imagine how I worried, all those years you were growing up, I never knew. I never knew anything. Where you went or to whom, and I feared, always, I was mad with fear sometimes, that they were cruel to you or didn't love you or—"

"They were excellent parents. Fine people. I love them," she said, her voice softening. "And I have a brother. Also adopted. Younger than me. I love him too."

"Oh, I'm so glad to hear it. Oh, yes, they did fine with you. Look at you. You're beautiful and accomplished and you have a good job and people love you. Do they know you're here? To meet me?"

"Yes. They encouraged me to call you. They know that I have questions, and you are the only one who can answer those questions." She sounded as if she were proctoring a test at Aptos Elementary.

Rusty squirmed "I'm sure that's a good idea. Yes. I mean, I guess. I don't know."

"Do your daughters know you are here, meeting with me?"

"No. I wanted to meet you myself first. Later, I can take you home." *Melissa.*

"I have a home already. Do your daughters know about me? That I exist at all?"

"No," she confessed, dry mouthed, ashamed for something she could not name. "My husband. I told him. My ex-husband. Listen!" The restaurant Muzak was playing Debussy. "We did that just last season. The symphony, I mean. I work for the symphony development director. It's a fine job. A wonderful job. I get season tickets, half price. I get to meet all the conductors and soloists when they come to the office."

This clearly was of no interest to Suzanne. She studied the menu. The waiter returned. She ordered the pasta with red pepper and garlic sauce. She said she was a vegetarian. Rusty ordered the same and said she wasn't. She asked for another pot of herbal tea. After the waiter left them, and the Debussy ended, there was a silence punctuated only by the fountain across the nearly empty room.

"I mean, I'm curious about myself," said Suzanne.

"I'm curious about you too."

"You don't look like what I thought."

"You don't either," Rusty confessed, studying her daughter. Her dark eyes were her best feature. She wore small gold hoop earrings that twinkled through the straight dark hair framing her face. Her mouth was the Manning family mouth, Rusty noted sadly. Suzanne did not look like Rusty, but there was enough Manning there to be disconcerting.

Suzanne unbuttoned the cuff of her long-sleeved blouse, rolled it up to her elbow, and laid her bare arm across the table. "Put your arm next to mine." Her skin was brown, a smooth nutmeg color contrasting with Rusty's fair, freckled arm. "You're much more pale than I expected."

"It rains up here a lot," said Rusty. "Everyone is pale."

"Can't you see what I'm asking you, finally and at last? You wrote me two years ago that you wanted to meet me. Here I am. I want to know. Who am I, Rusty? Who am I?"

You're not Melissa, thought Rusty. Not Melissa. How can you not be Melissa? It never occurred to me that you wouldn't be Melissa, that I wouldn't know you. "You're my daughter," said Rusty, mustering a bit of dignity. "You're their daughter too, of course, those people. The Potts, I mean the Posts. What are their names again?"

"Carol and Stan."

The waiter brought their orders, did all the waiterly things with pepper and Parmesan while Suzanne glowered and Rusty watched the wallpaper with the pictures of the gondolas. He inquired if they wanted something further to drink.

"I'll have a glass of wine," said Rusty. "Have a glass of wine," she said to her companion. "We should toast our reunion. Mother and child reunion. We should celebrate," she added hopefully.

"I'll have a glass of wine. Merlot," Suzanne instructed the waiter.

They declined a half carafe. They ate without speaking till he brought them each a glass. Rusty lifted her glass tentatively, but Suzanne made no such gesture. Rusty sipped her wine, thinking what Melissa would have done.

"Who was the man, Rusty?"

For a terrible moment Rusty saw before her the image of her old father, furious, hopping with rage and outrage, ready to beat out of his daughter the answer to that very question, who was the man? She took a sip of wine, remembering the torrent of abuse, of violence that had ensued when she had finally answered her father's questions. "He was not a man," Rusty said at last. "He was a boy. A Mexican boy. I was a girl."

"So you couldn't get married? You were underage?"

Marriage? "What are you talking about? Marriage. Underage. He was a Mexican boy. You don't understand, I guess. How can I explain? I don't think I can."

"You have to explain! You have to tell me! Why do you think I came here? Why do you think I called? Look, I'm here now! I came! Isn't that what you wanted?" Suzanne rebuttoned the cuff at her wrist. "I may not ever come back. Please, just tell me the truth, now, once and for all and let's be done with it."

"I don't want to be done with it," said Rusty quietly. "That's not why I wanted to see you."

"All right. Sorry," replied Suzanne, evoking less Rusty's old father. "Please tell me the story."

"I've written it all down. I wrote it all down as a memoir. I could send it to you. I could give it to you. I could bring it by your hotel and give you the memoir I wrote. I explained everything there."

"Yes. Fine. Send it. But tell me now. Who was this boy? Why didn't you marry him?"

"There was no question of marriage." Rusty got the waiter's attention, indicated another glass of merlot for herself.

"Aren't you driving home?" said Suzanne when he set the glass in front of Rusty.

Embarrassed in front of this waiter to be chided like a child, by her child, Rusty colored. None of this was going as she'd hoped. She did not want to be or become Charity Manning all over again, cowed and submissive.

"He abandoned you altogether then?" asked Suzanne when the waiter left.

"Who?"

"The man. The boy."

"He never knew."

"What?" Suzanne put her fork down midway to her lips. Consternation lit all her features and her composure deserted her. "He never knew at all? He never knew I existed?"

"He never knew."

"Does he know now?"

"He never knew," she repeated stubbornly. "Not then. Not now." She could feel some of Charity Manning's old hidden resistance stirring within her. And like Charity Manning, her next instinct was to run away. But the snowy gondolas on the walls around her seemed to rock slightly, as if the silvery water beneath them whispered, you're here. Use it. Tell the truth. Tell it. Tell the truth to this girl. To Suzanne. You promised yourself you would take this chance. All right, she's not Melissa. Tell Suzanne. Don't lose her again, even if she's not Melissa.

Rusty took a deep breath and began as if she were in court and under oath. "He was a Catholic. A Mexican. The son of Mexican pickers. We were high school students who fell in love. In those days, the schools were integrated, but the kids were not. The white kids ran the schools. The black kids kept to themselves. The Mexican kids kept to themselves, socially, I mean. The Japanese kids and Chinese kids, same thing. You'd have classes together, and everyone went to sports events, but the whites and the Mexicans and the black and Asian kids did not mix. So when we fell in love, it was a secret from everyone."

"What was his name?"

Why had Rusty not thought this far ahead? How many years had passed since she'd said his name? Rusty had kept Melissa alive always and before her, but Duardo? She had buried him, except for one day annually when she remembered him, almost religiously. "His name was Eduardo Arias. The teachers, the white kids called him Ed or Eddie. Everyone else called him Duardo. I called him Duardo."

"He didn't know he had made you pregnant?"

"No one knew. No one outside my immediate family, my parents, my sisters. I don't even know if they told my brothers, they were so ashamed."

"Surely in a small town, that sort of thing . . ."

"You don't understand." And then Rusty tried to help her to understand what it was like to be a girl in a family that hated women, saw them all as daughters of Eve, a family that kept their women enslaved with Eve's old transgression. Rusty tried—in a flopping, flapping, inadequate, and inarticulate fashion—to explain to Suzanne what it was like to have admitted she had loved and lain with anyone outside of marriage. Much less a Mexican Catholic boy. How her parents thought the Catholic Church was the whore of Babylon, and the Mexicans right down there with the Negroes, with the Chinese and Japanese, in short, everyone who wasn't white. What it was like to hear her father vow to kill Eduardo Arias, and to hear her mother talk him out of it, not because murder was a sin, but because if he killed Eduardo, then Rusty's sins— the biblical sins and the social sins—would be known by all and further tarnish their family. What it was like to have her father who, when he was done smacking her around, made her promise never to see Duardo again, never to return to that school, never to step out of that house except to get on the bus, the next morning, for Nevada. What it was like to be exiled to Elko, Nevada, and to be pregnant in a remorseless home with two loveless hags. To have borne that beloved child and lost her. To have heard that child crying crying crying all the time and to be powerless to pick her up, to comfort her. She did not say the child's name was Melissa. She did not say she had gone insane.

When Rusty had finished, she fought tears, but she steeled herself against crying. Suzanne was not tearful. She was quiet, assessive. There was a determined pinch to her lips that Rusty found altogether foreign. Certainly she had not inherited any such thing from poor old Charity Manning.

The waiter cleared their dishes. Suzanne ordered coffee, Rusty another pot of herbal tea. Bring it with a big syringe, she felt like asking the waiter. Calm me down. Put me out of my misery. When Suzanne finishes her coffee, she will leave. Maybe forever. Nothing had gone as she had planned. Rusty toyed with her hair. Auburn #7. She could feel her daughter's disappointment, condescension. She wished she'd sent glamorous, cool Francine Hellman to this meeting in her stead.

Suzanne lowered her voice. "Where is he now? This Eduardo Arias. What happened to him? Why do you think I came to you? I want to know who I am. I've decided I need to find my biological parents. Not my real parents," she insisted. "My real parents are Stan and Carol Post."

"Be grateful that you have them. Lots of women do not have fathers and mothers they can admire."

"I don't think you quite understand," said Suzanne. "All I need is some information. I'm a specialist, remember? If you give me some information I can find this Eduardo Arias. I found you. Now I want to find him."

"No, Suzanne, I found you. Two years ago."

"Are you faulting me for waiting two years?"

She was, of course, but she had no right to. Why was this reunion going so badly? "If I tell you now, will you still read the memoir I wrote for you? Or someone like you." Rusty gave a weak smile.

"Yes."

Rusty began guardedly. "Eduardo Arias was a year ahead of me in high school. He was a football player. He was built like a rock." She blushed for what the remark implied, but in saying so, she realized that Suzanne had Duardo's strong sturdy body. Only Melissa looked like Rusty. Suzanne looked like Rusty's father. "Duardo wasn't big enough for the big leagues, or even the Pac Ten universities, but he was fast. Anyone who ever saw him play football knew how fast he was, and he had this will to win that made him unstoppable. He wasn't the player who got all the praise and attention, but he was the one who won the games for them. The whole town turned out for these football games. Even the church I belonged to, even though we couldn't dance or go to movies, people in our church went to the high school football games. The young people from our church all went together, everyone in a big mass, like a chain gang or something. A church chain gang. You couldn't leave the bleachers without a buddy. Even if you had to go pee. We traveled in tribes." Rusty could all but smell the popcorn and feel the hard bleachers under her bottom. Before she fell in love with Eddie Arias, she had admired him from afar, watching him on the football field. After they were in love, she was in his heart and on the field with him and his every triumph was hers and his every injury hurt her too.

"When did you last see him?"

"I guess that's the information specialist talking."

"I guess."

"I don't remember. When I finally came home from Nevada, my parents told me that Eddie Arias had gone to prison for stealing, and that was the kind of low trash I had fornicated with. Committed sin with. I didn't believe them, I mean about his going to prison, or his being low trash, but I believed them about the sinning. How could I not? Sin was in the air my family breathed, in the water we drank, in the dry grim food we ate." For the first time since they had taken her infant from her, Rusty actually put aside her own pain and loss and saw the ravages that might have been. Clarity overcame Rusty, and her throat tightened. "You were lucky, Suzanne. You were lucky they took you away and gave you to good people. I would not have been a good mother to you. I would have tried, but I was powerless. I could not exert myself against my family. I was barely seventeen and I had nothing and nowhere else to go. If I had kept you, my parents would have brought you up too. They were monsters. Not even well-intentioned monsters. You would have been theirs and not mine. I suffered for the loss, but now, really, when I look at you, at the woman you are, with good parents, good family, I thank God for that. I never thought of it before. The prism changes."

"What?"

"You can see the truth only through a particular prism in time, and when you hold it up to the light or time, it changes."

"Excuse me?"

"Never mind. I would have been your mother if I could have. Truly. I loved you always. Always. But now, really, I see it was for the best that you were taken from me. But I loved you, and I'm sorry you don't think so."

"What makes you say that?"

"I'm old, I'm frumpy, I use Auburn #7. I'm only a secretary and not a media specialist, but I'm not stupid."

Suzanne remained unperturbed. "I just have to get used to the idea."

"Which idea? That I loved you? Or that I let you go?"

Suzanne seemed to consider the question, but she did not answer it. She observed instead that Rusty had escaped from the Mannings and their narrow, harsh world. "That shows you weren't completely powerless."

"That was years later. I didn't leave until I knew they'd taken my mother's education from her, and she didn't even miss it. I'm tired of talking. It's all in the memoir I wrote. You can read it if you want. Tell me about your parents, your brother. Carol and Stan Post," she said, fixing their names carefully in her mind.

"I have fine parents, and they love me. I have a brother, and I couldn't ask for a better family. But I still want to know about you and my father, this Ed Arias. I still want to know," she added emphatically. "Did he go to prison?"

"His brother did. Later. Not then. His younger brother went to prison for grand theft auto, my cousin said."

"What happened to Ed Arias? Did you just let him go? That easily? Your parents said he went to prison, and you accepted this as the truth?"

Charity Manning had never believed the prison bit, but at the time she was too beaten up and beaten down, too sick at heart and wrung worthless with a sense of sin for which she could never atone. She hadn't the strength to fight it or deny it, much less look for Duardo. Charity—hearing her baby cry night and day, unable to hold that baby—broke down and had to be sent to the state hospital for the insane. Rusty regarded her daughter, the information specialist, and decided she could not tell this crisp, cool, determined young woman that she had been insane. Suzanne Post wanted to know why she had dark skin and that was all she wanted. Very well, then. That was easy.

"When I came back from Elko, an unwed mother, though I had no baby, I was forbidden to leave the house," said Rusty calmly. "No school. No nothing. They thought I'd race out and sin again, find some other boy and fornicate. But finally, they let me go out, to the grocery store, maybe with my mother, or one of my brothers with me. Finally, months later, maybe a year, my mother sent me to the store alone. I stole a dime from her. I went to a pay phone and called Duardo's house. I wanted to tell him about you. I thought maybe together, he and I could run away and find you. But his brother answered the phone, and the brother said Duardo had gone to San Jose State. He was playing football for San Jose. And then the brother asked who I was, and I wouldn't say. He just laughed and said, all you Anglo girls are the same, hot for Duardo, all hot for Duardo. You gringas just can't get enough of his Mexican ass. You want to try mine? I'm right here."

"That's all?"

"What else is there?"

"You never tried to contact him again?"

"Don't you understand, Suzanne? Try to think what that did to me."

"I don't have much imagination," she confessed.

"I was just another Anglo girl to Duardo. Another gringa chick who was hot for his ass. I would never call him again. I would never tell him he had a daughter."

Suzanne put her napkin down. The reunion was over.

"Tell me about the Posts. Tell me what it was like growing up. Tell me what your life is like now, Suzanne. I don't know anything more about you. I want to know everything about you."

"Next time." Suzanne got out her credit card and motioned for the waiter.

"Will there be a next time? When? Tomorrow? You're still in town tomorrow."

"I don't know. I have these meetings."

"Any time. Any time at all."

"I'll have to call you."

"I hope I haven't been a disappointment to you."

"You're not what I expected."

"What was that?"

"I don't want to say."

"Say." Rusty shrugged. "Hey, we're family," she added, but the joke fell like a stone.

"I expected someone more in control of her own life."

The young waiter arrived with the check and Rusty protested and fumbled for her bag and insisted on paying. This was her treat. But Suzanne would hear none of it. No, she had asked for the meeting—she really called it that, a meeting, not a reunion—and she would pay.

Suzanne gave her credit card to the waiter, and when he left them, she regarded Rusty Meadows in silence, as if searching for a familiar house in a strange neighborhood. "I was hoping to meet someone more in control of her own life. I would have thought if you could give up a child and move on, then you would be the sort of person who had some direction and focus."

Rusty began to fathom what had drawn Suzanne to meet with her. "That's what you're looking for, isn't it? Direction and focus."

Evading this, Suzanne asked, "How did you meet this Eduardo? How did you manage to sleep with him, if your parents were so strict?"

"How do teenagers ever manage to sleep together? Anyway, we didn't spend the night together in beds, if that's what you're asking."

"All right, how did you manage to have sex?"

"We did not have sex. We made love." The thought, so long foreign to Rusty, pleased her. She could recall the danger and excitement, the heady cocktail of sex and love and sin and the smell of Eduardo's sweat. She had loved the smell of his sweat. It was like tonic. Oh, yes, Charity Manning, the girl of headstrong pride. The girl who loved Eduardo Arias and risked everything to lie with him. "I met him every chance I could. We parked and got in the backseat of cars. We lay in the fields and groves. We found barns to be together in. We were kids. Surely you were a kid like that, groping around, unsure about sex and fascinated by it." She frowned. "Weren't you?"

"That wasn't what I was asking. I mean, you said the whites and

Mexicans in your school stayed separate. How did you meet him at all?"

"Driver's ed. We were in the backseat of the driver's ed car and the teacher fussed all over the other student, a girl named Barbie Adams. I remember all this because I've been writing this memoir, and once you start to write about the past, you can't keep to some straight garden path, everything bordered. It's not. You're plunged into a thicket and your feet sink down and your shoes get dirty and you remember things and people you never thought—"

"Barbie Adams? Go on about Barbie Adams."

"Mr. Price just doted on Barbie. He liked to put his hand over hers on the steering wheel. On her knee, for all I know. Anyway, he paid no attention to Duardo and me, and we were always in the backseat. We got to know each other. Once a week, Saturday afternoons for a whole semester. It was like a double date, really, like Mr. Price and Barbie Adams in the front seat and me and Duardo in the back. Sometimes Mr. Price even took us to the A&W drive-in for root beer floats. I never had a date in high school. My parents didn't allow me to date anyone, ever, of course, so it seemed wonderful to me to be riding around in the backseat, even if it was the driver's ed car. Duardo seemed wonderful. Even Mr. Price and Barbie seemed wonderful. We were all in love. I can't answer for Barbie Adams, but Mr. Price was in love. It was a spring semester. There was jasmine everywhere. And slowly, Duardo and I, our hands met in the middle of the backseat, out of sight of the rear-view mirror, or Mr. Price or anyone. That's how we started. We held hands in the backseat of the car. Like any other young couple."

"Do you think you really were just another Anglo girl to him?"

"How could I judge these things? I had no experience with boys. No experience at all. I had no friends. Not even any girlfriends who weren't from the church and always looking out for the devil and for sin. I had no idea what the rest of Duardo's life was like. I only knew what he had with me, and what I had with him. And maybe it wasn't the same thing."

"That happens," said Suzanne as though she were putting a cork back in a wine bottle. She picked up her purse. "I have to go."

"Wait! I have one last thing. Maybe you would like to know this one last thing, Suzanne." Rusty put out her hand. Withdrew it. But at least Suzanne put her bag back down in her lap. And looked at her expectantly. Maybe Rusty could not offer her daughter focus, but possibly a little direction. "I had a cousin," Rusty said slowly, "Leah. When I ran away from home and came up here to Portland, my family just figured I'd gone to the devil and that was that. I didn't hear from any of them for years, and even now, hardly ever. But my cousin Leah and I were always good friends, the rebels of the family, really. She couldn't wait to get out of there. Leah was younger than me, the same age as Duardo's brother, the one who went to prison. About fifteen, sixteen years ago Leah's husband got a job at Boeing in Seattle, and they were driving through Portland, and she called. I said they should spend the night at our house. It was summer, and we pitched a tent for them in the backyard. But Leah and I didn't sleep. We stayed up all night, just laughing and talking, and pretty soon I brought the conversation around to the Arias family. That's when she told me that his brother went to prison and that Eddie was a high school football coach over in Stockton. His teams went to state finals nearly every year. Leah said he had a will to win like no one else. She said that everyone in our town was pissed off, I mean, annoyed, because Stockton beat us regularly. They still take high school football very seriously there. Leah said that everyone thought Eddie Arias was ungrateful to the town that had been so good to him. Leah and I agreed that was a crock. That town wasn't good to anyone, much less a family like the Ariases. I asked if he was married and she said yes."

"Did he marry an Anglo chick?"

Rusty shrugged. "His sister told Leah he married someone he met at college. Anyway, I can tell you this much, he's still in Stockton."

"How do you know that?"

She could see Duardo now in Suzanne. The intensity. The will to win. The dark hair and eyes and high cheekbones. The nutmeg skin. Suzanne's resemblance to Rusty's intolerant father had receded, though not vanished. Still, Suzanne was nothing at all like the easygoing Amy or Diane or Kevin. This woman—whomever she called her mother and father—was the daughter of Eduardo Arias. "Once a year, I call Stockton High School, home of the Stockton Bulls, and I ask to talk to Mr. Arias. I get his voice mail. I hear his voice. He answers, but I do not speak. I know it's him. I never leave a message. I call every year on May fourth."

"My birthday."

"Yes."

"Thank you."

"You're welcome."

"I have to leave now."

"I know you do."

"Where are you parked, Rusty?"

"I'm going to sit here just for a minute more, if you don't mind."

"That's fine. I just . . . I have things to do."

Rusty thanked Suzanne for the lunch. Suzanne thanked Rusty for taking time from her weekend to meet with her. It was all very cordial, even empty promises to call. Rusty wanted to cry, but didn't. Rusty had brought pictures in her wallet of Diane and Kevin and Amy, but she did not offer to get them out.

"Good-bye, Rusty."

"Good-bye, Suzanne."

Rusty ran her hand through her hair. "This is my real color," she said just as Suzanne turned and walked away. "Not now. But it was. Auburn #7 was the color of my hair when you were born."

"Are you all right, madame?" inquired the young waiter, refilling her water glass. The bill had been paid. The dining room was empty. It was a fine day in spring. Why was this old girl sitting here alone so long after the other one had left? "Shall I call a cab for you?"

"I'm fine. No, I'm not fine. But I'll leave of my own accord in a bit. Just give me a bit."

"Of course."

"I've just had some bad news, that's all."

He said he was sorry to hear it, but he wandered away before Rusty could say what it was, before she could say that in finding Suzanne she had lost Melissa. The child whose cries had driven Charity Manning insane was not Melissa but Suzanne Post, whose looks and demeanor and intensity all suggested a strange cocktail, brewed from three parts Eduardo Arias, the man with the will to win, and one part Charity Manning's implacable old father. Fortunate Suzanne had been spared life with Mannings. But Melissa had lived that life. With Charity. Melissa: the beloved daughter Rusty Meadows had kept alive. But Rusty had not borne Melissa; she had created her with bits of Kevin and Amy and Diane, and some recollection of herself as a girl. Charity. She had almost forgotten about Eduardo altogether. Except on May 4 annually. Memory had failed her with Eduardo until she met Suzanne. But Melissa was not a memory. Melissa was a void that Rusty had filled with imagination and longing. Farewell, Melissa. Here in La Gondola, a death in the family. A black funeral boat rocking on gray painted waters.

9

A Carthage of Her Own Making

IN MARRYING A JEW, MARY FRANCINE SULLIVAN HAD deeply wounded her parents. Their initial shock and disapproval at her runaway marriage might have eased into something like tolerance had she raised her sons Catholic, but she didn't. In fact, Mary Francine shed her religion once she and Marc left Gonzaga and moved to UC Berkeley. Over time, her relations with all the Sullivans cooled and then hardened into polite exchanges that no one trod upon or beyond. Marc's parents were less able to turn away from him since he was their only child and they adored him. They had not wanted him to go to a Catholic university in the first place, but he got a full scholarship, and Gonzaga was so far superior to anything else in the region, that of course they agreed he must go. They believed he had made a disastrous marriage outside his faith. They disliked his wife. They were shyly devoted to their grandsons. But so intense was their connection to Marc that when he died from cancer—so advanced and undetected, or at least untreated, that doctors gave him only six months to live—his parents scarcely outlived him. Less than two years after Marc died, both his parents had gone as well.

Francine did not go to their funerals, but Jesse and Eric did. They flew to Boise from the East. After they had seen to all the legalities and witnessed the utterly unfamiliar Jewish rituals for the dead, they took the quick flight to Portland. They stayed with their mother for two excruciating days, sleeping in their boyhood rooms.

Of their experience in Idaho, they remarked only that the Jews were very strange people.

They knew nothing of the Jews. Nothing of the Catholics either, for that matter. Their parents had evaded rather than resolved the religious conflicts of their marriage. Jesse and Eric Hellman had been raised in that happy American commercial spirituality that celebrates Christmas with toys and Santa Claus, that acknowledges Easter with bunnies and pastel baskets, where all things are comfy and possible. In this vapid spiritual terrain, there are no irrevocable tragedies, no sense of sacrifice or humility. And yet, both Marc and Francine, from different faiths, were aware of the possibility of tragedy, the necessity of sacrifice, and both had a sense of humility before mysteries greater than mere mortals. They did not acknowledge or discuss these things. They were practical and ambitious people. But they knew that such things existed.

Thus, the letter from Yu-Chun Liu struck Francine with the force of a thunderbolt delivered by an angry God. An Old Testament God. She opened the letter at the kitchen table. A hand went inside her chest, the hand of the Old Testament God, for all she knew, and squeezed her heart. She could not breathe. She thought she was dying. She dropped the letter and her vision blurred, but she did not call 911. She read it again and again, then believing she would die if she did not get away from it, she left it there and made her way, slowly, clumsily, clinging to the bannister, upstairs and to bed. Not her own bed that she had shared with Marc, but to the guest room. Twenty-four hours later, Francine went to the Catholic church.

She knelt in front of a brilliant bank of votive candles, tiers of colored brightness. She lit her first candle, as her mother had taught her, not from a match but from the flame of someone else's prayer. Coming on the heels of an another prayer, her mother said, God would hear yours better. Francine knelt, folded her hands. She no longer had a rosary. She didn't need it. She remembered. You don't forget things like that. She was grateful to utter, over and over, the simple Hail Mary, because the longer she knelt there, the less she knew what to pray for. She started with a simple request.

"Let it not be true, Lord, that this woman, many years Marc's junior, his graduate student, let it not be true that she slept with my husband and bore him a daughter named Marcella. Let it not be true." She lit another candle and shoved another dollar in the box and went on. "Let it not be true, what I suspect, that my husband, my husband, my beloved husband, the joy, the delight of my life, betrayed me with this woman, with other women. Betrayed me often with many women. Let it not be true." From the flame of her own candle, she lit another. Another dollar in the box. "Let it not be true that my own sons, flesh of my flesh, Lord, knew of this betrayal all along. Kept me in darkness and plotted with their father to betray and mislead and hurt me." Another candle. Another dollar. "Give me some sign, Lord, that all these things are false and that the man I loved above all, the man for whom I sacrificed everything, loved me too, that he was loyal as I was loyal, that he did not betray and desert me, that my sacrifices were not in vain, and that I was loved as I loved him."

All in all, there before the bank of votives, Francine Hellman contributed some forty dollars to the coffers of the church. And when she was done, the only sign that came to her was the conviction that everything she'd asked to be a lie, was in fact the truth. Everything she had believed was an everlasting truth about her life and her marriage was a lie, false and filthy. And on the recognition of this, Francine's bowels loosened, and she had to run for the church ladies' room, where she remained for quite some time.

Francine had fallen into the void. What was it Penny had said of Jill's memoir? There was a void that memory could not fill. She no more knew who she was than Jill McDougall knew who she was. The difference between them? Francine knew who she had been.

She had been the woman for whom no effort of her sons was quite up to her standards, and no effort of her husband's was anything less than perfect. She had stood by Marc's side. The worldly, shrewd, politic, and charming wife had manipulated his career with every tool in her power. With her inborn acumen, Francine had helped him achieve financial comfort, stability, security beyond the wildest dreams of the Idaho haberdasher. She had invested their money and manicured their lives. Marc was allowed, no, expected to do nothing except *be:* to be brilliant, to be the great scientist, the caring husband, the father of perfect sons. In short, her mar-

riage was Francine's lifelong achievement. For this she had sacrificed. What? These sacrifices were all so long ago that she hadn't
any damned idea now what they were.

What had she given up? She didn't get her BA. She quit Gonzaga
and typed Marc's thesis instead. Okay. She didn't need the university degree. She was Mrs. Marc Hellman. If it came up, she lied
and said she was a Gonzaga alum. What else had she lost? She had
given up her faith, and she had not raised her sons Catholic. But
even that loss was so far in the past that she could not imagine her
life other than what it had been religiously, a cheerful, commercial
agnosticism. What else? What else had she sacrificed for Marc
Hellman?

At home Francine flung herself around her house, the bed. She
couldn't sleep at night, not even in the guest room. She couldn't
stay awake during the day. She couldn't eat. When she tried to eat,
she vomited. She did not answer the phone. She picked up the
mail with the greatest trepidation. She ached as if she'd been physically run over by a truck. She considered doing just that, walking
into the street, in the path of an oncoming car. Or something very
like it.

The fact that she couldn't remember what she'd given up for
Marc Hellman meant she had given up everything. It meant that
Marc had betrayed everything in her life.

It meant to this passionately proud woman, whose regard for the
world's opinion was something of a internal compass, that everything she thought she had achieved had turned to dust, to cinder
and ash, just as Yu-Chun's letter turned to ash when she burned it
in the sink.

The letter had arrived on Thursday. The following Wednesday
she burned it. When she remembered that the Memoir Club was
coming that night, she picked up the phone to call Penny. Cancel
tonight. She was sick. Oh, yes. That was the truth. Francine Hellman was sick unto death. She dialed Penny, but the phone just
rang and rang. No answering machine. She dialed Jill, and a man's
voice answered, "Empress Ice Cream." Colin. That must be Colin.
She hung up. She looked at the clock. Six on the East Coast.

The conference call with her sons was easily arranged. What was
not so easily arranged was Francine's own part of the conversation.
She was not a spontaneous or exuberant person in the best circum-

stances. She took a pen and wrote out exactly what she intended to ask her sons. She wrote as well what she would not ask. Or say. It must be done right.

She had already flung everything in Marc's study, books, papers, pens, pencils, reprints, manuscripts, Rolodexes, the old pipe tray from when he used to smoke, yes, she had already pulled all that from the shelves and the desk and left it in a stinking heap on the floor. The mess symbolized the wreck of her life with Marc. She made the call from this room. At his desk.

Later she might fall down weeping, cry into the carpet, barf, flail, fail to sleep. But by God on the phone with these men—not her boys, but these grown men—she was going to be in control.

"I assume you knew of this," she began. She kept the steel thread in her voice.

"What?" They answered in unison.

This was a reply that Francine did not dignify. And into the silence there wafted gradually bits and broken pieces of understanding. Yu-Chun.

"How long?"

"How long what?" said Jesse and Eric together.

"Don't toy with me," said their mother.

And into that ensuing silence, flotsam and jetsam drifted. And the answers were variously, a while . . . some time . . . not the whole time. No. Never that. But some time. Some recognition, yes.

"Yu-Chun was something special to Dad," said Jesse, the Wall Street stockbroker.

"Asshole," said Eric. "Shut up, asshole."

Francine excused herself and sipped from the bottled water she kept beside her legal pad. "Others?" she asked, checking off the next item on her agenda. "Were there others?"

"Other what? No others, Mom. None."

"Other women. Not other children. Were there other women?"

The silence here was quickly broken with noisy denial. Too quickly. What was the point of pursuing? "Who else knew of this? Of Yu-Chun's relationship with your father?"

"No one."

"Few."

"Hardly anyone."

"Boys," declared Francine, "I am sick to death of lies. I do not think you quite understand how sick to death I am. I want no comfort. I want the truth. Please. For the first time in forty years, I want the truth."

"Mom, Dad loved you. He did. He loved you best."

"Better than the others?" inquired Francine.

Into the silence the younger one, Jesse said, "Yes. He adored you, Mom. He—"

"Asshole," said Eric, his response remarkably terse for an MIT scientist.

"Who knew of this relationship?" She again cautioned them against lying. "You lie to me and I will make you pay. Both of you," she added fiercely, though she had no idea how she could make them pay, since it was clear to her, even at this distance, that her suffering brought forth from them nothing more than chagrin. She could hear it in their voices. They were embarrassed, but they were not heartbroken for and with her.

"Some people knew," said Jesse. "Not everyone. Some."

"Marc's colleagues?"

"Some. A few."

"Maybe."

"All these people I have written to asking them to tell me in some detail what it was like"—the steel string in her voice went taut, harsh—" 'to bask in his presence.' You have the list. You know to whom I wrote. You know what I said. Those people—did they know?"

"Some. Not all."

"Most?"

"Many," Jesse said again, churlishly. Like a boy caught torturing a cat. His brother again called him an asshole.

"And locally?" asked their mother coldly. "Is this common knowledge here in Portland?"

"No," they both agreed. Not at all. They were most emphatic.

"And Marc's other women. Were any here in Portland?"

No. But they were not as emphatic.

Francine checked off another item on her legal pad. Her icy control, the protocol she followed made her feel like she was in court, though she never had been in court. Not so much as a speeding ticket. A charmed life. "Did Ted Swanson know any of this? Our attorney. Was he aware of—"

"No." Both sons leaped into the breach, assuring her again that their father's, well, his, his other family, you might say, were not locally known.

"So that's what they are? Your father's other family?" When silence greeted this observation, Francine continued. "In this letter there is reference to some money to be sent to this, this child." Marcella Liu, Marc Hellman's half-Chinese daughter. And suddenly, in a sort of swift throb, Francine thought of Jill McDougall, her diffidence, her soft voice, her spiky hair, her youth, and her sense of having already failed in life because she did not know her parents. And yet Jill herself was so alert to others' pain. There was much the same sense in the letter she had received from Yu-Chun. Yu-Chun had not written to inflict pain and begged forgiveness for doing so. Yu-Chun wrote on behalf of her daughter who, in a few years, would be of university age. Except for her daughter's well-being, never would Yu-Chun inflict suffering on Mrs. Hellman. But things had not gone well. Not as well as they should have. Yu-Chun's own horizons had, alas, contracted over time and especially after Marc's death three years before. Marc had sent money while he lived, and now there was none. Moreover, in the last three years, Yu-Chun phrased this delicately, his ideas had fallen into a sort of scientific disrepute, or limbo, anyway. Yu-Chun, his student and protégée, had not been promoted. She had to leave her post. She went to another university, but only as a research assistant. She had not married. Taiwan was expensive. Taiwan was limited and limiting. Her daughter must have an American university education. Yu-Chun could not do this on her own, and she wanted this for her daughter. Marc would have wanted Marcella to go to an American university. Indeed, Yu-Chun knew Marc wanted this, because she had a letter from him to this effect. Written some weeks before he died. Three years ago. Marc wrote that Marcella would have money from his estate. The inheritance would be coming from Jesse and Eric. But in these three years, Yu-Chun had heard nothing.

"What happened to the money?" asked Francine.

She let Jesse and Eric dribble out inquiries, *The money? The money?*

Then she added, "The money each of you was to give, to send to Yu-Chun from your father's estate. Half. That's what she said in the letter."

"That's a lie," said Jesse.

"A damned lie," said Eric.

"Marc never spoke to you with regard to each of you giving half to this, this girl?"

"No."

"Never."

"Marc said nothing to the effect that when I die you two would inherit all the rest of the estate?"

"Never."

"I am executor of the will that Ted drew up, so I know what's there, what's actually written. There's nothing of that sort in his will. So the only provision your father made for her, for this girl, was asking the two of you to give up half, and writing a note to this woman. Yu-Chun."

"She's lying," said Jesse.

"She's a lying, moneygrubbing bitch," said Eric. "Isn't it enough that Dad sent her money all those years?" And then he knew he had said too much. They had known all along.

Francine drew a long sigh. She was very nearly at the end of her resources, her strength. She debated hanging up the phone immediately, but they both burst into promises, offers to come to Portland. To leave tomorrow. Drop everything and come to see her. To help her. To explain. To be there for her. With her. Their words were so heartfelt, and in this past week there had been so little comfort, that she wanted to cry. She fought tears now. She thought maybe she should have her sons, her boys, nearby in this crisis. She bit her lip and began to imagine everything they could be and say to one another. Then she suddenly saw the future as the past. The implied structure, as Penny Taylor might have said, arced over the void. If Eric and Jesse came to Portland—she could see it as clearly as if she was writing a memoir—Francine would forgive her sons their betrayal. It would not happen without many tears and curses, gnashing, sobs, and all the dreary like, but it would happen. It would have to. Eventually, inevitably, her forgiveness would extend to all the Hellman boys. Marc too. They were all she had. If Jesse and Eric came to her, if they put their arms around her, she would crumble. She would forgive. She was not ready to forgive. Not yet. Certainly not now.

"I don't want you to come to Portland," she said. "I want to know what happened to the money. Why did you not do as Marc asked?"

They both denied that he had asked. For this Francine had nothing but contempt. But she hadn't the energy to pull the truth from them. So she went on the assumption that they were weak liars who had ignored a dying man's request. She said as much. She asked again what happened to the money.

Eric, the MIT scientist, mumbled words to the effect that six months after his father died, he had bought a condo on the Charles River. "The address alone," Eric explained, "cost a fortune."

"It's gone then," asked Francine, "your part of the money?"

"Yes."

Jesse said he had lost his half.

"Lost?" she inquired. "Like lost it in Central Park? Lost it in a cab? Lost?"

"I'm a stockbroker, Mom. I lose money all the time."

She hung up on her sons and waded into Marc's study, through the mess she had made, and grabbed a handful of reprints of his scientific papers. She went to her own painfully neat desk in her own painfully neat study, and she collected all the drafts she had written of her memoir. Marc's memoir. She loaded it all in a box and pushed the box into the kitchen and there, following Caryn's suggestion, she got out a box of stick matches and she burned the whole of it. Piece by piece.

That evening when Nell and Caryn, the first to arrive, knocked on the front door, there was no answer. They tried the door and it opened. "Smoke," they said simultaneously, dashing through the living room and calling Francine's name. In the kitchen, smoke hung like a curtain, palpable and grainy.

They found Francine, still in her robe, on the kitchen floor, eyes closed. Her face was streaked with grime and smoke. There were empty boxes all over the floor and the burned ends of stick matches all over the counter. The sink was black. The smoke alarm, its batteries disemboweled, lay on top of the trash.

Caryn swiftly knelt, took a pulse, pressed her fingers on Francine's throat. The touch of Caryn's cool hand roused Francine with a start.

"Should we move her?" asked Nell.

"Not yet."

"She hasn't taken anything, has she?"

Caryn peered into her eyes, made her open her mouth and stick out her tongue. She reached in and swabbed out her gums. "Smoke on her gums. Nothing else." Caryn stood, washed her hands, and moved about the kitchen, opening windows. Nell supported Francine.

"Francine," Nell asked, "what's happened here?"

"Dido."

"What? What is she talking about?"

Caryn didn't know, either. Just then they heard other footsteps running from the front, Sarah Jane and Jill came in, Rusty right behind them. They dropped their purses and papers and gathered around Francine. They raised her up from the floor and sat her at the table. Nell handed her a glass of water.

"I can't," said Francine. "It will taste of smoke. Ash."

"Let's go into the bathroom, then," suggested Jill. "Come on. You can just rinse out your mouth. And wash your face."

With her arm around Francine's shoulders, Jill escorted her out. In low voices they murmured among themselves as Nell energetically cleaned out the sink and washed down the counters. Rusty moved the empty boxes outside as Caryn swept up the ash from the floor. Sarah Jane put water in the kettle; she hauled out a big pot and filled it with water and put it on to boil. She dug through a cupboard and found a two-pound bag of macaroni.

When Francine returned, the streaks of soot were gone from her face, and she was pale beneath. Her customary carriage, her thin-lipped, assessive expression had been altogether altered, and she no longer looked like herself. The planes of her face had hardened; her eyes, ringed and red with crying, were still vacant. This time she could drink a glass of water. She sat hunched at the kitchen table, and she still did not speak.

Jill asked Sarah Jane what she was making.

"Oh, I don't know. Something starchy or greasy and rich and heavy and bad for you. Something so you know you've eaten. The kind of food you need when something terrible's happened."

"We don't know what's happened," said Jill.

"But we know it's terrible." Sarah Jane opened the fridge and took out a brick of cheddar cheese, a few eggs, and a half carton of milk. "We know that."

And knowing that, they waited.

Finally, Caryn, in her best professional voice, asked Francine what was so terrible that she had burned what looked to be a vast part of her life.

"Dido," said Francine again. "In a Carthage of my own making."

Nell looked around to see if this explanation eluded anyone else.

"Dido was the queen of Carthage," said Sarah Jane, pulling a bowl and a cheese grater from the cupboard. "When her lover left her, she burned everything around her. Including herself."

"What did you burn here today?" asked Caryn.

"Marc. My life. My past. Paper. My, I don't know, really. The memoir. Oh, yes, that."

"After all that work?" asked Rusty.

Her eyes seemed to clear, and she shook her head with a mournful little smile. "Penny Taylor is always telling us, structure and voice are everything in the memoir. But in the past? The past is not a literary construct! The past is the past, its own place! Its own thing. I lost the past. How can I write about it when it's gone? And the voice? Narrative voice. She's always going on about narrative voice." Francine wiped her nose with the back of her hand. "I cannot bear the voice. Marc's voice."

"So you burned it?" said Nell.

"The past was already destroyed. The burning was nothing." Francine lifted her chin and knotted her fist at her chest, as though keeping a rag against her breast for warmth. "He had what is coyly known as another family. He had many other women. But he certainly had another whole family, a daughter with a woman who was his graduate student." The Memoir Club's sympathy came out in one choral sigh. "And now I can see everything. I can see, I can imagine all Marc's women. I can look back, and look around, and I see them smiling at me. My friends. Marc's women. The women from the university. The women in Symphony League"—she nodded to Rusty—"no doubt. They all knew who they were. Probably Ronald Oliver knows who they are. I finally understand that a man who could sleep with his graduate student could sleep with his neighbor's wife or his wife's friend. I can all but name the names. The man who could betray once could betray twice. Or more. That is the terrible truth."

"The truth is always terrible," said Caryn.

Francine began to weep. "You're the only people I can say it to."

"So say it."

"I have been widowed twice by the same man. Once when Marc died and now, again, three years later when the dream of him died, and when the love and respect and loyalty and my marriage and all that died. He was my life's work. Really. Think of it. Some women paint pictures. Some women teach generations of kids. Some women are doctors, or nurses, or therapists, or run whole offices, or guide tribes of Cub Scouts and soccer teams, or make a business out of ice cream, but my life's work was Marc. His well-being. His career. He was the gem. I was the setting. And now, old as I am, I see that my life's work was squandered. So was my life. My whole life," she said, amazement momentarily lighting up her face, until extinguished, and she went gray again.

"You have your sons," said Caryn. "Your children."

Francine shook her head. "I don't even have them. Or if I do, I can't bear them. My sons had the chance to do right, and they ignored it. They have proved themselves weak, shallow, mean-spirited. They betrayed me too. Betrayed us both, really. If they're all I have, then I have nothing. Here is the truth of it."

Their hands wrapped around coffee mugs full of strong tea, they sat in the diminishing light of the spring evening as long mauve threads of twilight draped at the windows and across the floor. They listened to Francine tell the truth. Not the artfully constructed memoir, but the messy, ragged, unstructured truth, the truth that ran off here and there and came back around on itself, bit its own tail, spilled its own guts, bled, barked, wailed, wept, and had no pride. The truth that went ragged and unclothed.

"How can I live?" asked Francine in the enveloping dusk.

"You can," said Caryn at last, when none of the others was equal to this question. Caryn put her hand over Francine's. "I know you can. I know anyone can live through anything, whether she wants to or not. I know that the body goes on, dragging the broken heart behind it like a ball and chain, and all you want is to be rid of that broken heart. Even if it means being rid of your life."

"Are you speaking as a doctor?"

"No." She glanced across the table to Nell. "Nell knows. Nell has kept me alive these past few years, haven't you? Insisted on it.

Kicked and screamed and pummeled and bullied me into living. The St. Bernard."

"Go ahead, Caryn," said Nell. Then she got up, took the last of the stick matches, and lit the two candles on the table. "It's all right. Go ahead."

"I know you can live through anything, because I have lived through the worst there is. I have never spoken of it before. These Wednesday nights have been the only place I could come where my losses, my catastrophes, my disasters were not the defining fact of my life, but they are. They are the defining facts of my life, and I have accepted that. I wouldn't have thought so. I'm not an accepting sort of person. I'm not the kind who turns her palms up and says, all right, this bitter cup is mine and I will drink from it. No, I'm a striver. I always have been. Nell and I, we're both strivers."

"Athletes," said Nell, "and women of medicine."

"So I've given up striving. Even given up fighting. I live. I breathe. I eat. I sleep with my children's toys. I hug their stuffed animals. I put their baby shoes under my pillow."

"We didn't know you had children, Caryn," said Rusty softly.

"I don't. Not here. They're still mine, of course. I just don't have them here. Sometimes I have nightmares that someone is trying to pry the baby shoes out of my hands. I fight to keep the baby shoes, but I know I've lost the children, and nothing will bring them back to me here." Caryn looked at the faces of each of her friends. In the flickering candlelight, Nell was crying. "I will have to go to them."

They listened to Caryn tell the truth. On the face of it, hers was a simpler truth, since the betrayals were only those of fate. Hers was a truth that could be stated but not described. A truth from which there was no retreat. From which all advances would be painful. Caryn did not finish telling this truth. It finally finished with her. And when it did, to the alarm of everyone there, the kitchen light suddenly came on and Penny Taylor stood in the doorway.

"Sorry I'm late. The time got away from me. What have I missed?"

10

Cherry Guava

THERE WAS NO SHORTAGE OF ICE. THERE WERE MANY freezers. You couldn't be in the ice cream business and not have a lot of ice and freezers, but the windowless warehouse was still stifling in the unseasonable spring heat wave. The warehouse office where Jill and Colin lived was even more close and airless. Jill could not even open the back door to admit a breeze for fear the Rose City Industrial Park security patrol would come by, have a little glance in, and see that the Empress of Ice Cream was actually living on the premises.

"We should have got offices somewhere else, where they didn't pride themselves on their security, all those little cars and men with flashlights," said Jill as Colin brought in another fan from the warehouse itself. In his other hand, he tugged a wet gunnysack along the concrete floor. "It'll be a hundred and ten in there tomorrow morning," she cautioned him. "Maybe you should leave the fan out there."

"It'll cool off overnight. And besides, as long as the electricity doesn't fail, what do we care? The ice cream's in the freezers."

"The electric bills are going up," she replied, giving him the bad news straight, no chaser. "So is the rent on the warehouse. Starting next month." She fanned herself with the notice.

"Home sweet home? A man's castle? The Empress's palace?"

"Colin, you really are maddening. What's that you have in the gunnysack?"

"Close your eyes. Don't say anything, Jill. Just close your eyes and when I call you, come in the bathroom. It's a surprise. Go sit on the bed and wait for me."

"I know what you're doing."

"No you don't. It's a surprise." He went into the bathroom and closed the door. "Eyes closed," he called.

"I can still hear."

"Just close your eyes and sit still!"

Jill padded, barefoot, over the concrete floor to the high bed. She wore only underwear and a T-shirt, and she dutifully sat on the bed and listened to Colin in the bathroom. She knew exactly what he was doing. He did it every time there was a heat wave. He brought in a bunch of ice and ice cream from the freezers and he put it in the bathtub they had installed. The ice cream was Cherry Guava, she suspected. It was a failure as a flavor. An expensive failure, too, she thought reflexively. That's what businesspeople thought of: how much money you had to put into something in order to get money out. Colin had lavished a lot of money on the guavas, and the cherries, for that matter, to say nothing of the cream and all the experimenting, and still, Cherry Guava was un-worthy of the Empress name. They would not sell it, but they kept it. Colin was in the bathroom now rubbing it all over his body. And shortly, she knew, Colin would rub it all over her body in the cold tub and lick it off and she would rub it all over his body and lick it off and however hot it was and however broke they were, they'd end up in the sack, sticking to each other and the sheets with ice cream all over them like two miscreant puppies.

"Are you ready?" she called out. She smiled to remember the Peach Macaroon fiasco last summer, and how they had found bits of macaroon all over the place for months.

"Just stay where you are."

They would have gone on for maybe ten minutes, calling back and forth, but Jill heard a car outside. It pulled away. Then it came back, as though it were circling the warehouse. It did not have the tinny rattle of a security car. The engine was bigger. Lower. Purring. Maybe it was Rose City bigwigs, and they were on to the Empress. "Colin!"

"Just stay where you are, Jill. You're going to love this."

"Colin, there's someone outside. Don't you hear the car?"

"It's just security."

"It's not. It's someone else. Listen."

Eventually he came out of the bathroom. He was slathered in Cherry Guava, his fair skin pink with guava and nubbed here and there with bits of cherry. Jill would have laughed, but the car continued to circle the warehouse. Then it stopped. They heard the motor turn off. Jill froze. So did Colin. They heard steps coming toward the back door that led up the loading dock and into the office.

"Jill! Jill?" A woman called out. "Colin?" An unfamiliar voice.

Jill got off the bed and moved slowly to the door while Colin stayed rooted, paralyzed into inaction in the middle of the floor.

"Security are all men," whispered Colin.

The knocking was more insistent. Jill opened the door.

"Oh Jill!" cried Francine. "I was so worried—"

Jill yanked her inside and locked the door. Francine was rendered speechless to see a naked pink man across the large room. Colin bolted into the bathroom, slammed the door behind him, and Jill realized just how naked he was and how utterly weird they must look to Francine Hellman of the French doors, the china cups, and the Aubusson carpet. "We weren't expecting company, Francine. We never have company. You can't stay here, really. Your car, you know. If security comes by and sees your car, well, they'll think you're a prowler or a trespasser."

"Not in a Mercedes," replied Francine. "Trust me."

"They'll think we live here, and we're not supposed to. They'll throw us out. They'll—"

"This place is stifling! How do you stand it?" Francine took it all in at a glance. The high bed in one corner. The long counter with about ten home ice cream makers, four or five grinding away. The kitchenette with an industrial-sized fridge and freezer and gleaming stove. The futon set up before a television. The drain in the concrete floor. The desk near the door that led to the warehouse. Two computers. The air stagnant despite the whirring fans. The high ceiling with the unadorned bulbs. Posters of seascapes and gardens on the gray concrete walls.

"I've come with a proposition," said Francine. "We need to talk." She walked to the kitchenette and sat at the small plastic table. "I won't be long. I need to talk to both of you."

Jill went to the bathroom door. "Can you come out, Colin? It's Francine. From my memoir class. We meet at her house. You remember?"

"The one who just found her husband had another whole family in Taiwan?"

"Shhh." She turned back to Francine. "He'll be just a minute."

"Jill. My clothes."

Jill thrust some clothes through the bathroom door. She quickly pulled on a pair of shorts and returned to the table with Francine. What could she possibly say? She asked Francine if she wanted something to drink. No. Francine got out her own bottled water and sat it on the table. Colin joined them, and to Jill's surprise, Francine introduced herself to Colin as the one whose late husband was discovered to have had another family.

"Naturally," she said, "you can imagine the shock."

"Naturally," they both said.

"I'm sorry," said Colin with a look to Jill begging for direction.

"You don't have to be sorry. I'm actually glad that Jill told you. Now that you know, we don't have to cover that old ground. It saves time."

Jill unaccountably remembered the Alice books, the Red Queen instructing her, "Curtsey while thinking what to say. It saves time." Seeing bits of cherry still stuck to Colin's hair and an ice cream smudge on his shorts, she felt as though she had stepped through the looking glass, all right. But all she could think to say, without quite bobbing for a curtsy, was, "Would you like some ice cream, Francine? It's fresh."

"Later. Not now."

Five timers went off, one after another. Colin got up and turned off the ice cream machines. He came back and sat down. Without the purring ice cream machines, the place seemed wretchedly quiet.

"The Memoir Club can continue to meet at my house, of course, but I am no longer looking to the past. I am looking to the future," declared Francine. "I was going to sell the house and move back east, and sit out what would undoubtedly have been my dotage either in New York or Boston. But I'm not going to do that after all. My sons, I'm sorry to say, have betrayed me. They were privy to information that I ought to have had, and they did not share it.

They have betrayed their father as well in agreeing to a dying man's request and then ignoring it. I'm disappointed in them." She gave a short, harsh laugh through her nose. She sipped from her water bottle. "That's what I always used to say to them. 'Boys, I am disappointed in you,' over cleaning their rooms, or mowing the lawn, or not putting the groceries away, or setting the table incorrectly, or not putting the toilet seat down. 'I am disappointed in you.' If they failed to make the varsity track team or came in second in a music competition. 'I am disappointed in you.' If they brought home less than straight A's, or left the bed unmade, or didn't clean the hair out of the sink. I scared the shit out of them with that phrase. Isn't that astonishing?"

It was certainly astonishing to Jill that Francine would say "scared the shit," and so she nodded.

Following her cue, so did Colin.

"I could wield that one little phrase like an ax. I took pride in it, really, proud that my sons needed but one phrase from me. I was the Lizzie Borden of *you have disappointed me*. I raised them right. I created this lovely home and lovely atmosphere, and helped my husband, but there was ruin all around me, and I never saw it." Her voice broke and her lower lip trembled.

"Oh, Francine, you do create a lovely, warm atmosphere! We love coming to your house on Wednesday nights. I look forward to it," said Jill, fearing that the whole of Francine's family fiasco would come tumbling out all over again and Francine would be here for hours and security would drive by, see her Mercedes, and wonder what the hell was going on.

"Anyway, that's neither here nor there anymore." Francine reached into her purse for a tissue, used it, and nodded as though reassuring some apparition only she could see. "I'm still selling the house. But I'm not going back east. I'll get a small apartment here in Portland. What I need, what I want," she spoke slowly carefully, "is some thread to stitch together a new life and identity. If I cannot be who I was, then fine. If I cannot write the past, then I must write the future. Even the future becomes the past, eventually." She took a deep breath. "I want to take the money from the house, the money that I have, and put it into a new career for myself. I want to go into business. The ice cream business. Empress Ice Cream."

Jill absorbed this statement slowly. Colin, clearly, couldn't quite absorb it at all. Finally, Jill said, "We're not really looking to expand our markets at the present moment. We're artisan ice cream. We're local."

"I wasn't thinking of the ice cream business per se. I was thinking of what you wrote, Jill, about the restaurant. About Colin's wanting to have a small restaurant. What was your phrase? Nothing snooty, just the best?"

"Oh, that's just a dream," Colin protested. "Just something. Someday. Like the guy who wants to sail around the world."

"We can do it. Together, the three of us, we have everything we need to succeed. Colin has the creative genius in the kitchen. You have the business background, Jill. I have the money." She glowed at them. "I've thought it all through. Believe me. This is not impulse. I am not an impulsive woman."

Jill spoke carefully. "What Colin and I were thinking of, well, when we thought of it at all, it was just an idle dream."

This was not the truth. They had lain awake naming the place as a pregnant couple might lie awake naming their unborn child. They put white tablecloths on small tables, and small vases, votive candles in cut-glass containers. They polished the wooden floors. They brightened all the bottles behind the small bar. They rested their arms on the marble pastry board. They shined up the pots and knives, all hanging within easy reach. Colin cooked, perfected items they always said they'd want to have on the menu. They rolled their eyes and said how good everything was. They knew they would recognize their customers.

"It's like Colin said, it's just a dream."

"Well, the difference between a dream and ambition is doing it," declared Francine. "What about what you wrote about how you wanted to be rich?"

"That was a silly college girl's ambition. I'm a happy woman. I don't want to be rich anymore."

"And you, Colin? Was the restaurant a college boy's ambition? Never mind. Everyone has dreams and some have ambitions. Here's my ambition. I want to be part of something that isn't a lie. I want to be part of something that has a future and not a ravaged past. I want to be needed, to be part of something that will engage my time and my enthusiasm, and yes, my money. That's finally all I got out of my whole adult life! Marc was my whole adult life. And what's left? The money. The house. And the money the house will bring in when it sells."

Jill thought back to last Wednesday night. Unexpectedly memorable. They did not read or comment on anyone's work. They stayed in the kitchen with the thin pall of smoke still present. They listened to Francine: what she had burned and the things she had discovered and the losses she had endured. *How can I bear these losses?* Caryn Henley had started to cry. Then Nell started to cry while Caryn told them what she could not bring herself to write. The plane crash. The two children. The ex-husband. The unthinkable pain of it. Then everyone had started to cry. By the time Penny had arrived, long after class should have started, no one could face the ordinary. They did not tell Penny what they had said to each other. She did not ask. She left and said she'd return next week. But Jill had wondered how they could even continue with the Memoir Club at all. And certainly, in the face of such suffering as Caryn and Francine had endured, Jill's memoir, her identity dilemma—whom to take on her first class trip to Korea—seemed paltry and small and scarcely worth the ink, much less the gnashing she'd expended.

"After what you've been through," Jill said softly, reaching for Francine's manicured hand, "who could blame you for wanting some antidote to your suffering. But this is too big a step. Too much. Too soon."

"Don't you see? I can't wait for happiness to find me. I'm getting old. I don't have that kind of time. I want to be part of something that is outside of what I've suffered. I want us to go into the restaurant business. Together."

"These things are a gamble," Jill said reasonably. "They fail all the time. It's a terrible business, restaurants. The risks are awful. Do you know how many go under every year? Even just here in Portland. You should put your money into a small press, or something where you know you'll lose money, and you can still feel like you've done something important. The restaurant, well, when it's over, what have you got? A bunch of dirty aprons and old menus. Too risky."

"The risk would be yours as well as mine."

"But it wouldn't be our money," said Colin. "We don't have any money."

"We're just getting by. As you can see." Jill nodded toward their living quarters. "And we have no collateral to borrow money, unless you want to take a note out on all the equipment in the other room and the Empress minivan, which wouldn't exactly be useful to you, would it?"

"I don't want to lend you the money. I want to be partners with you. Three-way partners. I don't want to just sit and sign checks. I want to work there. I could be the one who greets people. Who puts them at their ease. I could do in this restaurant what I did for over thirty years for my husband to advance his career. Now I want to advance *my* career. I'm serious. I'm committed to this. We can get Ted Swanson to draw up papers. You remember, Jill? My lawyer from the winter class."

"The one with the judge for a father."

"Yes. I'll have him draw up the papers making us a business partnership. In the meantime, you two can move out of here and come live in my house," she added to their surprise. "It's a big house. Huge. There's no reason for you to live here in this . . ." She did not continue and noting a bit of pink drying on Colin's cheek, she went on, "You can have the master bedroom. It has its own bath. I don't sleep there anymore. I've moved into the guest room."

"We couldn't," said Jill, Colin echoing her.

"Of course you can. The master bedroom looks to the back. Every morning you can open the window and see the garden." She pointed to one of the posters. "The real garden."

"We're fine here."

Francine gave her thin-lipped disapproval to the concrete floor, the fans, the unmade bed, the long fluorescent tubes of light. "It'll only be for a bit that you stay with me. Say, six months. My house will sell by then. We can be looking for restaurant locations while my house is on the market. Then you two can find an apartment."

"I don't see," said Colin with a cryptic look to his partner, "how we could afford an apartment if we're putting money into a res-taurant. We can't afford an apartment now."

"You're putting genius into the restaurant," said Francine. "Jill is putting her MBA."

"I don't have an MBA."

"You can't just shake out a few white tablecloths and open a restaurant," said Colin. "There's licenses, and—"

"Yes, yes, but surely all that is just a matter of time. A liquor license might require a little more, but that's why you have a lawyer, so he can do these things. Ted can speed them along. He's very good, not just competent, but excellent, and very well connected. He takes care of his clients."

"I don't see how we could even think of it," Colin said. "It's out of the question. I, we, wouldn't dream of going into business where we couldn't put up anything. You don't need a bus ad degree to know that much."

But Jill knew that tucked under socks in the top drawer of the bureau there were two round-trip first-class tickets to Seoul. Redeemable, refundable whenever. Money to fund a dream. "This is the chance of a lifetime, Colin," she said softly. "A dream. How many people have the chance to see a dream to fruition? We couldn't do it alone."

"Oh, Jill. We can't do it at all. It's too much."

"We need to think about it, Francine."

"That's fine. Of course. I have a neighbor who sells commercial real estate. I'll contact him. Jill and I can do the first round of looking for a place. And when we have a few candidates, then Colin can come check them out."

"We need to think about it," Jill repeated.

"Think about it. What'll we call it? Surely you have names in mind."

"You don't even know us," Colin protested.

"You forget. I know your pasts, your families. I know about the talking kimono. I know about Sybil and John and how they made Jill and Lisa and Katherine watch TV while they did their silly sacred thing together. I know about Lisa's awful wedding. I know, Colin, that your parents call each other Tooter and Twinkie, and that your family taunts you with "Mary Had a Little Lamb" from the ice cream truck."

"Well, taunt's a little harsh," said Colin.

"Whatever I wrote in the memoir, Francine, it's not always the absolute truth," Jill hastened to correct Colin's impression. "It's narrative construct, like Penny is always telling us."

"Here's what I have learned from Penny Taylor," Francine declared. "The past changes. I want a new past. Which is to say, a future." Then she smiled at Jill. "You ask the talking kimono."

That night Colin pointed the big fan toward their bed and Jill tenderly lay the blue kimono on tissue paper beneath her pillow. She smoothed it out and made sure the little toggles were fastened.

Colin lay down, troubled. "The talking kimono can't answer this one, Jill. This one's too tough a question for a baby's jacket."

Jill put her pillow over the kimono, turned out the light and lay down beside him. "I'm not asking a question tonight. I think I've found the answer."

"Really? This is kind of sudden, isn't it?"

"So was Francine's coming over here. That was sudden."

"I don't think we should do this. It's too risky. You're the business person. You know that's true. We could lose everything. Even what we have now. Anyway, why are we even talking about it? We don't have any money."

"We do. Some. Not a lot. Not maybe capital, but something we could put toward this venture."

"What?"

"The ticket. The first-class round-trip, anytime-refundable ticket to Korea. That ticket is a little bank account. We haven't made any interest off of it," she added, the reflexive bus ad observation, "but we haven't lost anything, either. Let's cash it in and use the money for the bistro. The Empress Bistro."

"No. I got that ticket for you. A gift for you. I never intended it to be used to fund my dreams."

The fan whirred. She snuggled up close to him; she could smell the Cherry Guava. "I want to go to work every day in a place where I don't live. I want to see the faces of people who think our ice cream is the most divine thing on the face of the planet. Here, we sell it, but we never see the satisfaction on the faces of people who eat it. Just think. The Empress Bistro. Think what it would mean to us. To both of us. It's my dream, too."

"Do you mean that, baby?"

"I mean it. I know who I am, Colin. I don't need to ask the talking kimono questions anymore. Right now I want it to listen. To take a message for me."

"What's the message?"

Jill closed her eyes, breathed deep his familiar scent. "Good night, little kimono, and please take a message for me to the hands that embroidered the little white flowers. Please thank those hands, and tell whomever those hands belong to that her daughter is well and happy. Tell her that her daughter is loved and loves in return. A wonderful man." She squeezed his hand and he kissed her forehead. "Please tell her that her daughter has two sisters, Lisa and Katherine. Lisa has Mary McDougall's nose and Katherine has her hair, and I, Jill, have Mary McDougall's eyes. I know who I am. The Empress of all the Ice Creams, an American original."

Being Preggers

FUNKY AND FREE OF CHARGE, THAT DESCRIBED WOMEN'S Uptown Clinic. Holly Go-Homemaker did not do Lamaze at the Women's Uptown. At Women's Uptown, Amy Meadows recognized women she'd seen prowling the maternity racks at Valu-Village. This is where Amy had done her shopping, and early on, because she had started to show almost immediately. At Valu-Village, Amy had tried on maternity smocks and declared to her sister Diane that all these women must have given birth to pencils. By now, late in her pregnancy, Amy was as big as a house. She was out of maternity and into muumuus. A hot Hawaiian mama, she told her sister.

Certainly it was hot. Amy sulked in the passenger seat as Diane drove to the Women's Uptown. Diane's driving was so timid, Amy wanted to scream at her, but she needed a Lamaze coach. Chuck wasn't equal to Lamaze. After the first prenatal doctor visit, Chuck went into what Amy thought of as his aw-shucks-I'm-just-a-dumb-guy act, pleased to be a father but in awe of female competence. Diane was with Amy from the very first ultrasound. Diane knew the baby was a boy even before Chuck did.

A bookkeeper studying to be an accountant, Diane had her Wednesday afternoons free now that tax season was past. She was the perfect Lamaze coach, even though she was a bad driver, over-correcting and overreacting. Since she had been sick all through high school, Diane had never had driver's ed. She missed a lot more than driver's ed. Diane lacked high spirits; she measured everything carefully, her time, her money, her calories, her energy, and her patience. Amy had used up her share of Diane's patience on the way over here.

They pulled near Women's Uptown. It was a low, one-story stucco building with a big marquee in English and Spanish. There were no windows, and there was a wrought-iron screen in front of the door. The unseasonal heat sweltered up off the treeless pavement.

"Just park the damned car, Diane. There are plenty of spaces."

"We're supposed to park around the back," said Diane. "They called and said to park in the lot that says Staff Only. I mean, look over there, Amy, those guys in the back of the pickup truck. They're the ones I read about in the paper. They're taking pictures with a video camera and broadcasting them on the Internet all around the world."

The video camera was mounted on a tripod. The sign on the truck said FAMILY CHAMPIONS, and the men were apparently changing shifts, filming everything and everyone who came in or went out of the front door of Women's Uptown Clinic.

"Never mind that asshole, Diane. Park. There's a place right in front. I'll put the dime in the damned meter. I gotta get out of this car before I die of the heat."

"But Amy, they said to park round the back."

"Like I care. I'm not going in for an abortion, am I?" She patted the bulge sitting peacefully over her lap. Suddenly it leaped and twisted.

"Little Chuckie's active."

"Don't call him that," snapped Amy, who was growing more sensitive by the day. This and the heat and Diane's driving, Chuck's increasing zeal for the navy, and the fact that Amy had not seen her own knees in months, these all made her especially testy.

Amy got out of the car and locked her door. She put a quarter in the meter. She turned to the Family Champions pickup truck across the street and gave them the finger. Twice. Right hand and left hand.

"Oh, Amy, look, now you've done it. That one guy is crossing the street. He's coming over here!"

"Shit on him," muttered Amy, though she was a little alarmed to see the bearded man dodging traffic and coming toward them and the clinic. "Pick on someone your own size!" she cried out. "You weenie!"

Diane hustled her sister around the back of Women's Uptown and in through the staff door. From there, the door to the waiting room was open. Almost every seat was taken. A uniformed policewoman, belted, armed, wired, and sweating like a pig like everyone else, stood with her hands clasped in front of her, her back to the front door. Ever since the Family Champions started filming outside, a policewoman stood guard at the front.

Amy took a seat beside a drooling drug addict and let Diane check them in for Lamaze class. She picked up *People*. She felt like crying.

Ordinarily Amy liked the Women's Uptown and the other people in her Lamaze class, most of whom were here with their mothers or their girlfriends for coaches. Amy and Diane were not the only sister act. Hardly anyone had a husband, even Amy. Chuck wasn't equal to it. Chuck was equal to the cineplex and Bongo's, a bar where he and his friends hung out. He was equal to his cousin's town car service where he was a regular driver. He was a good dancer and he had fab abs and a cute butt. Chuck was equal to the gym where he could do breathing and stretches; he could bench-press his own weight, but he could not help Amy hold on to a big pillow in Lamaze class.

The Women's Uptown waiting room was crowded. The presence of the uniformed policewoman made it more crowded. Her dark blue uniform, her dark hat, her dark skin and hair absorbed light and gave off heat. Her black name tag with white HODGES gave off heat. The black pistol strapped to her thick black belt with a black walkie-talkie and a black radio gave off heat. The place was sweltering, and the fan only moved the stagnant BO around the floor. Amy thought she might gag.

Diane came back and whispered to Amy that the Lamaze instructor was a little late today; she was afraid of the Family Champion video cameras. "I told you it was serious," Diane added.

"BFD," said Amy.

"You shouldn't have flipped them off. You shouldn't have called him a weenie."

Diane had to sit apart from Amy. There were not two seats together. Diane took her accounting class text from her backpack and started to read.

Amy noticed that many of the children waiting for their mothers had snotty noses. Well, that was funky. The kids played with toys, mostly all broken. Doublefunk. At least no one was seriously looking at *Gourmet* and *Sunset.* No, the best-thumbed mags here were *People.* Often, the women waiting commented on the marriages and breakups and rehabs and live-ins of Julia and Cameron and Denzel and Whoopi and Halle and all the rest of them. Like they just lived down the street. Funky family values.

Today Amy was not in the mood. The heat. The armed cop. The drug addict who smelled especially bad in the heat. But it was more than that. Amy had started to have second thoughts about this baby. And she had no one to talk to. There was no one to whom she could say, well, maybe being preggers wasn't going to be so fun after all. Diane was an okay Lamaze coach, but she was useless as a confidante. Diane was not looking for fun in life, so she was not disappointed when she didn't find it. Amy felt differently. Amy was sick of sick. Amy had enough of sick growing up with Diane. Tired of drear and fear and bickering parents and stifling family life. As soon as she had got a job, full-time barista, Amy got an apartment with her girlfriends. She expected to have some fun. And she did. A lot of fun. Then there was the surprise of finding out she was preggers. Amy and Chuck were in love, but they hadn't planned on getting preggers, and the shock of it was like *Days of Our Lives,* only no commercials and no music.

Amy told Chuck first. They gnashed and fretted and cried together, but it was Our Secret, and they loved each other. Our Secret, Our Baby brought them even closer together. Then Amy told her roommates. Their eyes all got big and they said, oh, Amy! Like she was noble or doomed or somehow set apart like a character in a movie. It was less like a movie after she stupidly told another barista at work and that bitch told everyone there. No more secrets. By the time Amy and Chuck told their families, everyone had an opinion. Oh, God, not pregnant! Everyone nattered at Amy and Chuck. Amy's mom, Diane, her dad and his wife Linda. Her friends and roommates. Chuck's parents, his brother, his friends, and his roommate cousin with the town car service. Abortion. Adoption. Marriage. Rusty said Amy wasn't ready to be a mother and have her whole life change, that Amy was lucky abortions were legal, and she ought to do it soon. Some, like Amy's dad and Chuck's whole family, were for getting married. Chuck and Amy declared they would make their own decisions, thank you, that they were partners.

Amy got through the months where you barf and feel yucky. That was no fun. Then Dr. Henley said she had to watch her weight and stay off her feet and give up the barista job. The manager said he'd heard she was preggers and he was going to fire her anyway. Amy took off her apron, quit on the spot, and called him a weenie on her way out the door. With no job, however, she had to move out of her apartment and back in with Mom and Diane. That was not fun. Getting her room ready to share with the baby, this was not fun. They bought a Valu-Village crib and it took up the whole room. Amy had to put her stereo under the crib till Rusty pointed out to her that she couldn't be playing the stereo under the crib. The baby had to sleep. Rusty said that having a baby was serious business, and who promised you fun in this world, Amy?

Well, no one promised her fun, but Amy had expectations. Only now, she had second thoughts. When Amy sat down, she could not see her knees. When she stood up, she could not see her feet. No one cared. Worse, there was no one to whom she could say she was having second thoughts. Amy could not share her fears or misgivings with her girlfriends, even those who had given her that fine surprise baby shower just a few months ago. Where were they now that her time was drawing near? They were going to clubs and dancing and meeting men and having dates. They were taking men home to their apartments. They had their eyebrows pierced. They had jobs and classes, and they wore sleek, fashionable clothes. One had a belly button ring she showed off with low-slung pants. Amy feared her own belly button would never be cute again. Her ankles were always swollen. Her feet looked like water balloons. Her boobs felt like inflatable dinghies. She was wearing pup tents. She sweated from every pore and orifice. Her mother had promised all that would pass.

"Your body will come back to you," Rusty had told her, "but your life will never be the same."

There was a knock at the door of the Women's Uptown Clinic. The armed cop took a step forward, turned the lock, opened it a crack. "Go around to the back," Hodges ordered whoever it was. There was protest, demurral. "All deliveries, all patients go around to the back for now. The back door is open." She closed the door and stood in front of it, hands crossed in front of her body. She glared at Amy. She looked like a linebacker.

The heat in the waiting room made Amy miserable, itchy and wretched. The boy baby—the little fetal penis ultrasound detected made Chuck happy—kicked all the time. Amy feared that Chuck was falling out of love with her. He talked about the navy all the time. He talked about the benefits navy men received, but he did not talk about allotments for their wives. What about the navy wives, Chuck? But she could not bring herself to say it. She wondered if she and Chuck were falling out of love. Of course they didn't need a certificate from the state of Oregon to prove they loved each other, but Amy had started to wonder who was going to raise the kid. At night she would lie alone in her bed and look at the empty crib nearby. She wondered if she would be a navy wife. If she would like being a navy wife. Chuck said he wanted to join up soon. He didn't want to be too old. He said the navy likes to shape its men. Chuck was twenty-two. For the first time Amy saw him for the boy he was. A boy with a penis, just like his soon-to-be son.

Penis, vagina, sperm, ovum, pelvic and pubic, Amy had started to think like that. That's the way Lamaze described everything. Nobody talked about fab abs or cute butts. Buttock and labia, fetus and embryo, placenta, uterus. There was none of this MTV *baby baby lemme have you inside me, gotta gimme mora your lovin'* in Lamaze. On MTV good-looking men bounced on the balls of their feet and pointed at their crotches *right here, right now, right there.* In Lamaze class there was none of that. There was no *baby lemme do you right* with Chuck either. Not anymore. Amy was too preggers. Chuck didn't seem to be missing it. This suggested to Amy that while she was incapacitated, preggers with Little Chuckie, Big Chuckie was *doing it right* with someone else, that Chuck was flexing his fab abs with another girl.

Like father, like son? Another kick from the baby rolled across her abdomen, so intense it rattled the pages of the *People* magazine she held in her hand. A few of the tired, hot mothers in the waiting room smiled. And then Amy wondered how, if she got Chuck to marry her, could she endure being married to him? How could she be the one to be reproducing Chuck, little penis and all? How could she be here, great wings of sweat beneath her arms and probably a great puddle of sweat where she was sitting preparing for childbirth, when Chuck was off somewhere having fun? She was stuck with this kicking infant. Even after it was born she would be stuck with it. She would be stuck with it for twenty years.

Amy had once suggested to Dr. Henley that maybe she wasn't feeling all the maternal feelings that she should. Maybe there was something wrong with her. But Dr. Henley had been so reassuring; Dr. Henley said there were many things to feel, that one was not right and another wrong. This was a big step, and to feel fearful and inadequate, well, that was part of it. All would be well, said Dr. Henley.

But all was not well. It wasn't fear and inadequacy Amy felt. She felt stunned, like that deer her father once hit in the road. Mom was home with sick Diane, and Dad was driving Amy and Kevin back from Hood River in a terrible rainstorm. The windshield wipers were worthless against the onslaught of rain and her father leaned forward over the steering wheel, trying to see. Suddenly something huge and dark appeared in front of them and there was a sickening thud, and another and another. Amy and her father were both thrown forward. He turned the wheel furiously and pulled off to the side of the road. He got out of the car, swearing, and Amy got out behind him. The deer, though struck, got to her feet and staggered about, as though merely uncertain. The deer did not know she had been struck by a Ford station wagon going forty miles an hour. The deer fixed them all in her gaze while Dad swore and Kevin cried, but Amy could make no sound. The deer and Amy stared at each other. Amy saw in that deer's eyes what she now felt. The deer took a few more steps before the enormity of what had happened fully dawned on her. Then she fell flat in the road and another car struck her and went out of control, and there was blood everywhere.

Amy looked around the waiting room. They were all old and tired, these women. They'd all done this before. Even the cop had the big breasts and the don't-mess-with-me demeanor of a woman many times a mother. They had no lives except their children, these same snotty children who were so happy with a few broken toys. These women could sit in this stifling room and wait for the months to pass, because it would all be the same for them anyway. But Amy was young! Amy had her whole life in front of her. Amy was too young to be preggers. Amy wanted to have fun.

It was fun being preggers when she was the focus of the whole family's attention and ire and excitement. Sort of like what Diane must have felt like all those years she was sick and everyone had to care and be careful of her. But hey, I didn't really mean it! Amy wanted to shout now. She wanted to scream, I didn't want it to be for twenty years! That's a life sentence! That's forever! She all but stood up and cried out. Did she love Chuck? Had she ever loved him? Tears welled in her eyes. She glanced over at the only other young patient in the Women's Uptown waiting room. This girl was Amy's age, slender and tall and beautiful with dark curling hair and pale skin. And her eyes, like that deer's, were round and black with foreboding, stunned, struck, and filled with fear.

The nurse, Nell Faraday, came out, clipboard in hand. "Darcy Reeves?"

12

Alternative Education

THE WRITING WAS ON THE WALL, ONLY NOT IN THE way Darcy expected. It said: *Pregnancy and Alcohol do not mix.* She did as she was told, stood on the scale, answered the nurse's questions. "What does any of this matter?" she asked irritably. "I'm here for an abortion."

"Follow me. We'll be in number eight today. End of the hall."

In the small, stifling examining room, chrome stirrups, chrome trays, chrome lights overhead all gave off a dull gleam. There were calendars on the wall and anatomical posters of burgeoning uteruses and female reproductive systems. Nell took her blood pressure. High.

"I'm nervous," said Darcy. "How could I not be?"

Nell made some further notes on the chart. "I don't think you want to go through with this, Darcy," she said, not looking up from her pen. "I think you've been pressured. I think you may have been bullied into this."

"It's my legal right."

"Look around you, girl. This isn't Oprah. There's no TV audience. There's only the voice inside you."

"The child?"

"If it's a child to you, then why are you here for this procedure? Answer me that." Nell added when Darcy did not, "Dr. Henley wanted you to get counseling. She referred you, if I'm not mistaken. Did you do this?"

"I don't need counseling."

"Everything about your chart and your behavior indicates a woman very conflicted. Now you're right at the moment of decision. It's your life. Your choices, Darcy."

"My choices are to be chosen. I have been chosen for this work."

Nell gave a short derisive snort. "You mean like you told Dr. Henley, that having this baby was your job? Is that what you mean? Having a baby is a big job. Raising a child is an enormous responsibility."

"It is my work," Darcy maintained coldly.

"Your gown is there behind you. Dr. Henley will be with you shortly." Nell left, taking the chart with her.

Darcy Reeves took off her sandals. Shimmied out of her jeans. Pulled her T-shirt over her head and took off her underwear. She slid her arms into the holes of the thin cotton rag and tied it at the back of her neck. She went to the mirror and pulled a few clips from her thick dark hair and it tumbled, curling to her shoulders. The fluorescent light was unflattering to her pale skin. Her eyes looked gouged out. She wanted to fall to her knees and pray, but something kept her upright. Fear. Praying would suggest, even to God, that she was uncertain about the course ordained for her. Praying would suggest that she wavered. Maybe not if she prayed for strength, she thought. Just strength. Just the strength to do what was obliged of her. What she had been selected for. Much as Mary had been selected to bear the infant Jesus, she reminded herself, Daniel's voice, his inflections echoing. Much as Joshua had been selected to bring down the walls. Much as David had been selected to bring down the murderous Goliath. Darcy Reeves was of this select company who know that God has chosen them to make His vengeance known, His displeasure felt, to effect His changes in this sinful world.

The writing was on the wall.

The sign over the door said simply SEEKERS. Well, that described Darcy's older sister Janeen, a simple, decent woman who had sought out one church after another, looking for a faith that would explain why her husband Slim was an alcoholic wife beater. The Seekers met in a big room, once a billiard parlor in a suburban strip mall that time and new commercial arteries had left empty. Businesses died here, and nearly all the storefronts were empty. But religion seemed to flourish. The Seekers were a small congregation, steadfast under Daniel's leadership. He alone led the Seekers, and any pastoral support was volunteered within his congregation.

Daniel gave himself entirely to the Seekers. He personally paid the rent on the storefront. He lived frugally, renting a room in the home of an old widow. He worked five days a week as a sales associate in a chain computer store. He did well there. He didn't jolly people along. He was serious, and he knew that buying a computer or a stereo or a television was a serious purchase; he listened. Management told him he spent too much time with individual customers, but his sales were unflagging. There were noises about a promotion.

Daniel was serious about God too. On Sundays he could tell you what God wanted for and from you. He was bearded like Jesus. He could be gentle as in Suffer the Little Children, but he could also be like Jesus on the rampage, when He flung the Pharisees out of the temple, fearless and physical.

Darcy's sister Janeen had been a Seeker for about a year. She had confided some of her miseries to Daniel. When Janeen became pregnant again, she confided she wanted an abortion. Daniel counseled her away from this in no uncertain terms. It was murder, he said. "Well, that may be," Janeen replied tearfully, "but I'm the one dying here. My husband is killing me, just as surely."

One Sunday morning, Janeen came to church wearing dark glasses. She did not take them off.

Just as Daniel was warming up—he did this, warmed up, as an athlete warms up, working himself and the congregation into a state of mind to believe and receive—Daniel stopped his preaching. He walked down the center aisle. People scuffled and craned their heads and turned their knees, scooting out of his way as he moved relentlessly through Janeen's row. He removed her dark glasses. To the rest of the congregation, which included by this time Janeen's parents, Bert and Billie Jean, and their youngest child, Darcy, still a high school student, he blasted forth. He seared right through all of them, words to the effect that God doesn't like the innocent to suffer. God doesn't like the unprotected to be victimized. God will not rest easy while His children are being abused. Daniel touched the shiner that had spread all around Janeen's eye, her nose, and her cheekbone. Janeen winced. He said to her, "That is the last time that man will strike you. You have my word on it."

This was not an idle offer. The story made it to the police blotter. It made one column inch in the *Oregonian*. It made it into Superior Court on charges of assault. Bail was granted, though it was not the first time Daniel had been arrested for doing God's work. He was fearless. Janeen's family and the Seekers congregation got together his bail and got him out. Janeen drove him not to the rented room in the widow's house, but to her parents' comfortable home in a working-class suburb where Billie Jean had cooked a fine meal. Daniel said grace. The assault charge was later dismissed.

The story of Daniel's zealous wrath on behalf of the downtrodden varied only in its particulars. The thrust, as it was told among the Seekers, was that Daniel had gone to Fritzy's, the bar where Janeen's husband Slim habitually drank. Daniel went to the bar, asked the bartender which one was Slim. Without so much as an introduction, Daniel said to Slim if he ever laid another hand on Janeen or her children, that Daniel, acting as God's instrument, would kill him.

In and of itself this would not have been enough to get him arrested, but the husband took this as an affront to his manhood and demeaned his ability to do whatever he goddamned wanted to his own goddamned wife. Daniel told him that kind of language would land him in hell. The husband struck him. This, clearly, was what Daniel had intended all along.

The cronies scattered, the bartender called the police as Daniel hammered the husband, pummeled him, crying out that this was what it felt like to be the butt of violence, smashing Slim's jaw, nose, guts, and kidneys, telling Slim that God hated him. By the time the police got there, Daniel had beaten Slim senseless. It took two armed cops, and a gun at Daniel's head, before he'd stop. They called the ambulance for Slim, and the police took Daniel away in handcuffs. He did not resist them.

Daniel's physical strength, his willingness to confront evil, his refusal to accept injustice—all these became Janeen's strength. She moved out of the trailer she had lived in with the husband. She and the three kids moved into a cheap apartment. Grim but cheap. Daniel had something to do with the rent being so low. It belonged to a Seeker. The congregation furnished the apartment. Janeen got a restraining order against Slim who, for all his bleating bravado, found himself another woman to bully. He paid no support, so Janeen got a job. For her prenatal care with the baby she was carrying, her third child, she went to Women's Uptown.

Some version of this saga, amplified according to the needs of the speaker, or the listener for that matter, traveled well beyond the Seekers. The congregation grew. They had to rent more folding chairs, and on Sundays the former billiard parlor filled up. Many came to Daniel with their own woes, their fears and trepidation and tales of people who had done them wrong. They hoped he would take upon himself their troubles and effect their deliverance, but though he would counsel Seekers, he only rarely took upon himself the mantle of avenger. However, Daniel might speak to your oppressor. He could be frightening. Daniel might find a way to help you find God's will. He believed that God had a will, and it was up to God's people to find it, follow it. He was not the gentle, joking pastor people were accustomed to. He had no sense of humor.

The widow in whose home Daniel rented a room died, and her children tried to evict him. He said the widow had changed her will and left it to him. It was his house, and he refused to move out. Whatever the widow had promised Daniel, she hadn't actually changed the will. The house was left to her children, who made dark innuendos that Daniel had killed her off thinking he'd inherit. These came to nothing. Save that he had no place to live.

Bert and Billie Jean Reeves invited him to live with them. They had only one child left at home, their youngest, Darcy. They had an empty bedroom. They would be honored to have him live in their home. And in time they were honored to have him fall in love with their daughter.

Darcy Reeves was one of those coltish girls whose journey into womanhood is swift and certain. The difference between Darcy Reeves at fifteen and Darcy Reeves at sixteen or seventeen was stunning. She was the youngest by many years in her family, and in effect had grown up like an only child in a grave household of elderly adults. She was not high-spirited or boisterous or giggly as most high school girls; she had no gaggle of friends who slept over. Darcy was one of those young people who tolerate their goofy adolescence, knowing they must go through it to come to the other side. She dutifully placed herself on the swim team sophomore year. She played the flute in band. She had a job at Dairy Queen. She looked after her high school boyfriend as if he were one of her little nephews, driving him here and there in the car that she had bought with her Dairy Queen wages. When the boyfriend started playing bass in a rock band with some loutish friends, she dropped him, not because she was jealous of the band but because it was such a squanderous waste of time. That band was going nowhere but the drummer's garage. Face it. She had a calm, middle-aged sensibility concealed behind great youthful beauty. High school was trying to her. She wanted to drop out and work full time.

Bert and Billie Jean looked to Daniel to counsel her against this, and he did so. He urged her to go to an alternative fundamentalist school, one that gave students unstructured classrooms and more freedom but demanded more responsibility and religion from them. Alternative education suited Darcy, and she graduated from this school. Daniel stood her tuition, part of which, it would later emerge, was paid in missing inventory from the big computer store where Daniel worked.

Daniel Phillips, for the first time in his thirty-one years, was in love, smitten as if struck, blinded by the light of Darcy Reeves. He could not accept this. Did not trust it. Everything for Daniel had to be tested to be certain it was free of sin. Everything had to be heightened, brought up a notch or two on the significance scale. Soaked with significance. If not, it would be ordinary, and this was intolerable to Daniel. He was no ordinary man. God had chosen him to speak, after all, to lead. But Darcy was so beautiful and Daniel was so smitten that he distrusted her altogether. What if she were the devil come to tempt him in a pleasing form? What if God had sent Darcy Reeves to tempt Daniel Phillips, to test him? In truth, he was never quite certain. But lust was not available to him as an option, so it must be love.

After a fashion, he proposed to Darcy. He explained to her and to her parents, Bert and Billie Jean, both good-natured, easily awed people, that he could not, at this moment, marry her according to the laws of the state of Oregon, man's laws. He did not say he was still married. Twice. Once in Wisconsin and once in Montana. That would later emerge too. Daniel assured Bert and Billie Jean that if they gave their permission for their daughter to be One with Daniel, God would smile on everyone.

Darcy, listening, sitting very straight, her composure unruffled, but her full lips curled in a half smile, agreed. Darcy was not very concerned about God's smile, or any of that. Darcy knew only that Daniel was the most exciting man she had ever met.

She did not stop to think that other than her teachers, her brothers, and her brothers-in-law, her male acquaintance was pretty much limited to boys. Janeen pointed out to the whole family that Darcy was just a kid, that she didn't know shit from Shinola and she didn't have enough experience to judge. Darcy denied this. Then Janeen said that a thirty-one-year-old man should find a woman his own age and not pick on minors. Daniel questioned Janeen's fitness to be a Seeker.

Daniel also questioned Darcy's fitness to be One with him. This meant long excruciating sessions in the Reeveses' living room, going into all aspects of her life in front of her parents. Sometimes even Bert and Billie Jean were called to account for their own actions and beliefs, and made to feel small and insignificant, though honored to be the parents of the girl Daniel Phillips had chosen to be One with him. Among other inquiries, he asked if Darcy was a virgin, and she said no. Her parents both blubbered over this admission, feigned shock, and hoped Daniel would not think her unworthy. Darcy informed them that she had bestowed her virginity on the bass player in the backseat of the car bought with the Dairy Queen wages. Bestow was the word. No peer pressure. Darcy bestowed her virginity, and the boy was unbelievably grateful. Darcy had sex, because it was an experience crucial to adult life. Did she love the bass player? Yes. At least until she drove him home and dropped him off at his house. Did she love him now? She loved only Daniel now. Now and forever.

And so Darcy and Daniel were united not quite in holy matrimony but something very like it. He conducted the ceremony himself. They waited till Darcy turned eighteen and everyone was happy with this, except for Janeen, who left the Seekers altogether. Her family cut off all connection with her.

Becoming a married woman accentuated those qualities that made strangers stare at Darcy. Customers in the Dairy Queen sometimes forgot their Blizzards just to look at her. She moved through the world with an instinctive grace, filling up even the Dairy Queen uniform with her beauty—more than that, an elusive maturity that would have enhanced a much older woman and was dazzling on one so young. When Darcy became Daniel's woman, her youth and beauty were enlisted—her dark eyes, her cascading curls, her fine skin and bright warm lips, her high-breasted body, long legged, erect, elegant—to his cause.

Daniel became the effective head of household in the Reeves home. Bert and Billie Jean lived in awe of him. They lived in awe of Darcy. Her standing among the Seekers altered. She became the leading lady to the Seekers' leading man. She had her own place to sit every Sunday. Paths parted for her. If there was a line at the women's restroom—and there always was—other Seeker women let her go first. People came up to her with little gifts, little tokens to be shared with Daniel. They treated her in some ways as if she were herself a shrine to Daniel.

Darcy was not unhappy with this. She didn't feel that her life had been submerged in his; after all, she was not part of a clique of friends who went sashaying through the mall on Saturday. On the contrary, Darcy felt as though Daniel heightened and brightened and burnished her life. Through Daniel the whole world recognized her worth, and through her the world would recognize his worth. She was his vessel. A vessel must not crack or spill. A vessel must not waver. A vessel is only as beautiful as it is useful to the man who carries it. Carries her. Their sex was not the joyful, spontaneous coupling of lovers, nor even the tender newfound intimacy of newlyweds. Sex was sacred. Sex was significant. Sex was important: the way their bodies could evoke the union of their souls.

Daniel scrutinized his wife's every phrase and thought and article of clothing. She never protested or complained. She followed his instructions. His smile of approval somewhere beneath the thick beard thrilled her, truly down deep, physically she could feel the flutter of his approval. She did everything he asked of her. She was being groomed for something great. She was certain of it. This was alternative education at its most intense.

Later, in court, even in privileged conversation with her public defender attorney, Darcy Reeves could not really remember when the issue of abortion had come to absorb Daniel's religious and pastoral attention, his whole waking life. She said it had happened slowly.

The public defender, Arnetta Hughes, gave her some dates. Darcy did not contest them, but she could not confirm them either. Yes, Daniel was the founder, the founding father, if you will, of the Seekers. And yes, he was the founding father of Family Champions and the Embryo Protection League. Were they part of the Seekers? They met in the Seekers' building. She knew that. She'd been present. But when? How long? She could remember only that over time his obsession with this issue came to blot out everything else he did or believed in. And yes, as this happened, a lot of the old Seekers left the assembly. New ones joined, people who believed that the slaughter of the innocents was everywhere at hand and Americans were doing nothing to stop it.

Conferring with Arnetta Hughes in a consulting room in the Portland jail, Darcy didn't always respond to her questions. Arnetta asked two or three times. "At these meetings of the Family Champions, was there talk, did Daniel talk of violence?"

"Yes. Some. Not at first. Some."

"Was there a difference between the Family Champions and the Embryo Protection League?"

"Some. I can't remember. I spent so much time in the church and the meetings. Especially after I quit the Dairy Queen."

"Would you recognize these people now?"

"Yes. Some."

"Didn't it alarm you that they were talking about murder?"

"But they weren't. They were filming. They were going to shame these women before the world."

"When did this plan get hatched, Darcy? The one that eventually went down?"

"I can't remember when."

"But you heard it."

"Of course I heard it. I was there. Always. I was his wife. Well, sort of his wife. They tell me now he had other wives."

"That's true."

"It doesn't matter. I was his vessel. I was the one Chosen. My child was Chosen. Daniel was Chosen, and God had chosen all of us. We were a sort of holy family, see?

Arnetta Hughes broke her pencil in half. She stood, paced around the interrogation room. She was a young attorney, sassy, her black hair in neat, fashionable cornrows, though her stiff unrevealing clothing made her look like a briefcase with legs. Arnetta thought that in six years as a public defender, she had seen it all. The good, the bad, and the ugly. But this? This was one for the books. "Darcy, who told you all this?"

"Everyone. Daniel. My parents. God."

"God."

"God."

"Did they tell you what a reckless and terrible act they had in mind for you to commit?"

Darcy raised her dark eyes to Arnetta's face. "They said no one would convict me, young as I am. No record. They said it would go easy for me. I'm pregnant. The writing was on the wall."

"And Daniel? What did he think would happen to him?"

"The writing was on the wall for him too. He knew he would be called to suffer as Christ was called to suffer."

"And he was like Daniel in the Bible, and he could read it and no one else could?"

"Yes."

"Did he tell you that you too would be called on to suffer?"

"Those who suffer for God's will are not condemned, but blessed. They will go easy with me. No record. The writing is on the wall."

"Are you retarded, Darcy? Are you? Answer me!"

"Of course not."

"So why didn't you use your brains to think this one through?"

"That's what she said to me. Dr. Henley said to me, think this one through. I liked her. I did. I liked her a lot. I wanted to tell her the truth."

"Did you?"

Darcy did not reply. Looked only at her hands.

"Didn't you ever, ever think to yourself, *never mind what Daniel told me, this is wrong. This is a sin.* Yes, that's what it is, Darcy. Were you Daniel's zombie always?"

"Not always."

Darcy's conviction of Daniel's correctness had started to unravel when she knew or guessed that she was indeed pregnant. And she knew by this time why she had been made pregnant. It was part of Daniel's plan. God's plan, her mother would sometimes whisper to her. Darcy quit the Dairy Queen. The mother of the Chosen One doesn't sling Blizzards for minimum wage. As her body underwent these changes, Darcy's feelings toward the child and the man began to change. She had been told that she and her child had been Chosen to bring the world's attention to the slaughter of the innocents. It was part of a plan, God's plan, that she and Daniel were to enact. Daniel's voice, whether he was lying beside her in bed or in front of the Seekers or addressing the Family Champions, was so soothing and full of such conviction and correctness, it felt hypnotic. Darcy sometimes felt her eyes droop as her will dissolved into his.

However, at their first appointment at the Women's Uptown, she heard another voice. Dr. Henley. Dr. Henley's voice did not put you to sleep with its rich, lulling invitation to give up. Dr. Henley's voice made you wake up. The whole place made you wake up, all those women, old and young, washed and unwashed; there was noise and stink and screaming, oaths and rippling laughter at Women's Uptown. To Darcy it was strange music. Forbidden. As music was forbidden.

After her first appointment, other forbidden things occurred to Darcy. Doubt, for one. Could Daniel's plan be wrong? Are we really sure of God's will and plan and needs? But Darcy did not say that to the Chosen, especially not since he had chosen her. You cannot look weak, cowardly, vacillating, and stupid. Darcy wanted to call up Janeen and talk to her, but she didn't. She feared if Daniel caught her talking to Janeen, Daniel would know she was weak, cowardly, and vacillating.

In private, now and then, when she could, Darcy began to suggest to Daniel that the filming from the pickup truck should satisfy

God's purpose. Hadn't they got on the nightly news with that alone? Look at all the press and media attention. National media. Ten zillion zaps on the Family Champion Internet site. Another ten zillion on the Embryo Protection League Web site. She made these observations more than once. Over time. Gently. Then she brought them up at mealtime, hoping her parents would back her up, but they kept their eyes on their instant mashed potatoes and said nothing.

After one such meal, and back in their bedroom, Daniel brought his bearded face right up to hers. He spoke so vehemently that little sprays of saliva burst into her eyes. "No one else sees abortion for what it is, the slaughter of the innocents, just like Herod in the Bible. No one but me knows how to stop it."

Gently, quietly, Darcy pointed out, "Other people have tried violence, but it hasn't worked."

"That's because no one has gone inside the very temple of death. That's what you're going to do. What we are going to do. You and I and our firstborn son. We are chosen. If these miserable sinners think they're risking their own miserable lives, their own rotten deaths, no one will come to an abortion clinic. They're happy to commit murder on the unborn, but if they have to face it themselves, believe me, it will cease."

"I believed this," said Darcy to Arnetta Hughes.

"So you just went along with it?"

"No. Well, yes. I guess I did. I believed he was right. I believed I was chosen to do this, you see? I was Darcy, chosen by Daniel and God chose him, and God chose me, and I was given into a state holier than marriage, to Daniel, chosen to conceive and carry his child. To conceive and carry out his ideas, his plans. To bring his seed truly to fruition."

"That's what he told you?" asked Arnetta.

"Yes. That's what I believe. Believed."

Arnetta wanted to throttle this girl. "You are such a little goddamned sheep that you're still thinking all this is fine because he chose you to do it?"

"Please, don't." Darcy started to cry. Put her head on her arms and wept. "What do you want from me?"

"Let me tell you instead what the judge is going to want from you. You are not the fucking angel of death or anything else, get it? Let me tell you what the jury's going to want. Let's start with a little remorse, huh? Let's start with some regret, Darcy. Some *oh, God, if only I could undo my actions!*"

"Do you think I don't regret it? Do you think I don't wish I could undo it all? I tried to get out of it! I did. There was an earlier appointment, you know," Darcy blurted and wept, great blubbering snotty sobs. And in some ways this is exactly what Arnetta wanted from her: an end to the damned composure. Darcy choked. "I made an earlier appointment. I was going to do this weeks before, but I told Daniel I was sick and I couldn't do it when I was sick. I had to be healthy to have lots of courage."

"And what did he do?"

"Nothing. He said I was disappointing God. He said that I was weak, that God and all the unborn relied on me and what did I do but wussy out of it. He said to make another appointment."

"And so the second time you didn't wussy out? Oh, that's great, Darcy. The second time, what in hell did you think?" Darcy did not answer. "Tell me, that second time, you sitting there waiting, what did you think about?" No answer. "What in hell did you think?"

"I thought I should pray."

13

Writing on the Wall

WHEN SHE FINISHED PRAYING, DARCY GOT UP OFF the cold floor. She went to the backpack she had brought in with her and unzipped it. She took out the revolver Daniel had bought for her, registered in her name for her self-protection. Six bullets. She put it under the flimsy hospital gown. The metal was cold on her thigh, and she left it there to warm it up. She burst into a great volley of sweat in the unventilated room and thought for a moment she might pass out. She concentrated on Daniel. The plan. Their plan. God's plan. Daniel would have left the pickup truck by now; another Family Champion would be operating the video camera. Daniel would have crossed the street, and he would be waiting at the back of the Women's Uptown. Waiting to hear the shots and screams. Waiting for Darcy to bring his seed to fruition. For all hell to break loose. Then, armed and terrible, he would join her, and they would end the slaughter of the innocents.

She heard voices outside the room, Dr. Henley and the big nurse, Nell. She could hear them take her chart from the rack on the door. They spoke, low murmured exchanges, and then Dr. Henley opened the door, Nell behind her.

"So, Darcy," said Dr. Henley, "termination is what you've chosen after all."

"I hope you will forgive me," Darcy blubbered.

"I'm the doctor here, not the priest. Maybe you need some more time. Is that it?" Caryn reached out for her shoulder.

In that transparent sliver of time, Darcy knew that if Dr. Henley so much as touched her, all her resolve would crumble. All Daniel's teachings, all their planning and praying and hours of practice would come to nothing. She knew too that Daniel's wrath would be unimaginable, devastating, and it would crash upon her. His wrath and God's too. She feared Daniel's wrath more than God's. She reached under her gown and took out the revolver.

Dr. Henley gave an astonished, squealing little gasp as though strangled and went a ghastly greenish-white. But Nell, seeing the gun, seeing it pointed at Caryn's face, pierced the heavens with screams and thrust her weight against Caryn and pushed, flung her to the floor. Darcy pointed the gun to the floor, fired. She shot the doctor in the back. She panicked, because something was already wrong; her instructions were to shoot everyone in the head. Nell dropped to the floor, still screaming. Darcy got off the table, pointed the gun at Nell's head, just as she had practiced, but Nell's hand went up to strike her, and so Darcy shot her through the hand. Nell fell back. Darcy stepped over them both, their blood pooling on the floor.

She opened the door of the examination room and started down the hall. Behind her Darcy could hear Nell screaming for everyone to get out of the building. She thought this was odd. The nurse should have been screaming for help. Nurses, staff, patients were darting into the crowded hall. Darcy fired again and again. The writing was on the wall.

Darcy held the gun in both hands as Daniel had taught her. Alternative education. She didn't exactly aim, though. Even if she couldn't shoot them in the head, she could shoot them. She fired at anything that moved amid the screams and shouts and oaths. Another burst, a spray of blood, and someone slumped down the wall. A doctor? Nurse? She couldn't tell. Daniel had said it did not matter, anyway. After that first doctor who was prepared to murder the unborn, it didn't matter who Darcy hit or wounded. Patient? So what? Daniel would be right behind her. She listened for him. For his shots to ring out. The writing was on the wall.

Darcy fired, hitting one of a troop of heavily pregnant women waddling down the hall to an open door. They were following a woman with a clipboard high in her hand, all of them screaming and trying to scatter, but the hall was too small, too narrow, and the pregnant women were too many and too cumbersome. The youngest of them, Amy Meadows, stood right in front of Darcy, screaming to wake the dead, who were probably all around her. Darcy was sure there were more dead. Daniel was supposed to be behind her. She brought the gun to Amy Meadows's face. To Amy Meadows's nose.

"Don't! Don't kill me! I don't want to die!" Amy's urine released in a great gush down her legs and she thought she was about to give birth and die in the same moment. "I don't want to die! I'm too young! Don't!"

Darcy cocked her head to one side, looking at Amy with some of the old serious absorption she'd once given to the Blizzard machine at the Dairy Queen, or to Daniel's teachings, as though Amy had something important to tell her. Darcy raised her arm, pointed the firearm, and pulled the trigger. A spray of ceiling tiles fell over all them; powdery shards fell like snow. Darcy regarded Amy's stricken face, gone ashen, with the residue still falling. And then, for all the sweat and adrenaline pumping, Darcy nonetheless put both her arms up high, like she was drowning, waving good-bye to the world before the waters closed over her. The gun fell from her hand, clattered to the floor. Her part was done. She had not yet heard Daniel firing.

The uniformed cop, Hodges, ran screaming toward Darcy; her weapon was drawn. Darcy had forgotten about her. Did Daniel know about the armed cop? While she was still in the waiting room, Darcy had wondered if she ought to go outside and tell the Family Champions in the pickup truck that they should do this on another day. But she hadn't. Daniel's wrath would have descended on her. Where was Daniel, anyway? Surely her part was done now, and he could take up his own righteous wrath. But where was he? The hall was full of smoke and powdery bits of ceiling.

Officer Hodges, crying into the radio strapped to her shoulder, barreled toward Darcy, swiping at the screaming pregnant women who blocked her path. Their faces, white, brown, black, were contorted, and their mouths were open, screaming; their bodies bounced against one another. Hodges's face was a taut mask of fear as she tried to push past them.

Darcy remained beside Amy Meadows who was screaming now for Hodges not to shoot her. Hodges had the gun pointed at Darcy.

And Amy. Esther and Chantal burst out from behind Hodges. Though the cop called out that everyone should get back, Esther and Chantal tackled Darcy, knocked her off her feet. She landed hard on her backside.

Shots rang out down the hall. Officer Hodges, hearing the gunfire behind her, stricken, turned, swore, and ran toward the other end of the building near the staff room and the back door. "Get here!" cried Hodges again into the shoulder radio. "There's hell to pay!" She saw Daniel. Both his hands were wrapped around a handgun. "Drop your weapon, now! Drop it!"

Daniel fired at Hodges and missed, fired at a patient, felled her. Then he darted into an examining room, where there was more gunfire and screaming. Hodges, unmindful of her own safety, stood in the doorway, saw Daniel Phillips with his gun pointed at an old woman. The nurse he had wounded lay on the floor screaming. Hodges shot him. In the head. He fell, weapon still in hand.

Women's Uptown was quickly cordoned off, police and paramedics and newspeople, cameras and telephones and sirens all swooped down on the neighborhood, turning it into the war zone that it was. Across the street, the Family Champion cameraman continued to videotape until he was knocked out of the truck bed by a Portland cop, flung facedown into the street, handcuffed, and nearly run over by an ambulance. Police secured the building, finding that, in truth, Hodges had already secured it: there were two assassins, a male, gravely wounded, one female pinned to the ground by clinic employees.

Medical personnel tried to determine who was hit and who was just hysterical. The old woman, a drug addict, whom Daniel had been aiming at had gone into convulsions. One woman's water had broken, and two others had started labor. There was blood everywhere. Given the confusion and the narrow passages and the number of people, paramedics could not immediately get to the examining room at the end of the hall where Nell lay over Caryn, her arms encircling her, her lips pressed in mouth-to-mouth resuscitation while she tried at the same time to talk, to holler for help, to whisper to Caryn whose blue eyes had gone milky and her body limp.

14

Remembering Wednesday

Rusty Meadows did not park her car, just turned off the motor and left it in the street when the traffic bottled up and she could not get through. Drivers trapped behind her cursed as she got out of the car and started running toward the Women's Uptown Clinic. She kept her cell phone pressed to her ear, and she was still talking, crying out to Diane and Amy as she ran. Once in the vicinity of Women's Uptown, she had to push through the minicams and the TV vans, men with cameras, coiffured on-the-spot reporters, a flock of women and small children rescued from the waiting room, and spaced-out onlookers. Some of these leaned over shopping carts holding all their worldly goods, some clutched bottles in brown paper bags, shaking their heads and saying to each other, "No shit? No shit?"

At last Rusty broke through all that and up against a yellow police cordon and a uniformed officer blocking her way. "No one is allowed in there."

"My daughters!" Rusty waved the cell phone in front of his face, and from it there wheezed out the terrible, *Mom! Mom!* "You hear them? My daughters are inside! I have to go to them."

"They'll be bringing everyone out as soon as they can," the policeman cautioned Rusty.

"No, my daughters! I have to get to my children! They're in the Lamaze class!"

A female paramedic nearby stepped up to her. "You know your daughters are safe? Not hit?"

"Yes. Yes I know that. Here. Listen to their voices. They're all right." *Mom! Mom!*

"If I let you through, will you help me bring them out calmly? Calmly," she reiterated.

And so Rusty Meadows followed the paramedic into the Women's Uptown Clinic. The waiting room was empty. No one in there had been injured, none of the children. But chairs were overturned and tables too, lamps, everything. She put the phone in her pocket. She carried no bag. When Diane's call came to the symphony office, she took only the phone and her keys. Rusty turned to the paramedic, "There was a doctor here, Caryn Henley, and a nurse, Nell Faraday, good friends of mine, are they—"

"I don't have names for you. Don't ask me for anything. Just help me move these women out in an orderly fashion. The Lamaze class is in the third door on your left. Take your daughters out to the ambulances in the street. I'm going to let you go down the hall and get your daughters and bring them out. That's all. Touch nothing."

Rusty went through the waiting room door into the still-smoky hall; the walls were streaked with blood where the wounded and the dead had slid down them. "My God," she whispered. "My God." Paramedics jostled for position among the people who still lay there, jaws slack, eyes wide.

"Diane!" Rusty called out. "Amy!"

"Mom!"

Crowded into a small examining room, Rusty found Amy and Diane and some of the other Lamaze students, including a woman whose water had broken and who was having contractions. The instructor was trying to soothe her. The others were all crying, clinging to one another. Amy was sobbing into her hands, and Diane was holding her. For a moment Rusty thought Amy had suddenly aged overnight; her hair had gone white. Only when she took Amy in her arms did she realize it was some sort of white powder that had fallen all over her. She put her other arm around Diane and drew both to her, grateful to have them warm, crying, speaking, and uninjured. Screams sounded from down the hall.

"She could have killed Amy," said Diane, the words forming slowly and with spittle at the corners of her mouth.

"She could have!" Amy cried. "She was going to, Mom!"

"But she shot overhead," said Diane. "She had the gun to Amy's face, but—" Diane could not go on for sobbing.

Rusty enveloped them both in her embrace. She soothed them and tried to quiet them, and when that didn't work, she said abruptly, "You and Diane, you're not injured anywhere? Are you? Anywhere at all?" They were fine. She kissed their foreheads, tasting on her lips the white powdery grit that had fallen over Amy. "All right, then, let's be useful. Let's be of some use to others."

"I don't care about the others!" Amy wailed.

"Yes you do," said Rusty. "You are not a child. You must help me."

Rusty took the elbow of the woman whose water had broken and told Diane to hold her other arm, and for Amy to follow behind them and to hush her screaming. The Lamaze instructor moved over to calm the other two women while Rusty and Amy and Diane escorted the woman in labor down the bloodied hall. She was breathing hard, writhing and crying out, but they got her to the main door where they had to stand aside for men bringing in a collapsible gurney.

"Take her on out," said Rusty to her daughters. "I have to find Nell and Caryn."

"Who are Nell and Caryn?" asked Diane.

"Friends," said Rusty, "friends from the Memoir Club."

"The what?"

And then Rusty remembered she'd never told Diane and Amy that she was taking a memoir class. And then she thought, this is Wednesday night.

With foreboding in her heart, Rusty moved against the tide of people streaming out the Women's Uptown Clinic into the blinding light of the treeless street, the roiling lights of police and ambulances, and the sounds of emergency all around her: feet running, wheels turning, orders shouted. On a rattling gurney, paramedics brought out a bearded man, bleeding badly, two cops on either side. Rusty walked past three cops encircling a single figure, a girl, handcuffed, raised roughly to her feet, her hospital gown

flapping open and her backside defenseless. The cops were arguing about getting her dressed, but no one knew where her clothes
were.

"I know this murdering bitch," Esther said to the cops. "She was
Caryn Henley's patient, and they had her in number eight. End of
the hall. You goddamned murdering bitch."

Darcy Reeves had lost all volition. She did not fight or protest,
not when she was shown outside, barefoot, her arms bound behind
her, with a cop clutching the back of the frail hospital gown, all
that stood between Darcy Reeves and the world.

Rusty walked down to the end of the hall. There, outside the
door of Number 8, was a gurney. Inside the sweltering room two
or three uniformed paramedics knelt on the floor beside Nell, who
clasped Caryn to her breast, crying, rocking, begging her, "Don't
leave me. Don't leave me, Caryn."

"Let us have her," said the paramedic, a woman whose blouse
was already stained with blood.

Nell still held, encircled Caryn's body with both arms, cradling
her head. Caryn's lips were moving, whispering. "Oh, God, baby,"
Nell pleaded, "don't talk. Don't. Just wait. Help will be here. Help
will."

"Help is here," said the paramedic. "Move away, please."

Nell looked up, but she did not move.

A young man knelt beside them; he took Caryn's pulse. He
spoke calmly to Nell. "Let her go. Please."

Caryn's lips moved again and Nell bent to hear. "She's cold. Get
me a blanket," Nell demanded. "I've got you, Caryn. I'm warm.
You can have my warmth. Shh. Don't talk. I'm here. I won't let
anything happen to you, ever."

Caryn's mouth relaxed into a half smile.

"Dr. Henley," said the young man, "we're going to lift you now.
We're going to take you to the hospital."

With the last of her physical strength, Caryn touched Nell's
cheek, felt over her face. Her voice was ragged and blood dribbled
from the side of her mouth.

"Oh, God, don't leave me. Don't leave me here, Caryn. Don't
go with them. Stay with me."

"You need to let her go," said the paramedic more harshly. "If
you want to save her life."

Nell clung to Caryn and spoke low insubstantial words of love and encouragement. She put her lips against Caryn's and blew fiercely. "Breathe! Breathe!"

The young paramedic told Nell to give up and let go.

"Don't tell her to give up," said Rusty, standing in the doorway. "She'll never give up."

"What's her name?"

"Nell. Let me try."

The paramedics made room for her, and Rusty knelt, focusing all time in this particular prism. She put her arms around Nell's shoulders. "Nell, it's me, Rusty. It will be all right. They need to take care of Caryn. Your job is done right now. You did your job. Let them."

Nell lifted her face. "Rusty?"

"We need to go to the hospital. Caryn too. They're going to wheel Caryn out, but you can walk, can't you? Big Nell." At that, Nell's hold on Caryn loosened and the paramedics were able to lift her to the gurney. "Can you walk, Nell?"

"She can't leave me," said Nell.

"We'll all go together. To the hospital. She won't leave you. Caryn's going on ahead," Rusty said just before Nell lost consciousness and pitched into a painless place of darkness. Nighttime on the old sea of grief.

Writing Your Memoir

PENNY TAYLOR, INSTRUCTOR

Things to remember

The memoir is not and should never be confused
with the truth.
The very act of writing creates a literary construct:
alteration is inevitable.
As a result, truth belongs to the teller.
Truth is relative to the teller.

PART III
Relatives of the Truth

15

Ultra Amy

I'm an immature slut, okay? Insincere, shallow, false, throw in stupid. Fine. Am I alone in this? Am I the only twenty-one-year-old who's made a mistake? Okay, a big mistake. Sorry. So, shoot me.

She tried. That crazy girl at the clinic, she tried. The gun was right in my face. My face and my brains and my life were about to be sprayed all over the hall, the wall, the universe. I, Amy Rebecca Meadows, would be dead. Finished. Kaput. That's what I thought, when I thought at all, which I didn't. I peed myself with fear. She shot at the ceiling, and then her hands went up and she dropped the gun. Someone wrestled her to the floor. Down the hall more shots rang out. There was screaming, shouts, and oaths. The cop started shooting too. I thought, I'm dead, the cop is going to miss this crazy girl and shoot me and I'm dead.

All of us Lamaze types, we hug the walls, or try to. I'm shaking and sweating and peeing, while my sister Diane is clutching my arm and screaming at me that it's all my fault. Amy, they're going to kills us all because you flipped off those Family Champions with their video camera! You called him a weenie!

Call Mom, I tell Diane. Will you just do something useful, Diane, and call Mom and shut the fuck up?

Someone hustles all our Lamaze class into a tiny examination room, like a herd of little hippos. Diane gets out the cell phone even though she's still crying, whimpering, accusing me. She calls

Mom at work, begging Mom to come get us. But all I could think of when I thought at all, which I didn't, was that I could be dead right now, me, Amy Rebecca Meadows. And my unborn child. Him too.

Mom shows up at last, and she helps everyone to restore calm and to get out of the building and into the ambulance. But does Mom come with us? No, my mom says she has friends here at the clinic. She has to see about her friends. I want to scream at Mom, what about me, Amy Rebecca Meadows? I'm your daughter! She was going to kill me! Not your friends! But the woman standing next to me is going into for-real labor, her face all twisted with surprise and pain. They put her and me into the next available ambulance and close the door. They're slapping monitors all over her, an oxygen mask too. They tell her to breathe. The blood pressure cuff on my arm is about to explode. They tell me to breathe.

At the ER, they wheel me into this cubicle with a young nurse who has a voice like a melted Heath bar. She feels all over my belly and takes my blood pressure and pulse and makes soothing conversation, asking me if it's a boy or a girl and what I'm going to name it. I say I don't know. I start to cry. I tell her I could have died.

The nurse says gently, smiling like Mr. Rogers, even if you had died, Amy, your baby could have lived. If they'd got to you soon enough, we could have saved your baby no matter what.

I said, you mean if they got to my dead body soon enough?

We could have done a C-section and saved your child.

And you know what? I thought that was damned unfair, that I should die, and Chuck's kid should live. And you know what else? I didn't care that they could save the baby. I know that makes me a hard-hearted whore, but I didn't give a shit. When that crazed girl had her gun in my face, when I'm looking down the long silver barrel of eternity, and I know I'm going to die, was my last thought for the kid? No. Take out a bedpan and beat me, but it wasn't. It was for me, myself, and I, Amy Meadows. I did not know then that the wacko Darcy Reeves had killed Dr. Henley and injured the nurse. I did not know my mother knew Dr. Henley or the nurse. I didn't know anything except I was going to die and I wanted to live. I did not want Amy Rebecca Meadows to die, even if she is a selfish, immature brat, a stupid slut who made a big mistake. It isn't like they say, your whole life flashes in front of you. Not for me. It was what I *haven't* done, all the living I would lose and never know, that flashed in front of me.

Don't kill me! I just kept screaming at the Reeves girl.

Now her face is all over the evening news, the TV, the radio, the Portland papers, *USA Today,* the *New York Times,* and the *National Enquirer.* Everyone in America is looking at Darcy Reeves, twenty years old, eleven weeks preggers, following the instructions of her wonko Embryo Protection League president boyfriend, Daniel Phillips. Daniel Phillips convinced Darcy and her parents that she'd been Chosen to bear his Chosen child and to stop the slaughter of the innocents by signing herself up for an abortion at the Women's Uptown Clinic, and bringing a loaded gun in her purse, and murdering the doctor and anyone else she could off.

So thanks to Daniel Phillips, our Lamaze class, expecting nothing more than another lesson in how to push, waddles toward the classroom, and we hear these shots. We don't know that Darcy Reeves has already shot the doctor and the nurse in the examining room. Then Darcy Reeves, her hair wild, her face white, still wearing her flimsy gown tied in the back, walks out into the hall and fires again. Someone screams and we all turn and look at a woman who slumps to the floor, leaving a long trail of blood on the wall. The hall fills with smoke and screams. Darcy Reeves comes up to me, personally, Amy Meadows, and puts the gun up my nose. Darcy Reeves stands so close to me I could have kissed her. But all I could do was shriek and tell her I didn't want to die. But while I'm shrieking, I look at her and I can see it's like she's not even mad. Or angry or anything. A little confused, maybe. She gives me this look, sort of, well, like she's got something real important to tell me, like she knows something important is happening, but she's just not sure what it is.

Then she shoots overhead, drops the gun, and gets tackled by the receptionist. Officer Hodges shot and killed Darcy's wonko boyfriend, Daniel Phillips, after he busted in the clinic back door, shot a nurse, and gave an old bag lady a heart attack.

By the next day, police had arrested all the rest of the Family Champions who had parked a pickup truck across from Women's Uptown and were taking video pictures of everyone who came in or out and putting their faces all over the Internet. Police arrested

the whole Embryo Protection League and anyone who belonged
to Daniel Phillips's personal church, the Seekers, too. They arrested Darcy Reeves's awful old parents, who stared into the TV
cameras like two people whose quarter got eaten by the pay phone
and they can't get it back. Everyone in America is talking about
the Women's Uptown bloodbath and the plan to assassinate everyone there. Columbine for clinics. The whole city, the whole country, really, is in a right to life furor. Weirdos, nationwide, are
crawling out of the woodwork. Armed police are stationed at all
the clinics and hospitals that perform abortions. TV cameras like
vultures in the streets in front of these places. Here in Portland,
we have all these newspeople and TV types interviewing us, Diane
and me, everyone who was there that awful day, asking how we felt.
Asking if we think the Reeves girl is insane or evil. Or both? Is that
a no-brainer? What? I want to ask them back, have you got turds
for brains? How would you feel?

I felt all kinds of awful emotions that night. But the worst wasn't
even at the Women's Uptown, Darcy with the gun up my nose. The
worst was after the ER people were finally through with me, poking,
prodding, telling me how brave I am, how baby and I are fine, and
I can get dressed and I can go home. I tell them I have to pee. I
go into the bathroom, all shiny steel and fluorescent light. I look
in the bathroom mirror. Whoa! Who is that old white-haired hag?

Why, it's Amy Meadows!

No. Impossible.

Yes! One day Amy Meadows will have white hair and her eyes
are going to be big craters in her skull and her jaw will be hanging
slack, and she'll drool and her skin will be the color of ash or
oatmeal or both. That's who I saw in the mirror. Hello Amy Meadows in 2050? 2060? Hello Amy? Good-bye life? Because even
though that shit-for-brains crazy slut did not shoot me, I knew,
staring at that mirror, that even though this was just powder from
the ceiling tiles all over my hair, I knew one day I would die. I
never thought I would die.

I'm only twenty-one. I'm supposed to be having fun. Not being
gunned down. I'm supposed to be having the time of my life, not
this damned baby. Not loving, caring for a helpless babe, moved
to maternal sacrifice and heroism. Thanks but no thanks. It's not
me. Sorry.

That night, the hospital releases us, and Diane and I go out to find Mom in the ER waiting room. Mom is sitting there with an old lady who has pink and purple streaks in her hair. They are holding hands and fighting tears. Mom says this woman is Sarah Jane Perkins. Like I care. Mom says she can't take us home. She says she's staying at the hospital, waiting till there's word of Caryn and Nell.

Nell? Who's Nell? I never heard of Nell. How can that be, Mom? That this person Nell is more important than your own daughters? Excuse me, Mom. I know it's shocking and all, but who is Nell, and how did you know Dr. Henley? I didn't think you went to Women's Uptown. I mean, you have health insurance.

Oh, God, Amy! Mom chokes out. I can't explain everything to you now. Call Chuck or your dad to come get you.

I tell Diane to call Dad. I don't want to lay eyes on Chuck.

Diane and I finally get back home, and right away the phone rings. Diane gets it. Chuck tells Diane he's mad with worry. He wants to be with me. I tell Diane I can't talk to him or anyone else. I tell Diane, tell him come over tomorrow. Not tonight. I have to get out of the clothes I have peed in, but I don't say that.

Next day Chuck comes rushing over, just full of . . . full of . . . all I could think of was jam. Like I was a piece of toast, he was slathering jam all over me and petting it on, thick and luscious, and once he'd got it all over me, he would take a big bite and eat me up.

Chuck was upset. Chuck was sorry. Chuck was jumping up and down with sorry and worry and questions. Like why didn't I call him right away? On the cell phone. Right after it happened. Why didn't I let him come rescue and protect me? Why didn't I take him to Lamaze class with me? How could I have put myself and our baby in all that danger and not call him immediately?

I wanted to say, Chuck, put a sock in it. But I couldn't. Why couldn't I tell him to shut the fuck up? I don't know why. But I just sat there like a piece of toast and agreed with everything he said, all his love and concern and caring. I acknowledged his suffering. Poor Chuck has suffered too. My suffering is his. My pain is his. My child is his. The baby kicks across my abdomen. Chuck puts his hand over it and gazes into my eyes.

But I'm looking at someone else, Ultra Amy, let's call her. Ultra

Amy has somehow squirmed out of my body, though not through any physical passages, I can tell you that. I'm all too well acquainted with those nowadays. Ultra Amy is sitting across the room from me in the La-Z-Boy, lounging there, one ankle resting on her knee. Ultra Amy is thin. She's wearing low-slung pants and a T-shirt that lets you see her tanned tummy. She has spiky-heeled sandals and streaked hair and frosty lip gloss, and makeup that makes her cheekbones sparkle. She is nibbling her French manicure and shaking her head. Ultra Amy is one good-looking babe, while I— Ultra Amy informs me—am stupid and fat, a great bag of retained water, and soon to be a mother to this guy's brat son who will grow up and be just like his asshole father.

What the fuck are you doing? Ultra Amy asks me. Look at this guy. She says, this is the man you're going to marry? This is the till-death-us-do-part love of your life? Look at him, Amy. He's already got a bald spot. He's not even twenty-two, and his hair is thinning.

From my vantage point, I cannot see the bald spot, because Chuck's head is on my shoulder and I'm patting his back and comforting him.

And never mind his looks! says Ultra Amy. I mean he's kind of cute in a muscle-bound Pillsbury Doughboy sort of way, I guess, but is this what you want to be carrying through life? You nearly died in that shootout! You're the one who faced down the killer! You're the one who was in danger! You're the one who was brave and saved your own life and the lives of all the other Lamaze students. You ought to be leaning on the arm of someone strong and handsome, like Mel Gibson.

Mel's too old.

Okay, okay, someone younger, but you know what I mean.

Yes, I certainly did.

You're a piece of toast hugging a jar of jam, says Ultra Amy. You're pathetic. And you'll do this the rest of your life. Till you look like that woman in the hospital bathroom mirror. You'll have white hair. You'll look like shit. You'll feel worse. What's wrong with you, Amy? You almost died, didn't that make you think at all?

Ultra Amy nibbles some more on her French manicure, and I realize I haven't had one since I got preggers.

Well, it was all too much for me. I peeled Chuck off of me. He was still pretty broken up. I said he should go get a Coke or something from the fridge.

Do you want one, Amy? he asked.

I, personally, Chuck? I want a great big snort of straight vodka. A hit on the bong. A little stab of Ecstasy. But I just shook my head.

When Chuck came back out with his Diet Coke, I gave it to him straight. I said, Chuck, I'm not a piece of toast.

Okay, so I didn't give it to him straight, but I let him know I was sick of feeling what everyone thought I should feel. I was up to here with smiling and being the good little mommy in the cute little smock and being all preggers and excited for Baby. I told him how I knew that demented Reeves chick in the Women's Uptown was going to kill me, and I would never have lived, and it was no comfort to me that this child would live, even if I died. I told Chuck I didn't love him. I didn't want to marry him. I would never marry him, and I did not want his baby.

Well, I had to wait while he crashed his way, protesting, carrying on through all of that. But I didn't let him come near me. Oh, no. You gotta stay in the La-Z-Boy, I told him, no putting your arms around me, no blubbering, no calling on my finer instincts, which I don't even think I have anymore. Ever since the shooting, I've been hurting everyone's feelings, right and left, pissing everyone off, Mom, Diane, Dad, my friends. No one understands I just want to be myself. Is that so much to ask? I just want to be Amy, not Chuck's wife and mother of his son. No, and not Chuck's partner and mother of his son. I don't want to be anything to anyone except my old sweet self.

It's not true love I'm missing. It's not a career I'm missing. I don't want to be the CEO of anything. All I want's a job to pay the rent on my own apartment, a few classes at the community college with my friends. A little skiing in winter. Summers, I want to go to rock concerts at the Gorge, windsurfing on Hood River. I want to have a few beers, a few moves on the dance floor, and some guy to tell me I'm pretty and how he can't wait to get me into bed. Brunch the next morning and then it's over. Hey, I just want a few laughs and some fun. Of course, I want the guy to be nice and have a good sense of humor. That's all I really want right now. Is that so much?

So when Chuck was all done thrashing through *what do you mean,*

Amy!, clueless as a hamster on a wheel, I told him, Chuck, I'm going to the social worker tomorrow and I'm going to ask for papers to give the kid up for adoption, and I want you to sign them. We'll agree on this, right?

You don't know what you're saying, Amy! You're preggers and pregnant women don't know what they're doing.

I know, Chuck.

I love you.

Sayonara, Chuck.

You'll regret this.

No, Chuck, I said, never. Wrap your gray cells around this thought: never.

I knew I'd win, but it wasn't as easy as I'd thought. Took a long time. All afternoon.

And of course I had to take shit from Chuck's parents. They came over that evening. Oh, God, you'd think I'd left the baby in the crosswalk with the light about to change. I told them they could adopt the baby if they wanted. Hell, let Chuck take it into the navy and teach it to salute. I don't care. Get it?

Chuck and his family, they were a piece of cake compared to what I got from Diane. My own sister accused me of cruelty and crass immaturity and not living up to what people expected, of running away from life and acting like a big baby myself.

Like I hadn't already suffered enough. Eight and a half months! That's a long time. I said to Diane, I have already suffered eight months with this baby and that's enough. I'm not doing eighteen years with him. Eighteen years, Diane! Think about it: that's my whole up-till-now lifetime, just about. And then I said, Diane, if you're so hot on maturity and responsibility, how about I give the kid up to you, and you keep it. In the family, so to speak.

And that was the end of that. But she heaped more abuse on me for even thinking of giving away my child. It was my child and my responsibility.

The only one who understood, who supported my decision, was my dad. Dad said he and his wife Linda agreed with me. Personally I could give a toasted turd what Linda thinks, but Dad kind of undid me. Dad said, *Amy you're too young and irresponsible for this. You have no idea what it means to bring a child up. What it costs. In every way.*

Then I wondered, for the first time ever, what did we kids cost him and Mom? I didn't ask. I didn't want to know.

And then there was Mom.

Nothing, nothing prepared me for Mom, except maybe Darcy Reeves with the gun up my nose, because Mom went ballistic. Mom went Godzilla on me. Mom thrashed and screamed at me, yelled, *I told you this a long time ago, didn't I? What is wrong with you, Amy, that you can't listen or learn or think about anyone but yourself? How can you be so fucking stupid?*

Yes, she really said that. My mother said "fucking stupid" for the first time in her life, and it was to me, her pregnant daughter. I took offense. Yes I did. I said, you're not supposed to say that to me. You're supposed to be supportive. I don't need your permission for this, you know.

Ultra Amy, I could feel her smiling at this, and so I repeated it more emphatically, I'm not asking your permission.

Well, Mom turns Mount St. Helens Meadows. And she rages and erupts and spews all over me, wanders all over the house crashing into things, knocking them over, swearing and screaming at me and at someone named Melissa. Finally Mom just goes in her room and slams the door, and I can hear her in there, lying on the bed, sobbing. Worse than she did during the divorce. Worse than when Diane was so sick they thought she would die. I don't know what to say, but I'm not heartless, so I take her in a glass of water and put it by the bed and say, Mom, I'm sorry I upset you.

Mom rolls over. Her eyes are vats of pain.

Mom, I shouldn't even have brought this up now because I know you've been under a lot of stress about your friends, about Dr. Henley, and your friend, the nurse whose hand is all shot up. I didn't know they were your friends. I never heard of the Wednesday night Memoir Club. Okay, Mom, I never thought to ask where you went on Wednesday nights. Is that what this is about, Mom? That I never asked why you weren't home on Wednesday nights? That I didn't ask about your friends? I know you're really upset about them. I know it's especially hard for you since there was no funeral service for Dr. Henley, and you didn't get to say good-bye, and I guess I haven't been very supportive like I should be, and I'm sorry.

Mom sits up, mops her face with her arm, swills the water, and stares at me. Like Darcy Reeves stared at me before she shot the ceiling tiles. I know I've missed something important here, but I go on: Mom, I'm sorry I brought this up while you have all this other stress, but I did.

I expect Mom will put her hand on my arm and weep a little about her friends, and we'll agree all this is really really sad, but no. Mom's features are doing a little tango around her nose, like she really can't believe what she's hearing, but I have to go on now, don't I? I say, Mom, I'm really sorry I didn't take your advice months ago, about the abortion, I mean, but I didn't. How could I know how things would turn out? This is for the best, Mom. It's best for the baby and for Chuck and for me. I don't think we'd be good parents. The baby will be better off with someone who wants it.

Who wants *him*, says Mom. It's a boy. Your son.

And right then that baby kicks me, oh, he kicks me and it made me mad. If I could get mad at a fetus, imagine what I'd do to a kid. It's best to give the kid up for adoption.

Amy, says Mom, you are dooming yourself. For the rest of your life, you will feel this loss as an unfillable void. You've gone too far now. You have to go through with it. If you let this child go, all your life you'll look for this boy. This man. He will be the great emptiness in your life, no matter what else you fill it with.

No, I won't, Mom. Chuck feels bad, but not me. This is the right thing to do.

Chuck is a moron, Amy. The dumbest thing you've ever done, and I do mean ever, way beyond shoplifting at Nordstrom, was to get knocked up by a guy who is—she flung her arms around, hoping to catch the word in left field—that thin.

Chuck's not thin.

His brains are like gruel. He's a good-looking oaf, and you fell for it. He's dumb as a chicken. He's—

Mom! Stop! You're being a little harsh on Chuck. And on me. After all, I love him. I loved him.

Before God, it's true, she said bitterly. I'm glad you're not marrying him.

Well, I won't be keeping his baby either, I say, putting a hopeful spin on it. There'll be no more Chuck.

But if you give up your child, your life will never be the same.

Sorry, Mom. Like with that little shoplifting incident, what could I say but sorry and return the goods. I wish to hell I could return the goods this time.

You don't know the meaning of sorry, girl. You'll never forget this boy's birthday. You'll remember it better than you remember your own. Every year, you'll suffer on that day. You'll look at every male child and wonder if he's yours. You'll never quit asking yourself, who is raising my son, and are they good to him? How are you going to feel in thirty-some years when some man comes up to you and tells you you're his mother? You gave him away. You abandoned him!

Mom, I can't answer that. How do I know how I'll feel? That's too far away. I might not live that long, I add optimistically.

Oh, Amy, if you lived past Darcy Reeves, you've got a long old road in front of you, and it is going to Regret, as in a place, Regret, Oregon. That's where you'll live.

I won't either.

Sit down, Amy. I have something to tell you.

Then she tells me this long, gruesome story. About Melissa. Really, right out of *Days of Our Lives*. I had a sister named Melissa. Born out of wedlock when Mom was still in high school. And how she loved Melissa and they took her away from my Mom and gave her away. Mom could hear the baby crying and crying, even though the baby was long gone and far away with strangers. The crying drove Mom insane. My mom in a mental hospital? Mom's family thought she was a whore and going to hell. Mom had to run away from home and never saw her family again. When she told my dad about Melissa thirty-some years after it happened, he couldn't hack it, and that was the last straw for their already rocky marriage. Oh, God, it was a saga. Really, all these emotions running amok in my mom? And for all these years? It didn't seem right to me that something that long ago should still matter so much, but here's Mom spewing her guts and breaking her heart and crying her eyes out.

And now, she says, here, just a few months ago, she had met this Melissa, the beloved child she had loved and missed and cared for, and it wasn't Melissa at all. It was someone named Suzanne. Mom was a wreck in the telling, crying and then falling apart and scraping herself together and going on. Took me twenty minutes to figure out Suzanne *was* Melissa. All this pent-up sorrow comes flooding out, but I am the one there drowning in it and trying to be a nice person, thinking, I don't want to know this. I'm a little curious, I guess, about this Melissa or Suzanne or whoever. But all this anguish for something that long ago?

Finally, for the fifth time she shakes me by my shoulders and says don't I see how and why I cannot do this? How terrible it will be for me? How I will suffer for it in the future?

I try again to say it won't be like that for me. It will be different. But this just sets her off all over again.

Finally, I take her hands in mine and I say, I'm sorry for everything you've suffered. I'm sorry Suzanne was not Melissa, and I'm sorry you lost Dad and your own family and all that. Really, I mean it. I am sorry. But I'm not you. You're the one always telling me I'm too irresponsible and too flighty and all that. You ought to be glad I see that at last. You were right, Mom.

I thought for sure that would bring her around. All moms like to be told they're right.

All right, Amy, she says, nodding, her head bobbing up and down rhythmically like she's talking to Ultra Amy too, or at least someone invisible to the rest of the world. She says yes, and I will be right in thirty years too.

She gets up off the bed and goes into the bathroom. I can hear the water running in the tub. The phone rings and I pick up. It's a guy named Eddie Arias, and he wants to talk to Mom. Who? Eddie Arias. Well, I tell him this is not a good time, no not right now, and I take his long-distance number and I tell him she'll call him back. Sometime. Not right away. That's for sure. And it's then I feel it, not just a kick and a thud from the baby, but more. Lower. A great dull roll of pain that takes my breath away. I forget everything I learned in Lamaze. I hold my breath and wait for the next one.

16

The Sea of Grief

SARAH JANE'S HOUSE IS STRANGE AND WHIMSICAL. Everywhere you look there's something that isn't quite as it should be. Something to make you think about the ordinary in an extraordinary way. I do not want to think at all. Give drugs. Kill pain. That's all I want. I came here to stay with Sarah Jane after the hospital released me. My friends moved me here like a piece of furniture, like an old wooden bureau, barged up, heavy, and full of secret cupboards. And, like a piece of furniture, I didn't protest. Give drugs. Kill pain. Put me wherever you want. Sarah Jane wanted me here. Said she could look after me till I could look after myself. They must have thought I'd protest. I didn't. Let me feel no more than furniture feels. Put me out of sight. This back bedroom, upstairs in Sarah Jane's modest clapboard in an old neighborhood near Reed.

But to wake daily in this room, to emerge slowly from the drugs and pain, is to come to life in the funhouse. Like Oz. When I first get out of bed, I notice the door handles. They're all on the wrong side of the doors. Sarah Jane says that's the point, the ordinary things you do by rote, you should think about them. You should make yourself aware. Not just me. Everyone. To relearn and replace and rethink. My left hand is shattered, and I am left-handed, so I have to rethink everything, consciously, in a way that is itself painful and time-consuming and irritating. I do not want to think. I want only to float on the sea of grief for Caryn Henley, my friend of twenty-some years, my colleague, my companion whose well-being was my reason for being.

In bits and pieces—not while it was all happening, because I was in a fug of pain and painkillers and understood nothing—but now, slowly, I've heard how things happened in the days after Caryn's death. The Henleys came from Michigan. I did not see them. They did not ask to see me. They dealt with police and lawyers. They had a lawyer read terse statements for the media, which daily offered more newspapers stories, television coverage, all of which raised again the spectre of the long-ago plane crash, and Caryn's devastating losses. Dr. Caryn Henley, stalked by tragedy.

Caryn's family went through her house, hired a company to move some things and sell everything else, even the swing set. They put the house in the hands of a realtor for sale. They asked for no help from Caryn's friends and did not accept what was offered. They had no interest in her friends or her life at Women's Uptown. Caryn belonged to them. In death the family simply claimed her. After all the official inquiries were past, Caryn's body was cremated, and the Henleys announced there would be no service.

The authorities were grateful, though doubtless the media was disappointed. The police and Portland hospitals didn't want any more antiabortion Seekers crawling out of the woodwork with their guns and thirst for martyrdom. The prochoice forces were massing for a giant memorial rally, as if Caryn were a cause, a disembodied cause, a symbol, not a woman at all, not the tragic alignment of her time and place and profession and her caring for this girl who killed her. For once, I'm on the Henleys' side, grateful that such an orgy of politics and public farewell will not, did not take place. The Henleys took Caryn's ashes back to Michigan. Fine by me. I don't want her ashes. I want Caryn. I want the pain of losing her to cease. And then I don't. The pain of losing her is all I have left.

But I have to pee, don't I, so I get out of bed and reach for the bedroom doorknob and find the handle's on the wrong side. They're all on the wrong side of the door, all over the house. Everything here is an irritating surprise. The bathtub knobs have ceramic faces. One has a rubber face over the knob and it's shocking to touch the faucet and have it go soft on you. The toilet in the downstairs bathroom responds to weight on the seat and sings a little electronic version of "We've Only Just Begun." Enough to scare the shit out of you. I found it damned annoying. It got in the way of my grief. I was cross and irritable like Caryn used to be. Now I know why the guy in snow sometimes kicks the St. Bernard, why he wishes to be left, frozen and immobile.

Sarah Jane is no St. Bernard. No pouncing like I used to do with Caryn. Yoga! Therapy! Travel! Memoir class, for that matter. Sarah Jane Perkins is a marvel of indirection. Oblique. Like the ideas in her little classic book, *The Laughing Cat*, which I'm only just reading as I come off painkillers, when I can read at all. She is constantly putting tasks in my hands, both hands, taxing me at every turn. She gives me potatoes and a peeler, and I nearly weep because I cannot do it. Me. Big Nell. Women's soccer MVP at Notre Dame, and I cannot peel a damned potato.

But she is protective of me, turns away the press. Sarah Jane stays cheerful, never abrasive or aggressive. Even when she's at her most adamant, she phrases her responses like questions, variations on, really, even if Nell knew why Darcy Reeves and Daniel Phillips went on their murderous rampage, why should she sacrifice her strength to sell newspapers?

I don't even have the strength to deal with my friends. Another good reason to stay here with Sarah Jane. If I went home, they would be all over me. I'd have frozen hamburger casseroles filling up the freezer and flowers enough to choke on and houseplants all dying from thirst. I'd have cards and condolences and offers to help whenever I need it, from everyone, including Mike, my ex-boyfriend, who came to see me in the hospital. Esther, Chantal, the Uptown Women, they'd take turns being there and being good to me, and every last one of them, however well-meaning, would pull my plug. I'd have to respond and I can't. They will have to wait. Everyone will have to wait except the Memoir Club. Six months ago I didn't know that Francine and Jill and Rusty and Sarah Jane and Ted Swanson existed, and now they are the Nell Faraday Bucket Brigade.

When I came out of surgery that first night, the first person I saw was Rusty Meadows. Some awful predawn hour, and Rusty and Sarah Jane had waited for me all night. But when Sarah Jane asked to see me, the hospital staff said family only. So Rusty said she was my sister. She was there when I came out of anesthesia and there the next day too. She stood between me and the telephone, thank

God. She answered the phone, fended off my family whom I could not bear to talk to. Not then. I could hear my sister, calling from Indiana, asking if I wanted her to come out to Portland and bring me home. Rusty gently told her that I was home, that I had people here, and I would call her when I could talk.

When my mother called, I shook my head. Rusty put the phone between our ears and we both listened as my parents, horrified that I could be on the evening news, asked how could I be involved in a gun battle? Rusty tried to explain, but it was no-go.

"Tell Nell," my mother instructed Rusty, "that I've always said that Uptown Clinic is not respectable. If it was respectable, you wouldn't have people shooting it up." I could hear my dad's phlegmatic voice: two dead, one born, how many injured? I turned away from the phone and let Rusty finish the conversation.

When the police came to the hospital to talk to me, I told them that after the first shots, I was on the floor with Caryn in my arms. I didn't see anything else.

When the Deputy DA came to see me, I said all I knew of Darcy Reeves is that she went on a murderous rampage at the behest of her sick bastard boyfriend who slunk out through death's door, and if they were going for the death penalty for Darcy, I'd testify for the defense. Darcy killed my best friend, that's true, but Caryn cared for her. Caryn knew she was troubled. Darcy Reeves is guilty of holding the gun, yes, but the man who put that gun in her hand and that baby in her belly—who begot a life in order to commit murder—the truly evil Daniel Phillips died that night. Hodges saved everyone else's life when she shot Daniel Phillips. He would have seen us all dead, but Darcy? Darcy's no killer. Amy Meadows told reporters Darcy fired into the ceiling and dropped her gun. Raised her arms. Darcy gave herself up, and I will argue for mercy for her. The DA thought I was being noble. But I'm not. Caryn would have done the same thing if I had died there instead of her.

For now, the time being, I stay with Sarah Jane at her odd house. There are no more Wednesday nights at Francine's, and no one's heard from Penny Taylor, but I wish I could write a new memoir now. About Caryn. About the past. And the future. My future is my past. I have already lived through terrible grief. With Caryn. But I did not expect to live through grief *for* Caryn. I cry for Scott and Elise and Caryn and even Andrew. Now they are all gone. They are all together, and I am alone. I understand how she could prefer drowning in the sea of grief to swimming to the unknown shore.

The windows of this second-story bedroom look out to a small back garden and a weedstrewn easement that separates Sarah Jane's from other small gardens and frame houses just like it. Except that Sarah Jane's backyard has flowers growing out of men's top hats and out of old working boots and battered saucepans and broken cups. A clematis vine weaves in and out of a rusting iron bedstead, climbs up through the wire springs and covers them. As if you could lie there in summer, and the vine would support your body. You could sleep in a sea of purple. There is a four-foot-high container of some sort with a big begonia sprouting out of the top and shelves that drip with ivy. You can't even tell what this is till you come right up to it and then you see that it's a doorless icebox. At the very back, by the gate, there is the body of an old pickup truck, from the twenties perhaps, covered in ivy and with a bed of daisies in the back and hollyhocks and foxglove where the engine used to be.

At Sarah Jane's, you have to look before you sit down or you'll sit on something that will squeal piteously, like you've lowered your bulk on a kitten. There are whoopee cushions all over, even in the kitchen. In the front hall there is a hatrack with all old hats, straw hats, golf caps, men's fedoras, women's little net numbers from the fifties, and big-brimmed big-bowed church lady hats, as if all these people await you just inside. And on her front porch there is a department store dummy, clad in a thirties housedress and a checked apron and a big hat, a basket over her arm for the mail. The doorbell is wired to her nose with an arrow that says RING THE BELL. You have to laugh. Everyone does. That's the point.

This house is Sarah Jane's classroom. She gives workshops and seminars here three or four times a year. She used to teach at Reed College, but she has no advanced degree, though she stayed on there a long time. And then maybe twenty years ago, they did not renew her contract. She was adjunct and had no means of protest or grievance, though now she says she's grateful. Otherwise her ideas would have been confined to Reed. Instead she's traveled and broadened her notions; she's written books, that first one, *The*

Laughing Cat. She gives seminars all over the country and she still works locally, too, with autistic children and in clinics with the mentally ill. She makes the rounds of the assisted living and convalescent homes where she works with stroke patients. She says when I am better, I can come too. Thanks but no thanks. Give me the funky old Women's Uptown any day, people trying to get by and live, not getting ready to die.

But Daniel Phillips killed off Women's Uptown as surely as he killed Caryn Henley.

Ted Swanson brought me this news. Sarah Jane put a potato and a peeler into his hands too. She says using your hands, being aware of what they can do, is essential, even if one of them is shattered. Especially if one is shattered. She says our experience is like color. Color is always relative to what's next to it and so is human experience, and that's why we are porous, and experience flows both ways. Personally, I've never talked like this in all my life, but I do now. It's contagious or something.

Ted and I sat around the wooden kitchen table, and every time we moved, the whoopee cushions under us gave out little fart noises. It was hard to hold this serious conversation there, and then I knew that's why Sarah Jane didn't invite us all to go outside and sit in the fleeting sunshine in the wicker chairs that had no whoopee cushions.

"They're closing Women's Uptown," said Ted, applying himself to his potato in a methodical fashion. "After what happened, they say that no patients will ever go there again."

"They probably mean it would cost too much to clean up the blood. The place needed a good cleaning, and it's easier to close it." I was bitter, though my days as an effective nurse are over. I can't even take a patient's blood pressure, much less write it on the chart.

"Well, they're moving the patients to other clinics in better neighborhoods."

I put down my potato. "Does it take a great mind to see that what happened at Women's Uptown had nothing to do with the neighborhood? It wasn't gangs or drug addicts or the homeless who did this. It was a middle-class white guy who worked in a computer store. This is the very neighborhood that needs a clinic, a place where women can go, where their health and welfare and safety are important. Our patients need us there, right there at the bus stop, right there not far from the freeway underpass. Right there where we were. All of us." I stared at the vegetable peeler in my right hand. Useless. Both hands. I bit my lip and fought tears. "I want my old life back. I want Caryn to come back, Caryn and the clinic and Wednesday nights at Francine's."

Ted took the vegetable peeler from me and put his hand over mine, and I thought how much he could have done for Caryn. I swallowed the great hairball of tears in my throat. I asked, "What about the staff? What about Esther? She's been there longer than anyone. What about Chantal and the women in the office? What will happen to them?"

"I don't know any more than what I told you, Nell. I didn't want you to hear it on the television."

"How did you hear it?"

"I'm a lawyer. I hear things."

"Like a priest."

"I can't give absolution." He squeezed my hand again and returned to his potato, peeling methodically.

"You knew what could happen, didn't you? You knew we were in danger. I thought the Family Champions were just bozos gone wonko with the possibilities of the Internet. I never, ever connected them with Darcy Reeves. Caryn told me that you wanted to stop them legally. If you had taken them to court, then Daniel Phillips's name would have come out, and we would have connected him to Darcy Reeves, and we could have prevented all of this. I can't imagine how I could have been so blind. I was always there to protect Caryn. I failed her, didn't I?"

"You never failed her." He put down his potato and rested his level blue eyes on me. "The more I knew Caryn, the more I admired you. I admired your loyalty and your tenacity. She was fortunate to have you. She knew it, even if she didn't say so. The kind of strength you have, that isn't given to everyone, and I admire that too."

"I should have made her listen to you."

"Don't fault yourself. I should have insisted more vehemently." Ted put down the peeler. "It's hard, Nell, to go on living after such a loss. No one knew that better than Caryn. But I don't think she'd want us, any of us, to wallow around in recrimination, in what we could have done."

"No," I agreed. "She wouldn't want us to, but that's what she did. I was always looking for the Grief Slayer."

"Caryn told me there was a picnic every year. The anniversary of the crash. She had asked me to go with her. With both of you," he added, seeing some surprise on my face. "She said you wouldn't mind."

"I wouldn't. It wasn't a competition."

"If you want to go, I'll go with you. We can still go together."

"I couldn't bear it."

"It might be good for you."

"How could it possibly be good for me? I always went to find out what had worked for other people. It was like a seminar or something."

"Aren't you still looking for that Grief Slayer?"

"Caryn is gone."

"You're not. I'm not. It's not a spectator sport, grieving."

"Those people have all had years and years to come to terms with their grief."

"You will too."

And that's when it struck me. I would live, but I would never be the same. The old life was gone, and what had I to put in its place? I saw how hard it would be for me to make a new life and how swift and easy would be an overdose of painkillers. Only, what if . . . what was it Caryn said? *If it's true and killing yourself is a sin, then I wouldn't ever get to be with Scott and Elise and Andrew. I couldn't bear that. I can bear this world only because I feel certain that somewhere I'll be with them again.* She believed that every day she did not die, she had endorsed life. Well, now I understood, didn't I? "Why would you want to go to this picnic?" I asked Ted. "The Families of the Victims are nothing to you."

"They're something to you. To Caryn. And I'm like you now, Nell. I'm looking for the Grief Slayer, as much for myself as for you."

I went to the picnic with him, but it was a huge mistake. Caryn's violent death had flattened everyone who was there. It was compounded grief compounded, and we had to leave after an hour or so. I cried all the way back to Sarah Jane's. We came back to Sarah Jane's exhausted, and she took one look at us and said we should go outside and lie down, and she'd bring us out something cold to drink. It wasn't even that hot.

"There's no place to lie down out there," I said.

"Sure there is. The bed."

"The bed with the clematis vine?"

Sarah Jane nodded.

"That's a damn silly idea," I said.

But Ted walked out, down the garden path, sat on the coiled springs with all that tender greenery twining in and around it, and lay back. Closed his eyes.

"Go on," said Sarah Jane.

So I walked out to the bed. The garden was awash in late afternoon shadows, though the sky was still light and the warmth hadn't yet dissipated. The air was full of neighborhood sounds, voices of unseen children, a barking dog. I looked at Ted. He lay there, stretched out, eyes closed. He was breathing regularly, but he was not asleep. He had left room for me beside him, so that my right hand would be beside him. I lay down. The leaves I crushed with the weight of my body gave up some tangy scent utterly new to me. We lay side by side, as if we were longtime lovers, so comfortable and easy with one another. I had liked Ted Swanson when he loved Caryn, and I wondered now, a fleeting, first-time question, if I could love him. If he could love me. I wondered if it could work the way of some old ungainly syllogism of the heart: I loved Caryn, and Ted loved Caryn, did that mean that Ted and I could love each other? Would not Caryn always come between us? Everything Ted had done for me since the shooting, had that been loyalty to Caryn? And what about my loyalty to Caryn? Me. Big Nell. Would loving Ted make me disloyal to Caryn? Did I love Ted? I don't know. Could I love him?

He took my right hand. We were lying hand in hand, on galvanized steel springs, bedding courtesy of just-budding clematis. I felt as though the little tendrils of the vine came up behind my ears and along my neck and shoulders and arms, as though they were caressing me. I felt the warmth of Ted's hand in mine. I relaxed.

I eased for the first time since I saw Darcy Reeves pull out her gun. Ted must have felt it. The pressure of his hand tightened and then released, and I knew this was a man I could love. We lay there like the twin prongs of a tuning fork till the sun dipped below the rooftops and chill came on and the woman in the next yard called for her children to come in to supper.

17

Perkins Finest

We were all in the boat, including the dog, even though he fell out and drowned. He jumped out of Georgieanna's arms and fell into the river. The current carried him away and pulled him under while we watched, Georgieanna screaming till Ma slapped her, and the rain sluicing down. We would have all gone down with the dog and Perkins Hotel, but for Mr. Jasper. A commercial man, he was, did a nice little business up and down the river, always wore a bowler and a vest and carried two big cases and a pack on his back. It might have been the Depression for everyone else, but thanks to Mr. Jasper and men like him, it was fine high times for us at Watson's Landing. Pa painted a sign, said PERKINS HOTEL, but it was always Watson's Landing. It was never ours.

Mr. Jasper said he'd only just got off the boat for a minute. It was tied up out there at the landing. The steamer was a small shallow-bottomed, flat-deck boat, mainly used to fetch men and supplies back and forth from logging camps and farms upriver and down to Mt. Vernon and other towns on the flats and finally on out to Puget Sound. The boat would not be back up here till the rain ended. The river was too high and hazardous.

Mr. Jasper suggested we take such cash as we had and come with him to safety. At least Pa should send the missus and the sprouts. Ma snorted at this. She said wasn't going to let a little rain chase her off her property and leave every last thing she owned, including the Cornish pipe organ, the velvet settee, and the fine rattan rockers with their cushions of green taffeta and pink silk tassels, unprotected from thieves and scavengers. Pa said he would stay here, protect our property and care for the animals, and we should go with Mr. Jasper. Ma said no. Said if Pa cared to abandon his wife, then fine, he should take the children and go with Mr. Jasper. She could always make things sound like that, fine and vile. In the same moment.

Mr. Jasper said to my father, Amos, you live on this river, but you are not of this river. I'm a river man, Amos, and I'm telling you, this is no ordinary rain. Upstream, the Skagit River is raging and gouging out new channels. With all the soil and weight in it, likely when it gets down here, if the rain keeps up, it'll change course, plow itself out a whole new bank, and there'll be hell to pay. It could happen anywhere along the river. It could happen here. A river's like a woman, Amos—he said this with a look over to my mother who was pushing taters and a slab of pork around in a fry pan—there's times you just want to stay out of her way, and then there's times you want to leave.

Pa never did believe in disaster, whereas Ma believed in nothing but. Thanks to Mr. Jasper, Pa got the boat ready, oars, buckets, stout lines and cleats, canvas for shelter. Maybe he wasn't a river man—like Mr. Jasper said, Pa was a logger till he lost his leg—but the day of the disaster, Pa watched the rain with special care. He saw trees floating by and then he saw some cows, bloated up, bobbing down the river in the rain, half a barn, and that's when he knew that Mr. Jasper was right and upstream the river had changed its course, had carved itself out a whole new channel, and we had best get to higher ground.

Everyone to the boat, said my father. Now. We're going to the island.

It's getting dark, Amos, said my mother.

It's darker in the grave. Now, everyone to the boat.

My brother Virgil begged Pa to let him take the Jumbo and drive downriver. The Jumbo was our truck, and Virgil loved that truck with all the love a thirteen-year-old boy has to offer two pair of wheels, a motor, and a chassis. Virgil loved that truck better than he loved the dog. He said he would drive the Jumbo to safety. Pa said he needed Virgil's strong arm in the boat, and the roads were probably all washed out anyway, since they were mostly mud tracks. Pa said he needed a man with two legs to help get us to safety. Virgil was boy with two legs, but Ma was every bit as strong as my father. Ma was broad and solid and held herself well and upright. She always wore a long-sleeved cotton housedress, a cardigan in winter, and a checked apron till it shredded. Then she found another checked apron. She had big blue eyes and a full mouth, fine skin, and might have been a good-looking woman, but she cared little for her own looks. She left good looks and any charm you might need to run a place like Perkins Hotel, she left all that to Pa who was bearded and quick, a lithe, lanky man, as befits a logger.

Take nothing, Sarah Jane, Pa called out to me. Just get in the boat! I grabbed *Heidi* and *Robinson Crusoe*, presents for my tenth birthday just past. Georgieanna got the dog and her doll. Ma took such cash as we had and the baby, though he wasn't really a baby by then, but four years old. We just called him the baby. She always carried him under one arm just like a little piglet.

Even as we hotfooted it to the boat, we could see that the river had already washed over our land. The poplars along our bank still stood, but the river had uprooted trees upstream. You could see them churning in the roiling brown water, crashing into one another. As we hastened into the boat, we could see that the farm and garden, potatoes mostly, had vanished under the big brown river and the sheds were awash too. The river had jumped its banks. It was coming after the cow. The cow was too stupid to protest, but the hogs were outraged. The chickens were squawking and flapping. Anything that couldn't climb a tree was eaten by the river, devoured by the rain. Pa and Virgil rowed, hard, as best they could, but the minute we untied from the landing, we knew the river was going to take us where it would take us. And just to prove it, the river took the dog.

Make for the island! cried Pa. Remember that, Virgil! Make for the island!

The roar was tremendous, but even over it, we heard the crack and the crumble of wood and we weren't too far downriver when our own sign, PERKINS HOTEL, floated past us.

Pa and Virgil kept fighting off what the river had chewed up, trees, sheds, carcasses, even an old Model T. We saw a corpse too. A woman. Her housedress ballooned up, her breasts keeping her afloat like buoys. Face gray-green and awful. We didn't know her. She was gone and we let her go. Pa kept shouting out, make for the island! Don't let it pass. Virgil, he cried out, make for the island! That river was like wrestling a huge brown snake, like something biblical rising up against Sodom and Gomorrah that would eat us alive. The November afternoon was short. If we lost the light, we couldn't see the trees and debris that were coming at us and the boat would bust up and we'd drown. The island wasn't but a mile downstream. It had high ground and lots of trees, and Pa knew it well. Pa had a neat little distillery set up there, high in the woods, far from the Internal Revenue men.

The island came in sight, but the river didn't want to go there. Ma put the baby in Georgieanna's arms and told her to hold him and not let him go or he'd end up like the dog. Virgil, Pa, Ma, they fought toward that island shore, knowing if we didn't get there, it was death for us on the river. I bailed water out of the boat while they paddled and pulled and struggled, but the island seemed to be going past us. For sure, the riverbank with the high pilings that Pa always used to tie up the boat, those were gone, drowned under. The river pulled us past all that, and still we were midchannel and not yet close to land. I prayed and bailed, and looked up at the island with every bucket I flung out of the boat. The tall trees at its summit were lost in clouds that hunkered over us, the rain still pounding. If we got swept past the island, we'd never get back to it, the current was too strong. Night was coming on. The river churned, and we would be smashed up by torn-up trees and barns and boards and things we couldn't see.

Keep at it! Pa shouted. The island! Anywhere on the island!

But the island seemed to be moving past us, as we rowed and got nowhere. Oh, God, God, I prayed and bailed, don't let this river kill me. By the grace of God and the power of prayer, I'm convinced, we grappled our way out of the central channel and struggled toward the rocks, the trees, the island, got close, the boat banging and shoving against unseen rocks and trees. The riverbank was gone altogether, swallowed up by the raging river, all brown and so high that we ran right into the trees themselves.

Virgil grabbed the towrope and leaped out, pulling with all his might, pulling us up, high as he could. Planting his feet against the tree itself, he wrapped the rope around the great belly of a cedar. Pa, leaping out of the boat as best a one-legged man could, held the line with Virgil, his wooden leg sinking into the wet earth around the tree, his other foot pressed against its trunk. Quick, Ma! Quick! cried Pa. Jump! Ma, with the baby under her arm, scrambled out. Now you, Georgieanna! Only Georgieanna was crying and wouldn't move. All right, you, Sarah Jane! Jump, cried Pa. And I did. Now Georgieanna, you! Jump! Georgieanna wailing that she couldn't jump, and Pa yelling at her, do it girl, don't look, just do it. I went back and hopped quickly into the boat and slapped Georgieanna a good one and made her jump, pushed her out of the damned boat. That's when I knew I was more like my mother than my father.

Once we were out, Pa and Virgil tried to secure the boat to the tree, but they lost it. Off it went, and everything in it, cash, Georgie's doll, my two books, down to the bottom of the river.

We climbed uphill through the trees till darkness was complete, and then we all huddled up and stayed that night in the woods. Wet, cold, hungry, footsore, our hands scraped raw, our arms just about pulled from their sockets from the fight with the river. I slept anyway. I wished I hadn't lost *Robinson Crusoe*. It might have done me some good.

At the first watery light of dawn, Pa said, let's move out. Pa always had this unerring sense of direction. He could follow the sun to China. We followed behind him, not talking, the baby whimpering how he was hungry. Georgieanna sniveled a little, but quietly so she wouldn't get smacked. For a one-legged man, Pa was unstoppable, climbing, up through the woods toward the island summit where he had his still. By the afternoon, we came upon it. It looked like the promised land to me, that little cedar shake cabin, there on high ground, tucked away from the revenue men and a haven to all of us. It had a steep roof, with hardly any leaks, neat wooden shutters over the two windows. If it was one thing my father knew, it was timber. Just like a real house in town, it had a lock on the door and the key was still on its little hook at the back of the first step. Any other time I might have laughed to see it. The revenue men could have let themselves in any old time if they'd ever found the place.

There was a good-sized stove inside and dry wood. It was a still, after all. There was food in tins on the shelves. There were rain barrels with freshwater. There were some blankets. There were maybe forty bottles of hooch on some shelves, all lined up with their bright painted labels. Pa painted the labels. Perkins Finest. Pa opened one and poured us each a tin cup full and said, drink this.

It seared up your insides as it went down. Warmed you. Didn't take the stink of the river off of you, but your innards were toasted everywhere that hooch went in your body. Perkins Finest.

Well, Amos, Ma said, how long must we live on this? She looked inside her tin cup. It was empty.

Well, Eliza, said my father, we been living on it for about six or seven years now. You surely don't think that Perkins Hotel been supporting us all this time, do you? You surely don't think the fine cooking, the good beds, and the hospitality would be why travelers put up at Perkins Hotel? Maybe it's escaped your notice, Eliza, but hardly anyone puts up with us overnight. Didn't you never think, Eliza that it might just have been a bit of this—he poured some more in her tin cup—kept travelers coming back to Watson's Landing?

Didn't you *ever* think, she corrected him. She was looking around for someone to slap, and I knew it. I pulled the baby on to my lap. She would never slap him. Georgieanna quit sniveling, and Virgil backed away.

Pa went on: didn't you never wonder, Eliza, why our guests sometimes just tied up at the landing, came in for a quick jaw, a bite to eat, if they was desperate and starving, and a few bottles of Perkins Finest? A few commercial men like Mr. Jasper and others to make a little detour for this island and collect enough to go on selling all over western Washington? Didn't you never marvel that a poor shop like Perkins Hotel provided you with a Cornish pipe organ, a red velvet settee, and rattan rockers with silk embroidered cushions? The money Perkins Hotel brought in would have scarcely kept us in seed potatoes and benzine. Perkins Hotel was a losing venture, Eliza. Why do you think Watson sold it and left his own landing? This is the age of the motor. River traffic ain't what it used to be, Eliza, and never will be again.

Isn't what it used to be, Amos. And the less said of Mr. Watson, the better.

Well, Eliza, children, I do not mean to be bragging and immodest here, given our perils, but you can all thank Perkins Finest for what you have received over these years, the comforts you've enjoyed. The ease. The books, Sarah Jane. The Jumbo, Virgil. All that's thanks to the Finest.

It's fierce, Pa, said Virgil, swilling down the last from his cup. Virgil was fair and thin-skinned, and he was all flushed.

The Finest is always fierce, said my father, and you could see he really did take some pride in this stuff, which was vile by any standard. I finished my cup and could feel my face flushing too. The fire in the stove was toasty and my clothes had started to dry on my body and they were stiff with mud and river water and they smelled bad. I could feel mud sludging around in my drawers.

Perkins Finest is what draws 'em back and keeps 'em happy, Pa went on. I never did have to advertise nor nothing like that. My name is legion all over western Washington, blessed. I am probably immortal, and my knack with the potato heralded all the way to Alaska. He swilled the last of his Finest from the tin cup. He was flushed with pride. My mother could not abide this, and so she asked, now that he had got us to the island, how he proposed to get us off.

We stayed on that island for ten days. The rain had stopped, though it would be too much to say the sun shone. We ate everything that was on the shelves. Luckily Pa had a rifle there, so we ate squirrels. Ma said the least he could do was shoot a deer. It was disgusting to be eating squirrels, but she stewed them just the same. Late one morning, we heard thrashing through the trees. Ma said it was a deer and Pa should go shoot it. But it was Mr. Jasper without his packs and cases but still with his bowler. He and some other men had gone up and down the river looking for survivors or corpses and finding, alas, a few of the latter and, mercifully, a good many of the former, some people living in trees, clinging to them. Mr. Jasper said our place was washed away completely, the river had claimed it back, but he had known where to find us. Mr. Jasper and the others, including the sheriff, took a few bottles each of Perkins Finest for their rescuing troubles.

We joined the other survivors they had picked up. The steamer that took us downriver to the town of Euclid where Ma had once taught school. We and the other survivors were all put up at the Euclid Methodist Church. Mostly we had little to say to the other survivors after they all had told their terrible stories of ruin and rescue. The baby played with their babies, none caring for their peril. One by one these families left the Methodist church; their people came for them. But my parents had no people but each other. Ma was from Canada. That's all she'd ever tell of any of her past. A schoolteacher from Canada. Pa's whole family had been wiped out by mushrooms.

We six Perkinses, the last remnants of the flood, were the only family left, sleeping on the pews. You could see that the Methodist pastor was having his holiness taxed. Only its being Christmastime—no room at the inn and all that—kept him from expelling us. As it was, we had to sit out many of his sermons, so many so we turned into Methodists. At least he had something to show for his begrudging goodness. Various families in Euclid took turns feeding us. When we came back to the church after one of these dinners, and lay down with our blankets on the pews, Ma said, Amos, you had better think of something because I will choke on more charity. I am sick to death, Amos, of thanking stupid people for their kindness. I never thought I would be sleeping on a church pew and saying thank you to women who are all but illiterate. Women who have nothing over me except their luck.

Lying there alone on my own pew in the dark church, I knew it wasn't their stupidity that incensed her. It was their kindness. It was both the thanking on her part and the kindness on theirs. She couldn't abide either one.

Well, what were we to do? A one-legged man isn't exactly the man you'd be looking to hire even in the best of times. This was the Depression. Besides, there was no call in December for a sign painter. That's what Pa was good at. Give him a brush and he'd paint you as fine a sign as could be seen anywhere, Seattle, anywhere. He was good at that, and of course he was good at making Perkins Finest out of old potatoes, a fire, a few copper coils and some glass tubing, and a bit of what else he never would say. Pa was an artist. But the sheriff was one of our rescuers, and more or less told Pa he was shutting him down, no arrests, nothing like that, but no more hooch either. And what did it matter? Prohibition ended the very next year. Our cash was at the bottom of the river. We had no money at all, and no property either. There wasn't even land to sell. It all belonged to the river now.

It didn't always belong to the river. Sixty-five-some years later, it belonged to a couple, Patricia and Ben Holtz. I was driving north from Portland last summer on my way to Vancouver Island for a vacation with some friends. I was on Interstate 5, driving across that great apron of farmland we always called the flats. In the distance to the east, there were the mountains, majestic peaks, shrouded always in snow, often in clouds, even now, late June. To the west, in the distance was the Sound, but you could not see it, because the land and water met, melded into one another, even though the air was so clear and clean, the colors bright as jewels. On either side of the freeway, fields rolled away and gulls speckled these fields, white punctuation on an otherwise green page. I saw an exit for Thornton and Euclid. I took the off-ramp and drove east, inland, all the way to where the two towns had now basically combined, united by a single four-lane avenue full of fast food and name brands, parking lots. I checked in at a nondescript Comfort Inn on this thoroughfare and asked the kid at the reception desk for a map, knowing it was useless to me. I had inherited my father's sense of direction. Why else would I be here? I had never been back to Watson's Landing since I'd left there in a boat, but I knew I must go now, knew it as surely as if I heard my mother wheezing on the Cornish pipe organ or the dog barking on the porch.

Beyond, east and inland of the four-lane strip mall, you could follow almost any road up, over the railroad tracks and come on the old part of these towns blended now, more or less, bound by commerce. In what was old Euclid, the Methodist church still stood, but it was a School for the Dance. The schoolhouse and the little cedar shake shack out back of it where my mother had first lived alone as a teacher and where the six of us lived after the flood, gone, replaced by a minimart and a doughnut shop. Only a few of Edison's old buildings, the bank, the Odd Fellows, remained, the ones of brick and stone. Some of the houses I remembered. Probably I could have got out the phone book and looked up some names, but what's the point? If the place had so changed in sixty-five years, imagine what time had done to those people. What had time done to me, for that matter? Who would ever say to me, Sarah Jane Perkins? Sarah Jane, is that you? And what would I say back? Well, I guess so. That's my name, but is it the person I was?

The city graveyard was well tended, with streets and a directory, just like town, I found my parents' graves, a plaque in the grass:

PERKINS, AMOS AND ELIZA.

No dates, even. Ma put up the plaque after Pa died. Ma said her children would know when she and Pa went and who else would care? Nearby were the Perkinses who had all died of mushrooms. Virgil's name was on a plaque with other men who had perished in the war. Virgil had joined up the day after Pearl Harbor and lived through the whole thing except the Battle of the Bulge. The baby, whose real name was Ethan, lived in LA. Georgieanna had ended up in Colorado. We scarcely knew each other and hardly ever talked. None of us would be buried here.

I drove east and east again, in no particular hurry. It was a high, hot Saturday late in June. The best of days. The ripest. The summer up here, western Washington, the mountains sloping down to the Sound, the summer is the gift God gives you for living with the rain all the rest of the year. The best summers in the world are right here. In June you believe they will go on forever, but in five weeks' time, August, death will already be on summer. Yellow leaves will twinkle in and around the green. The cattails will be dry and rusty, the shallow parts of lakes all boggy and hedges dried up and the blackberries gleaming red and unripe on the brambles. But you would not believe that in June.

I came to a road that said WATSON'S LANDING ROAD. Well, I didn't recognize this road, but as I said, the landing was never ours. The Watsons left when they sold the place to my parents, and yet they had endured here and we had not.

On either side of the road there were perhaps a dozen tract houses lined up, with maybe a quarter acre each. Neat little pastel homes, alike as gumdrops. Someone made a bundle selling those lots, I thought, and it wasn't the river. I drove maybe a mile or two past the tract houses till I came to a line of tall poplars to my left and, beyond them, the river. I could see the river, bits of it through the trees. I could feel it. Smell it. Time had not changed that. To my right and set back from the river there was a modest house, set on a high foundation, a deck of bright new wood wrapped round the back and a BMW and an Audi parked by the picket fence, awash in climbing red roses.

This was the home of Patricia and Ben Holtz. They were a career couple, no kids, midforties, with computer jobs. They were weekend farmers who loved the land, this land especially, and they prided themselves on doing most all the work themselves. They had grapevines and fruit trees and a big garden and beyond that a meadow where the spires of a thousand foxgloves waved. There was a barn they didn't use except for tools. They saw me looking all around and came outside. Ben was especially nice, hearing my tale of how I had lived here, or at least close to here. I couldn't be sure. The river had changed everything.

Ben was a bearded man, soft-spoken, lanky and pale, and his wife was small with a restless energy. Maybe that's why she took off, running errands. Ben offered to walk me all over the property. We went out to the poplars and stood there on the bank and watched the river roll by, muscular, green and brown, and an eddy here and there, gnats overhead catching the sunlight like bubbles. Even fish jumping, splashing. That old sound. I closed my eyes. I breathed. I listened. Though I was a stranger to Ben Holtz, though I was an old woman to whom he owed no particular courtesy, he showed real grace, I thought. He left me there alone and walked a bit upstream. I tilted my face to the sky. Was this the same light pinking my skin? The chatter of birds stirred in the poplars and the flies buzzed over the oozy banks. The slow, thick green water whispered and lisped. The scent came up and over me, the river scent, and the smell of the grass. I opened my eyes to see finches swooping and darting over the water and a butterfly struggling to make its way across the watery expanse. Was this the same river that had tried to kill us?

Ben Holtz told me every time they tilled their land to put in the garden, they were always finding bits of this and that, a pot, a pan, a bolt or hinge, a bottle. He said they kept most of it in the unused barn. He asked if I wanted to see it. I could have anything I wanted.

Have you ever, I asked him, found bottles with bright labels that say Perkins Finest? But Ben said none of the bottles they found had any labels at all, so I thanked him but said, no, I didn't need to see the old junk. I wanted nothing. It probably wasn't my family's, anyway. The river had covered everything, miles upstream, I told him, and it carried a lot down with it.

Oh, yes, said Ben, don't we know it. We had our high concrete foundation reenforced on this house, which was built maybe 1948. Every spring in the six years they had lived here, he said, there were days when it rained so much they could look out from their deck and their whole property looked like a lake. Or a darkened mirror.

And in that darkened mirror, I thought, no telling what you'll see.

Ben walked me back to their house and asked me to stay for a glass of homemade wine, from their own grapes. He said although the growing season was short, their produce was terrific. The flooding could be a problem, of course. But not dire, not like in the old days. They had flood control now. I listened to him, nodding agreeably, but I thought, there'll come a day, Ben, when you'll wish you had a boat tied to this second-story deck of yours. I knew, as Ben did not, that when the river wanted your land, the river took it. My father always said some lucky bastard would truly inherit the earth, our earth, that one day Watson's Landing would be prime farmland with good topsoil. And so it seemed to be for Ben Holtz and his wife Patricia.

For Amos Perkins and his wife, Eliza, Watson's Landing grew potatoes. Enough to feed those travelers who had bowels of steel and us children, four in all, Georgieanna and the baby born there at Watson's Landing. My mother's cooking was heavy on lard and flour, pork, mush, puddings of a sort, plain fare seasoned with salt and pepper, maybe, nothing more. Grits. Grains. Fruit and vegetables in season. She didn't put anything up, no canning against the coming winter, and when, now and then, she made jam or applesauce, she was chintzy with the sugar. Her fruit pies were runny and thin, the crusts like bricks. Most of the potatoes went to the island for Perkins Finest, that sterling imitation of vodka.

We moved to Watson's Landing after my father's accident. I don't remember living anyplace before, but Virgil remembers the logging town.

Hardly a town at all, a sawmill and a settlement of loggers' families in the mountains south and east of here. Men. Machinery. Mountains. The smell of fresh-cut wood, bleeding trees. Pa and the other loggers lived five days up at the camp. A hard life, but for a skilled man, a steady man who didn't drink, didn't hold with foolery, who had good hands, and yes, good luck, it was good money. My father was a skilled man who didn't drink (at that time), didn't hold with foolery, who had good hands. It wasn't his fault his luck gave out.

The loggers at the camp eventually cut a wooden leg for my father from the tree that had felled him. His leg was gone below the knee. The worst kind of catastrophe for a logging family because we had nothing. None of the loggers did. The house we lived in, credit at the company store—all that belonged to the company. And what kind of work could a cripple do? All the loggers and their families knew the company would cut off our credit. They would make us move and free up the company house for an able-bodied man. Not right away. But soon.

Pa was on morphine and knew nothing, but the outpouring of help and concern was intolerable to Ma. She had no grace about her whatever. Slowly the other families drew away from my parents. They quit bringing by meals and offering to take the baby (me) off Ma's hands while Pa slept or while she changed his dressings. After a time, the women just left hot food, wrapped up in towels or blankets, on the front steps while my father recuperated. My mother was supposed to wash these cast iron pots and leave them and the folded blankets out for the donors to collect. It was too much for Ma, like putting food out for a dog. People were afraid of us, Ma said. They weren't cruel, said Pa, just superstitious. The Perkinses seemed cursed. Ma quit returning their cast iron pans and their blankets. People stopped leaving food on the step.

Then, as I heard it, there came word from Euclid where my mother had been a teacher and had been courted by my father in the days before his whole family succumbed to mushrooms. Word came that Watson's Landing upriver was for sale. Drink had made a mess of Watson already. He drank up his own profits. And with Prohibition, well, a fuddled man can't balance all that's necessary. He didn't pay his bootlegger. He had to leave the landing. So people said the land, the outbuildings, the hotel and its furnishings, including a player piano with a hundred piano rolls— all that was going cheap. My father said a hotel was just fine for him. He said that anymore he was only good for loping after customers, limping after travelers. But it was there, at Watson's Landing, he picked up a paintbrush for the first time. A brush instead of a saw. He was an artist, my father. He could transform things. Isn't that what an artist does? He could take potatoes and transform them into hooch. Say what you will, that's transformation of a sort. He could take an old board, sand it down, finish it off like glass, and paint across it, in great brilliant letters, red and gold and blue three feet high: PERKINS HOTEL.

The sign was too fine for what it was supposed to describe, a rambling wooden frame, rooms added on willy-nilly in Watson's time. Each room had a couple of iron bedsteads with lumpy mattresses, some of the lumps so big they looked like goiters. There was a big kitchen where Watson had only a fireplace and a rusty little box he called a stove. We prospered there. Pa didn't have to pay a bootlegger; bootleggers like Mr. Jasper paid him. We put in a great big cast iron cooker with a large drum for heating water and copper pipes that went to the white ceramic sink nearby. The sink had brass taps. Our water came from a well, but the pump was indoors and it was my job to keep the big drum filled. We had everything except electricity and telephone. We subscribed to *Life* and the *Saturday Evening Post* for the reading pleasure of our guests, and in this way, the great world came to Watson's Landing. From the central kitchen, down one hall were the family's own rooms, and here we had the pipe organ, the settee, the rattan chairs with their taffeta cushions, and real velvet drapes across with white lacy inserts in the window. Georgieanna and I shared a bedroom, Virgil had his own little room. The baby, Ethan, slept with Ma and Pa. The guests hardly ever stayed the night. They ate a little and drank a lot in a big public room with tables and some chairs, the player piano, a fine stone fireplace, and a long bar, where my father served Perkins Finest, though it was Prohibition and the bottles with their colorful labels were kept well out of sight. The sheriff was well taken care of, but my father never was a flaunter or a braggart. As I said, he was an artist.

Except for the stone fireplace, Perkins Hotel, Watson's Landing, whatever you wanted to call it, the whole place was nothing but flimsy cedar shake, shingles put over a frame, drafty in winter and damp all the time, a sort of shambling building, shilly-shallying this way and that with a steep roof and a covered porch. So poorly built, no wonder it went down in a flash when the river came to claim it. It could just as easily have gone up in a flash and burned to the ground. Lots of them did.

I do not remember moving there, but Virgil told me there were three or four little one-room cedar shake cabins out back, not too far from the

hotel, all within an easy trot of the privy. Virgil remembered these burning. Ma told me nothing had burned.

Pa told me—later, much later—that Watson's Landing, before it was
Perkins Hotel, was less of a hotel and more of a dance hall. Men came
there who weren't even traveling men. Even couples came up from Thornton and Euclid on Saturday nights when Watson hired a band. Pa said
the cornet player would stand on a chair and blast that horn till the
whole place shook. Pa said he'd once brought Ma there before they were
married, though she would never go again when she figured out that
Watson provided some men with more comforts than just food, drink, a
fire, and a cornet player on a chair. Some men enjoyed a fine haunch of
female flesh in the bed next to them. These little outbuildings were theirs,
and Watson, that geezer, extracted rent from the girls.

Pa told me that on moving the family into Watson's Landing—we came
by steamer, up the river—one of these girls came up to Pa and said, same
terms as Watson, only no ironing and no poker nights. Pa said, what's a
man with a wooden leg want with poker? He said it without laughing,
and then he split a gut laughing.

Ma was not laughing. Ma told that steamer captain to stay at Watson's Landing for fifteen minutes, that he would have three more pas-
sengers. Then she said to these girls, that's all the time you have, go
collect your things. Without another word, she went into the hotel
kitchen, built up the fire in the stove. She had a way with fire; she could
start a blaze going, keep it going better than anyone I ever knew. She
found herself a nice dry branch of pine lying about, lit it, and went out
to the cabins and torched the one closest while the girls cried and
screamed and swore and collected their things, all right, in smoking
haste.

Finally Pa stumped out, faster on one pin than many a man with two,
crying out, Eliza! Eliza! Don't! He stopped her at the last little cabin. He
said they might need it. For the chickens. And so they did. And after the
first crop of potatoes came in, it proved a handy dandy hiding place for
the Finest, so that a stroll to the chicken house always netted my father
a tidy profit.

We Perkinses, we never referred to it as Watson's Landing. It was
always Perkins Hotel. After all, we had the red, blue, and gold sign in
three-foot letters to prove it. When my father took up the paintbrush,
there was no stopping him. When Ma said she always thought she'd have
wallpaper where she lived, he painted her wallpaper, and he painted a

fine carpet in the room with the Cornish pipe organ, the velvet settee, and the wicker rocker with the taffeta cushions. He painted carpet designs all over the floor of the hotel public room and along the halls leading to the bedrooms. He painted some not very good family portraits hanging on those walls. He was best at stopping your eye with color. The place was a riot of color, a feast for the eyes, which was good because that was the only feast possible at Perkins Hotel. The cooking was awful.

In the room that had the pipe organ and settee, Pa whitewashed over one whole wall where he'd originally painted rosebuds up and down in the imitation of wallpaper. He painted there instead a library. A whole wall full of books. They looked so real, you could go up and rub your hands along the spines and expect to feel leather. Everyone in the family got to say which books would be on our shelves. Ma filled up her shelves in no time with all the Great Books she'd read, and even some we had read, since she taught us at home. Watson's Landing was too far from any town for us to go to real school. Virgil's shelf stayed empty, because he cared for nothing except motors, and he couldn't think of any books about motors. Georgieanna had some books I don't recall. The baby couldn't read. But my shelf had so many titles! *Robinson Crusoe* and *Heidi*, books I had read over and over, got from the Euclid library when Pa would take me into town. Those books were a special and a sweet gift to me for my tenth birthday, even if it was just months before they were washed away with everything else.

On my shelf in the painted library, next to my favorites, my Pa painted maybe half a dozen books. No titles. He said to me, Sarah Jane, those are the books you are going to write one day. We can't be putting titles to them now, because they aren't written. But they will be. And when they are, Sarah Jane, you come back here to the Perkins Hotel, and you fill in these titles, you hear me, Sarah Jane? You come back and knock on the door and tell whoever is living here you only want a moment of their time, but you have to put your name and your titles on these books. They'll let you in. They'll be good to you, Sarah Jane, no matter what they're calling the Perkins Hotel then. They won't be using the rivers then. Nor even the railroads. Not like they do now. I can see it coming.

Pa said the same thing, about the rivers and the railroads that terrible day on the island while we were drinking Perkins Finest, while the mud, drying on our clothes crinkled and stinking, stuck in our underwear, and we were footsore, homeless, anguished, and hungry. We were as deep in poverty as any poor Okie blown out of the Dust Bowl. We were in for the Depression.

Perkins Finest bootleg hooch gave my family the only period of prosperity we had ever known or ever would know. Prohibition and potatoes and the river trade, commercial travelers like Mr. Jasper gave us a golden age. Sarah Jane, my father would sometimes say to me, sitting in a boat, our poles out in the river, the fish flinging themselves into our boat, Sarah Jane, even though my wooden leg still hurts, even though it remembers the pain of being shattered, infected, gangrened, and then cut off, there are still times when I bless that tree that broke me up. Yes I do, Sarah Jane. I bless it. Could I ever have bought your mother a Cornish pipe organ, a velvet settee if I was still a logging man?

Well, Pa, I felt like saying all those many decades later when Ben Holtz left me there on his high deck, well, Pa, why don't you just rise up from that little dateless grave in town and come out here and bless the river too? Because at least with the flood, we had something to blame our woes upon. We had something we'd never forget, ten days there, stuck on that island eating squirrel meat, not knowing if anyone would ever find us because the whole point of putting an illegal still on an island in the middle of a river is so that no one will ever find it.

Pa could see it coming, and he was right. Rivers and railroads were finished. For a hundred years, all over the Northwest, people and timber and fish and foodstuffs, goods and religion moved by river. The rivers all led to the Sound. The Sound could be navigated by ships, down south to Seattle, up north through and around all the San Juan islands to Canada, to Victoria and Vancouver, and beyond, to Alaska. But the roads were few and difficult. The roads were made for logging, for mules at best, primitive trails that only the most foolhardy would navigate in a Jumbo or a Dodge or an old Franklin. Who in those Prohibition years would ever have thought I could drive up on Route 5, the Interstate like a gray gleaming ribbon, or that I could wend my way back to Watson's Landing on fine, smooth paved roads with a white line telling you which side to stay on?

Yes, Pa, I thought, sitting there in the sunshine and shadow of a June afternoon while Ben Holtz fetched me glass of his homemade wine. Pa, you should kiss that river and salute that flood. Otherwise, there just would have come the end of Prohibition, and we would have failed anyway, slowly, painfully, out here with no one to come to Watson's Landing anyway. Because right after the flood there came the advent of the CCC and the WPA and FDR putting all those jobless men with two legs to work building roads across the Northwest, and building bridges across the rivers, and building tunnels through mountains and highways over peaks, and building dams, magnificent dams that would forever change the course of those rivers and confound the fish for the next millennium.

The Christmas we spent in the Methodist church, the pastor made such a fuss over our being homeless in this sacred season, Pa said he feared we'd find ourselves in the vestibule with a few sheep and the baby in a manger. I told Pa the baby was too big for the manger, but I could see he had a point. I could see too, and so could he, that once Christmas was past, our usefulness as sermon fodder would be at an end.

Pa went looking for work every day, but there wasn't any. He'd lost all his paints and brushes. There wasn't any work in Thornton or Euclid, not for a one-legged man, and there wasn't any money to get us out of the Methodist church and out of Thornton or Euclid and maybe down to Seattle, or somewhere where my parents could have done something or other. My mother grew grimmer by the day. We three older children stayed out of her way. We didn't even go in the church if we could help it. We played in the cold till the pastor's wife invited us into their house. We played with the pastor's children in their nice warm kitchen and hated them for it.

Then, just as with most disasters, you look desperately in one direction, and salvation comes from somewhere else. There came a telegram from the Euclid schoolteacher who had gone home to Walla Walla for the Christmas holidays and who would not be returning. She would stay in Walla Walla to marry her long-ago sweetheart, now a widower with two little children. "Life is full of blessings," she wrote.

Little did she know.

We moved into the cedar shake cabin out back of the school where the teacher had lived alone, the same cabin where Ma had first lived on her own on coming to Euclid as the teacher. The same cabin she'd lived in when Pa courted her. Only now there were six of us. People donated some dishes and spoons and blankets. Ma and Pa and the baby got the bed. Virgil took the floor, Georgie and I took turns in the chair, but I was too big for it. So it was the floor for me too. The bad thing about the floor was mice. I do detest mice, all rodents. They'd scamper, keeping me awake with their noise and with the fear they'd gnaw at my blanket or, worse, my toes or my nose. I couldn't sleep at night, and Ma would smack me if I fell asleep in the daytime when I was supposed to be working.

And then, maybe a month after we'd moved in, one night there's this calico cat. Where she came from, I never did know. She just appeared and she would wreak terror on those mice. I'd watch her dashing through the moonlight like a calico ghost, chasing away the mice. Then she'd come back and sit on a chair and grin at me. I swear, she would grin in the dark.

After that I could sleep, and there was less reason for Ma to visit her wrath on me or my students, the babies. Probably Ma put me with them because she had no patience whatever for children that young. Except for her baby. He was different. He was the only one Ma never slapped. Ethan never felt the leather switch. In winters, she kept him in her class, the side with the stove, even if he couldn't read. I don't know why she so loved him, for he was a stupid child and not even that pretty. When he was about ten he said he was tired of being the baby and wanted to be Ethan. I don't know if he ever did learn to read. Georgieanna could read but had no wish to. After I left for high school in Mt. Vernon, Ma tried to make Georgieanna teach the babies, but she would have no part of it.

And my father? One-legged though he was, he turned that one-room teacher's cabin into a fine house. He built on a porch and an actual bathroom with a tub. He painted the porch and the bathroom and the tub too. The tub was dripping with what looked like wisteria, long graceful blooms swaying on green branches. On the floor of our house, he painted another rug. Better than the last. And some wallpaper, and he even painted in a Cornish pipe organ and a maroon settee, knowing we'd never again own such things. To my knowledge, my mother never commented, saving to say we'd have to leave the windows open and let the paint smell out.

I wondered, always, how two such strange and dissimilar people as my parents had ever persuaded themselves they were in love. If there was any such answer, I found it not in poetry but in Professor Plunkett's classes, in biology, the science of what happens whether it's willed or not.

Professor Plunkett had an original mind, and he paid the price for it. His lectures at the University of Washington were always crowded, though lots of people thought he was a crackpot or a drunk. Most students, when they'd leave, they'd shake their heads and ask each other why he didn't follow the textbook and how could he make all these bizarre connections. But I didn't think they were bizarre. I could follow Professor Plunkett's train of thought. I was only nineteen, but I began to understand. Professor Plunkett believed that there were instincts, drives that lay in deep within not just mammals or vertebrates, but that lay in that great collective force in the universe that was Organic Life. Not individual little lives, not even in history, a sweep of human events, but in some surging force that brought the waves to shore and the rivers to the sea and grew the pines in the deepest black shadows of the forest where no sunlight could penetrate and nothing by rights should grow. Nothing could resist this force.

My parents, I began even then to believe, succumbed to something of this force he described. The old primordial instinct that urges the continuation of each species, the following of nature's commandments to the exclusion of all else, even at the cost of your health, happiness, well-being. Are we finless creatures any different from those poor salmon flinging themselves back upstream insensible to all else but nature's commands? My parents—who ought never to have married—met, married, bedded, begot four children. Though not perhaps in that exact order. At some point, after Ethan, they must have looked at one another, dazed and a little stupefied, dry-mouthed as if suffering from hangover. They must have wondered how in God's name they would live together for the rest of their lives, all those years before them. Their species propagated, they must have wondered what had even moved them to ally their fates and lives. How could this have been?

My mother Eliza could not say thank you, or tolerate a kindness. My father Amos could not admit an error in judgment. Amos made decorative what was merely functional. Eliza made functional what was only decorative. He had unending verve, and she had unending vengeance. She could cast him in a vile light and see nothing fine. He, in retaliation, refused to acknowledge anything vile, neither hooch nor the fate that deprived him of a leg. He stumped around Euclid and Thornton on his painted wooden leg, becoming eventually a figure of fun as she became a figure of fury.

By then they had forged something between them, shackles, maybe, unlovely but binding. Necessary. Maybe even noble. Now I suppose they would be pitied for staying together at all, but they were a staunch generation and would not have seen it that way. Certainly neither of my parents would ever have bellyached or bawled or moaned or twisted a tissue in the therapist's office. I do not say this was right or proper, or better than what people in similar circumstances might do today. It's the way they were, and to my way of thinking, it was noble. I admire their tenacity and their stubborn fulfillment of their vows. Would I want to live as they did? No. I have never married.

Last summer, I sat there on Ben Holtz's high deck, sipping wine pressed from grapes whose savor was drawn up from the wreck of my mother's Cornish pipe organ and the velvet settee, from the chassis of the Jumbo, and, no doubt, the carcass of the dog. I thought, well, perhaps I ought to do what Pa asked me. Ben Holtz had no painted shelves with titleless books to add my name to, but that June day, poplars whispering, fox-gloves nodding among the dry white daisies in the distant meadow, the whiff of mock orange and the scent of the river sweetening the air, it came on me. I ought to write something, especially since Pa always thought I would. I ought not to disappoint him. It shouldn't be scientific or a monograph, not even a collection of therapeutic notions and observations like *The Laughing Cat*. No. It ought to be decorative and functional. A memoir. I ought to write a memoir, and it ought to be something I could call Perkins Finest. Or at least as fine as I could make it.

So I finished the memoir. That was something. I made copies of the manuscript, one for each of them, Jill, Francine, Nell, Rusty. I thought of the manuscript as a kind of gift, thanking them for reading through all my various drafts, false starts, and early evasions. I decided to make an occasion of it and invited the Memoir Club, what was left of us, to tea after work. It was one of those high June days, perfect, summer in its full flush, almost a year exactly, I thought, as I laid out everything on the picnic table in my back garden, since I had sat on Ben Holtz's deck and decided I would do this. I had floundered about in the fall and then when I saw the memoir class being offered in the winter, I thought I'd do better working with others.

Odd to me, now, to think of the paths that had brought us together in Penny Taylor's class. This would be a subdued reunion, the first time the members of the Memoir Club have all been together since the tragedy. Rusty, Francine, and Jill came to my house from downtown after work. I collected Nell, who had moved back to her own apartment, but driving was still an ordeal for her. She and I fixed up everything in the back garden under the laburnum trees, with the creaking wicker chairs and no whoopee cushions. I put the teapots and the plates of food on the picnic table, not like Francine's elegant layout, but the thought was there, even if the execution was, as Penny Taylor would have said, wanting. Penny Taylor herself was wanting, though wanting quite what I could not say. Horace Plunkett might have had the words, but Sarah Jane Perkins? Well, I would just stumble along as best I could.

After I'd given them each a copy of *Perkins Finest*, and we'd had some time to rattle on a bit inconsequentially, subdued, as I expected, cheerful but chastened, I mentioned, sort of by the by, that when Penny returned that first draft of my memoir to me, she had returned my check as well. We'd each paid her separately for the spring class, three hundred dollars. She had folded the check and returned it with a note saying I could make better use of the money than she could.

"That's exactly what she wrote to me," said Jill. "And when I tried again to give her the money, she made me feel like I'd offended her."

"She could be testy," Rusty agreed. "She returned my check as well."

She had returned all our checks, as it turned out, which is what I had suspected. With that confirmed, I began my strange story. "It bothered me that we never saw Penny, or heard from her again after the tragedy at Women's Uptown. That was on a Wednesday night. She should have shown up at Francine's, but she didn't."

"It was all over the news," said Francine. "Everyone in this city heard about it."

"Colin and Francine and I were working at the Empress," said Jill, "and the carpenters had a radio on, and we couldn't believe it. A shooting at Women's Uptown? We tried to get through on the phone, but it was impossible, and they weren't letting anyone near the scene, so we all three went back to Francine's house and turned on the television news. We stayed there until the next morning at dawn, when we came to the hospital."

I nodded. I would come back to that, the hospital, later. "But why didn't Penny ever show again? As though she knew that the tragedy at Women's Uptown had finished off the Memoir Club. We knew. But did she? Or how did she? And why didn't she offer so much as a note? Nothing. To anyone. Not even to Nell. A student dies in a shootout and the teacher has nothing to say, not an ounce of condolence?"

"I thought of that," said Nell, eyes downcast. "Weeks went by before it crossed my mind, but I wondered."

We had all wondered, but no one could bring herself to say so, to point out that Penny Taylor looked to be heartless, devoid of any sympathy or even the most conventional courtesy. Since the clinic shooting, we had each concocted reasons for Penny's lapses. As we spilled them to one another, here in my back garden, offered them up and compared, they sounded not merely wanting but weak. We each confessed we'd tried to call Penny at the number she'd given us, but it wasn't in service.

"It never was in service," said Francine with a crisp finality. "I tried to call, to cancel the class the night I burned all of Marc's papers, the night you found me in the kitchen, but I just got the recording, the operator."

"That was the only night Penny ever showed up late," said Rusty. "She always got there before any of us, and she always left before we did. She was never late."

"Well, I have something to tell you," I said. "A story. No, it's my experience, so I guess it will pass as memoir, the kind of memoir, as Penny used to say, where imagination has to fill in the void left by memory." I closed my eyes and tilted my face to the sunshine. I felt as I had when Penny had thrashed over my schoolroom memoir, when she had sent me back to the river. I felt as though I were about to spit out a stone that had lain under my tongue ever since the night of the shooting. "I'm trained as a scientist. I have to look for answers. Even if I don't find them, I have to ask. After the tragedy at Women's Uptown. I went to University Extension. And when I said I was looking for Penny Taylor, no one had ever heard of her. Then I said I was in the memoir class last winter, and at that they hustled me into the program director's office, and the first thing she asked me is if I wanted my money back. I said no. I said I'd been one of half a dozen women who had paid Penny a fee to go on meeting in the spring. Then the program director, Ginny, got on the phone. The next thing I know, the divisional director comes in, introduces herself to me as Marilyn. She closes the door behind her and these two women look at me the way the mice used to look at the Laughing Cat. Like I was going to wreak some awful fate on them, and they weren't quite ready for it."

"Did Penny have a criminal record?" asked Rusty.

"Well, they didn't know. In fact, they didn't know squat about Penny. They asked me what I could tell them about her."

"They'd never met her?" asked Nell.

"They took her on as a teacher sight unseen. And she stayed sight unseen. When the New York author canceled, Marilyn and Ginny called every writer in Portland with any credentials at all, but no one could teach on three days' notice. Extension was desperate to keep the class going. It was going to be a moneymaker. It was filled, and they had fifteen people wait-listed. Then they got a call from Penny Taylor. She said she'd heard of their predicament from a writer who worked at the community college, a friend of hers. She said she could teach that very night, that she was a writer and had published memoirs and essays, mostly in anthologies and literary mags with bizarre titles. Marilyn couldn't remember any titles. Neither could Ginny. Penny said she'd send her résumé along later. They said okay."

"Those were her first words to us," said Rusty. " 'I have saved Extension's bacon.' "

"And that was the truth. Except that the writer at the community college had never heard of Penny Taylor. Her credentials, whatever they were, were false. Marilyn and Ginny didn't go into detail."

"I'll bet not," said Francine. "How humiliating, to have hired someone and then find out that they'd been duped. What else could they call it?"

"They did call it duped, but by the time they found out, the class was all but over. No one had complained. Not a murmur. They should have stepped in—of course they should have—and there in Ginny's office, they fell all over themselves apologizing that they hadn't. Well, that's an exaggeration. They said they'd refund my money for the winter course, but they had no responsibility for the spring."

"What about when they paid her?" asked Nell thoughtfully. It was the same question I'd asked, the question of a mind trained to look for answers. "Penny returned our checks individually, but they must have paid her. She must have signed a contract."

"Marilyn said Penny gave them a PO box as a mailing address,"

I said, "but the checks were all returned to Extension. The contract never did come back. No such PO box number existed. Even that took a while, given the bureaucracies, all of them, the PO, the university. Marilyn said as all this grew more questionable and murky, that, as divisional director, she decided not to investigate immediately. She didn't want to walk into a class and alarm everyone by calling the teacher a fraud and making nasty allegations. She said she'd take responsibility for the decision, like I was in charge of the firing squad, the squad that fires you from your job. Marilyn said she decided she would confront Penny Taylor after the class had ended and upbraid her then and tell her never to expect a reference from University Extension. No indeed."

All this time, Francine had been folding her paper napkin in an origami sort of fan. She placed it in its correct place and lined all the silverware up, perfectly parallel. "But she never wanted a reference, did she? She never wanted anything from University Extension at all. What did she want, Sarah Jane? Who was she?"

"What does it matter?" I shrugged. "We took the class. We stayed on with her in the spring because we had something to say, and we didn't have the words."

"Not me. I wanted the memoir class for Caryn. I thought . . ." Nell rubbed her uninjured hand across her forehead and through her hair.

I patted Nell's shoulder. "I have something else to tell you. Something I saw. Or at least that I think I saw. I feel obliged to tell you, even if you think I'm going senile, that dementia's setting in."

They all protested or assured me they would never think me senile, though Nell added, "You are pretty eccentric, Sarah Jane. And this must be serious because we're not sitting in the kitchen on whoopee cushions. Believe me," she turned to the others, her face lit by a smile, "when you live with Sarah Jane for a while, you never get used to anything."

I came on my tale in a straightforward way, answering their questions as they arose and taking care to keep it simple: that night in the hospital waiting room, late, waiting for word on Nell and Caryn. I was waiting by myself, since Rusty had lied to the nurse, passed herself off as Nell's older sister so they'd let her be with Nell when she came out of anesthesia.

The ER waiting room is fairly generic place. The lobby is across from a small reception area with semiprivate insurance booths and, beyond, elevators and a bank of vending machines. The carpet is a durable stubble of brown and gray. The walls are so off-white they look gray-brown. Fluorescent lights are on all the time, and there are few windows, so your sense of time passing is suppressed. The shifts change. The people in the little insurance booths, at reception, the nurses, come and go. Elevator doors hiss open and close. The uncomfortable chairs are lined up against three of the four walls. There are two interior lines of chairs too, facing each other sociably. All the chairs have wooden arms, so you can't stretch out and sleep, but by two in the morning, who cares? Even the television, the ubiquitous news and sports, is off. I stayed awake as best I could, dozing finally, my chin on my chest, waked now and then, embarrassed by my own snoring. After a while, I didn't have to be embarrassed. There were few people left, fewer each time I startled myself awake. Finally I was alone in the lobby and I didn't care if I snored or not.

I fell into a deep sleep, so deep that I was dreaming. I don't remember dreaming what, only that it was vivid, and then I woke, or rather I was roused by the sound of sobs, great breath-choking sobs. I struggled to come to consciousness, but the sound of weeping seemed to pull me back into the dream, to wrestle with me somehow for dominion over my consciousness. But I fought this, as anyone would, just on a human level. If you hear someone crying, you look to see what's the trouble.

As I came slowly out of the dream, I could see that across from me and down two chairs, there's a woman, hands over her face, shoulders shaking, crying. She was not in the waiting room earlier. In fact, she and I are alone here. I know enough not to move too close to her. I thought she was verging on hysteria, but I speak to her, softly at first. I ask her what's the trouble. She says she can't find her children. She's lost them and she can't find them. And I say, well, I'll help you. Let me help you. Tell me where you last saw them. But she can't. She just keeps sobbing into her hands, and I was about to move, to sit beside her and put my hand on her shoulder, when, from somewhere behind me, someone else emerges. I was near the wall, not the door. But someone walked past me and up to the weeping woman. She never turned around. She rested her hand on the weeping woman's shoulder, and she said, I heard her say: *I know where they are. Come with me. I'll take you to them. That's why I'm here.*

And just then, the elevator doors opened and I heard my name called, and I turned to see Rusty getting off the elevator, and when I turned back, they were gone. No one was there. There was noise in the waiting room, but no weeping. The televisions had come back on, and suddenly there was a face filling up all the screens. A toothless old woman in Turkestan or Khartoum or some remote place, a woman covered in a black shawl and pointing frantically to some rubble behind her, wailing about her children being lost. Buried in the earthquake. I did not understand her language, but I knew what she said. I knew exactly.

"When I got off the elevator," said Rusty after I had finished, "I thought Sarah Jane was alone in the waiting room. But . . . I was exhausted. I just fell into the chair beside you and started crying."

"That's when Rusty told me about the operation on Nell's hand. And that Caryn had died on the operating table. I didn't pay any attention to anything after that," I admitted.

There was a long silence, broken only by blue jays resident in my trees squabbling among themselves, scolding us for sitting so long and not leaving the crumbs and odd bits to them. They fluttered overhead, and from over the fence behind my yard, some kids were running through the sprinklers, laughing, squirting each other and vowing to tell Mom what the other had done.

"Who were these women you saw?" said Jill at last.

"I never saw their faces. The woman who was weeping never took her hands from her face. She had short light brown hair."

"Like Caryn," said Nell. "Nondescript hair. A doctor can't be fussing with her hair. What was she wearing?"

"Something colorless. Pale. No style. Just . . ."

"Like a lab coat or shapeless as scrubs?" asked Nell.

"I couldn't say exactly. Something like that."

"And the other woman?" asked Rusty.

"I only saw her back. But she was built like Penny. Older. Solid but spry. Dark clothes. A voice like Penny's voice, uninflected, sort of astringent. But I saw her shoes. At least I think I did. Athletic shoes. Grubby from the garden. Or the grave," I added. I had to.

"So you think," Francine began slowly, "that Penny Taylor came from the grave for Caryn?" She glanced at Nell, who had gone very pale.

"I don't know where she came from. I don't know what garden she toiled in. I don't know what she grew. I know what she came for. She came for us. I know that isn't a very scientific observation, but it's what I think nonetheless. How else would we ever have met? I think she came for us, but she left with Caryn." I plunged on, "I think she took Caryn where she needed to go to be with her children. I don't know where that is."

Nell, nodding as though in secret agreement with herself, then tried to tell us what Caryn Henley had lived through since the crash. "She was the bravest person I ever knew. There was only one thing she feared, and it wasn't the Family Champions, I can tell you that. And it wasn't even death. That's why I was always afraid she'd commit suicide. But when finally she told me why she hadn't—why she wouldn't—I was astonished. She said she didn't want to lose heaven. Caryn was a doctor and an athlete and a woman committed to the physical, the knowable, the scientific, but she said she didn't commit suicide because she was afraid such an act would make her unworthy of heaven. That's what she really said. I wanted her to recover, and she told me, that night, that I wanted too much, that I asked too much of her."

"What had you asked?" I said.

Nell looked at each of us. She gulped audibly. "Simple. We quarreled that night because I wanted us to go on meeting with the spring class. And she didn't want to. She'd had enough of Penny Taylor. She thought Penny Taylor was full of bullshit. I thought Penny Taylor was right. All those handouts about Writing Your Memoir, and the like, all that stuff I didn't really understand at first. But I was starting to. I think it's true, if you put a sort of narrative over your life, over your experience, you do impose structure on it, even meaning. Finally, Caryn agreed to go in the spring. She said she'd do it for me. I said, fine. And really, I did think she was getting better. Ted Swanson was part of it." Nell paused, held her own damaged hand. "He is a good man. He wanted to get a legal injunction against the Family Champions, but Caryn declined. She could endure anything, even Darcy Reeves and Daniel Phillips, though obviously none of us guessed that they were murderous. Ted knew they were dangerous, but Caryn was fearless. Caryn could endure anything in this life because she hoped—" Nell paused and struggled with her voice till she could command it. "Caryn had the hope that at the end, she would be reunited with her children. That's why she wouldn't commit suicide. She wouldn't risk that."

Francine handed Nell her origami folded napkin and Nell wiped her eyes with it.

"And if," I went on, since Nell could not, "if it seemed that she had died and lost that possibility, lost the children again, she would have wept like the woman in the waiting room."

"Was Penny capable of that kind of tenderness?" asked Jill. "She wasn't a gentle person. She had a way of asking bruising questions."

"But she never did ask Caryn anything very demanding," Francine reminded us. "All the rest of us—well, maybe not Nell—"

"Who cares about my Polish Micks!" Nell burst out. "Not even me. Francine is right. Penny Taylor asked all the rest of you difficult questions that made you, obliged you really, to wrestle with your pasts. But Caryn wrestled with her past every day."

"The woman who came for Caryn that night in the hospital didn't ask any questions either," I said, remembering the voice, what I heard. What I think I heard. "She just said she'd take her to her children."

Voices floated over the fence to my back garden, the mother who lived behind me, calling the children to come in, to turn off the hose and get dried off and come in right this very moment. The children grumbled, protesting that it was still warm and they wanted to play. Wherever Penny Taylor took Caryn Henley, I hoped that such bright voices were within her hearing.

Writing Your Memoir

PENNY TAYLOR, INSTRUCTOR

Things to remember

In a memoir, the author and the narrator
have an uneasy relationship.
What does the reader know of the author?
That the author lived to tell the tale.
What does the reader know of the narrator?
That the tale needed to be told.

PART IV
An Uneasy Relationship

18

Baggage Claim

Me-my, we-I, our-us. I tried my announcement out all sorts of ways. I have to say it. I have to tell my daughters I am meeting Eddie Arias for the weekend in Aptos, California. How am I going to do this?

I went to the still-under-construction Empress Bistro on my lunch hour to rehearse, practice on Francine and Jill. We sat on metal folding chairs beside the brand-new mahogany and marble-topped bar shrouded in tarps. It's the only piece of actual furniture here at the moment—unless you count the boards laid across saw-horses where the plans and drawings lie furled and the packing cases with the other fixtures. Colin said you could always cover a table with a white tablecloth and no customer would know the difference, but the bar had to be impressive. Invitational. People had to feel that they could come there and repeatedly have an experience they wouldn't have elsewhere, that the restaurant is special. After all, where else are you going to experience mahogany and marble? Jill said the bar was important, because people sat there, had a drink, then stayed for dinner, and that brought in revenue. Francine said they had both better be right, because the marble and mahogany bar cost an arm and a leg, a huge chunk of their start-up capital.

Jill and Francine were firm, absolutely I must say we. *We have been invited to our daughter's home.* After work that day, I drove out to Sarah Jane's house and rehearsed there. Nell rehearsed with me at Starbucks one afternoon. How strange that I could have lived in Portland all these years, worked, raised three kids, and yet the only people I could turn to were the Memoir Club. They knew the true past. Melissa and Suzanne. And their response was unanimous.

I felt like my own symphony orchestra tuning up for the curtain raiser, so I could go home and say to my daughters, we. *We have been invited to our daughter's home.* Carefully. It still sounds foreign to me, difficult and resting on my lips, exotic, like curry. *We have been invited to our daughter's home in Aptos for the weekend, and we are going.* Since I told Amy about my youthful disaster, the whole family knows. I'm relieved, actually. I don't have to tell the whole story as well as the fact that I'm going to Aptos. No one seemed particularly horrified. An illegitimate half-sister. They didn't even think of it like that. An unknown half-sister. Perhaps my story was softened because it came out after Amy decided to give her baby up for adoption.

Other than the births of my own children, going through that birth with Amy was the most intense experience of my life. Diane was there, her Lamaze coach, but only Amy and I knew the welter of pain and emotion, the effort to get something out and then to give it up. We three were together in the birthing room at the hospital. Chuck had signed the adoption papers, joined the navy, and left Portland just a few days before the birth. Chuck's family had ceased to speak to any of us. Tom, my ex and Amy's dad, waited outside for word. Give him that.

Amy told the nurse she didn't want to be brave; she wanted it over. And then it was. We were assured the baby boy was healthy and fine and that a fine family would raise him. Amy would have a month in which to change her mind. "I won't change my mind," said Amy without looking at anyone, closing her eyes, in fact. She had elected not to see the child. We all had to abide by her decision. Undergoing this, I was living through Melissa's birth all over again, the loss, the terrible loss.

When Amy was finally sleeping, I went out to the waiting room and sat with Tom. He put his hand over mine. He was glad to know that Amy would be fine and then he said he was sorry.

"For what?" I asked.

"For Amy. For having to go through all this, giving up the kid. For you. For . . ."

Tom Meadows was not very good with words, and he cast about for a way to describe what he meant. It took him a long time to say he was sorry that he had not been able to bear it when I told him about Melissa. I kept hold of his hand. I said it was all right. She wasn't Melissa anyway. She was Suzanne. "For all that, I added, even knowing all that suffering, Amy did the right thing. I didn't think so at first, but now I do."

"I do too," said Tom. He kissed my forehead and said he had to get home.

I know the pain of giving this child will follow Amy all her life, but not like it has been for me. The circumstances are not the same. Parallel, perhaps, but not the same. At least not until the day, perhaps thirty years hence, when she might conceivably meet the son she gave up.

Postpartum was especially difficult for Amy. She crashed into depression. At first she refused even counseling. She just told the doctors she didn't want to be brave, or explore the pain, or any of that. She called it bullshit. She wanted meds. She wanted to feel nothing. She got a three-month prescription. With these meds she seemed less like her old self and more like an underwater zombie.

The announcement of my going to Aptos, *We have been invited to our daughter's home,* roused Amy from her torpor into a froth of tears and temper. She raged at me that these people were nothing to me and I shouldn't go, that they were strangers, the house of strangers. She and Diane could stand the *notion* of the unknown half sister, but not the *fact* of it.

I had to explain again, gently, with many blurts and interruptions from Amy, that these people were not strangers to me. They had not been nothing to me. They had been and were important to me. After all, I had met Suzanne Post. The weekend before Darcy Reeves opened fire on the Women's Uptown Clinic, I had had lunch with her at La Gondola.

"You never take us to La Gondola." Amy's eyes narrowed, and she wept some more, as though the thought of lost entrées broke her heart. "You don't even take us to Denny's!"

I kept my voice even, offered that I had not paid for the meal at La Gondola, that Suzanne had. Amy sulked and asked if Suzanne had lots of money and if that's why I liked her best.

"Amy, I don't like her best. You know that's not true." She folded her arms over her chest. Diane watched warily, looking for her cue as I explained how Suzanne had got in touch with Eddie Arias. They had met. And he had asked for my phone number. And he had called me. Many times.

"Oh, we know that! He's been calling every day for weeks! Hasn't he, Diane?" Diane nodded. "Next time he calls, I'm hanging up on him," declared Amy. "He's got no business here talking to my mother. Who is he? A high school football coach! A married man!"

"He's divorced, Amy. Don't compound the errors here. I'm divorced. Your dad, if I'm not mistaken, has remarried. You went to the wedding, as I recall."

"This is a strange man, Mom! You haven't seen him *ever*, ever since you . . . since you . . ." Amy looked over at Diane who whispered, *had sex*. "Had sex! Yes! Since you had sex with him! How long ago was that? He could be a weirdo."

"He isn't. He wasn't then, either."

"In high school? School, Mom! High school! Listen to yourself!"

"I did have sex with him, but I didn't think of it like that. I thought of it as making love and committing sin. I thought of it as giving myself and breaking God's laws, I thought of it as doing what cost Eve Eden, and not even caring, of feeling something irresistibly ecstatic to have him in my arms. I thought I was putting my soul in peril, and I didn't care. I was young and that was how I felt."

Diane and Amy stared at me, jaws slack, unable to take all that in.

"Of course it's not nearly so complex anymore. Really, I have to agree with you girls, having sex is so much simpler, more straightforward and to the point. So let me say it that way: I had sex with him many years ago, and now our daughter has got in touch with him, and he has got in touch with me. She has invited us both to her home in Aptos for the weekend. I am leaving on Friday and I will be back on Sunday."

"And will you sleep with him again?" Amy demanded. "Have sex again?"

"I have had sex in the interim, you know. Your dad and I had sex."

"Don't try to get out of answering."

"I don't know."

I almost asked if Amy would sleep with Chuck again, but I didn't. It would have been cruel. Amy had got her body back, and soon she would have her equilibrium back, and then she would find a job, and she would have her life back. She never spoke of Chuck or the child. At least not to me. She'd taken up smoking again, as if to convince her body that truly her life was her own again. She went outside to smoke. Diane went with her.

Before going to Aptos, I refreshed my Auburn #7 and bought new clothes, putting them and the ticket to San Francisco on credit cards. I took off half a day from the Symphony League, telling Ronald Oliver only that I was meeting some old friends for the weekend. I packed a single bag and took the quick flight to San Francisco, and when I got off the plane, I was weak in the knees. My La Gondola reunion with Suzanne had been such a failure. She didn't like me. Did I like her? Probably not. So brusque and businesslike. I had met Suzanne and lost Melissa, and I had gained nothing. Except maybe that wasn't true. I had gained the sound of Eddie Arias's voice. That was worth having. I wouldn't have asked for more. I didn't want more. I should not be here.

I got off the plane and sat, collecting myself, in the departure lounge before going down to baggage claim. I tried to remember why I had agreed to come.

When Suzanne had called and offered this, she was clearly trying to mend fences with me. "If we could do this, be all three together, even just for a few days, it would solve something for me. I don't quite know what. But I want us to be together."

"A family reunion?" I had asked, trying to make a joke.

"Yes, I guess so. And I want it to be in my own home, not in a restaurant. I don't want it to be like when you and I met, Rusty. I was, well, I don't know what came over me. I was angry, and I didn't know why. I'd waited two years and never replied to your letter, and then when I met you, I acted like an information specialist gathering data. Not like a woman meeting her mother for the first time. I was rude, and I hope you won't hold it against me."

"I understand ambivalence. Of course I won't hold it against you."

"Then come to my house. You'll like it here. Eddie's coming."

And then Eddie called me and said he would drive to San Francisco and pick me up at the airport, and we would drive down the coast together. Aptos is near Santa Cruz. We would drive together to see our daughter. Like parents. As though all those years between us and our daughter could be erased? No. But could the old void be filled?

And now, I am riding the escalator down to baggage claim, thinking of how time's prism has changed me and how no doubt it's changed Eddie Arias, who has been married and divorced and, like me, is the parent of three grown children. I look down into that vast hall with the speakers blaring and the milling throngs and the carousels starting and stopping and the thrill of reunions all around, and I see him at the foot of the escalator. I see him before he sees me. He is still stocky and solid. His hair is mostly gray. His face has gone fleshy, but the high planes are still there, the strong jaw, the eyes alive with intelligence and engaged with the world. What does he see in me? I don't know, but whatever it is, his face lights up. Though I have brought but one purse and one carry-on, I am coming to claim the baggage I have carried alone all my adult life. And now, swiftly, he takes it from me. He kisses my cheek, shyly. He says, *Charity*. I say, *Duardo*.

19

Learning Experience

Dust and plaster and paint flew all over the Empress Bistro dining room, or what would be the dining room. The marble and mahogany bar was covered in a tarp, and tinny music spewed out of a boom box while painters and carpenters and plasterers worked. When Jill interviewed for server positions, she had to conduct these interviews in the office, a euphemism for a closety space, infernally hot because right next to it was the utility room where the boiler and the hot-water heater chugged along. Now in summer the boiler was off, but the place was still close, and she dabbed some perspiration from her nose. Oh, well, she thought, if you can't take the heat, get out of the kitchen.

Colin hired the kitchen staff, but the waiters were her responsibility. In all her bus ad experience, Jill had never actually hired anyone. Or fired anyone, for that matter. Now, readying for the Empress Bistro opening, she'd interviewed perhaps twenty people and chosen only three, four including the bartender. Opening day was coming near. Maybe she'd been too picky. In this new venture, she tried to keep before her a sense of what her sister Katherine would do. Katherine, with her fine job at the Honolulu hotel, was used to deadlines, screwups, and lots being at stake. Katherine knew how to delegate responsibility. But right now, for Jill, there was no one to delegate to, and she couldn't be like Katherine, or like Lisa, for that matter. She checked her watch. For starters, she had already decided, anyone not on time for their interview would automatically not be hired. It was two minutes to ten.

Ten on the dot, Colin showed Amy Meadows to the office. Jill greeted her, noting that she did indeed have clean fingernails, a requirement for the job. She even had a French manicure. "Please, sit down, Amy." Physically, Amy looked a lot like Rusty, though she did not have her intrinsic modesty or kindness. Amy was surly and expectant.

"I know you wouldn't even be interviewing me if it wasn't for Mom." She slumped in the chair by Jill's desk.

"Well, that's true." Jill got out Amy's application. "But you've had some experience. We require some experience."

"I was a barista, not a waiter. I'm not going to lie to you. I made espresso. I haven't had the kind of experience you want, but I really want the job. I'll learn fast. I need work, and I can pick it up all really fast." Amy added more plainly, "I don't want to go on living with my mother."

Jill nodded without commenting.

"You were part of Mom's Wednesday night Memoir Club. So I guess you know my whole story."

"The whole country knows your story. You nearly died at the Women's Uptown Clinic."

"I gave the baby up for adoption."

"Will that affect your ability to work for us?"

"I don't think so. It was different than I'd thought. I mean, the whole experience. I didn't want to be a mother. Anyone's mother. Maybe I've just had too much time to think about it. I haven't been able to find a job. That's why I'm here."

Jill looked over the printed application. "This is a nonsmoking restaurant. You've checked here that you don't smoke. I mean, you can go outside in the alley if you want, but—"

"Mom told you I smoked! How could she? I gave it up. I only started again to prove to my body I wasn't preggers. It's a stupid habit and I quit."

"Well, that's good." Jill checked off an item. "Now, let me tell you a little about the job, so you can judge if it's for you. Working in a restaurant is always a pressurized situation, and the better the restaurant, the more the pressure. However, the customer can never suspect that. The customer must always believe that everything is smooth, that flourish and good service are delivered without anyone so much as dropping a bead of sweat. That's where the serving staff must shine. And here, at the Empress, there will be even more pressure than usual. In this next year, the Empress will be creating a reputation that can make us or break us. We will have to live with what we do this year for a very long time. It has to be the right reputation. This is a serious job and a serious business for everyone who works here. If you think you're not equal to this, for any reason—"

"I'm equal to it. I want to succeed here."

Jill smiled. "Well, we all want to succeed here. You'll start part time. I'm starting everyone part time for three months. That's part of my business plan. If you do well, you'll be put on full time. If you don't, you'll be let go, and you can't use us for a reference. Clear?"

"Yes. Thanks for the chance, Ms. McDougall."

"Jill. I'm just Jill. We'll be having some orientation classes as soon as we get the serving staff in order. You'll be on the payroll, and we insist you come to the classes. We want everyone to be, as they say, on the same page with regard to the service."

"I'll be there. I know you're hiring me because of Mom, but I'll prove myself. I'll be good at this."

"All right, then." Jill's pen flew over the page. She was finished with this interview. "You have any questions?"

"Who cuts your hair?"

Orientation for the Empress serving staff was held at Francine's home, recently sold and now in escrow. Everything was set up for the first meeting. Francine had all the dishes and the silverware out, everything to teach the young serving staff, to correct their mistakes here in her kitchen and not on opening day. How to serve. How to set the table. How to remove dishes correctly. How to uncork and pour wine. How to be attentive but not obtrusive. All the things she had learned in thirty-some years of forwarding Marc Hellman's career. Francine's lessons would follow after Jill. Jill was going to talk about money. Francine was going to talk about manners.

All the Empress's new servers were under thirty, a rainbow coalition of attractive young people with clean fingernails and not visibly tattooed. Some were students, none were married, their schedules were flexible, Brent the bartender, Destiny, Servando, Kylie, Jenni, Josh, and Amy. They had some experience working in a restaurant, even Amy Meadows, if you count the espresso bar. In truth, of everyone gathered in this kitchen, only Francine and Jill really had no experience at what they were about, a fact they had agreed to keep between themselves.

"I'm glad to see you're all on time," Jill announced when they gathered in Francine's kitchen. "Anyone who wasn't would not be coming back. We run on a schedule and so will you. I'm going to talk to you first about the business." Jill glanced at her agenda. She pretended she was Martha Stewart, all smiles to the public, all knuckles and know-how when it came to money. "A restaurant operates on one principle. Food comes into our kitchen. In the kitchen, we process that food, we alter it, we even transform it if you like, and it goes out into the dining room and it makes money. A restaurant that doesn't make money, whatever else it does, it is worthless. We have opened this to make money. The food is only part of this equation. The ambience is part of it. The serving staff is crucial. This is where you come in. We have strict rules about what you can wear and what you can't; Francine will go over all that with you. But more important, it's your demeanor as a server that is part of the place. What we're trying to give our customers, besides great food, is a sense that the Empress is a place like no other. Invitational, warm, where there is camaraderie and no chaos. People have enough chaos in their lives. You represent the Empress directly to the customer. The service is part of what they pay for. We're charging plenty. Live up to it," she added in the sort of voice her sister Katherine would have used. Or Lisa, for that matter. Jill sat down, pleased with herself.

Francine stood up, her hostess smile in place, her blood pressure slightly elevated. She had never taught a class, and that's what she was about to do here. She greeted them individually, and she began with attire: hair, hands. Earrings were fine on men and women, no nose or lip or eyebrow rings. The restaurant would supply the servers with black pants and white shirts. They were to wear as well the Empress Bistro black-monogrammed apron. As the restaurant was prepared to pay for laundering these items, there was no excuse ever to be less than immaculate. They were to wear comfortable shoes. No athletic shoes, no sandals.

"As important," Francine continued, "is your demeanor. Naturally you are expected to be crisp, efficient, watchful, but absolutely not cozy. No telling them your name and chatting them up with personal stories. If you're told to push a certain dish that particular day, you do it with enthusiasm, even if you personally have never put it to your lips. To be a success at the Empress is to help make the Empress a success. We all have a stake here. For your part, I'd encourage you to think of yourselves in the European tradition of waiters: a profession, people at once charming and shrewd, not as part-time servers with other things on your minds."

"Like the old waiter in 'A Clean, Well-Lighted Place,' the Hemingway story?" asked Servando.

Francine said that was a good analogy.

"Tips are split nightly among all the serving staff," said Jill, returning to questions of money. "So it's in your best interest, everyone, to do your job well. If two old girls come in and you look at them and think, they won't tip, you must still make certain they get good service."

"And what if the restaurant critic from the *Oregonian* or the *Tribune* comes in?"

"They get great service," said Jill.

"And if they come in from the national mags? *Gourmet? Bon Appetit?*" asked Destiny with a smile. "Do we fall down and salaam them?"

"Not where they can see you," said Jill.

"We want you to think of yourselves," Francine added, "not just as servers in a new bistro, but as helping to build something. To be part of something grander than yourself."

"Like the navy," said Amy, wishing she hadn't.

After the fourteen hours of labor, after she gave the child up for adoption, after the baby stuff had been got rid of, and after her breasts dried up and her stitches had healed, and after she had got her hair cut and a French manicure, and her body had gradually assumed its old shape and she could see her own knees again, Amy was certain she'd have her own life back. Hey, it was summertime, wasn't it? Rock concerts at the Gorge. Windsurfing on the Hood River. Clubs, bars, dancing. Even if she was still living with Mom, Amy could do all this. Amy was over twenty-one. She could stay out all night if she wanted. She could smoke cigarettes. And she did. To prove that she could.

Her mother reproached her, said there was more to getting your life back than smoking and sex. Amy flew into tantrums. Then back into depression. She couldn't find a job. She gave up smoking, but the fog around her heart and mind did not lift. She would not admit as much to her mother. She couldn't.

She remained angry with Rusty. For everything. Diane had more or less given up being mad about Eddie Arias and Suzanne Post, but Amy stayed pissed off. She was rude when they called. And they called all the time. He was Eddie now. He called Mom Rusty. If Amy took the call, she sometimes didn't give the message. When Suzanne called, Amy couldn't stand to talk to her; she had to hand the phone on to Diane. She didn't want a sister. She didn't want a son and she didn't want a husband. She didn't want any more damned family. She didn't want to tell her mother that she felt this crushing sense of loss.

Not loss of the child. Some parents somewhere were very happy, said the social worker. And certainly not the loss of Chuck. Her doctor offered Amy meds for postpartum depression and she took them. Eagerly. She asked for more, a request that was denied. Instead, the social worker assigned a counselor to Amy, the fee paid by state medical services for a month. The counselor had listened gravely to Amy's woes and done what? Squat. Collected his fee. Who was there to help her?

Her girlfriends, well, they were no help. Amy Meadows had had an experience they did not have. This experience had changed her. Her girlfriends didn't want to hear it. Diane at first was sympathetic and supportive, but even Diane finally said, what did you think, Amy, that it would all be like before? Well, yes, she had. But she didn't say so to Diane. And the men she met? Amy went out dancing and met men, and none of them cared about this crushing sense of loss that oppressed her. Like a weight on her chest. She could see her knees, but she had a weight in her heart, and no one could help her. No one wanted to hear or know that she'd given up a child.

But when she said that Darcy Reeves had held a gun to her head, when, over a few beers or casual conversation, when the murderous rampage at Women's Uptown came up in the conversation, when Amy could tell how Darcy came *this close* to shooting Amy just before she surrendered, now that was something people wanted to hear!

Amy could never say what she felt for Darcy Reeves, which was a kind of sick kinship. Why? She didn't know, but it was inescapable, undeniable. One evening on the television, a newswoman speculated that Darcy Reeves's child would be put up for adoption since no one in her family wanted to bring up the child of Daniel Phillips. Darcy's own parents were accomplices to the crime, and they would be going to prison. Her sister did not want the child. Darcy Reeves did not want the child, or want it to suffer in foster care while she was serving a prison sentence. Darcy Reeves agreed to give up the child for adoption, as Amy Meadows had given up hers. And like Darcy Reeves, Amy Meadows was free of the man whose child she had borne and free of the child as well—but something besides her belly button would never be the same again.

20

Friends of the Empress

PREDAWN, ON A SUNDAY, YOU COULD DANCE IN THE middle of Yamhill, and this particular Sunday, Labor Day weekend, no one was likely to ticket the minivan parked outside the new Empress Bistro, the motor still running. The driver, Jill McDougall, stared at the French doors, the windows, all still curtained but lit from within. Jill smiled to see it. Took heart. Opening day was set for next Wednesday. But today the first meal would be cooked and served at the Empress, a celebration for a selected clientele. Invitation only. Friends of the Empress. It was like planning a wedding, and Jill felt like the bride. Except that she also felt like the groom, and like the parents of the bride and groom; she felt like the caterers and the orchestra and the ushers and the people who pitch the marquee and do the cleaning up. This private opening of the Empress Bistro had all the anguish of a wedding: deadlines unmet, shortened tempers, usual screwups, unusual screwups, the tensions of much at stake. Not just money. Dreams. Intentions. Making good on promises, vows to yourself and others. Jill was a wreck.

She felt the more inadequate because she knew Katherine would know how to handle this. At the Honolulu hotel, Katherine dealt with weddings all the time. Lisa would know. When lawyer Lisa married her lawyer husband in Chicago, the wedding was incredibly extravagant, incredibly screwed up too, but Lisa never lost her cool. No, not even when the best man showed up drunk, and the ring bearer peed his pants, and the flower girl had a tantrum and refused to walk down the aisle. Not even when they remembered at the last minute that the groom's grandparents kept kosher and nothing had been ordered for them. Lisa never lost her cool, not even when John and Sybil showed up with their brat son, Travis, despite the fact that the invitation had expressly said no kids, not even when Travis referred to the sisters as the Three Chinks, in Sybil's hearing and she did not rebuke him. Lisa kept her cool even when all three sisters were being fitted for their dresses, and Katherine—annoyed that she was a mere bridesmaid, and the groom's sister had been chosen to be matron of honor—acidly remarked that the gowns Lisa chose were so unflattering, the groom's sister looked like a pork chop in a tutu. Lisa never lost her temper, or anything else, until just before the ceremony Mom burst into the bridesroom, tearfully insisting that Paul the Greek walk Lisa down the aisle and not John McDougall, that Paul the Greek had been as much father to her . . . etc., etc. Then Lisa's cool deserted her and she flew into an astonishing rage that nearly melted the wallpaper. No more was said of Paul the Greek. Or John. Or the pork chop in a tutu.

Now Jill, who had considerably less native cool than Lisa, would have to deal with Mom, with Paul the Greek, with John and Sybil and, no doubt, Travis. For this opening celebration at the Empress, the staff had lined up square and rectangular tables end to end down the length of the dining room. Not trusting to chance, Jill put place cards out, so that John and Sybil were at one end of the table, and Mom and Paul the Greek were at the other. Never the twain shall meet, Jill vowed. But she counted on Katherine's help with their parents, and much else. Katherine was coming in from Honolulu, the red-eye overnight flight, cutting it too close for Jill's taste, but Katherine was airy about such things. She promised she'd catch a cab from the airport and be here early on.

Jill drove around the back and parked the minivan in the alley, their one parking place. Space was at a premium downtown. In the kitchen Colin and Gregory, the sous-chef, were already outfitted and the stove was fired up and steam wafted from a stockpot on the back burner and there was the rhythmic thump of Gregory chopping vegetables. If Gregory hadn't been here, she would have confessed to Colin how terrified she was.

"Hey, Jill, you want to go out front and make love on the marble bar?" Colin called to her. "Before anyone gets here. Gregory won't mind, will you?"

Gregory shook his head and laughed.

"Oh, don't joke with me, Colin."

"I'm not joking. I'm hot for it."

From his corner, Gregory chuckled.

"We have time," Colin added. "No one'll be here for hours. Just a quickie. Just have a little sex on the bar, or the floor. The floor would be okay."

"Are you having a breakdown, Colin?" Jill's fears intensified. "Sex on the floor?"

"You know, like those old European peasants used to do. I'll bet Korean peasants did it too. In the spring, they'd go out into the fields and fornicate to ensure a fruitful crop."

"Where did you ever hear such nonsense?"

"English class. Poetry."

Jill laughed, relieved. "The bar is too narrow, the floor is too hard. We'll go home to our new apartment and make love."

"Did you get new musicians? After the other ones pooped out?"

"Yes, an accordion player, and a string bass and a soprano sax man."

"That sounds like an odd combination. Where did you find them?

"Francine found them through her contacts with the symphony. They're coming at twelve-thirty to tune up and get ready. I told them they are absolutely not to play "Mary Had a Little Lamb" even if your father requests it."

"He'll slip them money. They'll have to. Get used to it, honey, if you're going to stay with me."

"Of course I'm going to stay with you! What kind of question is that?"

"Well, you know what they say. If you're going to marry someone, look hard at his family, because whatever that family has that you can't abide, that you detest, your spouse has got it too. It'll come out, sooner or later. One day, Jill, you'll be angry, and you'll turn to me and say, *You're just like your awful old father,* and you'll be right."

"You're not like your father."

"I probably will be one day. I might not be able to help it. And what if one day, in anger, I say to you, *You're just like your mother*?"

"My mother isn't awful. Besides, I'm adopted."

"What does that matter?" asked Colin.

Jill knew he wasn't joking. She felt her mouth go dry and her palms pop sweat. She asked him what was wrong.

"Well, if you really can't stand my family, then we should just call it quits."

"What are you talking about? Quits! This is opening day! You want to break up on opening day! Don't do this to me!"

"Well, answer the question, then. About my family."

"Not now, Colin."

"Now."

"What question?"

"What is it about my family that you can't bear?"

"Well," Jill dithered slightly, "all right then. Now and then your family drives me wild. They're—boisterous and noisy. But there's nothing I detest about them. Just never call me Twinkie, and I will never call you Tooter."

"If I promise you that, will you marry me?"

"What?"

"Seems like a good time to announce our engagement. How long have we lived together?"

"Sort of eight or nine years."

"That's long enough. Let's get married. What do you say? Will you, the Korean Empress, take me for your lawful wedded husband as long as we both shall live? I promise always to walk behind you respectfully, to take no concubines, and to bow on command."

Jill looked around the kitchen. "Did I say something to bring this on? Did I mention that all this seemed like planning a wedding?"

"You want me to propose on one knee? Here." He knelt and assumed a plaintive position.

Though she had lived with him long enough to expect the unexpected—round-trip tickets to Korea, ice cream lickings in the bathtub—a marriage proposal here in the kitchen on opening day, this she would not have guessed. "Don't be silly. Stand up."

He stood up, busied himself at the stove, lifted the huge stockpot, moved it to a front burner, and said, "Go on, have a reach in my pants pocket. Yes, that's the one! Feel around some more. Oh, Jill," he groaned, "I love it when you do that." Greg chuckled but he never took his eyes off the knife he was wielding. Colin writhed and moaned. She poked about in his pocket. She pulled out a small ring. Gold with a single small diamond.

"I put it on the credit card, by the way." He faced her with a smile.

"The credit cards are maxed."

"I found one. I'm serious about this. I want to marry you. I want you to marry me."

She slid the ring on her slender finger. "How did you know my ring size?"

"Haven't you missed your college ring lately?"

"I haven't worn my college ring since college."

"Well, there you have it."

"Can I think about this later?"

"You've had eight years. You said it yourself."

"I know, but I always thought of us like we were married."

"Well, we're not, and we ought to be."

"Do you really just think we should do this, so casually?"

"What makes you think it's casual? Today's a good day to launch things. Ask the Empress's astrologer." He lifted his eyes to heaven. "O Great Astrologer, do the heavens shine on us?"

"Yes," squeaked Gregory from the chopping block.

He turned to her. He took her shoulders. He met her eyes seriously, all humor evaporated. He spoke slowly and carefully, as though already making vows. "One day, I might be like my father, boisterous and noisy, but I will never be like your father. I'll never leave you. It's not in me. I love you. I'll love any children we have, and any ice cream we make. I'll love any home we have and any bistro that's ours. I loved you from the day I met you. I'll always love you."

Jill started to cry. She pressed her forehead against his white chef's coat and her mascara smudged all over his chest. "I'll always love you. I am yours and you are mine."

"Repeat after me, *I want you to marry me, and I want to marry you.*"

She lifted her lips to his gently. "I want you to marry me, and I want to marry you."

"I thought you'd never ask."

He took her arm, and they walked out of the kitchen into the dining room. The place was flooded with warmth from three dozen wall lamps with soft green-glass shades. He drew a great, expressive breath. "For as long as I can remember, this is what I wanted and hoped for. My dad knew it. He knew a chemistry degree wouldn't do me any good, that one day I'd have to own a restaurant."

"Well you stayed with the chemistry of the kitchen." Colin was too much of a dreamer ever to be a bus ad major. That was Jill's forte. The Empress represented their respective strengths. "I'm still worried," Jill confessed.

"Don't be." He put his arm around her shoulders. "All the time we've been building and remodeling here, I just still didn't quite believe it, but now I do. The real work lies ahead, of course, but a smallish place like this, a nice ambience, good food, the Empress is what I always imagined you'd find in a good Paris café. Even if they don't really exist like that anymore, even if they never did exist, that's how I imagine a good Paris café. I want the Empress to be that kind of experience. I want to offer people a kind of pleasure that isn't usually available, the kind of warmth and service that exist probably only in the imagination. When they come here, they'll feel like they've known this place all their lives."

"And the food," said Jill. "Don't forget that. You're the artist, you know."

"Good cooking is an art form, but it's in a disposable medium. It's not like a book or a movie, where you can go back to it. Once it's eaten, once it's past and everyone's gone home, then taste and flavor exist only in memory. And I always thought, if I ever have a place, I'd want to be where that past could be reproduced. You could come back to it."

"Like writing a memoir," she said with sudden inspiration.

"Yes."

Francine Hellman had been holding on to things her whole life. Now she was practicing letting go. It did not come easily. When her youngest son had gone away to college, she had got rid of the dog. That dog was the only thing Francine Hellman had parted with willingly since she was seventeen years old.

She actually practiced in the shower, letting go, an exercise Sarah

Jane had taught her: holding her arms out in front of her, fists furled. Slowly she unpeeled her fingers, leaving her hands open, empty, ready to receive. It seemed to work. At least it gratified Francine to stand in the shower, pelted with water as she imagined grief, guilt, anger, and any anxiety that did not directly relate to the opening of the Empress Bistro flying from her outstretched hands. In spite of this laudable exercise, Francine knew she was fighting her own nature in parting with the past.

She had parted with the house, which had sold for top dollar. And she had parted with a huge bundle of money to launch the Empress. And she was getting rid of everything that would not fit in the apartment she would rent. She would sell what she could, and give to Colin and Jill what they wanted for their small apartment. Before she could dispose of any of that, of course, Eric and Jesse had first choice. Jesse and Eric were coming in the night before the Friends of the Empress luncheon. They would have to be invited. This nettled Francine, but she let it go. She stood in the shower and practiced letting it go.

When Jesse and Eric pulled up Friday evening in their rented car, their childhood home was empty and silent. Both sons blamed the artsy-fartsy memoir class for their mother's distress. They blamed the class for the letter she had written and the letter she had received from Yu-Chun—a letter that had put them in a less than noble light. In a roundabout way, they convinced themselves that the memoir class was responsible for their father's infidelity and for their mother's finding out about it after all these years. They certainly blamed the University Extension and Penny Taylor for putting Francine in touch with people so flaky that they lived in a warehouse and made ice cream, a pair of restaurant con artists who had got hold of Francine's money. They were appalled to be called back to Portland at such short notice. They were irritated to be told to come get what they wanted from their family home and to know that were it not for the imminent sale of the house, their mother would not have wished to see them at all.

They dropped their bags off in their respective rooms and wandered through the house, where packing cases were already stacked and packing materials were strewn about the usually gleaming floors, and various items were already tagged for the Salvation Army, for storage, for sale, for moving. The disarray suggested that their mother was in a hurry. In such contrast to the usual well-ordered magazine-perfect home they were used to, it no longer felt like theirs at all. The master bedroom was empty, the bed stripped and marked for sale. Their father's study was absolutely bare, nothing on the bookshelves, the desk and lamps and computer and furnitue, the very curtains gone. The room looked like Marc Hellman had never inhabited it. Only the vague scent of his pipe smoke lingered. They missed him. It was a genuine emotion and shared, but they said nothing.

In the kitchen they found a note: *I will be working late at the Empress for Sunday's opening luncheon. You are both of course invited. Go out for dinner on your own. I will be home late. Don't wait up.*

"She didn't sign it Love, Mom," said Jesse, handing it over to his brother.

"So what? What has Love, Mom ever meant from her?"

"I don't know. It was nice to see, anyway."

"How can you be such a sentimental ass and still be a stockbroker?"

Jesse resented this. Mixed himself a drink and went out on the back deck. The house depressed him. He wished he had not come at all.

Eric made his own drink and joined him, lit up a forbidden cigarette, and broke out his cell phone. He dialed and asked to talk to Ted Swanson, who was surprised to hear from him.

"Are you both in town for the big day tomorrow, the opening of your mom's bistro?" asked Ted, noting the late afternoon hour and loosening his tie.

"It's hardly Mom's bistro," snapped Eric.

"Well, it's certainly partly hers. They're all three working very hard."

"It's her money."

"Jill and Colin put up some money. I drew up the papers, and it's all very clear. I don't think you have to worry about your mother."

"You actually let her do this! You didn't tell her it was foolish? Empress Ice Cream? Ice cream!"

Catching the drift of this conversation, Ted leaned back in his chair and let Eric natter on. He looked at the pictures on his desk, his father and mother, his father in judicial robes, his three grown children, a baby granddaughter, and a framed snapshot of Nell Faraday on vacation. Napa. Last month. Nell at a table, dappled sunshine all around her, smiling. At him. He was all but reliving the vacation, when Eric shouted that his mother was nothing but a cash cow to Empress Ice Cream. At that, Ted involuntarily laughed.

"What's so fucking funny?"

"Cow. Ice cream."

"This is not funny, Ted. You were supposed to protect her. My father expected you to protect her. I don't see how you can look her in the eye after this."

There was a concentrated silence on the other end of the phone as Ted considered his response. In a lawyerly tone, he went on, "Did either of you get my letter?"

"What letter?"

"Well, it will be waiting there for you when you get back east."

"What letter?"

"It's actually a copy of a letter I wrote to a woman named Yu-Chun. Your mother asked me to. It was too painful for her, so I took care of it."

Eric glared at his brother. He stomped out his cigarette.

"I understand there were provisions to your father's will that he never divulged to me. Before he died, your father made informal arrangements with you and Jesse with regard to his estate. I knew nothing of this, of your father's daughter in Taiwan."

"What's that got to do with it?"

"I did not see the letter Francine received from this girl's mother, but she told me about it. Francine took this very hard." He waited for a response, which was mumbled and grudging. "In my opinion, this venture, the Empress Bistro, is a way of dealing with the shock and sorrow that this letter caused her. Not only the shock of discovering that Marc had another family. She's very much disappointed that you and your brother were called upon to protect this girl, and to protect your own mother from finding out about this girl. And you didn't do it."

"That's not your concern," snapped Eric, hearing in the back of his mind his mother's low-key, everlasting, devastating *You have disappointed me.*

"That may be, but at her request I wrote a letter to this child's mother in Taiwan, and I told her that when the girl was ready to apply to colleges, that she should write to me here with her list of choices, and that by that time, the money would be found."

"What money?"

"The money your father asked you to put aside for this girl. Your mother figures that gives you a few years to find it, or do whatever you have to do. Sell some stocks," he advised.

"She can't hold us to that."

"Tell her," said Ted, knowing neither of them would. "I applaud Francine's restaurant venture. She's finding a life and finding work and some meaning for her time and effort and the energy that she puts into it. She looks better than she has in years."

"If Mom loses everything to this restaurant business, I'm going to hold you responsible. You should have told her she couldn't do this."

"I advise. That's all. I cannot guarantee her money. No one can. But I can tell you this, they're all working very hard and I admire them, all of them, Jill and Colin too, and I'll look forward to seeing you both there tomorrow. Good-bye."

"Like hell." Eric put the phone down. "I'm not going."

"Oh, yes you are." Jesse stretched out on the chaise. He handed him the note. "Read it and weep. *You are both of course invited.* You know what that means."

"I'll go," said Eric. "But I'll be late. That'll piss her off."

"Is that why we're here?" asked his brother. "To piss her off? I thought we already did that."

They were already late, and then Rusty Meadows got lost on her way to the airport. She was so tense that by the time they got to the airport hotel, Auburn #7 had probably worn off, and she would be gray at the roots.

Diane looked out the car window. It was a hot day. "I don't see why I have to come to the Empress opening. I don't care about the Memoir Club. Jill and Colin and Francine, these people you always talk about, they aren't my friends. I don't care about their restaurant or whatever it is."

"They've been good to us. They gave Amy a job. This is their special day. We're invited."

"So?"

"It's not just the Empress, Diane. I want you to meet Eddie and Suzanne. Suzanne wants to meet you. So does Eddie. She's your sister, after all."

"She is not." Diane spoke without defiance. Just the resignation of someone who has been long and often ill, often disappointed, often without the energy to contest the will of others. Diane wished Amy were here. Amy would say something smart and self-centered, and Diane wouldn't have to.

Rusty wished Kevin were here. Kevin would be easygoing and amenable. But Kevin had begged off. No way was he going to some downtown bistro opening, especially not in the company of his mother's high school boyfriend and the father of her illegitimate child. Kevin was officially out of town. In truth he was drinking beer in front of his television and watching sports. Rusty suspected as much, but she did not press it. There was no escape for Diane. And there would be no escape for Amy. Both girls would have to meet Eddie and Suzanne. Rusty herself had chosen the day of the Empress opening to invite them to meet the rest of the family. The phrase itself was difficult to say. She wanted her new family to be part of her old family. At least she wanted to try.

Arriving at last at the airport Sheraton, Rusty parked the old Toyota. She and Diane walked into the lobby, which was dripping with Muzak and had that peculiar odor of impermanence endemic to hotels, no matter how much marble and brass they use to cover it up. Rusty used the hotel phone to call Eddie's room and then to call Suzanne's room. "We're in the lobby," she said. She went back and sat down beside Diane, who seemed listless, even unwell. She took Diane's hand. "Please try to keep an open mind, Diane. That's all I ask."

"Do you love her better than you love us?"

"Of course not! Don't be silly."

"I think you love her more. You suffered more for her and so you love her more."

"Diane, honey, I suffered most for you, when you were sick, when I thought we were going to lose you. Those were the worst moments of my life. Suzanne for me is like meeting an old friend after a long time has passed. She was not who I thought she was. I thought she was someone named Melissa. But I made Melissa up. I'm not making Suzanne up. I have this chance."

"To?"

Rusty dared not describe what she truly felt or hoped from this reunion. Not even a reunion. These people had never met. "I don't love her more than you and Amy and Kevin."

"But you're asking me to love her."

"No, I'm not."

"You are, Mom. Get real."

"I'm hoping that you like her. I like her."

"And him? Do you love him?"

Suzanne and Eddie came into the lobby together, and Rusty watched them with a flush of happiness. Beside Eddie, Suzanne was so clearly his daughter that it took Rusty's breath away, as if they were the two sides of the same coin: one male, one female. Beside Eddie, Suzanne looked much less biologically allied to Rusty's old father. She introduced Diane as her daughter, then with just the slightest catch in her voice, introduced Suzanne as her daughter too. Suzanne was crisp and friendly. Diane was passive, limp. In that moment, Rusty knew how very like Charity Manning Diane was.

"You are the image of your mother," said Eddie, giving Diane a warm handshake. He was used to dealing with young people, and he always granted respect. Respect had to be in place before there could be any affection. His white teeth showed up bright against his skin tanned and toughened by years of football practice in the central California sun. His coarse, curly hair was shot through with gray. "Your mother was a great beauty in her youth."

Rusty flushed to the roots of her Auburn #7. "I was never a great beauty."

"You were always beautiful. You just didn't know it."

"You don't look anything like us," said Diane, considering the smartly clad, olive-skinned Suzanne.

"But I recognize you from the television," said Suzanne. "In the aftermath of that awful shooting at the clinic. I heard the name Meadows, and I knew Rusty had two daughters. Like the rest of the country, I was appalled and horrified to think that the two of you were in the thick of it."

"The shootout sisters," said Diane. "Everyone wanted our story for fifteen minutes of fame. Amy never got over it. Not the fifteen minutes. Darcy Reeves with the gun to her head. It changed Amy forever. Amy gave the baby up just like Mom did."

Rusty wondered if she somehow deserved that. Sweat beaded at her hairline. "Amy's doing fine," she added, though no one had asked after Amy.

"Amy's suffering. She'll never be the same," Diane repeated. "Never. In thirty years maybe the same thing will happen to Amy." Diane looked at Suzanne. "How can you not know your own child?"

"We better go," said Rusty. "It's a party, after all, and Jill is very particular about people being on time." She said this though they were already late and all her premonitions said *disaster, disaster.* She took out her keys and walked beside Eddie into the September sunshine. He did not take her hand or touch her.

When they got to the Toyota, he said, "Maybe Amy made the right choice, Rusty. For her, for the baby. Did you ever think of that?"

"I've thought of everything, Eddie. It was the right choice. But I know what's ahead for Amy, and she never will be the same."

"Maybe that's true, but it doesn't mean she can't be happy, can't fall in love and get married and have children she wants one day."

Rusty squinted against the sunlight twinkling off the cars, certain that's why her eyes were moist. "Tell me, Eddie, if you had known before this year that you and I had a daughter, would you—"

"We've been all over *if*. It's a playing field you can never win on. Let's go with *when*, now, here."

She started to put her key in the door when Diane called out to her. She had been walking behind with Suzanne, and she jogged now to the car. She glanced briefly at Eddie. "Sorry, Mom. I shouldn't have said all that about not knowing your own child. I didn't mean to be so . . ." Bitchy was the word. But instead she apologized again and said she would drive.

"You don't like to drive."

Diane insisted that she would drive. Suzanne, getting in the front passenger seat, looked pleased with herself.

In the back, sitting by Rusty's side, Eddie Arias held out his hand, palm up, and his eyes met hers, and just as all those years before, she willingly put her hand in his, the old backseat promise of their driver's ed days renewed, refreshed, almost like vows.

Francine thought of herself as a conductor. Yes, just like the symphony. Today, for the opening, the Friends of the Empress—these disparate and unconnected people—would have to be brought into a kind of unison, like tuning up the orchestra before they were to play the overture. The notion pleased her, though the only musicians present were the accordion and bass players, the soprano sax man. They were on time. Musicians are always on time.

They offered up all kinds of songs, cheerful, soulful, brisk, sweet, as guests drifted in. Friends of the Empress. Colin's family arrived first, his parents, his two look-alike sisters. To Francine's chagrin, his parents introduced themselves as Tooter and Twinkie. Mercifully, Colin had warned her they would do this. Moreover, Colin knew that Francine Hellman was not the sort of woman to address people with silly names. He told her their real names were George and Liz. When she greeted them at the front door, she called them George and Liz. They laughed. George strolled over toward the musicians, a couple of twenty-dollar bills laced around his fingers.

Next to arrive were Jill's fragile, irresolute mother, Mary, and her boyfriend, Paul the Greek, a short, barrel-chested man, clearly uncomfortable in a suit. Francine, who had read Jill's memoir, used her every ounce of charm to put the couple at ease while she braced for the appearance of Jill's father, John, and the dreadful Sybil. She was surprised at how much Mary McDougall reminded her of Jill when they first met. But Jill had changed. It came as something of a surprise to think, we've all changed.

Francine brightened visibly to see Ted and Nell and Sarah Jane enter. Sarah Jane carried a huge bouquet of home-grown dahlias. Francine gave the dahlias to Amy Meadows and told her where to find a vase. Then she did the intros all around, grateful that Sarah Jane seemed to take Mary and Paul the Greek under her wing.

Then, suddenly, the front door opened and the Empress filled with fragrance and the commanding voice of Katherine McDougall. "I am running late," she announced as she burst in. She directed the cab driver, sweating under the weight of her bags, to put them in the ladies' room. When he protested, she led the way. He left the bags in the corner and Katherine tipped him, closed the bathroom door. She changed her clothes, refreshed her makeup, and returned to the dining room wearing a gauzy dress of tropical blue, her arms draped with ceremonial leis. One for Francine, one for Jill, one for Colin. To look at Katherine, you would never guess she'd taken the red-eye from Honolulu.

Francine was elegant in a raw silk pantsuit of emerald green, and wearing her everlasting pearls. She moved among her other guests gracefully, inhaling the intoxicating aroma from the lei. By her count, almost everyone had arrived, friends, family, longtime enthusiasts of Empress Ice Cream. Not yet here, late, in fact, were the dreadful John and Sybil, oh, and her own sons, Jesse and Eric. She wondered fleetingly if Jesse and Eric would come at all.

On her way into the kitchen, Francine stopped to freshen the collar on Destiny Johnson's crisp white shirt. At the stove she found Colin putting the finishing touches on the garlic and lemon mussels. Jill arranged the rolls of prosciuto, cream cheese, and arugula, which stood in colorful contrast to an array of pale provolone slices wrapped around steamed asparagus. Gregory fussed over Kylie as she stirred the saffron risotto, admonishing her to slow down, that risotto needed to be stirred soothingly, that it would absorb anxiety otherwise. Francine laughed out loud. "That's what Sarah Jane always says, experience is porous!" Gregory looked at her, puzzled, but Jill just smiled. "It's beautiful," said Francine, breathing deep, the smell of lamb roasting with rosemary and small golden potatoes coming from the oven. "I mean I just came in to check on the timing, and I know it's all beautiful and no one will forget this day. Not just us," she added, "but everyone who is here."

Amy came in with an empty tray. "No, no," Francine chided her, "Don't carry it like that. If you walk like that you'll throw your back out. Worse, you look bad."

She opened the swinging door for Amy and followed her out. They both saw Rusty, Diane, Eddie Arias, and Suzanne Post. Nell was introducing them to Colin's family and to Mary and Paul the Greek. Francine took the tray from Amy. "Go," she said. "Go talk to your mother. Be civil."

"I will," Amy grumbled, moving with no particular haste past the guests who were lining up at the marble and mahogany bar, sampling appetizers, aperitifs gleaming in their glasses. She came at last to Rusty. "Mom," she said gently, "you look beautiful."

Rusty hugged her, fighting tears. She introduced Eddie Arias and Suzanne Post.

Amy shook hands. "I'm Amy," she said. "I'll be your server. We're not supposed to say that. Francine thinks it makes the place too California casual. They're going for something else here. I haven't figured it out, but they have. I have a lot to learn." Amy, more astute than Diane, could see elements of Rusty in Suzanne, in fact, elements of her own looks, though cast in a wholly different way. "Finding you both has made my mother very happy. We never knew she missed you, but she did."

"We never knew," repeated Diane, tucking herself behind Amy.

"I like to think you find the people in your life when you need them," said Eddie, putting his arm through Rusty's. "I consider myself a fortunate man to have found Rusty and Suzanne. To have a new family. At my age, I had quit looking for victories, or even surprises."

Amy wanted to ask how he knew they were victories. She wanted to know how Suzanne had felt when she saw Rusty and Eddie together, if some broken off part of herself had been reinstated, as if identity could be fragile as a porcelain cup, and if a crack was worse than a chip. She wanted to know if once cracked or chipped, that fragile identity could be mended. Looking at her mother and Eddie Arias, Amy knew that some broken-off part of Rusty's had indeed been glued back in place. Rusty had loved this man. Probably she loved him still. Maybe she had always loved him. Could such a thing ever happen to Amy and Chuck? Never. Chuck had vanished into the navy and Amy could not even remember why he had attracted her. Or if he had. Or if she had fallen in love with him as swiftly, easily as she fell into bed with him. And with as little consequence or significance. Except for the child, of course. The boy. Amy did not allow herself to think of him that way. Amy's identity, however cracked or chipped, would be forged in the future. Not in the past.

Never minding Jill's express instructions, the band struck up "Mary Had a Little Lamb." On the count of three, Colin's whole family called out to the kitchen that the ice cream truck was going by and Colin had better run outside and catch it, ask for a few pointers. They all laughed themselves silly. Colin came out of the kitchen for just a moment, blushing. He hugged Tooter and Twinkie and his sisters while his mother and father trotted out the hoary old family joke and told it all over again with enormous relish to anyone who would listen.

Francine could not see how this should be so funny. It must be some sort of family reflex.

The French doors opened and Jesse and Eric walked in. Francine assessed them as men, not as sons. Good-looking men. But suspicious. Were they always suspicious and Francine had just not noticed? Or was this their new and still undefined relationship to her? She watched their eyes, their quick critical gaze take in the Empress, each in his own way disapproving. This, she realized, was their family's reflex: disappointment unspoken, maybe even unsayable, but so present and palpable she could smell it like the flowers at her shoulders. For a moment, Francine endured what she had inflicted on Jesse and Eric. When she had attended their youthful events, she would offer them a brief bit of pride and then the immediate, implicit *Why didn't you do better?* She felt a stab of regret for their childhoods.

They each gave her a perfunctory kiss on the cheek. They wanted to talk about the house. Francine wanted to talk about the Empress. Each in his own way let her know they couldn't imagine her in the restaurant business. They said it as though she had opened a pawnshop. At this, Francine decided to treat them as she used to treat some of Marc's more recalcitrant colleagues. She put on the air she had practiced and perfected, convincing people they were the very ones she had most wanted to see. But her sons recognized it as a tactic and resisted.

Nonetheless, Francine linked arms with them and brought them to the marble bar, where Brent asked their pleasure. When they both said scotch and water, Francine declared, "No, no, that's too boring for today. Brent, make them each an aperitif, something French. L'amer Picon, I think. Don't you?"

"I never heard of it," said Eric.

"It's old-fashioned, sort of bracing and bitter at the same moment. It's nostalgic."

"For what?"

"Well, I can't tell you that. You have to create your own memories. Ted! Look who's here." She drew Jesse and Eric, both glowering, toward Ted. He was cordial to the Hellman brothers, and they were clipped.

"And this is my good friend, Nell Faraday, another of the Memoir Club."

Nell could see in Jesse and Eric something of their mother's nervous intensity. "It must feel odd, knowing your house is sold, and you won't be coming back to it."

"It feels odd," said Eric, glaring at Ted, "to think of my mother in the restaurant business."

"Well, it's not really such a leap from what she did all those years," said Nell. "Before, she had one customer, your dad, now she has many paying customers."

"That makes it sound like she's moved from being a wife to being a madam."

"Oh, really, Eric. Give it up," snapped Francine.

Amy Meadows appeared with their drinks on a tray, and Francine introduced her as well.

"You look familiar," said Jesse.

"Television," said Amy. "You've seen me on television. My fifteen minutes." She picked up some empty glasses and walked away.

"The clinic shooting," Francine explained. "Amy nearly died there. And Nell was badly injured. Another friend of ours died."

"The Columbine clinic?" asked Jesse, going quite pale. "I watched it on the news, but I never thought it had any connection to you, Mom, or that you knew the people who were injured. I mean, the shootout was in some kind low-income clinic, wasn't it?"

"Maybe you'd be surprised what has connection to me."

This was an understatement. The Hellman brothers, unfamiliar drinks in their hands, looked around the room: the odd trio of musicians, a noisy couple telling a noisy joke about "Mary Had a Little Lamb," the old girl with the chartreuse-streaked white hair and the bad teeth, and a stunningly attractive Asian woman talking to an anxious matron who clung to the arm of a swarthy, mustachioed Greek.

"Let's go meet Katherine," said Francine. "Jill's sister. She just flew in from Honolulu. She gave me this." She held up the lei with a smile. "Isn't it lovely?

She introduced Eric and Jesse to Katherine, who was wearing a chic, gauzy blue dress with thin little straps holding it over her tanned shoulders. An Asian print jacket in the same light material floated around her. Katherine herself needed only a little paper umbrella to look like one of those cool tropical drinks, and Jesse stupidly said, "Blue Hawaii. You remind me of that drink, the Blue Hawaii."

"And you remind me of a Manhattan," she quipped. "Am I right? You sound like you're from New York."

"How did you know?"

"I work in the hotel business."

Jesse thought she winked at him, but he couldn't be sure.

"And this is Katherine and Jill's mother, Mary McDougall." Francine put her hand on the shoulder of the matron who did not look the least like Katherine. "And this is Paul the Greek."

She moved her sons along, offering introductions to the musicians and the staff as well as the guests. With each individual, Francine gave Eric and Jesse some context, who they were, who they were related to, how they happened to be here. In introducing her sons, however, she called them simply Jesse and Eric; she did not add MIT or Upper West Side to ensure their importance. Until today, she hadn't even been aware that's why she always offered their occupations—as appendages, definition, validation. Well, this time, she thought, if Jesse and Eric are important, they're going to have to do it on their own.

She brought them to Sarah Jane, who excused herself from a conversation with an Empress Ice Cream employee.

Francine introduced Sarah Jane as part of the Memoir Club and author of *The Laughing Cat*. Jesse and Eric had never heard of *The Laughing Cat*. "Well, very soon the Empress is going to have a drink called that. Brent is working on it."

"I'm the Empress's official tester," said Sarah Jane.

"I've been the Empress official tester for months now," said Francine. "Since Colin and Jill have been living with me, Colin's been practicing what we'll serve here." She took a deep breath. "You won't believe what you're going to experience today. You will never have tasted anything like it. Since Colin been cooking at home, I'm a new woman. Really." And she laughed in a way neither of her sons could ever have imagined. Francine looked around at the bistro, the mirrored bar, the tile work beside it, the glowing light fixtures, the beveled glass, the shining wooden floors, the tables lined up for the luncheon, immaculately white, beautifully set with a small vase of flowers, one at each place. These were her own touch. "I want you to like it here," she said to her sons. "I guess I want you to approve."

Jesse and Eric glanced quickly into their drinks as though wisdom awaited them there.

Francine abandoned them when another couple came through the door. Jill's father and his wife. Francine recognized John and Sybil from Jill's memoir. Not that Jill had described them physically, but Francine knew them from the very way they stood, their truculent air.

John McDougall was bullet headed, his skull and face so clean shaven that he looked to be all but polished. He wore casual clothes, starched. He had a strong jaw, a high nose, a thin mouth, and tiny little blue eyes. Though he moved in a lethargic way, his eyes darted about, seeking an exit. Sybil, in Francine's opinion, was a mess. She wore platform sandals, a short skirt, her midriff showing like a little tanned tire. At least, Francine looked behind them, they had not brought their awful son. She introduced herself as part owner of the Empress.

"Where's Jill?" John asked.

"Well, there's Katherine."

"And Paul the Greek," Sybil muttered to her husband. "We haven't seen him since Lisa's wedding."

Katherine waved to her father. She came up him, took his arm, said a cool hello to Sybil, and drew them both toward Mary and Paul. "Now," Katherine admonished all four of them, "behave."

"You don't need to tell me that," sniffed Mary.

"But I am telling you. All of you. This is not your day. This is Jill and Colin's day. This is the beginning. Isn't that right, Jesse?" she asked as he drifted toward her and her parents, abandoning his brother to Sarah Jane Perkins. "It is Jesse, isn't it?"

Jesse said it was a beginning, and in saying so, he felt something fall away from him, like something shedding from his shoulders that he had not known he carried. Like stepping out of the shell of a larva, even if he were only a moth beside this beautiful tropical butterfly.

There was a knock at the Empress door, and Francine moved toward it, but Colin's father bounded in front of her.

"Oh, that's for me!" Tooter was a big man, silver hair, flush faced, and he ushered into the bistro two men hoisting between them a big white box, flat and unwieldy, and two more young men with an ice chest. Tooter got the attention of Servando, whispered he wanted champagne glasses all around. He paid off the delivery men in cash and they left. His wife went over to the musicians and gave them some whispered directions. Their youngest daughter went to get Colin and Jill from the kitchen. Tooter was laughing the whole time, so was his wife, both them gasping, "This is going to be so great!"

On Jill and Colin's entrance, the musicians struck up "Mary Had a Little Lamb." Colin's father nodded to Servando and Destiny, who withdrew from the white box a cake: a perfect pastry replica of the ice cream truck, the wheels, everything perfectly worked in sugar, even the driver in his cap. In bright blue the truck's sign read Empress. Everyone cheered. Twinkie got out her hankie.

The applause died down, and Tooter put an arm around Colin and Jill. While his eyebrows bounced up and down, facial exclamation points, he went on at great length about the things a little birdie told him, a little birdie who had confided that there were other things to celebrate today, like a wedding, maybe?

Jill held out her hand with the engagement ring, kissed Colin, and the band struck up "Here Comes the Bride," all jazzed up, and "I Can't Help Falling in Love with You" as congratulations cascaded over them. Tooter and Servando and Justin popped champagne corks and the air filled with the faint spray of the grape and celebration. Destiny, Amy, Kylie filled all the glasses, and at Francine's nod, got glasses for themselves, before Colin's father, in a rare moment of gravity, offered a heartfelt toast to Jill, Colin, and the Empress, launching great enterprises and long-lasting love.

"It'll never work," Sybil murmured to her husband.

"She could do worse," John said.

Paul the Greek stepped closer to John and whispered, "I pity you and your wife. You are joyless thugs of the heart."

Francine heard John growl, and swiftly she moved between them. She linked her arms with each of these unlikely men. She announced that both John and Paul the Greek, as the men in Jill's family, should offer the next toast. They each went rather pale, blank, scuffling mentally through what they should say, especially since they wanted to outdo one another.

Francine regarded them with the look she had perfected as hostess for her husband. She slipped easily into this stance. Thirty-some years of practice. But to think of practicing these skills here at the Empress? In this company? On this occasion? Oh, yes, thought Francine, smiling, and all the occasions to come. She wished Marc could have seen her. He would have been so surprised.

Epilogue

WE CALLED OURSELVES THE MEMOIR CLUB, AND SO WE were. Are. We remain part of and important to each other's lives, though there are no more Wednesday nights. Ted and I try to meet, maybe once a month, with Sarah Jane and Francine, Jill and Colin for dinner at the Empress. We see Amy Meadows there too. Amy is much more interesting than I'd thought her. She seems poised, even astute in ways you wouldn't expect of someone so young. But then, like everyone else who was at Women's Uptown that day, we're all changed. Irrevocably so. I think of Amy as one of us.

When Rusty and Eddie come back to Portland from Stockton, we all meet for dinner at the Empress. Rusty and Eddie had their wedding reception there, the month before Jill and Colin got married. Katherine was Jill's maid of honor, and she certainly did not look like a pork chop in a tutu. The McDougall sisters, Jill, Lisa, Katherine, were a stunning trio, beautiful, accomplished, and they all three carried themselves with a kind of aplomb I think they must have taught each other. They may have been orphans to begin with, but they had certainly forged themselves into a family, never minding John and Sybil. During the endless round of toasts, Colin stood up and saluted his mother-in-law. He remarked that Jill had Mary McDougall's eyes and Lisa had her nose and Katherine had hair just like her mother's. Mary and all three of her daughters. Francine and I, and Rusty and Sarah Jane cried. Paul the Greek cried. A fine successful wedding.

But for a long time before those weddings, I lived in mourning. Not just for Caryn. I mourned my left hand. One day while I was still living at Sarah Jane's, she said to me, think about your right hand, Nell. Think about that right hand as though it were your child. The one child gone, dead, and you can't love the other one because of it.

I said it was stupid to compare the loss of a hand to the loss of a child.

My point, exactly, Sarah Jane countered. Then she asked, what would you compare it to?

I said, I am like a door without a knob.

Sarah Jane left the room, and I could hear her thrashing about in the hallway with a toolbox.

After a while, she led me back to the bathroom door, now closed and without its knob. When you have to pee bad enough, she said, you'll find a way to open that door. Your right hand looks all right to me. Your brains—she reached up and tapped me on the head—yes, they're still in place. And at that she smiled and walked away.

By the time I moved back into my own apartment in early June my grief for my hand had eased. I'm an athlete, and I worked at the therapy, like I was in training, and slowly some of the use of my left hand has returned. I bought a laptop and learned to type with my right hand. I could at least rejoin the working world. For therapy easing the loss of Caryn, I had Ted Swanson.

Falling in love with Ted was not like anything I'd ever experienced. I think that's because this is the first time I am truly in love, and loved in return. I am amazed how love changes the way I see the world. He's asked me to marry him. Ted is a lawyer and he likes things done correctly, neatly, legally. But more than that, he says that we should marry because you never know what will be given to you. Or taken from you. One day to the next. Who knows that better than I? Far from Caryn coming between, she is a bond we share. She unites us.

Ted and I will marry next year, but in the meantime, we each gave up our apartments and rented a modest house together. Ted wanted to buy, but I said no, not because I don't love him, or believe in our future together. I wanted to wait till I had a new job. I want to be a full partner in this venture, not the one who's needy. It isn't in me to be needy, but I'm learning that it's all right to need. Ted is teaching me that.

The job I found allows me to use what I've learned as a nurse, what I keep in my head, as much as my hands. I counsel juvenile offenders. This is fine work for me and makes me feel as though I'm doing something important. Maybe I can intervene for these kids before their juvenile offense becomes an adult tragedy. Darcy Reeves might never have succumbed to Phillips if she'd had someone to turn to. I never again want to see a young person, deluded, emotionally derailed, plead guilty to a lesser charge and face her adult life in prison for a crime that, in essence, someone else committed. Committed on her and on her child too.

This year, when the first anniversary of the shootings at the Women's Uptown rolled around, both sides of the political spectrum planned big public orgies of politics and remembrance, and there was a flurry of articles and editorials in the press. They again interviewed Amy and Diane Meadows and the other Lamaze students. They again commended Officer Hodges for saving lives. The Family Champions, the Embryo Protection League, the Seekers had all disbanded without Daniel Phillips, and they could not be found to be interviewed. Local television and the press called all of us who had worked at the clinic. Chantal and Esther and a few others offered statements. I declined. Ted and I took vacation time, closed up our house for a week, put our dog in the kennel, and went camping on Vancouver Island.

Those of us in the Memoir Club did not keep the anniversary collectively. Perhaps in writing our memoirs, we'd learned this much: It wasn't the day we wanted to keep or remember, but the woman, Caryn, we would never forget. I guess I personally have learned there are no anniversaries. There are days you invest with meaning and try to keep, but finally the day, the twenty-four hours allotted by time, ends, fades, even if the meaning lingers. Why shouldn't every day be an anniversary? Why shouldn't every summer be the last? Why shouldn't you say to yourself on any old day that rolls, ebbs, and flows into one another: I'm going to remember the light through these leaves, or the sound of the rain. I'm going to remember the steam wafting off this cup of tea or the taste of this ice cream or the tears on the face of a juvenile offender. I'm going to remember a child's distant laugh or the way my lover looks, sleeping on the pillow beside me. You won't remember them, not individually. They slip through the sieve of time, and congeal, but you can savor their significance, even if you can't save it.

Acknowledgments

FOR HER ENTHUSIASM, HER WISE EDITORIAL EYE, HER time, insight, and acumen, I am much obliged to my editor, Diane Reverand.

I thank Deborah Schneider—agent and ally—for her support, her energy, and her loyalty to my work. This novel, in particular, owes much to her.

I appreciate too the efforts of the Gelfman Schneider agency staff, especially Cathy Gleason and Britt Carlson; they have been ongoingly helpful, and always swift to answer questions.

For her longtime friendship, cheer, and appreciation, I am grateful to Juliet Burton.

Thanks too to my friends Sandra Thomas and Lucerne Snipes for providing inspiration, long talks, and memorable California afternoons.

To my memoir students over the past ten years: thank you. In developing these classes, I have learned to approach the narrative experience of the past from many different perspectives, as a reader, a writer, and a teacher. To the spring class of 2002, an especial thanks for a unique experience.

For the rest, let us round up the usual suspects. You know who you are: my sons, my sister, my parents, my longtime amigos. Applause, affection, and gratitude to all of you.

READING GROUP GUIDE

This is a novel about the past. Not just the pasts of the various characters, but about understanding the past, looking at it in new ways in order to achieve that understanding. Once these characters set out to write their memoirs, the understanding they come to is not always what they had expected. In some ways, the memoirs turn out to be different than the memories.

1. How does Mary McDougall's inability to confront her daughters' past fuel Jill's anxiety about the Talking Kimono and everything it means? How does the breakup of their parents' marriage affect the sisters? Why is Jill finally able to "retire" the Talking Kimono?

2. Francine discovers a great lie. Though she breaks down under the strain of the revelation, does she regret having made the discovery? At the end of the book, Francine thinks Marc would be surprised to see her in her new role. Is it really such a new role? Does this mean she's made peace with Marc's memory? With her sons? With herself?

3. When Suzanne finally appears in Rusty's life, what happens to Rusty's beloved Melissa and the memoir for Melissa? Why does Rusty finally part with that last secret she had always kept? What ongoing role does "Melissa" play in Rusty's life?

4. Amy says at one point she feels an awful kinship with Darcy Reeves. Why does she say that? Darcy Reeves committed acts Amy would never dream of. Does Rusty's long, troubled story have any impact on Amy at all?

5. Why, with her scientific background would Sarah Jane live in such a whimsical house? Why does Penny Taylor "send" Sarah Jane back to the river, and the flood? In writing her memoir, does Sarah Jane finally step out of her past, or does she embrace it?

6. How does the Memoir Club break down Caryn's isolation and enable her to speak of her grief? How does the advent of Ted into Caryn's life change Nell's role as the St. Bernard? What allows Nell to recover from her own losses? Why does the whole Memoir Club evade the anniversary that marked the loss that changed their lives?

For more reading group suggestions visit
www.stmartins.com/smp/rgg.html

St Martin's Griffin